# KISS THE WALLFLOWER

*Books 4-6*

## TAMARA GILL

# COPYRIGHT

Kiss the Wallflower
Books 4-6
To Fall for a Kiss
A Duke's Wild Kiss
To Kiss a Highland Rose
Copyright © 2019, 2020 by Tamara Gill
Cover Art by Wicked Smart Designs
All rights reserved.

ISBN: 978-0-6450581-3-0

# TO FALL FOR A KISS

## Kiss the Wallflower, Book 4

*Lady Clara Quinton is loved and admired by all. She has no enemies—excluding Mr. Stephen Grant. After an atrocious encounter with Stephen during her first season, Clara vowed to never befriend him or any member of his family. But when Mr. Grant saves her in Covent Garden from a relentless and lively admirer, Clara falters in her promise.*

*Disliking everything about the social sphere he now graces—including Lady Clara—Stephen wants nothing more than to steer clear of the indulged and impolite woman. Her contempt of him and his family has been made known all over the town. However, after coming to her aid one night in London, the vowed enemies come to a truce.*

*Now, a landlord at the property adjacent to her country estate, a storm leaves him stranded at the duke's home. Uncovering Lady Clara's secrets and vulnerabilities changes the way he sees the privileged woman. Will this newfound knowledge force him to see her through different and admiring eyes? And will Clara see there is more to Stephen than his lack of noble birth…*

# PROLOGUE

*Covent Garden, London Season, 1809*

Lady Clara Quinton, only daughter to the Duke of Law, gingerly backed up against an old elm tree, the laughter and sounds of gaiety beyond the garden hedge mocking her for the silly mistake she'd made. The tree bark bit into her gown and she cringed when Lord Peel would not give her space to move away.

Walking off with Viscount Peel had not been her most intelligent notion after he insisted she see a folly he was fond of. After her acquiescence, her evening had deteriorated further. If she happened to get herself out of this situation it would be the last time she'd come to Covent Garden and certainly the last time she had anything to do with his lordship.

"Please move away, my lord. You're too close."

He threw her a mocking glance, his teeth bright white under the moonlit night. His mouth reeked of spirits and she turned away, looking for anyone who may rescue her. What did he think he was going to do to her? Or get away with, the stupid man? "My lord, I must insist. My father is expecting me back at our carriage."

"Come now, Clara, we've been playing this pretty dance for years. Surely it's time for you to bestow me a kiss. I will not tell a soul. I promise."

She glanced at him. Lord Peel was a handsome man, all charm, tall, and with an abundance of friends and wealth and yet, the dance he spoke of mainly consisted of her trying to get away from him. There was something about the gentleman that made her skin crawl as if worms were slithering over her.

He'd taken an immediate like to her on the night of her debut several years ago, and she'd not been able to remove him from her side since, no matter how much she tried to show little favor to any of the men who paid her court. She was six and twenty and sole heir to her father's many estates. She wanted for nothing, and with so many other things occupying her mind of late, a husband did not fit in with her plans at present.

If she were to marry she would have to leave her father, and she could not do that. Not now when he was so very ill and in all honesty, there had been no one who had sparked her interest, not since Marquess Graham during her coming out year before he up and married a servant. Clara would be lying if she had not felt slighted and confused by his choice.

"If you should try and kiss me, my lord, I shall tell my father of your conduct. I can promise you that. Now move." She pushed at his shoulders and she may as well have been pushing against a log of wood. He didn't budge, simply leaned in closer, clasping her chin and squashing her farther into the tree trunk. She cringed at the pain he induced.

"Do not make me force you, Clara." His voice dropped to a deep whisper full of menace.

Fear rippled through her and she shivered, glancing beyond his shoulder. Should she scream? To do so would court scandal. People would come scrambling to her aid, and she would be left having to explain why she was alone with Lord Peel in the first place. Especially if they did not have an understanding. Clara could not put her father through such gossip. He had enough on his shoulders without her worrying him with her own mistakes.

"You're a brute. How dare you treat me like this?" She tried to move away once again and as quick as a flash he grabbed her, wresting her to the ground. She did scream then, but with his chest over her face her cry for help was muffled.

Clara pushed at him as he tried to kiss her, his hands hard and rough against her face. "Stop," she said, "please stop."

He merely laughed, the sound mocking, and then in an instant he was gone. For a moment she remained on the ground, trying to figure out what had happened and then she saw him. Mr. Grant, or Stephen Grant, the Marquess Graham's brother-in-law and a man she'd promised to loathe forever and a day. He stood over Lord Peel, his face a mixture of horror and fury. Somewhere in the commotion Mr. Grant must have punched Lord Peel, for he was holding his jaw and there was a small amount of blood on his lip.

Clara scrambled to her feet, wiping at her gown and removing the grass and garden debris from her dress as best she could. Mr. Grant came to her, clasping her shoulders and giving her a little shake. "Are you injured? Did he hurt you at all?"

Clara glanced at Lord Peel as he gained his feet. He

glared at Mr. Grant as he too wiped garden debris from his clothing and righted his superfine coat.

"You may leave, Mr. Grant. You're not welcome to intrude in a private conversation I'm having with Lady Clara."

"Private? Mauling someone on the ground is not what I'd consider a conversation, my lord. I heard her shout for assistance. I hardly think the conversation was one of Lady Clara's liking."

Clara moved over toward Mr. Grant when Lord Peel took a menacing step in her direction. An odd thing for her to do as she had never been friends with the man and to seek his protection now went against everything within her. But if she were to remain at Lord Peel's mercy, she would choose Mr. Grant of course. He had two sisters after all, and from what she'd seen over the years he loved them dearly. He would not allow any harm to come to her. Mr. Grant reached out a hand and shuffled her behind him, backing her toward where her father would be waiting with the carriage.

Lord Peel's eyes blazed with anger. "Of course it was to her liking. We're courting, you fool."

She gasped, stepping forward, but Mr. Grant clasped her about the waist and held her back. "How dare you, my lord?" she stated even as Mr. Grant restrained her. "I never once asked for you to pursue me and I never gave you any indication that I wanted you to."

Lord Peel glared at her. Mr. Grant turned her back toward the opening in the hedge where they had entered the small, private space and pushed her on. "Go, Lady Clara. I shall speak to his lordship. I can watch from here to ensure you reach your carriage, which if I'm not mistaken your father is waiting beside and looking for you."

Clara clasped Mr. Grant's hands, squeezing them. "I cannot thank you enough. You have proven to be the best kind of man for coming to the aid of a woman you may not be inclined to help under normal circumstances. I thank you for it."

He threw her a puzzled glance. "Should anyone bellow for help and I hear it, of course I will come. Now go, Lady Clara. The time apart from your guests has been long enough."

Clara nodded, turning and walking away. She reached up and fixed her hair, hoping it did not look as out of place as it felt. As she walked back toward the revelers, a little of her fear slipped away knowing Mr. Grant watched her. She glanced over her shoulder, and true to his word, Mr. Grant continued to survey her progress and ensure she arrived back at her carriage safely.

A shiver of awareness slid over her skin, completely opposite to what she experienced each time she was in the presence of Lord Peel. She'd always disliked Mr. Grant and his siblings, one of whom married Marquess Graham, her own suitor during her first Season and the man she thought she would marry. He did not offer for her hand, choosing to marry a lady's companion instead.

"There you are, my dear. I've been looking for you."

She reached up and kissed her father's cheek, her legs of a sudden feeling as if they would not hold her for too much longer. "Shall we go, Papa?" she said, taking his arm and guiding him toward the carriage. The coachman bowed before opening the door for them.

"Yes, let us go, my dear. I've had quite enough time in the gardens and watching the *ton* at play."

Clara stepped up into the carriage and sank down on the padded velvet seats, relief pouring through her that no one other than Mr. Grant had come upon her and his lordship in the garden, or the position that they'd been found.

Heat rushed over her cheeks and she picked up the folded blanket on her seat and settled it about her father's legs as the carriage lurched forward. Anything to distract her from the memory of it.

"Shall we ring for tea and play a game of chess when we arrive home, Papa? It may be a nice way to end the evening just us two together."

Her father glanced at her, a little blank and unsure. "I think I shall retire, my dear. It's been a tiring evening."

"Very well," she said, swallowing the lump in her throat that wedged there each and every time she was around her parent. She knew the reason he no longer liked to play chess, cards or even the piano, at which he'd once been proficient, was because he'd forgotten how. His mind over the last two years had slowly disremembered many things, even some of the servants who had been with them since she was a girl.

Unbeknownst to her father Clara had sought out an opinion with their family doctor and he'd agreed that her father had become more forgetful and vague, and that it may be a permanent affliction.

She sighed. The fact that there was little she could do to help him regain his memory saddened her and as much as she tried to remind him of things, an awful realization that one day he'd forget her had lodged in her brain and would not dissipate.

What would happen after that? Would he still be as healthy as he was now, but with no memory, or would whatever this disease that ailed his mind affect his body as well.

The idea was not to be borne. He was all she had left.

"Maybe tomorrow, Papa, after breakfast perhaps."

He smiled at her, and she grinned back. "Maybe, my dear, or you could ask your mother. I know how very fond of chess she is."

Clara nodded, blinking and looking out the carriage window so he would not see her upset. If only she could ask her mama, who'd been dead these past ten years.

☙❧

STEPHEN STOOD between Lord Peel and the man's exit at his back in the gardens. The moment he'd strode into the small, private area and seen a flash of pink muslin and a gentleman forcing a woman into kissing him a veil of red had descended over his eyes and he'd not known how he'd stopped himself from pummeling the man into pulp.

"You will leave Lady Clara alone or I shall speak to her father of what I witnessed this evening. Do you understand, my lord?"

Peel chuckled, the sound mocking and full of an arrogance that Stephen was well aware of with this gentleman. He was also aware that he'd once been married and that his wife had fallen ill not long after their marriage. Of course, upon the young woman's death, Peel had played the widower very well, and had enjoyed the copious amount of money that his young wife had left him, or so Marquess Graham had told him one evening when Stephen had noticed his marked attention toward Lady Clara. A woman who seemed to show little interest in the gentleman trying to court her.

Lord Peel tapped a finger against his chin. "I forget… Do I need to listen to you? What is your name… Mr. Grant, isn't it? Son of nobody."

Stephen fisted his hands at his sides, reminding himself that to break the fellow's nose would not do him or his sisters any good now that they were part of the sphere this mongrel resided within. He'd already hit him once, to bloody him up too much would not do.

"You are correct. I'm Mr. Stephen Grant of Nobody of Great Import, but I will say this… You're no one of import either if the rumors about you and your conduct are to be believed."

Lord Peel's face mottled red and Stephen was glad his words struck a chord in the bastard. He needed to hear some truths and to know that his marked attention toward women, his inability to grasp that he saw them as nothing but playthings for his enjoyment had been noted and talked about. He pushed past Stephen and he let him go, not wanting to waste another moment of his time on such a nob.

The gentleman's retreating footsteps halted. "Lady Clara will be my wife. I will be speaking to her father soon about my proposal and I will have her. I am a viscount. It is only right that Lady Clara marry a man such as myself, so if you look to her as a possible candidate as your wife, you'll be sadly mistaken. Move on and marry a tavern wench, that'll suit your status better. A duke's daughter is not for you."

Stephen glared at the man's back as he disappeared into the throng of revelers still dancing and enjoying their night in Covent Garden. "Yes, well, Lord Peel, she's not for you either and I'll be damned if I'll let you have her."

# CHAPTER 1

*Autumn — 1809*

Clara settled the blanket about her father's legs and sat on a settee beside the fire. They had returned to Chidding Hall a fortnight past, and autumn this year had been windy and wet, a sure sign that winter would be cold. The fire crackled and popped, and with the velvet drapes pulled closed, the candles burning in the library, the room was warm and inviting, a perfect place to relax and enjoy some time together.

Something that had been happening less and less. Her father, since the end of the season, had deteriorated so severely that she'd ended her time in London early and had returned home to Kent without delay.

He'd improved since being away from town, and the many outings she feared took a toll on him and made him more vulnerable to bouts of anxiety, clumsiness and confusion. Home at least, her father was more relaxed and he'd been better, but still, something inside Clara told her that his illness would only get worse. It was certainly the trajectory he'd been on at least.

"Did I tell you that I received word today that we have a new neighbor? Moved in last week."

Clara placed the letter from her friend in London down in her lap. "Really? What estate? I've not heard of any estate being up for sale or lease." She knew all the particulars regarding their neighbors in the county. Having worked with the steward for the past three years, there was little she didn't know now about her tenants, the land and surrounding neighbors.

Her father's eyes twinkled, no doubt pleased that he knew something she did not. "Oh yes, a Mr. Grant has leased Ashby Cottage, his brother-in-law's home. It's been empty for so many years. I've not seen anyone living there since Lord Graham's grandmother resided there. It'll be good to have someone in it again. I always believe that when a house sits empty it deteriorates. Lord Graham has maintained the upkeep on the estate however, so I do not think there will be much needed to be done by Mr. Grant to ensure his comfort."

Clara listened as her father rattled on about the gentleman and she ignored the fluttering that overtook her stomach at the mention of his name. Mr. Grant was their new neighbor? She picked up her letter, feigning reading. "That is good news, both for the estate and the local county. Another home open will mean more employment for the local people." She paused, folding and unfolding the corner of the letter lying in her lap. "I met Mr. Grant several years ago in London, on recent acquaintance his character has improved, I'm happy to say."

Certainly he'd been an ogre the first time they had met in Hyde Park. She'd come across him, his sister and Marquess Graham not long after his lordship's marriage. It may not have been the nicest thing to have done, but to see his lordship flaunting his new wife, and her brother growling at anyone who dared mention their less-than-pleasing heritage had brought out the worst side of her. She'd been terribly rude, but then Mr. Grant had also. After that she'd not gone out of her way to mend ties with the family.

"That is very good to hear," her father said, smiling.

"I shall have Cook send a basket of our produce as a welcome." That would do nicely and she'd include a small note stating her own thanks for his assistance in Covent Garden. That should do the trick and end any future need to associate with him.

Her father leaned back in his chair, crossing his legs out before him. "No, you shall deliver it, instead of a servant. We're the highest-ranked family in the county, it is your duty to invite him for dinner and welcome him properly."

Clara gasped, unable to hide her dismay at having to do such a thing. "A basket from our servants will be just as well received as one from me. I do not need to go, Papa, and now that I no longer have a companion I do not see the point in making my maid travel with me, through this cold and damp weather simply to deliver a basket of food. One of the stable hands can deliver it. That will do well enough."

Her father looked at her, his brow furrowed. "Why do you no longer have a companion?"

Clara blinked, fighting back tears at his inability to remember details of their life. "Mrs. Humphries remarried three years ago, Papa. Do you not remember? You gave her away in our church."

He blinked at her several times before his eyes cleared and she knew he remembered. "Oh of course, how forgetful I am. Well then, we'll have to get you a new companion."

"I'm six and twenty, Papa. I do not need one. Most of my friends are married now, if I design to go out with them, they can act as my chaperone." The reminder that she was the last of her friend set to be wed had caused her many nights of unease, but then as sole heiress to her father's estates there was little reason to worry.

After losing Marquess Graham to a servant of all people, the desire to marry had waned. Not because she was still in love with his lordship, for she was not. She'd long ago recognized that her infatuation with him had been a youthful folly, but having seen him with his wife, the devotion and love he showed her and the *ton* was what she wanted for herself.

During the past eight years since her debut, she'd refused to settle for anyone who did not make her heart flutter and her stomach too. Not only that, but she wanted a gentleman who was intelligent, could offer an opinion without worrying what others thought of him. All the gentlemen who had courted her had been less than pleasing.

"Even so, my dear, I think it would be best that you welcome Mr. Grant to our county. Your approval of him will ensure his acceptance from the other families of our set."

Clara sighed, preferring not to see Mr. Grant again, but then, she supposed she ought to thank him properly for coming to her aid during the Season. His intrusion had thankfully kept Lord Peel away from her, at least at the events that Mr. Grant also attended. She'd not been able to talk to him there, however. Shame washed over her at the reason as to why.

Her friends knew of her dislike of him and his sisters

and so she felt bound to keep up the pretense of indifference, even though he'd come to her aid. But then he'd not sought her out either, to see if she were well and recovered and so it seemed their association, no matter how short in duration, was at an end.

"Very well, Papa. I shall deliver a basket tomorrow. That will satisfy my obligations and we shall be done with any further need to show hospitality."

Her father chuckled, leaning his head back and closing his eyes. "You talk as if you fear Mr. Grant, Clara." He opened one eye and inspected her. She fought not to fidget under his regard. "He is just a man, my dear. Nothing to cause distress, I'm sure."

Of course he was right, but still, even now after speaking of him her wretched body refused not to squirm at the mention of his name. It was simply because he'd caught her in a compromising position and was a gentleman whom she disliked. To be indebted to someone you had always loathed was not to be borne and was the reason why she did not feel herself. She was silly to imagine anything else.

STEPHEN KICKED off his boots at the servants' entrance after having walked about the grounds of his new home. His brother-in-law, the Marquess Graham had offered to lease the property, to let him make use of the house and land as he chose. His lordship had been contemplating selling the estate for some time, due to being unused since his grandmother's time, subsequent to her passing.

The house was on a good-sized property with three hundred acres that his lordship had said Stephen could use for income. His brother-in-law had also been lenient and allowed him to lease the property for less than what it was worth and he'd forever be indebted to him. Stephen wasn't fool enough not to know he did any of this for him. The man was devoted to his sister Louise and would do anything to make her and her family happy.

Since the marriage of his sister, Sophie, the Marquess had gone to great pains to ensure Stephen remained close to Louise and wouldn't, too, hightail it off to Scotland and live there. They had been separated as children and the Marquess did not want that again for his wife.

He walked without shoes into the foyer, his clothing damp and muddy after tracking down to the local waterway that ran through his property. He ran a hand through his wet hair and came to a sliding stop at the sight of Lady Clara staring at him, her mouth agape and her eyes stealing over his person from head to foot.

For a moment he didn't say a word, merely took in her perfectly styled hair, a bonnet dangling from blue ribbons in her gloved hand. Her gown was of a deeper shade of the sky and with her overcoat, she looked warm and inviting. He shivered, aware that he at least looked the complete opposite to her, a wreck, a wet and muddy mess.

She raised her brows, meeting his eyes and his defenses shot up. He'd seen that look before, many times in fact in London over the years when she judged him and his family, looked down at him along that pretty, pert nose of hers.

He stilled at the thought. She wasn't pretty, and what the hell had made him think such a thing? He started for the library, needing to escape her presence and the falsehood he'd just told himself. "Apologies, Lady Clara, but I must get dry. I've been out overlooking the property and have grown damp."

She followed him, her light footsteps close on his heels.

"Yes, Papa said Marquess Graham had leased the property to you. How very fortunate you are."

He clamped his jaw shut, making the fire and turning to warm his backside. Heat seeped into his bones, a welcome reprieve from the chilling outdoors. "Mocking me already? I thought that perhaps my coming to your aid in London may have halted the barbed words that so often spewed from your lips toward my person." They had never been wont to hide their dislike of each other, and Stephen had always found when it came to Lady Clara, to speak frankly was always best.

She raised her chin, and his gaze took in her features before dropping to her lips, now puckered into a mulish line. Damn it, he'd always liked her defiance, especially when he said or did something that vexed her.

"What a delightful way of putting it, Mr. Grant. I see living in a gentleman's house, circulating within the upper echelons of the *ton* has not improved your common manners. You will need to do better if you're to fit in with our society here."

He shrugged, bringing attention to the fact his shirt was damp. He reached behind him and pulled it off over his head. Of course to do so was courting scandal and ungentlemanly to the extreme, but the woman was a vexing little prig and he wanted to shock her. If she thought he was so very common, then he'd act like a common man not afraid to undress before a lady. No matter who she was.

"I do not need to fit in with the society here. If they shun me, that is their choice and problem. I'll not change to please others. Unlike some people whom I've seen throughout the years I've been in London." Namely the chit glaring at him right now.

She gasped, dropping the basket he only just noticed

17

she was holding on a nearby table. "I suppose you mean me, Mr. Grant. How dare you be so rude? I demand an apology at once."

"I will not apologize for stating the truth and I did not name names, Lady Clara. You think too highly of yourself if you believe I was talking about your person." Although he very well meant her and her gaggle of silly friends, all of whom had married men whom he'd seen frequent the clubs about London and had seen the indiscretions they partook in. All but Lady Clara had succumbed to the marriage state. He narrowed his eyes upon her.

Why though, he could not make out. She was a duke's daughter, an heiress, a perfect catch for the gentlemen of London and beyond.

It was probably because no one exceeded her lofty aspirations of what constituted a good husband. He walked over to her, ignoring the fact her eyes slid over his now-naked chest like a caress. His skin prickled and he wondered what her hands on his skin would feel like.

Damn good he'd imagine.

He shook the thought aside, opening the basket. "What do you have here? A present for me?"

She rolled her eyes and he bit back a grin. "Father wanted me to welcome you to the neighborhood. He insisted I deliver it. Now that I have, I shall take my leave."

He glanced down at her, noticing her blonde locks were only partly pulled up on her head. The few strands that sat about her shoulders only accentuated her pretty neck. She was not a tall woman, only coming up to his chin, but even so, neither was she short, considering his height.

"You did not wish to deliver them yourself? I thought we may be friends after Covent Garden."

A flash of fear slid into her blue orbs before she blinked and it was gone. Even so, he'd seen and understood the fear his words had brought forth. Lord Peel's treatment of her that night obviously haunted her, and scared her still.

Stephen sighed, ashamed to have teased her just then. "I apologize, Lady Clara. I should not make light of that situation. Please forgive me." He returned to the fire, keeping his back to her. "I thank you for the basket. I'll be sure to call on your father in the coming days to introduce myself and give my thanks for your generosity."

When she didn't venture to reply, he turned and found her gaze locked on his lower back. Her eyes widened and she looked at him as if seeing him for the first time. He couldn't help the grin that formed on his lips. He supposed it was only natural. She'd probably not seen many men so scantily dressed in her life.

"Lady Clara? Did you hear what I said?"

She nodded, licking her lips. His body hardened at the sight of her tongue. For all her harshness toward him and his sisters, her lofty airs and disdain for those she did not see fit to wipe her boots, damn it she was beautiful. There was no use trying to deny the truth of that fact, and he was a fool to try to sway his mind that she was not. Lady Clara was a sweet little morsel that was ripe for plucking. Not that he'd be the one to pluck her, but still, he wasn't blind to her outer beauty. What a pity her inner self was so very rotten.

"Of course I heard and my current thoughts are those that I hope you learn to dress yourself better when you arrive. I was also charged to invite you to dine with us tomorrow evening. Maybe your valet can guide you on what is appropriate to wear around a lady. What you have on at present is not."

He ground his teeth, wanting to retort in kind, and yet he did not. His pants were uncomfortably damp and he needed her to leave so he could change. He doubted that

Lady Clara would appreciate it if he undid his breeches and pulled those off in front of her as well.

"I shall ensure I pass on your advice to my valet." A servant he'd not deemed necessary and actually did not have. He'd been dressing himself since he was eight, he wasn't now about to need another man to assist him. "Your advice is so very welcome, my lady."

She rolled her eyes and his lips twitched. "I will bid you good day, Mr. Grant. Dinner is at eight sharp. Try not to be late." He watched as she turned and flounced out of the room without a backward glance.

"I shall do my very best to read the time correctly, Lady Clara, so as not to disappoint you," he called out after her.

He chuckled at the vexed *argh* that came from the foyer before the front door closed softly behind her. Stephen walked to the window and watched as she jumped back into the waiting carriage parked in front of the house before it rattled off down the drive.

Dinner with the Duke of Law and his daughter. He shook his head at the thought of it. Who would have thought he'd be doing such a thing? Certainly he had not, but after Louise and now Sophie's exalted marriages he was forced to endure this society simply due to whom he was now related. An earl and a marquess.

Stephen turned and started for his room, ordering hot water from a waiting footman as he passed him in the foyer. He would do the pretty, play the gentleman, and then his duty would be done with Lady Clara and her father. He could tolerate her for one more night and do his utmost to be on his best behavior before the Duke. If not for the little hellcat who was his neighbor, but then for his sisters and the reputation they wished to keep within the society they circulated.

# CHAPTER 2

Clara sat at the dining table the following evening and fought not to roll her eyes each and every time Mr. Grant opened his mouth and talked to her father, or at least tried to. Her father this evening seemed quite preoccupied with the table decorations and was continually staring and touching them as if he'd never seen embroidered linen before in his life.

It was only the three of them this evening, and she regretted the decision in not making some of their other neighbors attend and make welcome Mr. Grant. With her father ignoring everyone it was left to her to ensure conversation flowed and it was not a task she wished to do. Not with Mr. Grant in any case. He may have saved her at Covent Garden, but it did not make up for the many times he'd been rude to her in town.

A small voice reminded Clara that she'd been rude also, atrociously so, and especially toward his sisters, so it was only logical that she would receive some criticism in return. Even so, his rudeness had been beyond what she thought was necessary.

"Are you enjoying the venison, Mr. Grant? The deer came from our lands, we have hundreds running about." She stared down at the meat on her plate, furiously thinking of what else she could talk about. If they resorted to talking of the weather the evening would be a terrible bore. Perhaps horses? Or even the tablecloth, at least then maybe her papa would take part.

"It is very good...deer."

She looked up and read the laughter glinting in his blue-green eyes, having not missed the double entendre to his words. Was he trying to be amusing? If so, he was not succeeding.

"How are your sisters, Mr. Grant? I heard Miss Sophie has moved to Scotland and is settled."

All amusement fled from his eyes and she marveled at her triumph. Good, at least the subject of his siblings he did not find amusing, especially when it was she who was querying about them. No doubt he'd steeled himself for her to be cutting in regard to his sisters. For years they had played this game of who could insult the other better. It was only natural he would assume she would not stop, even if before her father.

"Both my sisters are doing well. Louise has recently traveled to Scotland to be with Sophie during the birth of her second child. She has returned to London now, however."

"What a shame you did not go," she said, smiling to soften her insinuation that he ought to leave and never come back. "But I suppose moving into Marquess Graham's country estate is more important for a young man on the rise." She smiled sweetly. "I hope Lady Mackintosh came through the birth well."

He stared at her nonplused and she kept her smile

firmly on her lips. At least if he'd gone to Scotland she'd not be forced to host dinner parties and think of things to say to please their guest. In future, no matter what her father said, she would agree, but then not follow through on any such ideas. Her father had not taken part in the evening in any case, he may as well have stayed in the library where he was most comfortable for all the conversation he'd taken part in.

"Sophie tolerated the birth well. I will travel up to Moy in the coming months after I finish moving into Ashby Cottage. I wish to lord about the house and grounds for some weeks and think myself very grand and important. I must act, you see, just as my betters do. People such as yourself. I have little doubt that you keep a steely eye on all those working for the estate."

She raised one brow. Had he really said what he just did? Clara took a sip of wine, watching him over the rim of the crystal glass. "I do of course, just as any proficient landlord should. You forget, Mr. Grant, I'm an educated woman in possession of a brain and know how to keep not just one, but multiple estates running well."

"Clara dear, do you think the roses are happy being on our table? They look a little sad to me."

Mr. Grant turned his attention to the roses, reaching out to pick one. "I think, your Grace, that they are the happiest when before those who appreciate beauty, like now, as the centerpiece of your dining table."

Clara did not know what to say to Mr. Grant's kind words to her father. Very few, except for her father's valet, the butler and housekeeper knew that the Duke was falling ill of mind. Mr. Grant being here this evening could soon change that fact. He'd likely tell everyone he knew that the Duke of Law was addled completely.

He'd take pleasure in embarrassing her and her family she was sure, a revenge of sorts after the many years that they had not gotten along.

"You look a little tired, Papa. Do you want me to ring for James?"

Her father's eyes cleared and just like that she knew he was with them again. "Not yet, my dear. The night is still early." He turned to Mr. Grant. "I'm going to go on a fox hunt tomorrow. Have some friends coming up from London for the sport. Would you like to join me?"

Clara inwardly sighed as the fox hunt her father was talking about took place two years ago shortly before his decline.

"That would be wonderful, your Grace. I shall be here before eleven."

The Duke stood, seemingly finished with the conversation and Clara watched as he wandered about the room before walking out the door. She turned to a waiting footman. "Please escort the Duke to his room. James will take over from there."

"Of course, Lady Clara," the servant said, bowing and leaving to do as she bid.

She read the confusion in Mr. Grant's gaze and knew there was little she could do but to explain, as best she could in any case.

"Apologies for my father, Mr. Grant, over the last several months his heath has declined, his memory most of all. I need you to understand that there is no fox hunt tomorrow. The fox hunt he invited friends up from London for took place two years ago around this time, but we have not hosted one since."

He leaned back in his chair, a thoughtful expression on his face. "I'm very sorry to hear this, Lady Clara. You will tell me if there is anything that I can do. I know we're not the best of friends, but all of that is forgotten when one is in need."

She hoped she could believe that with this man. Certainly in the past he'd had an uncanny ability to speak his mind and to go into battle for those he thought were being mistreated. She'd certainly been on the receiving end of a tongue-lashing from him a time or two.

"Thank you for understanding. The doctor does not seem to know what has brought this ailment on, but he believes it'll be lifelong." Horrifyingly, tears sprung to her eyes at the thought of her father succumbing to his illness and she blinked furiously, lest the one man she was loath to see her upset saw her rattled.

"Truly, my lady. I'm sorry that this has happened to the Duke and yourself. I should not have come here tonight."

She waved his concerns aside, knowing there would be many more days like this one where her father would be vague before guests and tongues would start to wag. "Father invited you, and no matter that sometimes he does not seem to know where he is or what he's doing, having a little normalcy to his life is all I can do for him. If a friend visits, or he invites a new neighbor to dine with us, I will not stop him. In those moments when he is his old self, and I have not done what he's asked, I would never hear the end of his displeasure, so it's easier to be complicit."

Mr. Grant chuckled, the sound deep and warm. Clara studied his strong jaw, straight nose and features that were similar to those of his sisters'. He had a pleasing face for a man who was not nobility and did not come from such exalted stock. Her attention snapped to his attire, his wide, broad shoulders and arms that bulged a little under his superfine coat when he cut into his meal. For all that they were enemies, Clara could admit that as a woman looking at a man, he was far superior to the many men she knew. Pity he was so very far beneath her notice and social status.

STEPHEN CUT into his venison and tried to eat his meal as quickly as he could. Seated across from Lady Clara, he had the odd sensation that she was sizing him up and finding fault. He chanced a look at her and yes, sure as the sun rose in the east, she was inspecting him. He inwardly swore. *Please do not think of me romantically.* He wasn't interested.

When he married… No, *if* he married, he'd marry a woman who knew a day's hard work, a woman who was capable, intelligent and empathetic to those less fortunate. A woman who knew how to survive without servants at her every beck and call. Not like the duke's daughter across from him. He doubted Lady Clara knew what a broom was. Not that he would expect his wife to do such menial chores—they would have servants for such matters—but he wanted to know that she at least was capable. He certainly was.

He picked up his glass of wine, taking a sip. He would not let what Lady Clara told him about her father sway his idea of the woman. Her tongue was still as sharp as a blade, and the insults they'd passed between them were too many to count. Far too many to forgive.

He would, however, help her should she need it in regard to her father. To see a man well respected and liked within the society be brought low by illness was never a pleasant thing.

"If I should be fortunate enough to meet your father again, I will not make a scene should he become fuddled or confused, you have my word. Now that I know he's suffering from such an illness, I shall do my very best should I see him to keep him out of harm's away."

"Thank you, Mr. Grant. That is a comfort to me."

Stephen pushed his plate away. A footman offered dessert and he declined. It was time he returned home and he was sure Lady Clara wished to check in on her father in any case. "Please thank your father for the invitation to dinner, but I think I should return home. It's been a pleasure, Lady Clara."

She watched him from across the table, a small smile playing about her lips. "A little advice, Mr. Grant. Such words are normally spoken when one is taking their leave, near the front door or in the parlor after dinner. Not at the dining table."

And there she was again, the little *so and so* who couldn't help but criticize him or his conduct. He stood, walking to the door and leaving her gaping after him. "Goodnight, Lady Clara," he said at the threshold. "I do hope this door is adequate enough for me to take my leave, or do you want to escort me into the hall to satisfy your rules?"

He heard her annoyed sigh and left. The woman bothered him terribly. There was something about her that niggled under his skin like a maggot in cheese.

"Perfectly adequate, thank you," she called after him, taking the last word.

Stephen took his greatcoat from a waiting footman, the cool, fresh country air minimizing his annoyance at Lady Clara just a little. He waited while his horse was brought around and looked out over the ducal lands. The gardens were manicured, not a blade of grass dared be out of place, and even from where he stood, and the encroaching dark, he could tell the property would be even more magnificent during daylight hours.

Maybe if he were invited here again he would get a chance to see its glory. It was certainly the only thing he wished to see at the estate. Certainly the daughter was not a priority in future travels.

# CHAPTER 3

Several days later, Clara sat under ferns at the base of the garden. She squinted, focusing on a large hare that sat in the grass looking about for any threats. Clara adjusted her rifle that sat atop a fallen tree log in her hand, trying to get a better position.

The housekeeper had asked her about tonight's dinner and her father had requested rabbit. She'd not seen one of those yet today, but a hare would do well enough and her father would not know the difference.

It sat still, not moving from its own cover and Clara wondered if it would ever walk out into the open so she may have a clean shot.

A bird flew out of the brush and the hare darted away and out of sight. She cursed the little devil and stood, knowing she would have little chance of catching him now that he'd been spooked.

"Maybe tomorrow, Lady Clara," the gamekeeper said, a rifle over his arm and a small smile playing about his mouth. Mr. Wilson had been with the family for as long as Clara could remember. Her father was especially fond of him and his knowledge of animals and wildlife was beyond comprehension.

"Perhaps, but today will not be the day. Father is quite adamant he has rabbit, so do you think you could try and shoot one if you have time?"

He tipped his hat, reaching out a hand to take her gun as she gained her feet. "Of course, my lady. I will ensure the dining table has rabbit on it this evening for his Grace."

"Thank you." She turned toward the house when the sound of voices carried over to her. She stumbled at seeing Mr. Grant walking toward her with her father. He was looking at her curiously, and she could hazard a guess as to why. She supposed he'd not thought her capable of catching her own food. Which, in truth, she had not done today, but on many other days she'd had more success. Clara leaned up and kissed her father's cheek. "Papa. Mr. Grant. How lovely to see you again so soon."

Mr. Grant looked over to where their gamekeeper stood. Clara turned and watched as Mr. Wilson adjusted the guns and then walked into the trees.

"Lady Clara, I did not know you knew how to hunt."

She took her father's arm, leading him back toward the house. "There are a great many things I should imagine you do not know about me, Mr. Grant."

"She's an excellent shot," her father added to the conversation. Clara smiled, a burst of happiness filling her that her father should remember such a detail. There were times when she wondered if he recognized her, never mind what she was capable of.

"I'm not so very good at using a gun. I was not part of any shooting or fox hunting parties when growing up."

The reminder that Mr. Grant had been poor as a child eliminated the barb that she was about to say about a gentleman's worth when one could not shoot. Similar to those little insults often heaped onto a woman's shoulders. That being if they could not sew, draw or play the piano. Instead, Clara found herself saying, "Having your own estate now, Mr. Grant, we shall have to remedy that lapse."

Her father patted her hand with vigor. "Of course. Of course you shall. That is the best idea, my dear. And as you're so proficient in it, you shall be the one to teach Mr. Grant."

Mr. Grant mumbled reasons as to why that would not suit at the same time that Clara pointed out the facts as to why she could not teach him. She would need a chaperone and the gamekeeper was already too busy and so too was her maid to go trudging around the estate teaching a man how to shoot a gun.

"Nonsense," her father said, quelling both their words. "You're more than capable, Clara, and now that we're home you have time on your side. A day or two each week is not too much to ask for our new neighbor."

Clara fought not to show the dismay that coursed through her at the idea of teaching Mr. Grant anything. They were not friends, having never got along well in the past, and should her father be of his right mind, he would never allow her to escort an unmarried gentleman about the grounds for a shooting lesson. The idea was atrocious.

Not to mention that they could have a disagreement and she'd be tempted to shoot him in the foot!

"If you wish, Papa. Of course I'll help Mr. Grant learn the ways of a gentleman."

Mr. Grant met her eyes and she saw the challenge in them. She also recognized that he was dearly fighting to hold back some caustic remark that would annoy her.

She smiled. "Shall we return to the house for tea?" she asked, all sweetness.

Her father nodded, pulling her forward. "That sounds just the thing."

*HMM, yes, just the thing.* Stephen caught up to the Duke and Lady Clara, his hands itching not to strangle the little minx who at any opportunity afforded to her, bothered him. He no more wanted to learn how to shoot with her than she wanted to teach him. He was only here to see the Duke and ask if it would be all right for him to fish in the river that ran adjacent to his property and was owned by his Grace.

Another neighbor had said that there was good perch to be caught in the Duke's stream, but it was unlikely he'd allow him to fish there, stating his Grace was quite protective of his own fish and game. Not that he'd had any trouble in gaining approval, the Duke only seemed too happy to allow him to fish there after he'd asked.

"Oh, and by the by, my dear, I've given Mr. Grant the right to fish in our stream. You know the place, up near farmer Coe's cottage, on the bend where it is deepest."

She glanced at him in surprise. Obviously she was quite aware that her father did not give approval for such occupations often. "As long as Mr. Grant does not fish it out."

Stephen fought not to roll his eyes at the ridiculousness of the comment. "I'm sure I can control myself, Lady Clara. There will be plenty of fish left for you." And bull-headed came to mind when he thought of her.

She raised her chin, not deigning to reply. They strode for a time in quiet, just the sounds of the birds and the gardeners who worked in the beds could be heard. Stephen thought over the Duke, and his mannerisms and words the last two days. There was certainly something not quite right, and after Lady Clara's warning yesterday, he'd seen flashes of the Duke's mind coming and going. Even in the last half hour that he'd been here the Duke had been vague one minute and sharp the next. How much longer would Lady Clara be able to look after him by herself? And would the disease, whatever it was, become worse to the point that the Duke did not know or recognize anyone about him? Even his daughter?

A terrible thought, but one could not help but have it after observing him.

"Mr. Grant will not fish us out, my dear. I see no harm in it. Many people fish there and we've never had any issues yet with stock numbers."

Lady Clara rubbed her father's arm, a confused frown between her brows. "Papa, you never allow anyone to fish there, remember? Mr. Grant is the first you've ever approved."

His Grace stared at Lady Clara and Stephen could read the confusion, the blankness behind the eyes. The poor soul had no idea he'd given him the first approval ever.

"No, you must be mistaken, Clara. I cannot see myself being so difficult to my neighbors who requested such leave."

"Perhaps I'm mistaken, Papa," she conceded, obviously not willing to press the point. "Let us go indoors before it rains. I think there is weather coming in."

They walked up to the terrace and Stephen went ahead, opening the terrace door for the Duke. Clara stopped at the threshold, staring up at him. Her defiant chin rose, and her wide, blue eyes stared down her pert nose at him. How she managed it since she was shorter than he was, was beyond him. But she did and he found himself drawn to taking in every nuance, every little freckle that flittered across her nose and cheeks. He'd thought her skin had been perfectly unblemished, but it was not and it only made her more approachable, more real. He ground his teeth. He would not see her as an attractive woman. He'd be betraying himself should he stoop to such a level.

"You need not stay, Mr. Grant. You have your approval from Papa, no need to have tea."

He feigned injury, clasping his chest in mock pain all the while holding the door open. "You wound me, my lady. If I leave now, how will I ever recover from not taking tea with the most sought-after woman in the *ton* at her country estate? My reputation will never recover."

"Are you two coming in or are you going to have a tête-à-tête in the doorway for the remainder of the day?"

The Duke's words pulled him from thoughts of how fun it was to annoy the chit who stared up at him with loathing. He knew why she hated him so much—he'd been poor, and his sister had married her future betrothed. In her mind in any case.

The thought of her being married soured his temper and he stalked indoors, leaving her standing in the doorway alone.

She gasped and he ignored her shock. Stephen bowed before the Duke. "I thank you for the invitation for tea, your Grace, but I must be off. I hired a man of business and have to meet him this afternoon to discuss the estate and lands."

"Do not let us keep you, Mr. Grant." Lady Clara flopped down on a nearby settee, reaching for the teapot that a servant had brought in without having to be told. How delightful it must be to have people waiting on them hand and foot. He'd become accustomed to a similar life-style, but it never sat well with him. To this day he felt as though he were impersonating someone else, should be the one serving the lords and ladies instead of taking tea with them.

Lady Clara thought this way about him still and it irked. More than irked, it irritated the hell out of him. She was an uppity little snob.

"Are you sure, Mr. Grant? You're more than welcome."

His attention flicked to Lady Clara at the Duke's declaration and her little gag of repulsion was not hard to decipher. He shook his head. "Alas, no, but I will call again soon. You're more than welcome to come fishing with me, your Grace. It may be nice to get outdoors and away from meddling females."

The Duke glanced at his daughter and then burst into laughter. Stephen smiled, pleased to have made the Duke laugh and annoyed his daughter at the same time before his leaving.

"Father may attend any event he wishes, I shall not stop him." She picked up her tea and took a sip. "He shall be able to count how many you catch, ensure that you're not taking more than you're welcome to."

The Duke laughed harder and Stephen narrowed his eyes. He took a calming breath, bowing to Lady Clara also. "Good day to you both. I'll see myself out."

Lady Clara's smirk was enough to make him swear, or kiss her smart little mouth quiet. He strode to the door, thanking a footman who handed him his coat from when he arrived. A servant went to fetch his horse, and he kicked his heels in the foyer for a minute as his mount was brought around.

However would he survive living so close to such a woman? He would write to his brother-in-law in London and ask if he had any other estates that he'd like leased in other counties. Maybe he could move to Scotland and live in a cottage on Sophie and Brice's land. To live here, to have to put up with Lady Clara was too much, and yet on his ride home all he could see in his mind's eye was her pretty little nose up in the air as she met his barbs with some of her own and he cursed himself a fool for thinking it charming.

# CHAPTER 4

Clara stood and walked to the window, watching as Mr. Grant gained his mount and cantered off down the drive. She told herself it was because she wanted to ensure he left her lands, hadn't loitered about and managed to stay longer than he needed to. It wasn't, however, why she was staying where she was in the library, staring after him as his bottom sat snug in his saddle, his back ramrod straight as if he'd been riding his whole life, not only a few years.

He looked very well indeed on the back of a horse. She mumbled words no lady should know and turned back to her father. "It's started to rain. I think Mr. Grant will be soaked through by the time he arrives home."

Her father glanced up at her, a biscuit with jam on top partway to his mouth. "Mr. Grant was here? Why did he not come and see me? I like that fellow, good chap. We should invite him 'round for dinner one evening."

Clara nodded, biting back the sting of tears at her father's words. She looked back out the window and the rain that was falling much heavier, torrential even. A flash of light blazed outside the window followed by a boom of thunder that made her jump.

The thought of Mr. Grant out in this weather was not a pleasant thought, no matter how much they did not get along, how much they disliked each other's company. Mr. Grant out in this storm was dangerous. He could be hit by lightning or his horse could bolt with fright and leave him injured, or worse, dead in a ditch.

"Mr. Grant has just left, Papa, and the weather has turned terribly dangerous."

He joined her at the window, taking in the weather just as another flash of light and boom of thunder rattled the panes.

"Let us hope he returns home without injury. We'll send a stable hand over later today to ensure his safe arrival."

And just like that he was back again, his eyes clear of confusion. She bit her lip, wishing she knew what it was that ailed him so she may try to cure him of the disease.

"I think that would be best. I'll go and send word now to the stables. You may wish to ready yourself for luncheon, Papa. We'll be dining in an hour."

Clara walked from the room, and after telling the butler to send word to the stable, she was walking through the foyer about to head upstairs to change for lunch when the front door burst open and Mr. Grant stumbled in, water dripping from him as if he'd partaken in a swim since he'd left. He glanced at her, holding out his arms as if to stop his clothing from touching his sides.

"I do apologize, Lady Clara, but the causeway is flooded. It seems the storm hit upstream prior to hitting us here and I cannot make my way home."

Which was true, the Duke of Law's estate was in effect on a small island, surrounded by a river that when flooded made one housebound. She turned to the footman who looked at Mr. Grant with annoyance that he was making a mess on the floor.

"Have the blue room prepared for Mr. Grant, and tell Mrs. Pennell there will be three for both lunch and dinner today."

"Yes, my lady."

"Follow me, Mr. Grant. I'll show you the room. The chambermaid will be up shortly to place fresh linens on the bed." Clara walked up the staircase, fully aware of the tall, dripping-wet man behind her. Her skin prickled in awareness and she had the oddest sense that he was staring at her neck. The urge to run her hand across her nape assailed her, but she did not. Not for a moment did she want him imagining he had any effect on her whatsoever.

For he did not, nor would he ever have.

She turned toward the guest wing of the house, pointing out rooms that he may wish to use should he need solitude. "With the river flooding you'll be here for some days. It's quite deep and rises quickly, but unfortunately does not go down as rapidly."

She opened a door halfway down the passage, swinging it wide. "This will be your room. It has a lovely view of the maze and has a desk, not that you'll be able to correspond with anyone at present, but even so…" What was she saying? She was blabbering like a nincompoop. "There is a dressing room through there," she said, pointing to a connecting door. "You may change in there. I'll have Papa's valet find something to fit you and bring it in."

He threw her a tentative smile, running a hand through his thick, brown hair, pushing it off his face and for the first time in all the years she'd known Mr. Grant her stomach fluttered. "I'll instruct the maid to light the fire for you also. Is there anything else that you will need?" she asked with a sharp edge to her voice, annoyed to have reacted to him in such a manner.

He wiped a drop of water off his chin with the back of his hand and again her attention was seized. "No, thank you, Lady Clara. You're more than generous."

She turned without answer and walked from the room, before pausing at the threshold. "Well, I cannot have you stay in the stable. Father would never allow it." Clara walked away as fast as she could from the flash of disappointment she read in Mr. Grant's eyes at her words. She would not under any circumstance feel anything for him but contempt. He'd been rude and impolite to her during her first Season, which was unforgivable. That his sister stole her intended wasn't to be borne.

*He was never your betrothed...in fact he never showed you that much interest.*

She ignored the voice of reason and went downstairs to ensure everything was put in order for Mr. Grant before heading to her room where she found to her dismay that the rain had only grown stronger and now the wind had picked up. A day or two of Mr. Grant being at Chidding Hall may end up being a week.

Oh, however would she bear it?

※

THE FOLLOWING day Stephen sat in the upstairs parlor reading a book that the Duke had given him on the property he now leased. It was an interesting read and gave him more of an insight to his brother-in-law, the Marquess Graham, and his family on his grandmother's side.

The Duke seemed quite well today, bright and alert, and he was hopeful that maybe he would remain so, but after what Lady Clara had explained about his illness he doubted his day of clarity would last.

The door opened and a maid walked in, a few logs of wood in her arms. He stood, coming to her to take them. "Here, let me help you, miss."

She pulled them away, horror written on her face. "Oh no, my lord. I could not have you do that. I won't be a moment and I'll leave you in peace once again."

Stephen shook his head. "No, I insist. They look too heavy for you." He took them from her, surprised just how heavy they were when he grabbed them. He threw a couple of logs onto the fire before placing the others in the wood bin at the side of the fireplace. "I'm not a lord, merely Mr. Stephen Grant at your service."

The young maid grinned, a light blush stealing over her cheeks and he smiled in return. She was a pretty woman and the type of woman he'd always thought to marry one day. Before his sisters had married so very well and placed him in a precarious position. Related to people of high rank and yet without the funds to support such a lifestyle himself was oftentimes looked on with ridicule and pity. It was fortunate his brother-in-law was so very wealthy and could afford to lease him Ashby Cottage for a fraction of its worth.

"It's a pleasure to meet you, Mr. Grant. I'm Miss Daphne Smith."

The door opened and Lady Clara walked in. Her steps halted at the sight of them close before the fire and close enough to each other that to anyone it would look like a private tête-à-tête was at play.

She raised her brow and he knew what she was thinking. The chiding look she gave to Daphne was easy to read and the maid bobbed a quick curtsy before all but running from the room.

Stephen stared at Lady Clara in return and waited for the little minx to say something about his conduct.

She came farther into the room and sat over by the window, picking up a small basket he'd not seen there before, and pulling out a cushion that looked half completed along with needle and thread. "Cavorting with the help. I wondered how long it would be before you made trouble with one of our maids."

He sat, staring at the flames and counting to five before he answered, or stood and strangled the woman. "I was not cavorting, as you term it. I helped her with the wood for the fire and introduced myself. Had you found making a beast with two backs you may have an issue to discuss."

She gasped, her needlework halted in her hands. "Have you forgotten whom you're speaking to? That rough, uneducated speech is not appropriate for a Duke's daughter. Mind your manners, Mr. Grant."

"Mind your own manners." He glared at the flames, his hands flexing in his lap. Out his peripheral vision he noticed she stood, hands on hips and he ground his teeth. Now he was in for a tongue-lashing.

"I do not need to mind my own manners, sir. I know very well what is expected of me and how to go about in this life. You will never see me cavorting with a footman or giving the staff hope of an understanding that is beyond their reach and too beneath mine. From when I was very little, Father has reminded me of my duty, of whom I should marry and why.

"You're now the brother of a marchioness and count-ess, being such one would think that you too would under-stand your limits. Not to mention you're a guest in someone else's home and should conduct yourself with respect and propriety. Seeing you with our maid does concern me as to how you get on in London at your sister's home."

Stephen stood, storming over to where Lady Clara waited near the window. Her eyes blazed with annoyance and something else he could not make out. Even so, he was glad she was mad, for it only matched his own ire.

"You have a sharp tongue. One day, Lady Clara, someone will tell you to keep it still in that pretty mouth of yours."

Her eyes widened and her mouth opened in a pretty little O. He clenched his jaw, willing himself not to look at her lips. *Don't do it, man, you'll regret it* a voice warned.

"And you, Mr. Grant should decide to which social sphere you wish to belong. This one you're now circulating in or the one you'll find below stairs."

"Jealous I was not talking to you instead of the maid? Maybe if I complimented your gown more often, or asked you to dance you would not be so bitter toward me."

She scoffed at his words but her cheeks pinkened, making her even more alluring than normal. When she was angry, she was like a hellcat protecting its kittens and he found it extremely alluring. "To be jealous one has to have emotions involved. When it comes to you, Mr. Grant, I do believe you think too highly of yourself. I do not care what you do outside of these walls, but in this house, you'll keep your hands off my staff."

"Has anyone ever told you how pompous you are? How judgmental and belittling you can be to those who are not of your rank? Do not forget the people belowstairs that you find so beneath your notice keep this house running and everyone in it fed, clothed and warm. What do you do, *Lady Clara?*" He accentuated her name, wanting to add a little sarcasm to his words.

Vexing chit!

"I pay their wage, that's what I do, Mr. Grant, which is more than you can say for yourself."

He took some calming breaths through his nose, sure he was breathing fire. How dare she, but then, how dare he? He was being unapologetically rude and he would not be surprised if she did make him sleep out in the stables.

"Really? Or does your father pay their wage?"

"I do, Mr. Grant," she retorted hotly. "My father no longer controls the finances or running of the estates. That has fallen to me and our steward since his health has declined."

The reminder that her father was ill, that she had multiple stresses on her small shoulders shamed him. He stepped back, turning away. "I think, Lady Clara, that we should part ways before any more is spoken and if at all possible, start our acquaintance again. I apologize for my conduct here this morning."

"Apology not accepted. You think me judgmental, and you too judge me and my friends. I've seen you in town, laughing, throwing us mocking looks whenever the chance arose. Do not think for a minute that I do not remember how rude you were to me in Hyde Park several years ago."

He scoffed. "I was rude. You were throwing yourself at my sister's husband. Do you think I would sit by and watch you shame her so? I will never allow anyone to treat my siblings such, not even a duke's daughter who was angry because the Marquess had not picked her."

"He had not picked your sister either, if I recall correctly." She stepped closer to him, the breath of her words fanning his ire even more. "Am I wrong, Mr. Grant? Was he not found in her room by mistake?"

"That is beside the point," he mumbled, knowing she spoke the truth. "Their marriage is a love match and a happy union. You shall not speak of Louise again. I'll not stand for it."

She laughed mockingly. "You will not stand for it. Really? And if I do, what do you plan to do? Chide me like a child?"

Right at this moment a good slap on her ass would do him a world of good. The thought of touching her derriere pulled him up short and he ran a hand over his jaw. He didn't want to touch her any more than she wanted to touch him. Did he?

"Take my words as the truth that they are. I'll not stand for you saying another word about my sisters."

Her eyes narrowed, and she glared at him as if he were the worst creature in England. Their breathing was ragged, and Stephen's attention snapped to her bosom that rose and fell with each of her breaths. He cursed the ample delights that sat nestled in her gown. She was not for him to ogle or think about in any other way than the annoying, rude Lady Clara that he'd forever dislike. Not for a moment would he think her strong-willed, defiant, beautiful...

"You do not tell me what to do. Ever." The last word accentuated with a step closer to his person, almost putting her breast-to-chest against him.

He did not move away, nor did she seem to realize just how close they were. He glared down at her plump mouth, pulled into a mocking smirk and something inside him snapped. She seemed to sense a change in him and her eyes widened, but still she did not scuttle away. Nor did he want her to. In fact, right at this moment all he could think about was kissing her within an inch of her life. Taking the maddening wench in his arms and seeing if her fire burned as bright in his arms as it did out of it.

Stephen reached for her, wrenching her from the short

space that separated them and kissed her. His hand spiked into her soft curls and at her gasp, he deepened the kiss, thrusting his tongue against hers. She softened in his hold, her hands, tentative at first, clasped his shoulders before slipping about his neck.

She tasted like sweet tea and sin and he ravaged her mouth, punished her for being so obstinate and alluring at the same time. Punished her for all the times he'd been on the receiving end of her wicked lips while drawing him ever closer. His body hardened and he hoisted her a little off her feet, holding her against his person. She melted against him, her body undulating against his and he hardened at the satisfied moan she expelled.

Footsteps sounded in the passage and they wrenched apart, putting much-needed distance between them.

"Ah, here you both are. I've been outside and the rain does not seem to want to relent." The Duke walked over to the window, staring out at the weather. "No, my opinion on this is correct. The rain is here to stay. You may be stuck with us, Mr. Grant, for several days at this point."

Lady Clara moved over to the window and picked up her sewing. Her lips were swollen and there was a pretty rose hue on her cheeks that he'd placed there. For a moment Stephen couldn't move. That kiss. *Shit!* He had not meant for that to happen, but now that it had, all he could think about was why the hell had the Duke picked that particular time to interrupt.

He inwardly groaned. For all that was holy, he needed help if he were thinking about Lady Clara Quinton in a romantic light. "I think you may be right, your Grace," he said, joining him at the window and looking out on the weather. "I hope you do not mind. My stay here was not purposefully done."

The Duke chuckled, waving his concerns away just as a

muffled voice from behind him said, "I mind and the sooner you're gone the better."

He ignored her remark, making a note to take it up with her later. Or perhaps not. If he were tempted to kiss her again when they were alone it would probably be best if he stayed as far away from Lady Clara as much as possible until he could leave. If there was one thing he would promise himself, it would be to stay the hell away from her and the temptation she oozed.

She was not for him and he most certainly was not for her.

# CHAPTER 5

C lara had managed to stay clear of Mr. Grant over the next day, but after dinner the following evening, her father had complained of a megrim and had retired to his room. She'd been unfortunate enough to have to retire to the drawing room after the meal where she was joined by Mr. Grant.

He sat across from her, lazily crossing his legs and lighting a cheroot. She sewed in her own chair, ignoring the heat that sizzled across her skin from his gaze. It traveled the length of her like a physical caress and she cursed him for tempting her so.

After their kiss the other day, her body had not been its usual, calm self. Her skin heated at the memory of his touch, the slide of his tongue against hers made her stomach clench and heat to pool at her core. Two things that never had occurred to her before. Not with anyone. When he'd wrenched her against him she had been tempted to claw at his face, and yet the moment his lips touched hers she was lost.

All thoughts of refusing him fled and instead she'd

plastered herself against him as if her life were dependent on him holding her. She'd had the oddest sensations coursing through her blood, and her body ached in a way that instead of being painful was exciting, tempting, and something she wanted to do again.

How he must be congratulating himself on seducing her and making her jelly in his arms.

"Please can you do something else other than stare at me, Mr. Grant? I feel you inspecting me like some oddity on the street corner."

"You flatter yourself," he said, his voice flat and uninterested. Dismissive even. She hated when he spoke in such a way. Somehow it always made her feel unworthy. "Why would I stare at you? To do so would show an interest in the subject matter, which I do not have."

She ground her teeth. He was lying and she ought to call him out for such an untruth, but she could not. She was a lady after all, a duke's daughter. To call a gentleman out on his word was not the done thing. But his inspection of her was as true as the fact she was sitting across from him.

Her gaze flicked to the clock on the mantel.

"Trying to gauge if you've spent enough time with me?"

She shrugged, not willing to be polite if he was not. "You are right, which for you, Mr. Grant, must be a novel thing. It's not often I should imagine that you're right about anything."

He took a long draw of his cheroot before throwing it into the fire. He leaned forward, his elbows resting on his knees. "Do you want to know what else I'm right about, my lady?"

She shrugged again, curious and yet not. "I'm sure no

matter what my reply, you're going to tell me anyway, so you may as well just get on with it."

Not that she wanted to know, for the amused gleam in his eyes told her she would not like what he said. She had the oddest notion that he was laughing at her, or about to shock her. Which one it would be, she wasn't certain.

"That the kiss we shared made you as hot as it made me, and if I'm not mistaken, I would lay a gold sovereign on the table that it's all you've thought about since."

She stared at him, mouth agape before she closed it with a snap. Clara fought to find the words to tell him he was mistaken but they wouldn't come. Blast it. He was right of course. Every waking hour and sleep too she'd relived their embrace. His hands hard against her flesh, holding her against him as his mouth punished hers. What was wrong with her that she would be thinking of Mr. Grant, her enemy, in such a way? "How dare you be so crude."

"Am I wrong?" He lazed in his chair, his face suddenly serious, a dark, hungry glint in his eyes that made her stomach clench and her heart race.

"Yes, you're very wrong. I would rather kiss a fish than kiss you again."

"Liar."

She gasped, standing and throwing her sewing onto the floor. "Apologize or you will be removed to the stable like the common man who thinks he's speaking to a doxy instead of a lady."

He stood, striding over. Clara swallowed as he towered over her, his intense gaze, chiseled cheeks and full lips that she'd dreamed about last night staring down at her. Or more accurately, she'd dreamed about running her hands over those cheeks that were too perfect for a man. Of his mouth, soft and lush that had kissed her with such passion that she had woken up hot and flushed and aching in places she'd never ached before in her life except while in his arms. He was the devil's spawn. She hated him. Truly she did.

She did.

*Didn't she?*

"If I'm moved to the stable, you'll not be able to wield insults at me so easily. I would not deprive you of your sport, Lady Clara. I do believe you enjoy me."

Oh yes, she enjoyed him, that she knew with certainty. She'd enjoy having him touch her right now if only he would eliminate the need that coursed through her blood that only he seemed to evoke.

Blasted man.

"And you think I have a high opinion of myself. If I do, so do you, Mr. Grant."

He muttered something under his breath and clasped her face. Her hands came up to cover his, to remove his hold or keep him there she was not sure. The particulars did not matter, for within a moment he was kissing her again, and this time she met his tongue with hers, taking as much as he gave.

Clara ran her hands down his chest, the corded, strong muscles beneath her palms reminding her of what he looked like without his waistcoat and shirt. The thought did little to cool her desire.

He pulled back and she mewled in protest, having not had enough of his lips on hers. "You're too sweet. You should not taste as sweet as you do," he whispered.

Clara stared up at him as he watched her, his hands flexing on her hips and keeping her hard against him. "I dislike kissing you as well, Mr. Grant."

"Maddening chit." He kissed her again and she inwardly crowed. She'd never been kissed before Mr. Grant had moved into their home. His mouth moved on hers, drawing her ever closer. It was searing, wet and full of need. A real man's kiss that she'd only heard whispered about within the ballrooms of the *ton*.

Clara had always hoped to be kissed just so one day. So passionately that all her troubles would melt away and all she would be left with was the moment of the kiss. One that consumed and inflamed her body and soul.

Mr. Grant's kiss did all of those things and more. How would she ever make him stop?

His hand dipped lower on her back and Clara found herself no longer in control of her body. Somewhere between the start of the embrace to this point her body had formed a mind of its own. It also seemed to know exactly what it wanted.

*Him…*

When his hand cupped her bottom, pulling her into his hardness, comprehension dawned of just where they were and who could walk in on them at any moment.

She wrenched from his arms, his eyes heavy-lidded with desire and dark with hunger. Clara held up a hand to warn him off, to keep him at bay when he reached for her again. "I do not know what just transpired between us, but it'll never happen again."

He wiped his bottom lip with his thumb, as if erasing all traces of her off his person. She didn't like that he did such a thing. Did he not enjoy their kiss? Was he laughing at her?

"It was merely a kiss, Lady Clara. Not much different to the one we shared two days ago." He studied her a moment and expectation rippled across her skin at the thought he was going to kiss her again. He seemed to rethink his choice and she chastised herself for the disappointment that shot through her blood. "It would be a shame in my estimation if it never happened again. I rather enjoyed our kiss, both of them."

She bit her lip at his words and a small flicker of pride filled her before she shook herself back to reality. They did not like each other and nor should they be doing anything together, other than tolerating each other's presence while Mr. Grant was a guest here.

"Goodnight, Mr. Grant." She started for the door, but he wrenched her back, tipping up her chin to look at her. Her body rioted for him to kiss her again. She tried to mask her desires, but at six and twenty, she found her emotions were not always so easy to conceal, to push down. Now that he'd kissed her, twice, her mind screamed to run, but her body wanted nothing more than to lean up against him like a cat against a person's leg and do it again.

"Goodnight, Lady Clara." He stared at her a moment and hope bloomed in her chest that he was about to kiss her again, but then he stepped back, clasping his arms about his back.

She left, not caring if her departure looked like a scuttle or even a slow run. To stay in his company, to want such a man, a man to kiss her again. One whom she had never liked only meant one thing... She was deprived of the company of the opposite sex, of men who were eligible to court a duke's daughter. Mr. Grant was not one of them.

What would her friends say if they knew she had been so intimate with Mr. Grant? They would laugh, think it a joke at first and then they would probably oust her from their set. For years she had taken great pains to let everyone know of her acquaintance that she disliked the Grants, Stephen and his social-climbing sisters. To kiss the man, to allow such intimacies went against everything that she stood for.

Clara made her room, shutting and locking her door

before collapsing onto her bed. She frowned up at the ornate plaster ceiling. Worse was the fact that he kissed very well, not that she would ever tell him such a truth. He was kind to her father, did not amend His Grace's words when he made a mistake or did not remember what he'd said only five minutes before.

Had she been too quick to judge Mr. Grant? Had she been jealous that Miss Louise Grant married the Marquess Graham and she did not? She slapped the bedding at her side. Of course she'd been jealous, a raging lunatic if she remembered correctly. She could not have gone to any more trouble than she did during that Season to make Miss Grant feel unwelcome and friendless. Or her family.

She was a terrible person. After seeing the Marquess with Louise she knew that she never stood a chance of making him love her. He might not have known at the beginning of his marriage just how much he adored his wife, but it had become obvious quite quickly that he did. Seeing his lordship's affection had brought out the worst in Clara and Mr. Grant had been privy to most of her actions and caustic remarks over the fact.

It wasn't any wonder he loathed her for it.

With him staying here, and now after their two passionate encounters, it would only make the situation with him worse. She couldn't help but wonder if he'd kissed her to teach her a lesson, to tease her so he may use it against her when they were back in town.

Clara sat up on the bed and started unpinning her hair. She would not ring her maid, the last thing she wished for was company. When debating with oneself it was always better, in Clara's opinion, to do it in solitude. Then at least there was no one to tell you that you were a nincompoop and fool not just for one night, but for many years before.

# CHAPTER 6

Clara jumped in her chair the following morning at breakfast when her father bellowed at the footman. "What are you looking at, boy? Do you think you can stare at me? The Duke of Law?"

Clara reached out a hand to clasp his and he pushed her away. He stood, his chair flying backward at his abrupt movement and she gazed up at him, not recognizing the wild, crazy man who stood before her. What was going on?

"Papa?" she said, trying to clasp his hand once again. He stared at her, his eyes wild and vacant and the flitting thought entered her mind that he did not know who she was. "Sit back down, Papa. Your breakfast is growing cold."

He stormed around the table and she squealed as she tried to get up off the chair. She wasn't quick enough and he grabbed her, clasping her arms in a vise-like grip, shaking her.

"Who are you, you wretch? You do not dine with the Duke of Law. Get below stairs where you belong."

"Father!" she yelled. "It's me, Clara."

The door opened and Mr. Grant strode in. His eyes flared at the sight of what was going on and he stormed over to her, wrapping his arms about her father's and pulling him away.

"Your Grace, calm yourself." He pulled him back and Clara took a steadying breath, taking in the two footmen who stood idly by, their eyes wide with shock and their feet seemingly made of stone and not able to render assistance. "Leave us," she said, turning back to her papa, whom Mr. Grant still held and was edging back toward his chair.

"Father," she said again tentatively. "Do you know who I am?" Her eyes burned with unshed tears and she blinked to clear her vision, rummaging into her reticule for a handkerchief. Had he forgotten he had a daughter? If that were the case, she would have to ring for Dr. Miller and have him call on them as soon as the river dropped enough to be passable.

Her father's eyes cleared after a few minutes and Mr. Grant helped him to sit in his chair, kneeling beside him. "Your Grace, do you remember what just happened?"

Her papa rubbed a hand over his brow, frowning. "Did I spill the tea again, my dear?" he said to her, looking out over the breakfast table. "I do apologize if I did."

She smiled, although even to her it felt wobbly at best. "Are you feeling well, Papa? Would you like to lie down a moment?"

He nodded, not venturing to argue with her and that in itself was telling. Her father would never usually go back to his room throughout the day. He'd always been such an active, outdoors man. Loved to hunt, fish, ride his stallion. Whatever sickness that ailed him, it was only growing in severity. Mr. Grant helped him to stand and they walked him out into the foyer.

"I shall take the Duke to his room. Maybe you should

see what the staff can do about getting word out to your family doctor so he may be ready to call when the river is passable."

Clara nodded, not bothering to reply, but simply going straight to the housekeeper to give her instructions. Once she had ordered the servants to check on the river's height and prepare for Dr. Miller's arrival, she instructed Cook to make up a tisane and heat bricks for her father's bed since the weather had turned chill.

Clara walked back into the library, a sanctuary, a place that helped her remember that no matter what this issue with her papa's mind was, she would always have her memories of her father. Those at least could not be ripped from her.

"Lady Clara, are you well?" Mr. Grant walked into the room, coming over to her. For a moment she thought he may engulf her in his arms, but instead he looked about and then sat, staring up at her from the settee. He wrung his hands in his lap. "Your father is resting. Mrs. Pennell brought up a tisane that she said would calm him and make him sleepy."

Clara sat on a settee beside Mr. Grant, staring at her hands in her lap. "I've never seen Father so angry before. He's never raised his voice to his staff or myself. When he grabbed my arms it was like looking at a person whom I had never met." She took a calming breath, biting her lip to stop it from wobbling. "He's forgetting me," she said, meeting Mr. Grant's concerned gaze. "My papa is forgetting his daughter."

The tears did slip over her cheek at her words and she covered her face with her hands, lest he see her crying. A strong arm wrapped about her back and pulled her close. She went willingly, wanting the support, needing it more than she even knew. The horror of her father forgetting everything he'd ever been was too awful to face or accept.

*He was forgetting her…*

"I'm so sorry. I know this must be terribly hard for you."

Clara pulled back a little to stare up at him. What she found staring back at her gave her pause. She'd never seen Mr. Grant look at her with anything but loathing, or annoyance. Besides the two times they'd kissed, certainly he'd never shown a deeper emotion. His eyes were comforting, leaving her feeling warm and safe.

"Thank you for stepping in and assisting me. I could not manage to get Father to let me go and the footmen seemed to have been frozen from shock. That is twice you have rescued me. I will owe you a great debt by the time you leave for your own estate."

He rubbed her back, his thumb slowly working along her spine and making her skin prickle in awareness. The scent of sandalwood wafted from him, and she shut her eyes, liking that he smelled just as a man should, earthy and unpretentious.

"Has your father ever reacted like so before or is this a new development with his illness?"

"It's a new symptom and one that I never wish to see again. He was doing so well this morning, he sometimes does spill his tea or misses his mouth with his food or drink, but never has he ever forgotten who I am. Never has he become violent and grabbed me the way he did."

She looked up at him and met his eyes. "He's not getting any better, if anything he is getting worse every day. The decline has been so fast and now we're stuck here until I can get his London doctor out to see us."

Mr. Grant pushed back a lock of hair from her brow, placing it behind her ear. The action caused her to shiver.

Of all the times she would react so to a man's touch, now was not the appropriate time to do it. But how could she not when it had only ever been Mr. Grant who made her feel alive, was not scared to chastise her when he thought she was being unfair? It had only ever been the man beside her that had caused her to react in any way.

"The river will go down in a day or so and then we shall fetch the doctor. I shall stay with you until his arrival to ensure you remain safe. Not that I think that your father would ever intentionally harm you, but that does not mean that he will not unintentionally hurt you and when he does realize his mistake, it would kill him to know you were injured. I will save you both from that pain at least."

"Thank you, Mr. Grant." She threw him a self-deprecating smile. "You are a better man than I gave you credit for, I'm afraid."

He grinned, tweaking her nose. "Well, the fault lies with me too. I have not been the kindest to you either, so I would think we're even in that regard."

STEPHEN STARED down at her and the warm coiling in his stomach started as she stared up at him with her injured, sad, blue eyes. He wanted to wrap her up in a protective shell and save her from this sadness, but he could not. Her father was ill, possibly gravely so, and he would stay by her side and see this sadness to its conclusion, which he'd started to think would end with the death of the Duke.

Not that he would tell lady Clara such a thing, but the decline from the Duke was startling and he could not help but think it would only get a lot worse before it ended.

A tear slipped from her eye and he wiped it away with his thumb. It was never pleasant to see a woman upset, even Lady Clara who had been his enemy for eight years or so. To see her in this situation showed him another side of her. A loving daughter, a daughter who was frightened and scared for her parent and heartbroken at the outcome she faced.

"Do not cry, my lady. Your father will have a rest and he should be back to rights this afternoon."

She shook her head, her hands holding fast against his chest. "I do not believe he will be. I have this terrible, sinking feeling that he's not long for this world. He's become so much worse. I thought bringing him home would be beneficial, and it was for a time, but now... His outburst at breakfast has never happened before. What if he starts to do this often? Whatever shall I do?"

He rubbed her back, trying to give as much comfort as he could. "I'll not leave you alone in this, and so whatever happens, we shall deal with it together. Agreed?" he asked, meeting her gaze.

She nodded, a small downward tilt to her lips. "Agreed."

## CHAPTER 7

The road to London and to Mr. Grant's estate became passable the following day. The family doctor was summoned from London and would now be on his way to Chidding Hall. Clara sat in a chair in the conservatory, a blanket over her legs as the day, although clear, was chill.

Mr. Grant had set off for his estate early this morning, but had promised to return this afternoon, with everything he would need to reside here for the duration of her father's illness. After her papa's outburst, his physical assault of her, something he'd never done in his life, Mr. Grant had decided to stay. Even as a child neither of her parents had laid a hand on her, so for him to shake her, his grip punishing and cruel had been out of character.

The tisane, whatever Mrs. Pennell had made up, worked wonders yesterday, and they had given more to her father today. He was sleeping, which under the circumstances was probably best.

Footsteps sounded on the tiled floor and she turned, placing the unread book in her lap aside. Pleasure and relief in equal values ran through her at the sight of Mr.

Grant striding toward her. She'd never noticed his athleti-
cism before, but how she did now. Not to mention their
two kisses plagued her mind almost as much as her father
did. What did it mean, their slip of etiquette?

Did it mean anything at all or was he simply so angry
at her that he'd kissed her as further punishment? Not that
it had been a punishment at all. The sweet words he'd
breathed against her lips had not been a penalty to bear.
They had sent her heart to pound and her body to want
and need things she'd never known before in her life.

And now he was here to stay. However would she
behave herself with him?

"Mr. Grant, you're back." He smiled and the breath
in her lungs seized. When had he become so handsome?
His wavy brown locks accentuated his chiseled cheek-
bones and strong jaw. His nose was perfectly straight, and
his eyes, large and the kindest she'd ever seen, gleamed
with pleasure. She could not recall thinking of him so
fondly in London. Clara frowned as he came and sat
beside her and he reached up and smoothed her brow
with his thumb.

"Is something troubling you? Is everything well with
your father this morning?"

She nodded, ignoring the fact that his touch did odd
things to her. "He's asleep and better today. He ate breakfast in bed, but the tisane Mrs. Pennell made has put him
to sleep."

Mr. Grant leaned back on the stone chair they sat
upon, staring up at the sky through the glass roof. "The
doctor should be here this afternoon and that should alle-
viate some of the pressures on you, Lady Clara." He
turned and looked at her, his eyes skimming over her in
appreciation. She'd seen that look before from other
gentlemen in the *ton*, most especially Lord Peel, but with

Mr. Grant bestowing such glances affected her like nothing she'd ever known.

"Please call me Clara, Mr. Grant. I think we're past correct forms of address after all that we've been through these past few days."

He grinned and she had to look away lest she lean over, clasp him by his too-good-looking jaw and kiss him again. "This is where you may say in return that I may call you by your given name too."

He chuckled, leaning toward her and with one finger tilted up her chin. "You may call me Stephen, Clara."

Her name was but a whisper and she swallowed, biting her lip at the gravelly, deep voice in which he'd said her name. Never had her name sounded so evocative or, dare she say it, sensual before in her life.

"Stephen," she whispered, but even to her own ears it sounded like a plea. No doubt he heard the need, the want in her tone and without further prompting, he closed the space between them and kissed her.

Clara sighed at the rightness of having him in her arms once again, clasping his nape and kissing him back. His hair was soft under her gloveless fingers, his skin warm. He licked her bottom lip and she gasped as he deepened the kiss. His mouth covered hers with delicious wantonness and she could not get enough. For a man that she'd once reviled she certainly enjoyed his kisses.

She could no longer say that about Stephen, that she disliked him. Over the last few days he'd shown a side of himself as loyal and kind toward those in need. She supposed the night he'd helped her in Covent Garden she should have recognized that trait of his, a caring nature. With her, here and alone he was different. Gone were the harsh looks, the dismissing words whenever they had inter-acted. The man kissing her now could not be more different and she could not be more changed too, since seeing this side of him.

"I should not be kissing you like this." He leaned his forehead against hers, holding her gaze. "We're enemies, are we not?"

Clara clasped his jaw, kissing him quickly before pulling back. He let her go, but he watched her, his eyes wary and curious as to what she was going to say. "We are, or at least, we always have been in the past."

He leaned back in the chair, a small smile playing about his very kissable mouth. "Whatever we are, I will tell you this truth, Lady Clara. I enjoy your kisses and would welcome more of them from you if you were in agreement."

Heat bloomed on her cheeks and she bit her lip, not sure where to look at Stephen's words. She enjoyed his kisses as well, more than she ever thought she would, but what then? She was a duke's daughter, expected to marry someone of equal rank to her. Mr. Grant was only circulating in their social sphere due to whom his sisters had married. Kissing him could not lead anywhere. But it did not mean they could not enjoy this time together while he was a guest here at Chidding Hall.

A little doubt niggled at her conscience that she should not give him false hope that their newfound intimacies would lead anywhere permanent, but she also did not want to lose him. His support, protection and help in regard to her father. It was a selfish thought, but she had no one else. As an only daughter, there were no siblings to call on, she had no cousins, aunts, or uncles. Her father was all she had, and now Mr. Grant, who offered to help. She would not throw away such support, not for anything, not even the little guilt that taunted her that she was being unfair.

"I am in agreement," she said, sliding over to lean on

his chest. "As strange and new as all of this is to me, I'm glad that you're here. Thank you for your support with my father. I'll forever be grateful."

He pushed a lock of hair from her face, his thumb tracing down her cheek to run across her bottom lip. "The first time that I saw you in London I will admit to being a little taken aback at your beauty. Your golden locks, perfectly coiled atop your head most days, your brows," he said tracing one, "a faultless outline to the bluest eyes I'd ever seen. From across the room those eight years ago, I knew they were the color of a tempestuous ocean after a storm." He chuckled a little. "Little did I know just how wild a storm you would be."

Clara swallowed the lump in her throat at Stephen's words. No one had ever complimented her in such detail before. Oh, she'd had compliments on how pretty she looked, what a lovely gown, her perfect smile, but no one, not even her father, had ever explained in such detail her features and no admirer had ever said that when they had seen her for the first time that they had been taken aback, dazed into staring and taking their fill.

Which was what Mr. Grant had seemed to do.

"And then I ruined your illusion by opening my mouth and putting you in your place, if I recall."

He shook his head, frowning. "If I remember correctly, the first time we spoke it was I who put you back in your place for being rude to my sister."

Clara laid her head against his shoulder. His arm wrapped about her back and held her against him. "Please know that I am very happy for your sisters and their marriages. I will admit to being injured by Marquess Graham, that I hoped and thought his courting of me would lead to marriage. I suppose I did not take my ire out on his lordship and rather redirected it at your sister." She looked up at him and met his surprised visage. "I will apologize to her the next time I see her."

"She would like that very much. Louise is not the type of woman who likes to have enemies. I think if she could, she would enjoy having you as a friend, and I think you, Clara, could do with a friend who was honest and loyal."

She sighed. How true that was. Her friends in London were as fickle as they came. Most of them had married now, some were even parents of small children, but still they gossiped, made fun of debutantes who were less fortunate in looks or stature than themselves. They flirted and teased each other's husbands to the point where Clara had wondered if some of her friends were having rendezvous outside the marriage bed. Stephen was steadfast, loyal, and something told her his sisters would be as well. In the future she may need that sort of support if her father continued to decline and she was left with no one.

"I will make amends, I promise." She closed her eyes, lulled by the sound of his heart beating under her ear. How was it that in only a short time she'd become so very comfortable around him? The comforting thought was her last before sleep enfolded her.

STEPHEN HAD Lady Clara's maid pull back her bedding so he may place her on the crisp, clean sheets. He'd allowed her to sleep against his person for some time in the conservatory, before he realized that his back would cramp if he stayed in the position for too much longer. Even though it was not yet luncheon, Clara had a lot on her mind of late, so many worries and responsibilities it was only probable that she was exhausted. Caring for the Duke and the ducal properties would not be easy and would be time-consuming.

He headed back downstairs to the library. He would read for a time before the doctor arrived, which should be early this evening if his calculations of travel were correct.

At some point he too fell asleep and only woke to the sound of voices in the foyer, one of those a man's and Clara's, who was greeting the guest. Stephen rose quickly, checking his cravat and sliding on his coat as he stepped out into the foyer.

Clara spotted him, and turned the older gentleman his way. "Dr. Miller, this is Mr. Grant. He was unfortunately waylaid here for some days due to the river coming down and has been helping me with Papa. As I stated in my letter to you, it was Mr. Grant who stopped father from shaking me."

The doctor shook his hand. "Good to meet you, Mr. Grant, and thank you for your time here assisting Lady Clara. It is most appreciated, I'm sure. Now, shall we go upstairs and see his Grace?"

"Yes, this way if you please, Dr. Miller."

Stephen followed and stood at the back of the ducal suite as the doctor went about his inspection of the Duke, who was awake and sitting up in bed, his discarded mail on the bedside cupboard.

The doctor did what looked like a few tests with the Duke's hands, reactions, and then he spoke to him at length, questioning him about all sorts of subjects that Stephen wondered whatever had to do with anything. Even so, the doctor continued, before showing Lady Clara a vial of liquid that was to be added to his tea every morning. "Shall we discuss this further in the library, Lady Clara? I would welcome refreshments if it's not too much trouble," the doctor said, standing.

"Of course," Lady Clara said, settling her father before leaving the room. They headed down to the library. Clara rang for tea and biscuits, notifying the staff that there would be an extra guest for dinner and to prepare a guest chamber.

During the time the tea was being prepared they spoke very little about the Duke. When a footman brought in the tea and Clara asked for them not to be disturbed, only then did the doctor explain his findings.

"Regarding your father," he said, placing down his cup and saucer after taking a sip. "I do not have good news, Lady Clara. In the few weeks that you've been home I can see a marked decline in his cognitive ability and there is a slight tremor affecting his hands that you may not have noticed. In London I was not certain the Duke suffered from the affliction that I'd seen before, but upon inspecting him again today, I fear that he does indeed have a similar disease I've seen in only a few of my patients in the past. I'm so very sorry, my dear, to be the one to tell you this, but he will not survive its progress."

Stephen moved over to sit beside Clara, taking her ice-cold hand. He rubbed it, trying to force warmth into her body, but she was silent and still, shocked he had no doubt.

"My father is dying?" she asked at length, her voice almost inaudible.

The doctor nodded, reaching out to squeeze her arm. "I'm sorry, my lady. You must prepare yourself for the progression of the disease to strip your father of who he once was. He will forget how to do things for himself, he may become angry and upset and be quite pleasant on other occasions. His food will need to be cut up in smaller portions for him so he will not choke and I would suggest that you do not let him wander about alone. He may become disoriented and lost. He will become a danger to himself and I would suggest the hiring of a caregiver. I have one whom I can suggest and write to if you approve."

She did not answer and Stephen met the doctor's eyes. "Thank you, Dr. Miller. That would be most kind."

The doctor's attention turned back to Clara, concern in his gray orbs.

"Is there anyone we can summon to help you? Family or friends you may want here, my lady?" Stephen asked, holding her hand and hoping the terrible gray pallor of her skin would go away.

She shook her head and his heart broke at the sight of the unshed tears welling within her blue eyes. "I do not have anyone. Father is all I have, Stephen."

He pulled her into his arms, holding her tight as she succumbed to her tears, her body shaking in his hold.

"Do you have any idea, Dr. Miller, how long his Grace may have left?" Stephen did not really want to know, but with Clara as upset as she was, he doubted she would remember to ask such a question, and yet it was be something she would want to know. His surmise was right as she lifted her head, dabbing at her cheeks with the back of her hand.

"Dr. Miller?" she queried. "How long did your other patients have before the end?"

The doctor looked down at his hands clasped in his lap, his knuckles white. "Your father seems to be nearing the end stage of the disease. I would surmise three months if you are lucky, one if you're not."

Clara gasped, her face draining of color altogether.

"It is a shock, my dear. I know, but I would suggest you take this time to spend it with your father as best as you can. Try to keep a brave face in front of him, take him out on picnics or rides in the carriage, just be certain to have his caregiver or Mr. Grant with you at all times. The medication I gave to you will help calm him when the need arises. Give it to him in the morning and then he should be quite manageable during the day. When he no longer is, you know your time is limited."

"Thank you, Dr. Miller," she whispered, clutching at Stephen's hand. "I will make the most of the time I have left with Papa."

# CHAPTER 8

Clara had adhered to her promise to Dr. Miller over the next month and a half. They had made day trips to their neighbors, taken tea and cakes out in the woods surrounding the ducal property. At one point even a deer had walked up uncommonly close to them as they sat and ate. Her father had smiled and laughed at the brazen animal and the day had been one to remember.

Stephen had stayed at the estate during the entirety of her father's illness, helping the caregiver Dr. Miller had sent to them from London and being of any assistance he could. The man had done everything for the Duke that Clara could not do herself and she would be forever grateful for making her father's last few weeks comfortable and pain-free.

A quick rap upon her door pulled her from her sleep and she sat up so quickly the room spun a little.

"Who is it?" she asked

"Lady Clara, it's me, James. You need to come to the Duke's room. Straightaway, my lady."

Before her father's valet's words had stopped she was

out of bed and wrapping a shawl about her shoulders. She ran from the room to her father's. He lay still on his bed.

"He is unresponsive, my lady," the doctor stated, checking her father's pulse. "I cannot wake him."

"Father," she said, getting up on the bed to sit beside him. He had grown frail and much older than his fifty-four years during the past month and she was certain that if he were to walk into a London ballroom the *ton* would not recognize him today. "Papa, please wake up." Tears welled in her eyes, and she ran her hands over his cheeks, shaking him a little. "Papa…please, please don't leave me alone."

Her father opened his eyes, meeting hers and hope bloomed in her chest. He gave her a tired, little smile and her heart broke. She was losing him. Her only family and he was going away. "I will never leave you, my darling. I will always be with you. In here," he said, lifting his hand and pointing at her heart.

She nodded and tried to smile, but even to her it felt wobbly and uncertain. "I love you," she said, unable to stop the tears or the sob that escaped in front of all who stood behind her, Stephen included.

"The moment you were born you were the love of my life, my child. I'm proud of you, my dear."

She hugged him, holding him close as the last of his worldly breath left his body. The comforting hand of Stephen's slid over her back, stroking and supporting her in this time.

How would she ever survive without her father and Stephen, who too now would be going back to his estate? The realization made her heart ache even more and her chest burned as if she could not get enough air. She was going to be alone, an unmarried woman without a protector, without any family. Tears slid freely down her cheeks. However would she manage?

FIVE DAYS later she stood in the drawing room downstairs after having laid to rest her father in the family mausoleum. All of London looked to be in the room, her friends and their husbands had made the journey from London, including Lord Peel. The gentleman whom she had not seen since Covent Garden stood to the side of the room watching her as if she were a juicy piece of meat that his wolfish teeth wanted to rip apart.

Her childhood friend Julia, now Lady Davenport after marrying the Earl Davenport, sidled up to her, her face animated as if she were enjoying an evening out at a ball, not having just buried her friend's father.

"I suppose you'll be in mourning now for several months. How droll that will be. I will not mourn my own papa when he passes. I do not think he ever cared for me at all, certainly not enough to stop me from marrying Lord Davenport who is as droll as they come." Julia smiled, looking about the room. "Not that you will have any troubles finding a husband of considerable worth. Lord Peel is still interested if his fixation on you is any indication."

Clara glanced in Lord Peel's direction and watched as he saluted her with his glass of whisky. She looked elsewhere, anywhere but him, and found her attention locked on Mr. Grant who spoke to his sister and the Marquess who had arrived yesterday at his estate, or so he had said. The Marquess owning the estate adjacent to this one, and having been their neighbor in the past, thought it only right to pay his last respects to her father.

"I'm not interested in Lord Peel or anyone at present." She finished her glass of wine and summoned a footman for another. Not that that was entirely true, she was interested in someone, but that someone was not titled, not a land owner, not in his own right at least. As a duke's daughter there were expectations required of her, expected from her. Mr. Grant did not suit those requirements. He was, however, the only man whom she'd ever wanted in a physical sense, not to mention an intellectual one as well. "I will return to town for next year's Season and not before. Only then will I decide what I shall do regarding a husband."

"Oh my, would you look who is in attendance? That gauche family, the Grants. I see Mr. Grant and his sister still think that they are welcome at such events."

Clara shushed her friend, looking about to ensure no one had heard her unkind words. "Remember this is my father's funeral. If you would show a little respect for me and my guests, I would be thankful. You may say whatever you wish in London, but not here. Not today."

Julia raised her brow, her lips puckering into a displeased mien, but Clara did not care. She was not in the mood for petty hate, and derogatory references toward a man whom she had come to admire, depend upon and like.

She met his eyes across the room and her heart missed a beat. He threw her a knowing smile, and she could not stop the one he brought forth on her lips. How sweet he was, how kind and patient he'd been toward her and her many tears over the past month. Her father's ups and downs that had occurred due to the disease that wrecked his body and left him nothing like the man she'd once known. Stephen had been beside her the whole time, keeping her will strong and comforting her when needed.

He had not tried to kiss her again, although there were many times she'd wanted him to. She longed for the comfort of him, wanted to feel anything but the severing pain she always felt when around her papa. Now that her father was gone, what was she going to do? There was time to make a decision, but no matter how much time passed it would not change that Clara's social stature was so very different to Stephen's.

Not that she imagined he thought of her as his future wife, he'd certainly never brought up such subjects with her, but she could not help but wonder if he contemplated such things when alone.

"Lady Clara," Lord Peel said, bending over her hand and bringing it to his lips. "May I say how very sorry I am for the loss of your father, the Duke. He was a great man and well loved."

"Thank you," Clara said, pulling her hand away. "It is very nice to see so many of his friends and acquaintances here today." Not that Lord Peel had ever been friends with her papa. In fact, her father had disliked the man, long before he started showing a marked interest in Clara. She supposed now having learned more of Lord Peel and his inappropriate actions toward women when defenseless she could understand why her father had never offered friendship. Perhaps her father had known somehow of his ungentlemanly ways with the fairer sex.

"We will be sad not to see you in town, but I heard you say to Lady Davenport," he said, bowing to Julia who still stood beside her, listening to the conversation, "that you will return next Season. I shall count the days until we see you again."

*She would not count the days…*

She nodded, not the least thrilled about such an outcome. "I should probably greet Papa's friends before they start to leave. If you'll excuse me." Clara started when Lord Peel took her arm, guiding her about the room.

"Allow me, my lady. I shall escort you."

Clara took a calming breath, ready to tell the

gentleman that she did not need or want his type of support. His touch made her skin crawl and she could not help but marvel at how different she was when around Lord Peel than Mr. Grant.

"Lady Clara," Stephen said, bowing in front of her and holding out his arm. "I will escort Lady Clara about the room, Lord Peel. No need to trouble yourself." Clara pulled her arm free from Lord Peel's and placed it on Stephen's, turning quickly to thank his lordship for his help. "Thank you, my lord for your kind words. If you'll excuse me."

She ignored the glare that passed between the two gentlemen and allowed Stephen to guide her about the room to talk to her guests. "Thank you for removing me from his lordship. I did not ask for him to assist me."

"I gathered as much. His marked interest in you today is as forward and telling as it was in London. Be wary of him, my lady. I do not trust him to act honorably in his pursuit of you."

"What do you mean?" she asked, glancing up at him.

"Only that he's cornered you once alone already and would have done who knows what had I not heard your calls. I would not trust him not to try such things again."

"And I'm alone now. With father gone, maybe I should hire a companion again."

"I think that would be best, but you're not alone. I'm here, and I will be only next door should you need me."

She clutched at his arm, hugging it a little. "Thank you for all you've done these past weeks. I do not know what I would have done without you. You keep surprising me, Mr. Grant. I fear that we'll soon have to admit that we're friends."

He chuckled, the sound low and honeyed. It did odd things to her nerves. "I think we might. How terribly boring. I kind of enjoyed our verbal fisticuffs. Did you not?"

"I may have, but I do enjoy this kind of verbal discourse more." Clara tore her gaze from his before anyone noticed that they were both staring at each other, close and quite comfortable in each other's company. "How long are the Marquess and Lady Graham staying at Ashby Cottage?"

"They leave tomorrow. Will you dine with us tonight? I do not like the thought of you here alone."

She shook her head. "Thank you for your kind offer, but no. I feel tonight I want to be alone. Once everyone has gone, I shall retire early. I feel very weary all of a sudden. I think the past weeks have caught up with me."

"Very well," he said, patting her hand that sat atop his arm. "I will not push you to attend, but know, no matter the time or weather, should you need me, I will come."

"Thank you, Mr. Grant. I do not know what I would have done without you."

"You would have done exactly what I expected. You would have managed just as well as you did with me here. If there is one thing I know about you, Lady Clara, you're a strong woman, independent and loyal. Admirable qualities all. I'm in awe of you."

Clara blinked back tears, biting her lip to stop herself from crying in front of everyone. "Will you call tomorrow?"

"I will call as soon as my guests depart."

# CHAPTER 9

Clara could not sleep. She tossed and turned, rolled about on her bed, but in no way could she find a position that was comfortable. This was the first night that Stephen was not under the same roof as her, and she disliked the idea of being all alone, save her servants.

She glanced at her windows, the heavy damask curtains pulled closed on the cold, fall winds that had picked up in the afternoon. A howling could be heard from outdoors and even though she told herself it was just the wind against the house, she struggled not to clutch her bedding as if it would save her from some otherworldly ghoul.

Clara threw back her blankets and strode over to the fire, throwing a piece of wood onto the dying embers. She reached up on the mantel and lit a candle using the hot coals before going about her room and lighting the others.

She sat before the hearth, reaching out her hands to warm them, her mind consumed with thoughts of Stephen. There was little use in denying that she had emotions invested in the man, more than she should ever have allowed herself.

He was everything she wanted in a husband—he was kind, loving, caring and passionate. Certainly her every reaction to him had been telling, had told her more than once that he brought forth in her a passion she'd never had before. He spoke to her as an equal, did not dismiss or belittle her because she was a woman.

The wood caught alight and she watched as the flames licked at the wood, charring it. If only he were not so beneath her in rank. Should he be her equal in rank, fortune and property, he would have suited her in all ways, but she could not ignore the fact that he was not such things. That is was she who would bring the wealth and position to a union and she could not help but fear that somewhere, deep down inside, that was the reason for his liking her. Other gentlemen had certainly made it plainly obvious she was most sought-after because she was an heiress, but that wasn't enough.

She wanted a husband who loved her, not her money. If she married a man of wealth and position there would be no question as to why he wanted her for his wife. It would be because he cared for and loved her.

To marry someone out of that sphere would be a gamble and one she was not sure she could take.

A light knock sounded on the door and she started, holding still, unsure that she'd heard what she thought she did.

"Clara," a masculine voice whispered. "Clara, are you awake?"

Stephen? She stared at the door as nerves took flight in her stomach. He was here? Now? In the middle of the night…

She walked to the door and opened it. There, standing

before her in nothing but breeches and a shirt and great-coat was Mr. Grant. He was damp from the weather outside, and his hair was windblown, no doubt from riding his horse across the fields to Chidding Hall from Ashby Cottage.

"What are you doing here?" She glanced out into the passage and seeing no one about, pulled him into her room. "How did you get in?"

"The footman assumed I was still staying here and I didn't correct him on that assumption." He walked over to the fire and stood, warming his back. "I couldn't sleep."

"Neither could I," she said, going over to him. She had not thought to see him again today, but now with him before her, she was glad of it. In the few hours since he'd been here, she had missed him and that in itself was troubling. She wasn't certain what to do, or how their relationship would carry on now that her father had passed. All that she knew was that she liked Stephen and desired him more than anyone ever in her life.

He looked down at her, his eyes stealing over her and her lack of attire. She was dressed in her nightgown and little else and heat crawled over her face that he was seeing her thus.

"You should probably leave, Stephen," she said, not meaning a word she spoke.

His gaze heated and he reached out, running a finger along the lace collar of her nightdress. "Is that what you want?"

No. "Yes," she breathed as his hand slid farther down on her person to run along the flesh of her breast. Heat pooled at her core and she swallowed a moan when his hand flexed and he cupped her breast fully.

He followed his hands with his lips and she didn't stop him. Clara shut her eyes, clasping the nape of his neck as his tongue came out to flick her nipple. A shock ran through her at his touch and she was powerless to stop what was happening between them.

How could she halt this interaction that she'd wanted for so long now? With every kiss they shared, every look and touch over the past weeks she'd wanted him to do more. Now that he was, she was not about to stop him.

He moved and kissed her other breast and she moaned her acquiescence. His mouth was hot, wet and teased her with little licks of his tongue and full mouth kisses. Liquid heat pooled between her legs and she squeezed them together to try to quell the need that thrummed there.

Before she knew what was happening, he scooped her up in his arms and strode for the bed, throwing her onto the covers. Clara chuckled as she bounced before she watched in fascination as Stephen ripped his breeches buttons open and pushed them off his legs. His greatcoat, cravat and shirt soon followed and within a minute he was standing before her, as naked as Adam was with Eve.

Clara's mouth dried at the sight of him and she licked her parched lips, wanting to feel those corded muscles against her, pushing her down and taking her as she'd longed for him to for weeks now. His eyes darkened with hunger and she shivered, fully aware that she was still dressed in her nightgown.

"Take it off, my lady."

At his deep, rough command she did as he asked without question. At this moment in time she would do whatever he wanted of her so long as he touched her again. He reached down and took himself into his own hands, stroking his manhood until it jutted out before him.

Clara kneeled on the bed and wrenched the gown from her body, leaving her as bare as he was before lying back down. He kneeled on the bed, kissing his way up her body before settling between her legs. So many emotions rioted through her blood that she did not know what to do, but she could feel. Her body hummed with a need that she'd not known before, and all she craved was for him to take her. Make love to her.

"You're so beautiful," he whispered against her lips before kissing her with an unhurried air. He rocked against her core, making her gasp and she lifted her legs, hooking them about his waist.

"You're teasing me," she moaned when he nipped her neck before licking it better.

"I'm teasing us both."

Clara ran her hands over his back, feeling the corded muscle that ran down his spine. It flexed with each rock against her and she reached farther to clasp one perfect bottom cheek in her hand, pulling him against her. "Enough, Stephen. I want you," she demanded.

His hot breaths mingled with hers and he met her gaze as he reached down between them, placing his manhood at her core. And then, inch by delicious inch he slid into her. She gasped as pain ripped, stinging at where they joined. He stilled, kissing her lips, her cheeks and neck.

"I'm sorry, my darling. I did not mean to hurt you."

Clara shook her head, taking in this new feeling of him between her legs, the fullness and strangeness of being with a man for the first time. He felt too large, too wide and hard to go any farther, but then he rocked slowly forward and there was no pain, only pleasure and a throbbing ache that would not abate.

"Don't stop," she managed to say, liking the feel of his chest as it grazed hers with each thrust. She undulated beneath him, wanting more. There was no longer any friction, only pleasure, and Clara let herself go, to enjoy all that he could give her, tonight at least.

STEPHEN THRUST INTO CLARA, taking her as he'd dreamed of from the very first moment they kissed. She was so hot and wet, and clamped about his cock with a force that left him breathless and struggling not to spill too soon.

He needed her to climax, he had to make this night as enjoyable for her as it would be for him. It had, however, been quite some months since he'd slept with a woman and it was taking all the control not to climax like a green lad of eighteen.

Her fingers spiked into his back, drawing him close and he gave her what she wanted, thrust deep and hard into her willing heat. She threw back her head, gasping, and he kissed her neck, savoring her sweet perfume of jasmine as he pumped over and over into her.

Their breaths mingled, their hearts thrummed loud enough that he was sure he could hear them. Her legs rode high on his hips and he reached down with one hand, holding her ass as he took her.

"Oh yes," she panted, her eyes fluttering closed. "Stephen…"

Their actions were frantic as he pushed her ever closer to release and then he felt it, the small and then large tremors that thrummed through her core, dragging him along to climax. He pumped hard and deep, and she screamed, thrusting her hands above her head to push against the headboard as he fucked her without remorse.

For a moment he stayed in her, sweat covered their skin as he regained his breath and wits. Never before had he ever felt the way he felt with Clara. He flopped beside her, pulling her into the crook of his arm. Idly, he played with her hair, sliding it off her damp forehead.

"I hope I did not hurt you."

She rolled against him, laying her hand across his stomach to play with his ribs. "Oh no, you did not hurt me at all. In fact," she said reaching down to take his semi-hard phallus in her hand, "it only makes me more curious about what else a man and woman can do. Our first encounter was quite enjoyable."

He chuckled at her mischievous grin. "Lady Clara, you're a vixen."

She leaned over and flicked his nipple with her tongue, eliminating the concept of giving her time to recover from their first bout of lovemaking. He'd take her all night if she allowed it. "Only with you, Mr. Grant," she replied, doing it again and making his morals fuzzy. "Now, show me more."

Stephen groaned, and yet, was only too happy to oblige her ladyship. "Of course. Let us begin…"

# CHAPTER 10

Stephen arrived at Lady Clara's estate just after luncheon the following day and found her behind her father's desk in the library, a pile of missives and scrolls lying before her. She glanced up at him, pleasure written on her features when she saw him.

"Stephen, you've arrived at the most opportune time. Please take me away from all this work." She stood and came around the desk and walked to the bell pull on the mantel, ringing for a servant. "Shall we have tea?"

"Yes," he said, seating himself beside her and kissing her quickly. "How are you today? You look like you're very busy."

"Father's lawyers have left some estate paperwork for me, along with his will that they read here yesterday. I'm trying to take everything in that has fallen on my shoulders and catch up with correspondence that had arrived during father's illness. I think it will take me some weeks to get through it all."

Stephen glanced at the desk. There was certainly quite

a lot of papers to sort through. "When do you have to leave to make way for the new Duke of Law?"

She frowned, leaning back into the sofa. "I do not have to make way for anyone. The house and most of Papa's properties were not entailed. Father's family had a modest Tudor estate several miles from here that comes with the duchy, but this estate was owned by my mother's family. It was my great-grandmother's ancestral home and is handed down to the eldest daughter. We've always lived here as father preferred it to his own modest estate. So I do not have to go anywhere." She threw him an amused grin. "Are you sick of being my neighbor already, Mr. Grant?"

He shook his head. "No, never." He took in what she said and what it meant. She was an heiress, that he always had known, but now, the land and estates she must own, well, it placed her far above his expectations, his abilities to court a woman of such high rank. Disappointment stabbed at him that he could not be what society expected Clara's husband to be.

There was a light knock at the door before a footman came in carrying a tea tray. He placed it before them, then stood to the side. "Lady Clara, a Lord Peel is here to see you. He waits in the foyer."

Clara's eyes widened, and he noted the flicker of fear that entered her blue orbs. She glanced at him, and he squeezed her hand. "If you wish it, I will not leave you while you're speaking with his lordship." Although what Lord Peel needed to say to Clara, Stephen couldn't fathom. The man should return to London and stay there. He'd thought he already had, but even now that fiend loitered about Kent and near Clara.

"Show him in." She adjusted her seat and Stephen stood, positioning himself before the fire to await his lordship's entry.

They did not have to wait long before the strutting peacock walked into the room and stopped at the sight of Stephen.

"Mr. Grant. I did not expect to find you here." Lord Peel pulled off his hat and gloves, handing them to the footman who hovered nearby.

"I'm taking tea with Lady Clara."

His lordship came and without waiting for Clara to say anything, sat himself beside her. He poured himself a cup, thereby leaving Stephen without one. "I wished to call and to ensure that you are well, my lady. You have had a terrible personal blow and I wanted to show that you have my support in any way you choose."

Stephen raised his brow. *I bet she does, you cad!*

"Thank you, my lord. That is very kind." She poured herself a cup of tea, and for a moment Stephen watched as they enjoyed their repast. "What brings you back here, my lord? I thought everyone had returned to town."

"To offer my condolences once again, and to see that you have everything in hand. In times like these, please feel free to use my expertise in relation to running estates, investments, servants' salaries and such. I'm more than capable in running multiple properties, which you, with your delicate constitution, will not be."

Stephen masked his chuckle with a cough at his lordship's words. Delicate constitution... Was the man blind to her annoyance or simply too dumb to realize it? Either way Clara nodded as if his lordship spoke the truth and her mask of indifference did not slip.

"All is in hand, my lord. Anything that I find challenging I have my father's steward to guide me."

He reached out and patted her hand and Stephen glared at where he made contact with her. He didn't want Lord Peel or anyone touching one piece of her if he could help it. He stilled at his own thoughts. When had he become so possessive of her? When had he started to think of her as his and no one else's? He supposed their coming together a night past had something to do with it, but also over the last month of seeing her battle against her father's illness, seeing a vulnerable side of Clara, his heart had softened toward a woman he'd once thought the spawn of the devil.

"Mr. Grant has been a great help these past weeks. In the ones to follow I'm sure all will work out. He's my neighbor if you do not know, Lord Peel."

Lord Peel scoffed and, finishing his cup of tea, placed it on the small table before them. "Is that what you aspire to be, Mr. Grant? A steward, a bookkeeper for a great house such as this one? I'm sure I can ask around London and see if any of my friends are looking for a new employee in that field."

Stephen narrowed his eyes on the viscount, well aware of the game he played. He wanted Lady Clara for himself, that he'd known for some months, but to treat him with so little respect, to mark him as a person beneath the *ton's* notice would not be tolerated.

"I've leased Marquess Graham's estate and so I'm not in need of a steward. I have hired one already." Of course he would have preferred to have not had to rely on his brother-in-law's charity to enable him to make something of himself. What man did not want to become successful in his own right? But unlike Lord Peel, not everyone was born with a silver spoon in their mouth.

The Marquess may have enabled him to live the life which he now did. Had bestowed on both him and his sister Sophie a small sum of money, but it was not enough to keep him forever without occupation.

To keep the lifestyle he now lived, he would have to

work the land, budget and run the estate as well as any high-born lord would.

"Yes," Lord Peel said, rubbing his jaw as if he'd spied a delicious sweet. "I heard the Marquess had leased the property to you, and for a fraction of what it was worth. I should imagine no respectable man would accept such charity. You are obviously not such a man."

Lady Clara stood, coming to stand beside him. "Thank you for coming, Lord Peel, but I think it's time you leave."

His lordship stood, adjusting his cravat. "I do apologize, Lady Clara, but as an equal I feel it is my duty to remind you and warn you of those who would take advantage of your sadness. Other than his sisters' exalted marriages, we know nothing of Mr. Grant. He may be a charlatan for all we know."

"Would my fist in your face make us better acquainted, my lord? I can certainly bestow you the honor if you choose."

Clara set a hand upon his arm, stalling him from following through on his threat. How dare the bastard say such a thing? Stephen wasn't sure if it stung more because there was a ring of truth to what he said or the fact that it was simply because Lord Peel had said it.

He did not need the prig before him telling him that he was not worthy of Lady Clara. He knew that himself. A boy born and raised in a cottage in Sandbach with three rooms, an impoverished aunt and very little means told him that himself. Not that he didn't think he was worthy of her hand, he would do as well as any other husband, but she was a duke's daughter, he was the son of servants who worked for nobility. He knew as well as anyone that she could never be his.

Stephen fisted his hands at his sides and Lord Peel cast a glance at his hands before bowing before Clara.

"I look forward to seeing you in town when you're there next, my lady. I wish you well."

Stephen watched him go, glad when the sound of the front door shutting echoed in the house. "I apologize, Clara. I have little patience with the man and he well knows it."

She turned, surprising him by taking him in her arms, linking her hands at his nape. "I like that you stood up to him. He's a bully and thinks he can get away with it. Not with you it would seem."

He stared down at her, marveling at her beauty. He reached down and slid his thumb across her jaw, so soft and perfect. "I have a confession."

She grinned, a devilish light entering her eyes. "You do. What is it?"

Stephen wrapped his arms about her waist, holding her close. "I want to kiss you."

She threw him a knowing smile and then leaned up and kissed him. Stephen met her halfway, having thought of little else from the moment he'd snuck out of her bed in the wee hours of yesterday morning.

"I have a confession too," she whispered against his lips.

"You do?" he asked, pausing. "What is it?"

Her fingers played with the hair at his nape, sending delicious shivers down his spine. "I've wanted to kiss you again too."

CLARA WASN'T sure when she had fallen for Mr. Grant, but there was little doubt that her affections were truly engaged now. He'd supported her through one of the most difficult times in her life, never flinching or running away when days with her father had become too hard to bear. He'd been her rock, her support, the one person she could cry before and not feel shame. After taking him to her bed, there was no denying that she was falling in love with him.

She reached up again and kissed him. His lips were soft, willing, his tongue filling and inflaming her. His large hands clasped her hips, circling her back and pulling her hard against him. His previous kisses had been coaxing, teasing and soft in nature. She could not say the same about this one. Oh no, this one was demanding, hungry.

Starved.

His mouth covered hers, drawing her into a dance of desire and need. Clara squeaked and then chuckled when he swooped her into his arms, striding to a nearby leather chair and sitting down, placing her on his lap. She wiggled, making herself more comfortable as heat pooled at her core. He stared down at her a moment, their faces scant inches from each other and she reached up to clasp his stubbled jaw.

"What is it?" she asked, when he continued to consider her.

He shook his head, his lips remaining sealed.

She wrapped her arms about his neck, running his hair through her fingers. His locks were soft and thick. "Tell me," she pleaded, not wanting to have secrets between them.

"Only that," he said, pausing. "No matter how much time we have together, know that for me it will never be long enough."

Clara's heart ached at his words and although she did not know the full meaning behind them, she did wonder if he thought that their time would end. She certainly did not wish it to end anytime soon, there were so many more things she wanted to do, to experience with him. But that did not mean that Stephen had different plans for his future, different goals and dreams other than a wife.

She started at her own thought of becoming his wife. A duke's daughter, she'd not given much thought at all that this, whatever it was between her and Stephen, would lead anywhere.

She had been so against him in the past, cutting and dismissive. Shame washed over her that she'd been so awful and judgmental. Her friends would certainly be shocked at her turned-about opinion, and there would be some who would distance themselves from her over her choice.

His lips brushed her neck and all thoughts of her friends and their prejudices toward those who had less than them flew out of her mind. His hand moved up to cup her breast, which felt tight and enlarged under her gown. His finger and thumb found her pebbled nipple and he rolled it between his fingers. She gasped through the kiss, wanting him with a feverish need.

The kiss turned inflammatory as she explored his body. His chest was hard, his breathing as rapid as hers and she could feel beneath her palm the hard ridges of muscle that lined his stomach. There were too many clothes, too much separating them. All she wanted was to be rid of their clothing so she may see all of him again.

"Touch me." His voice was husky and low and she could hear the need that tremored through his words.

Clara stroked lower and the pit of her stomach clenched when her hand closed around his manhood. Thick and hard and ready for her.

"Clara," he gasped when she stroked him. "Stop," he said, his hand halting hers. "Or you'll find I'll lose myself in my breeches like a green lad."

"I don't mind doing this for you." She met his gaze and

without looking away, flicked open each of the buttons holding his breeches closed. A muscle ticked in his jaw, his face took on a hard edge and she marveled at how handsome he was.

She glanced down to see his member as it sprung free from his breeches. Perfect, just as she remembered. Veins ran the length of his manhood, and a little droplet of moisture sat at the head of his phallus. Clara wiped it away with her thumb.

He groaned, laying his head back against the seat.

"You undo me."

His words pushed her on and she wrapped her hand about him, stroking him, playing and teasing his flesh. Marveling as it swelled and deepened to a purple hue.

He wrenched her in for a kiss, her mouth opening for him as he devoured her. Moisture pooled between her legs as he moaned through their kiss and that's when she felt him push up into her hold, pumping against her hand as he found his pleasure.

Clara broke the kiss, her body aching for what she now knew he could give her.

"Now it's my turn," he said, his gaze heavy with determination and heat. Clara shivered, expectation thrumming through her at being with him again.

"What would you like me to do?"


WHAT WOULD he like her to do? What wouldn't he like her to do would be a better question. She'd brought him pleasure and now he was going to make her shatter in his arms. He hoisted her to straddle his legs, fighting with her black gown to pool at her waist. There was too much clothing, too much separating them and he wanted it gone.

She lowered onto his lap and he reached beneath her

gown, sliding his hand up her silky-soft thigh until he reached the apex between her legs. He slid his hand across her mons, delicious moisture met his fingers. She was ready for him, and his cock twitched at the idea of sheathing himself in her hot heat.

"I'm going to touch you now," he whispered against her neck, breathing deep her scent of jasmine. She smelled good enough to eat and the idea of doing just that, tasting her, kissing her to climax almost had him picking her up, laying her on the settee and delving between her legs.

She nodded, her cheeks flushed. He slid his hand over her flesh, cupping her. Her hands spiked into his hair, pulling his strands. Her body undulated above him as he found the slit in her pantalets and rubbed her sweet nubbin in a circular motion.

A breathy moan escaped from her lips as she continued to slide against his hand. Stephen slipped one finger into her hot core. She gasped, her hands frantically clasping his shoulders for purpose. The sight of her coming undone by his touch left him growing hard at a rapid pace.

"Do you want more, my lady?" he asked, reaching up and hooking his hand along the bodice of her gown. He slid the material over her ample bosom, exposing her to him. Stephen could not look away from the sight she made. That of a woman who was enjoying his touch, a woman learning of what pleasures can be had between a man and woman.

He leaned forward, kissing her puckered nipple before taking it into his mouth. Her fingers dug into his skin.

"Oh yes," she gasped, rocking against him. "Please."

Stephen took his hand away, reaching around to clasp one perfect buttock and hoisting her against his manhood. Her heat slid against his cock, wet and ready. Her eyes widened at the newfound sensation and damn it all to hell it felt good. Too good not to have again. Too good to walk away from.

He guided her to slide against his cock. "We can do this without going any further."

She nodded, her eyes glazed with desire and he grinned. He took her nipple into his mouth, scraping the puckered flesh with his teeth before laving it with his tongue.

Clara pushed her sex against his. He was rock hard and if she did not find her release soon he'd come again.

"Stephen," she gasped, her hips rocking and pushing against him with increasing tempo.

He held her steady, his balls hard and aching. "Come for me, darling," he said, pushing up against her as he pulled her onto him from behind.

She threw her head back, gasping as her body shattered in his arms. "Oh yes, Stephen," she cried. There was no use trying to stop, he climaxed again. Her breasts bounced before him and he reached up, pinching her nipple as she rode him through her pleasure.

Clara collapsed to his side, and he wrapped her up in his arms, loving the fact she fit him so well.

"Well, that was certainly pleasurable," she said, grinning up at him. "However will we stop such interludes?" He clasped her cheek, kissing her slowly.

"Yes, it was," he said when at last he pulled away. "And there are other things we can do besides that will be just as pleasurable if you're interested."

Her eyes brightened with interest and he inwardly chuckled. "Really? However will I keep away from you?"

He grinned. "That, my lady, is why you will not."

# CHAPTER 11

Three days later Clara received a note from her friend Lady Davenport from London regarding an article that had been published in the paper. Julia had sent her a clipping of the piece and Clara slumped onto the sofa in the upstairs parlor as she read words that hundreds of peers too would have devoured.

A little image had been drawn for the amusement of the paper's readership depicting a woman, similar in coloring to her and a man of similar features to Mr. Grant in a compromising position in a library. The article mentioned a daughter of a duke having been seduced by one not of her rank and implied that her stay in the country was solely due to being ruined by the fiend not worth her notice.

She rubbed her brow, pain spiking behind her eyes and for a moment the room spun. Who had written such a piece of malicious text and why? Clara read it again, certain that she could not be mistaken and again the words jumped out at her, taunting, laughing and ruining her.

The little drawing had the woman dressed in black and

there was no doubt in her mind that it was her that the article had been written about. And there had been only one other person who had seen her standing beside Mr. Grant in a library in such a way.

Lord Peel.

The urge to scrunch up the article in her hand grew the more she thought about the man who had tried to take liberties that were not freely given, and now this. To disgrace her in such a way when she had never done anything to him, other than rebuff his advances was not to be borne. Had her father been alive she was certain that he would never have been so disrespectful to her.

A duke's daughter.

Clara blinked back the tears and she stood, walking to the window to look over the grounds. Is this what society would do to her now that her father was gone? Or was this simply a taunt, a warning that she should remove Mr. Grant from her life or suffer worse embarrassments?

Something told her it was the latter.

The sound of footsteps sounded in the hall outside and she quickly wiped at her cheeks, turning to face the door and whoever had called. Although she already had an inkling of who it would be.

A footman knocked on the door, stepping inside and announcing Mr. Grant. She bade him enter, not moving from the window lest he see her upset.

"Mr. Grant, how good of you to call." Clara clasped her hands at her front, unsure of how to tell him what had been disclosed to her today. He would be furious she imagined and hurt, but would he see the implications for them at this affront?

The footman closed the door, leaving them alone and Stephen smiled, coming over to her and pulling her into his arms. She went willingly, breathing deep his scent of sandalwood and goodness. For he was a good man, no matter what she'd once thought of him. How wrong she'd been all those years ago, and what she was about to say to him would be very hard for them both to hear.

"Clara," he said, kissing her soundly.

She lost herself a moment in the embrace, not wanting to face the truth of their situation. Wanting to for a little while longer be cocooned in their bubble in Kent.

"I missed you."

"I only saw you yesterday," she said, trying to make light of his words and yet, they rang as true to her as they did to him. She'd missed him also. In fact, she'd come to realize of late with growing concern that she hated when he left.

"Come sit with me, Stephen. There is something you need to see."

A small frown played upon his brow, but he followed her to the sofa and sat beside her. Clara picked up the article from the small table where they sat and handed it to him. He read it quickly, his mouth turning down in disapproval, a deep scowl between his eyes.

"How dare the bastard? I ought to call him out."

She met his eyes, reading the truth behind his words. "I thought the same. This is most certainly the work of Lord Peel."

Stephen screwed the clipping up and threw it into the fire. "Do not react or show any concern over such an insulting piece. When he knows that we will not respond there will be little he can do."

*Except start to make up stories to suit his nefarious means. Ruin her reputation forever…*

Clara clasped her hands in her lap to stop their shaking. "You know Lord Peel. He's vindictive and doesn't like to not get his own way. My disinterest in his attempts of courtship have brought this on, and that you're the one gentleman whom he never thought to have to consider as a possible rival has led him to act out in such a way."

He grinned, taking her hand, his thumb running circles atop it. "Am I a rival for your hand, Lady Clara?"

Her gaze met his. Never before had they talked of courtship, that what they had been doing with each other these past weeks would ever lead to anything more lasting. Did Mr. Grant wish for there to be more between them, and if he did, did Clara want there to be?

"I had not thought about it." The lie almost choked her and she cleared her throat as Stephen narrowed his eyes on her. "A stolen kiss here and there is not marriage inducing, is it not?"

He pulled back a little, watching her warily. "I think what we've been doing is a little more than kissing, my lady." He studied her a moment before he said, "I will be honest and tell you that at first I did not think of such a possibility at all. You're far above me in rank and wealth and there is little that will change my circumstances. I do not need a London lord to write an article and draw a picture to tell me that truth.

"But I've come to care for you, more than I thought would ever be possible knowing our tumultuous history. I would be a liar if I did not admit that I've thought of you as my wife. As quickly as I thought such a thing I dismissed it due to our different circumstances. It does not mean, however, that I do not want such a future with you."

Clara pulled her hand away, rising and going to stand before the fire. She bit the inside of her bottom lip, not sure how she would get through this conversation that they had to have. A conversation long overdue.

"I do care for you, Stephen. So very much," she said, meeting his gaze. "But I cannot marry you. There is too much of a divide between us and this article is just the first of many such articles that will nail home what the *ton* would think of my marriage to you. We will be ridiculed, shunned, our children too no doubt. People will laugh at how changeable I am. They all know that I once despised you, and now look at me. I…" She stopped speaking, shocked that she was about to say a word she'd never uttered to anyone else ever in her life.

Stephen's face shuttered, all warmth seeping from his blue-green orbs. "All this time I thought that you had changed and yet you're still the same. A woman afraid of what others think of you. Do not forget who you are, Lady Clara. You're a duke's daughter, an heiress, no one can touch you if you do not let them."

She shook her head, wanting to believe his words but knowing she could not. She was not that strong. She may have seemed to everyone that she was formidable, cold and above reproach, but she was not. "Whether I like it or not, they're my friends. For the rest of my life I will have to attend the Season and be a part of that world. I cannot be ostracized. I have no one, Stephen. No family, nothing left to me that is blood. My friends are all whom I have left."

"You have me. Am I not enough?"

Oh, he was enough, he'd always be enough, but it could not just be the two of them forever.

"I cannot just have you, Stephen. There are other things to consider and you know that."

He stood and ran a hand through his hair. He strode toward the door and fear shot through her that he'd leave. "If you loved me I would be more than enough, Clara. You're certainly enough for me. You're all that I want in this world. I live to hear your voice each day, to kiss your lips, and breathe in your scent. I did not think I was alone in this emotion."

She took a step toward him and stopped when he held up a hand to halt her. "You are not alone in that, but I cannot marry you. My marriage should be the joining of two great families. For all that you are, your beautiful soul and heart, I cannot give you mine in return. I'm sorry."

"Spineless and cold to the very end. Had I not known you these past weeks I would not have thought it possible for someone to be so callous." He laughed, the sound mocking. "You do not disappoint, Lady Clara. A viper to the very end."

"Stephen," she pleaded, striding toward him. She grabbed his arm as he went to leave and he shrugged off her hold.

"What, my lady? What is there left to say?"

Her heart shattered at the broken look in his eyes. She'd made him feel that way. She had been the one to do this to him and she hated herself for it. "You're right, I am scared of what others will think, what they will do to me. Lord Peel's threat is there for all to see and next Season when I'm in town his little article may see me ostracized already. That world is all I have left. Please understand, I have no one left to protect me from them."

His face contorted into a look of contempt. "Nonsense. You have me, at least, you had me," he corrected. He turned for the door and wrenched it open. "Have a happy life with your lord, Lady Clara. May the nobility and all its trappings bring you joy."

She stared after him, his words echoing through her mind like a death knell. She swallowed the sob that wanted to wrench from her. Had they just parted? Parted forever? Her stomach roiled and she stumbled to the door in her haste to catch up to him. She jerked the door open only to see no sight of him.

Clara ran for the back of the house, ignoring the startled gasps and looks her staff gave her. She pushed open the servants' door that was a mere few short steps to the stables only to see Stephen pushing his horse out of the yard and toward his own estate at a full gallop.

"Stephen," she yelled, heedless of who heard her. "Stephen, wait!" *I've made a mistake...*

She watched until she could no longer see him and jumped when a clap of thunder sounded overhead. Clara looked up at the sky, watching as the first drops of heavy, large raindrops fell from the sky.

"Damn it," she muttered, turning for the indoors. She would travel over to his estate tomorrow and make it right. Once they had both calmed down and she was thinking more clearly, she would amend this riff. It was not over between them. Not yet at least.

# CHAPTER 12

*Scotland, Mid-March 1810*

"That's it, I've had it with you, Brother. Eat your breakfast, bathe and get on your horse back to England. You cannot mope about Scotland for the rest of your life."

"I can and I will," Stephen replied, moving about the one piece of bacon he had on his plate. He stared down at the food, knowing he was moping and that his sister was right. He really did need to return to his estate that he'd promised his brother-in-law he'd take care of for him. But how could he return there, the one place he knew she would be.

*Clara.*

He clenched his jaw, reaching for his cup of coffee. The thought of her always brought both longing and anger in equal measures. He'd not seen her since the day of their parting, almost four months ago now. He'd packed up his belongings that very day, placed his steward in charge of Ashby Cottage and rode for Scotland. Multiple times he'd thought to turn around, go back and fight for her. Make her see that he was more than what he'd been born, a common man with very little to recommend him other than his loyalty and good character. He was the man for her. If only the stubborn wench would see it.

Instead, she'd thrown him off. Told him to his face that he was not good enough for her exalted breeding.

He shook his head, throwing his napkin down beside him and pushing back his chair. "I'll see you at luncheon."

"No you won't," his sister said, standing and reaching the door before he had a chance to escape. "I've instructed a servant to pack up your things and at this very moment they are being bundled into a carriage. You're returning to England today and that is the end of it."

Stephen glared at his twin, turning to her husband who sat at the head of the table, watching them both with amusement. "Dinna look at me, lad. I'll not be going against my wife. I suggest ye shouldna go against yer sister either."

"You're kicking me out?"

His sister's shoulders slumped and she clasped his hands. Hers were warm and soft and it made him miss feeling such a way as well. He'd been cold since he'd left England, although he wasn't sure if it was because of the climate in the Highlands or because his heart had simply stopped beating.

"We would never use such terms, but we are setting you on a correct path. That being south and to London. You need to speak to Lady Clara. Maybe she has changed her mind. Your absence may have been the catalyst that had made her see that you were indeed the man she loved and wanted as her husband. Not some stodgy, old titled lord."

Laird Mackintosh cleared his throat. "I hope that isna

a reflection on what ye thought of me, my love."

His sister turned and the adoration that was etched on her face whenever she glanced at her husband made Stephen want to both retch and cry. He was a foolish fop.

"You're Scottish. I'm referring to the English only, my dear."

The laird chuckled and cut into his kippers. Stephen sighed. "She's probably betrothed by now. She had many suitors besides myself before her father died. Louise wrote in her last letter that Clara was back in town and taking part in the Season. What's left of it in any case."

"You know that I've never been fond of Lady Clara. Heavens, she was not the nicest to us, but if she was different with you, redeemed herself and you fell in love with that side of her, then you need to go win her back. Do not live to regret doing nothing, Brother. That is not who we are. We're Grants. We get what we want."

"'Tis true, I can vouch for that," the laird said, agreeing with his wife.

Stephen stopped himself from rolling his eyes. "I will go and I will see what is at play in London, but I cannot promise that anything will come of it between us. I've not heard from her, and nor have I written in turn. It is possible that it is too late."

"It is never too late to win back one's love. I can vouch for that." Sophie clasped his arm, walking him to the door in the great hall in which they ate most of their meals here in Scotland. "Go, my dearest brother. I expect to hear news soon of your impending marriage."

He threw her a small smile, not wanting to ruin her hope that he himself was feeling very little of. Even so, he would return to town and see what was afoot, and if Clara was as indifferent to him as her words of dismissal made her out to be four months past.

# CHAPTER 13

*London, April 1810*

Clara stood in the ballroom of Lord and Lady Davenport's home and only just stopped herself from gasping out loud. Tonight was the first time she'd seen Mr. Grant in some time, and for the first hour of the assembly, she'd not been able to look away from the striking appearance he cut within the nobility.

His superfine coat and silk breeches were cut to fit him perfectly, his silver waistcoat and faultlessly tied cravat accentuated his lovely jaw and sinful mouth. She'd not been able to look away, and not only because he made her body yearn with a longing she'd pushed down over their time apart. But because her friend, a woman whom she had at times vented her dislike of Stephen was currently hanging on his every word across the room from her.

Clara took a sip of her ratafia as she stood with a group of friends, all married and all thoroughly engrossed in their conversations regarding marriage and children. Clara had tried to take part as much as she could, listen and impart any advice that she could, but since Clara was unmarried and not a mother, her friends were often dismissive of her input and so she'd learned to stay quiet and simply nod when they looked her way.

It was easier than to tell them their conversations were boring and if she were not their friend she would have fallen asleep on the spot hours ago.

"Is that not your neighbor, Clara?" Julia said, staring in the direction that she'd last seen Stephen. "I did not know Lord Davenport had invited him."

Clara feigned surprise and glanced about until she spotted the dratted man. Oh yes, it was him, laughing and talking as if she did not exist. And she supposed she did not any longer. Not since she had told him he was not worth her time simply because he was not born nobility.

What a horrible person she was.

"Yes, I believe so," she said, matter-of-fact. "He must be back from Scotland."

"Visiting that dreadful sister of his, I assume. Remember, Clara what fun we had during Lady Graham's first Season?" Julia turned to the women about them. "We did not like them you see. Mr. Grant was quite rude and cutting toward Lady Clara and so we ensured we never went out of our way to befriend her or make her welcome. We succeeded too."

"Except Miss Grant became the Marchioness Graham. So I suppose we did not in truth," Clara said, wanting to remind Julia that Miss Grant had become a marchioness while she had only married an earl. As for Clara she had not married anyone.

Clara looked down at her gown of blue muslin with a silk underlay. It was so very fine and pretty, and she'd made the extra effort tonight knowing Stephen would be in attendance. All day her stomach had fluttered at the thought of seeing him again. He did not disappoint. He was as handsome as she remembered and after all they had suffered through together, she wanted to go up to him and speak to him again. She wanted to know how he was. Was he happy? Did he miss her as much as she missed him?

She swallowed the lump in her throat. She was not happy. Had not been so for a very long time and could not remember the last time she laughed. Certainly it would've been back when they were at Chidding Hall together.

"Why Mr. Grant is back in London is anyone's guess. It's not like he has a fortune. He's a son of nobody knows who. Surely he does not think to make an advantageous marriage within our sphere."

Clara cast a glance his way and from the way women of her acquaintance were lapping up his every word she concurred that Lady Davenport was wrong about that. He would make an advantageous marriage, especially for a woman of wealth who wanted the connection of nobility. Mr. Grant was, after all, the brother-in-law to one of the most influential marquesses in England and one of the wealthiest.

"You're wrong, Julia. Mr. Grant I should imagine will marry well and soon if his popularity is any indication. Do not be so judgmental. If you keep scowling, those lines between your brows will become permanent."

Julia gasped and yet her eyes were as cold as ice. "Clara, how could you say such a thing to me? I thought we were friends."

Clara shrugged, taking in all the sets of wide-eyed women staring at her after her words. None of them did she care about. Certainly, she did not care what their opinion of her would be, or if they would include her in forthcoming events should she follow her heart. Only one person did she care for and she'd thrown him away as if he were worthless, when in truth, this world she occupied, the fickle and fake friendships she'd made over the years, those were what was really worthless.

Not the genuine man who had aided, supported and loved her all of those weeks in Kent.

He did love her. That she was sure about more than anything else in the world, but did he love her still? He'd never said the words, but they were there, every day he showed his affection by being her pillar of strength, her support, in every touch and look, not to mention his wicked kisses.

"We are friends, Julia, but I find that my behavior over the last few years toward Mr. Grant and his family was shameful. He's a good man, just as his sisters did not deserve our slights and wicked remarks. We, all of us, owe them an apology. We should not like to be treated in such a way."

"No one would dare treat us in that way," Julia said, smirking as if Clara were making a joke.

"Not to your face at least," Clara said, dipping into a curtsy and leaving. She ignored the startled gasps from her friends, and sought out Lady Graham. She owed her an apology first and foremost and then she would find Stephen and remove him from the ladies who thought to win his affections. They were not his to give to anyone else for they were hers and hers alone.

Clara found Lady Graham standing beside her husband, the woman's eyes clouding in unease as Clara came up to them. She dipped into a curtsy, smiling a little to try to put the woman at ease. How awful of her to have treated her ladyship so appallingly simply because she had once harbored hopes toward the Marquess being her husband.

"Good evening, Lady Graham. My lord," she said, coming to stand beside her.

Her ladyship threw her husband a look of bewilderment before smiling at Clara. The gesture did not reach her ladyship's eyes and Clara sighed, hoping she could make things right between them. No matter what had happened between her and Stephen, she did want her feud with Lady Graham to come to an end.

"Good evening, Lady Clara. It is good to see you back in town."

Clara nodded, glancing back out toward where she'd left her friends. Most if not all of them had noted her location and many were watching with rapt attention. No doubt they expected Clara to be her usual, cutting self.

Clara turned to face her ladyship. "This may seem a little strange, and out of nowhere, but I wanted to apologize to both you and the Marquess. I have been abominably rude in the past, cutting and frankly a trial to be around, and neither of you deserved my atrocious behavior. This is quite forward of me I know to be so outspoken, but for whatever it is worth, I am sorry for my actions in the past and I want you both to know that it will never happen again." Clara glanced back to where she'd seen Stephen last and she shivered at seeing him watching her, his dark, contemplative gaze fixed on her person.

Lady Graham reached out and clasped her hand, squeezing it a little. "Thank you, Lady Clara for your apology. It is most readily accepted and I do hope we're able from this night on to be friends."

Clara turned back and smiled at her ladyship, pleasure coursing through her at her ladyship's words. "I would like that too, my lady. Very much."

STEPHEN WATCHED to see his sister's reaction to Clara coming over to speak to her, but from the delight and animated conversation they were now having after a stifled start, they looked for all the world to see as if they were old, reunited friends.

He narrowed his eyes, wondering at it. Inane chatter floated about him regarding the weather, gossip and the latest betrothals to be announced about London from his shadow for the evening, Miss Huxtable. He couldn't understand why she had taken a liking to him all of a sudden or why she and her gaggle of friends found his conversation so very interesting.

Stephen stifled a sigh, wanting to escape and yet not knowing how he could without causing offense.

"Do you not agree, Mr. Grant?"

His gaze shot to the women about him, each of their gazes set on him as if he was about to impart some grand advice they could not live without. "I do apologize, what was the question?" He shook himself out of being distracted by the woman who bothered him to no end and concentrated on the conversation at hand.

"We were discussing the merits of marriage. That a woman of wealth marrying a gentleman of little means is looked upon more favorably than a man of wealth marrying a woman of little wealth or connections. Do you not agree?"

Stephen swallowed, well aware that each of the women who stood before him were heiresses, but with fathers who were lower ranked on the nobility ladder. He supposed his connection to the Marquess Graham, one of the richest lords in England had something to do with his newfound popularity.

Not to mention he'd heard whispers about town that

his association with the Duke of Law's daughter had been noted.

"I must admit that I have not given the notion much thought, but I think that if a couple were to marry, I would hope that they cared for, if not loved, each other. I dislike the idea that wealth or connections would sway the union." Such as it had with Clara and him. He clamped his mouth shut lest he say anything else. The women before him did not know what had transpired between him and Clara, nor did they know their conversation grazed very close to his own truth.

That his love had been thrown back in his face simply because he was not titled. That Clara was worried what society would say about her marriage to him.

He knew what they would say. That he'd married her for her money and that she had married beneath her status. That his family had carried on their coup of marrying titled rich people of the *beau monde*.

Little did it matter that his sisters adored and loved their husbands and long saw past their husbands' titles to the men who were beneath all that finery. Stephen had seen past Clara and the decoration piece she was when in town to the woman beneath. The one who had a heart, cared deeply and loved passionately.

Now that he was back in London he wasn't sure if there was any future between them. Tonight was the first time he'd seen her in four months and the sight of her almost brought him to his knees. Her gown of blue muslin draped over her body like a second skin. Her lithe figure and creamy white skin were as perfect as he remembered and he ached to take her in his arms, to pull her close and kiss the little freckle that sat directly beneath her ear.

He wanted her, but he wanted her to want him too.

Love him for who he was, even if that was someone who was not of her stature.

He sipped from his glass of wine when the Earl Darwin bowed before her, asking for her hand in a dance. He gritted his teeth, finishing the drink instead of storming into the middle of the ballroom and ripping her from his lordship's arms.

Stephen inwardly groaned when the first strains of a waltz commenced and Clara smiled as his lordship pulled her into his arms. For a moment his gaze fixated on the bastard's hand as it held her waist before he bowed to the women about him. "If you'll excuse me." He strode from the room, heading toward the terrace doors. Anywhere but where he could see Clara smiling and enjoying herself in another's arms. A man's arms whom she deemed worthy of her rank. A man who by fortune of birth was an earl.

"Mr. Grant. Are you well? You left us so suddenly."

He let go of the balustrade he was leaning on. Damn it, he cringed at the sound of Miss Huxtable's voice behind him. Why the devil had she followed him? He looked up the terrace and spotted only one other couple. Relief poured through him that they were at least not alone.

"I'm very well, thank you. The room is simply a little warm."

Her gaze flicked over him in an assessing manner and he raised his brow at her candor. "You should return inside, Miss Huxtable before you're missed."

She sauntered up to him and he glanced back to where the other couple had been only to see that they had disappeared. He took a step back, his legs hitting the stone balustrade and halting his escape.

"Mama will not miss me." She grinned and he inwardly cursed. "Will you waltz out here with me?"

"Miss Huxtable, go back inside at once before you ruin yourself."

Stephen's gaze whipped to the doors and to where Lady Clara stood, a disapproving frown on her normally pretty visage.

"My lady," Miss Huxtable said, dipping into a curtsy and scuttling back inside as if the devil himself was nipping at her silk slippers.

Stephen leaned back against the railing, crossing his arms. "Lady Clara. It's been a long time." Too damn long. He took in every delicious morsel that was Clara, soaking her up after months of not seeing her, hearing her voice. He'd missed her more than he'd thought he would. Stephen had told himself it was for the best that they parted when they did. Before too many emotions became involved. Before anyone lost their heart. But seeing her standing before him, a look of disapproval on her face, well, it only hammered home how much he'd been fooling himself.

No matter what she thought or the words spoken on his lack of breeding, he was in love with her. Had been in love with her for quite some time if he were honest with himself.

She stepped out onto the flagstones, coming to stand before him. "What do you think you're doing out here with Miss Huxtable? If her father caught you in such a position, he'd have you married within the week."

He shrugged. "Miss Huxtable is a sweet girl. I'm sure marriage to her would not be a trial." The narrowing of Clara's eyes brought forth a wave of pleasure. He wanted her to be annoyed. Wanted her to see what she'd lost.

*Him…*

# CHAPTER 14

Clara fought not to scratch Stephen's eyes out over his blind stupidity. Did he not realize that if he compromised a debutante he'd be forced to marry her? Clara pushed away the knowledge that she only cared about such things because if Stephen married someone else it would mean he could not marry her.

She sighed, hating that she'd pushed him away. That she'd hurt him with a truth that held no sway on her anymore. Having been back in society these past weeks had proven to her that she no longer cared what her friends thought of those ranked lower than them. Those with more or less funds at their disposal.

Walking out onto the terrace this evening and seeing Stephen with another woman... Now that she did care about. It had taken all her years of learning to behave like a lady should to stop her from grabbing Miss Huxtable by her curls and hurling her back inside with an almighty push.

"Miss Huxtable is not for you."

He scoffed, shaking his head. "Let me guess as to why,

my lady. Because I'm not rich enough to satisfy her father? Some people, you forget, do not let such facts influence their choice."

"I suppose you mean that I allow such prejudices to influence my choices." She moved along the terrace and heard him follow her. "I suppose I have allowed such opinions to do so, but it was only because of the circumstances of my birth and my upbringing that guided me into that way of thinking."

"Does not change the fact that yet again you've stepped into my life and halted what could possibly be a future for me. Miss Huxtable is a delightful girl and who didn't seem to be inclined to care about my lowly birth. Perhaps it would be best if you returned inside and had Miss Huxtable join me again on the terrace."

Clara unfisted her hands at her sides, and fought to calm her heart. How dare he threaten her with such actions? She ought to call his bluff and return to the ballroom and do exactly what he'd asked. She cast a glance at him at her side, his hands clasped behind his back as they strolled along a darkened portion of the terrace. "How changeable men are. One moment you were courting me and here you are, at a ball in London and attempting to court others if my observations of you this evening are correct."

Stephen barked out a laugh, the sound condescending. "That opinion could be said of you as well, my lady. Four months past you were in my arms, all heat and passion, and here you are doing the same as I, since I'm not worthy of your hand."

Clara glared at him. "I ought to marry a lord, someone rich and titled, heaven knows plenty have been trying to court me." All true, since her return to town, her multiple estates and money had been a beacon of light for those who would court such wealth. All of the gentlemen had paled in comparison to the one who stood beside her. How she had fallen for the man who had vexed, challenged and rudely rebuffed her at times astounded her still, but she had and now no one else would do for her.

She wanted him.

Not that she was willing to spout such truths. The sight of him with Miss Huxtable had halted that notion. For the moment at least.

"Such an outcome would certainly make your friends happy."

Clara took a step back as he advanced on her. His eyes bored into her and left her steps unsteady. He looked so angry and annoyed and God help her, she was glad of it. Glad he was showing some emotion after all this time apart. She had thought him completely lost and indifferent only today after four months of not seeing him. His reactions to her words certainly gave rise to hope.

A hope that after what she'd said to him, she did not deserve to have.

"It would. It would make them extremely happy," she taunted.

Another step forward. Another step back. Clara slipped around him and started for the corner of the house. They did not need to be seen arguing and she had little doubt that was exactly what they were about to do. If not worse than they already were.

This side of the house they only had the moonlight to guide their way and Clara stood at the terrace balustrade, looking over the shadowy gardens beyond.

"Do you mean that?" he asked, his words low and tremulous behind her.

She shut her eyes, knowing it was the time for truth. "No. I do not."

STEPHEN LEANED FORWARD, unsure he'd heard Clara right. No? Did that mean... He turned her to face him, her beauty catching him by surprise for a moment before he steeled himself to find out the truth. "What does that mean?"

He didn't let her go. Couldn't if he were honest. He'd wanted to touch her for months now, to hear her voice, to be with her as they had been in Kent. His hands slid down her arms, the softness of her skin as smooth as the silk gloves she wore.

She glanced up at him and he read the longing in her eyes and he wanted to comfort her. To tell her the truth about their time apart, but he could not. Not yet.

"I was wrong, Stephen. So very wrong, and now I fear it is too late."

"No." It was never too late. Not for what he hoped she was about to say. "Tell me, Clara. Tell me what you're thinking." Or he would expire if she did not.

"Our parting has been one of the loneliest times I've ever endured. After you left I threw myself into looking after my estates, the staff and farms, but I could not get you out of my mind. I realized I made a mistake in sending you away. In fact, I came after you the day you left, but you could not hear me calling. And now tonight, seeing the many women fawn at your feet, well, I knew I had to tell the truth before it was too late."

He bit back a grin at her words, not quite believing what he was saying. "And that was?" he asked.

"I was wrong how I spoke to you all those months ago in Kent. After what Lord Peel wrote about us I was frightened I'd be ruined and my prospects along with it. But then being back in town I realized that I held more power than I gave myself credit for. Daughter to the late Duke of Law and all that position entails makes me immune to a lot of Lord Peel's nastiness. People know my character, and they will not believe his lordship's words. While some of my friends may slight me in society over my choice of husband, those who do are not the ones worthy of my friendship."

He closed the space between them, took her face in his hands and kissed her. She fell into his arms, holding him close and he deepened the kiss, having missed her so terribly. "I made a mistake too," he said between kisses, pushing her back toward the side of the house and away from prying eyes should anyone walk about the corner.

"You did?"

"I did," he said, kissing her again. "I should never have left you. I should have stayed and fought for you. Made you see what you had to come to realize on your own."

She clasped his jaw, scratching at the little growth of stubble that sat on his face. "And what was that? Remind me."

"That we're meant for each other. Even when we disagree we're perfect for each other."

He pulled back, kneeling before her. Clara's eyes widened and she bit her lip.

"You're the love of my life, Lady Clara. Marry me?" he asked, trepidation seeping into his blood even with the knowledge of what she'd said. Still the fear persisted that she would choose someone more equal to her.

She pulled him up to stand, leaping into his arms. He held her close, breathing in the delicious smell of jasmine and the wonderful future that was within his view. "I will marry you, Mr. Grant." She pulled back a little, her eyes bright with unshed tears. "I adore and love you too, even if you drive me to distraction most of the time."

He chuckled, lifting her off her feet and spinning her. "You bother me too, my lady, but promise me one thing."

Clara nodded. "Anything," she said, watching him.

"Don't ever stop being you."

She smiled and his heart thumped hard in his chest. He kissed her again, deep and long and with each brush of her lips across his, the fears he'd harbored slipped away and gave way to the possibility of them. The future was grand and he'd ensure always happy. For them both.

Always…

# EPILOGUE

Clara sat on the river back at Chidding Hall, her son stood beside Stephen, both with fishing rods in their hands as they tried to catch their dinner. She smiled as the two most precious people in her world spoke of the fish breeds available in Kent and what sizes they may catch if they were lucky.

"Did grandfather really not allow anyone to fish here?" their son, Maximus asked, looking over his shoulder at her.

Clara nodded, smiling at the many days her father had ranted and argued the point as to why no one should fish in this very stream, unless it was their gamekeepers of course. "Until your father that is. I probably should have realized at that point that your father was the one for me since father approved him."

Stephen threw her a knowing smile before turning back to look at the river.

"I wish I had known Grandfather, Mama."

She swallowed the lump that rose in her throat that always happened when they spoke of her dearest father and all the wonderful things he'd missed. "He was the best of men, Max. And he would have loved to have met you as well. I know he would be proud of the young man you've become."

They were all proud. Max had excelled at Eton and would go on to college when the time came. Their only child, she would miss him dearly when he left, but, she reminded herself, there were still some years to go before that happened, he was only thirteen after all.

Stephen placed his fishing rod down and started toward her, coming to sit at her side. He leaned over and kissed her softly, and her stomach fluttered as it always had from the first time she'd argued with him in Hyde Park to the day they had promised their lives to each other before God.

"What are you writing in that journal of yours?" He tried to take it from her and she snatched it away, holding it away from him.

"Nothing that concerns you," she teased. In truth, it concerned him and their little family in all ways. All their memories were in her journals, their lives, their travels, heartbreaks and triumphs. Everything written down so she would never forget, even if she one day succumbed to the illness that took her father. Not that she had any fears that her mind was failing her, but even so, at least she would never forget her life.

"Maybe one day you will let me read them."

Clara put down her journal and shuffled closer to Stephen, wrapping her arms about his waist. He pulled her close, his hand idly running up and down her spine, sending a delicious shiver through her person.

"One day I will, but not this day." She grinned up at him.

He reached around and slipped a strand of her hair

that had tumbled free of its pin behind her ear. "You're as beautiful as the day we met. I adore you."

Heat rose on her cheeks and she marveled that he could still make her blush after all these years. "I love you too."

Their son made a gagging sound and she laughed, knowing he disliked that they were so public with their affection. And they had been from the moment they were married, whether in town during the Season or at one of their many estates, they did not shy away from showing their love for each another.

Lord Peel had tried to mar Clara's character, but Stephen and her Scottish brother-in-law, Laird Mackintosh, had put paid to his lordship's continual threats by a good one of their own one day at Whites when no one had been about.

She grinned at the memory of it. Her fears that society would shun her for marrying a man beneath her social status had too been unfounded and instead of turning their noses up at them, they had never said a word. Certainly not to their faces at least, and she was content with that. Invitations arrived by the dozen each day as if she'd married a duke in lieu of a Mister.

How silly she'd been to have almost thrown away the one man who had made her life worth living. Had given her the gift of their boy, who squealed, reeling in his line all of a sudden.

Clara jumped and Stephen ran over to Max, helping him hold the rod as they reeled in the fish.

"I've caught one! It's a big one I think," Max said through his exertions.

She went over to them, watching as a large trout landed on the bank, gasping for air. Stephen patted Max's back, congratulating him.

"Well done, Max. I don't believe I've seen such a large fish being caught here for some years," she said.

"Not even father has caught one so big?" Max asked, his eyes bright and excited.

"Well, I'm sure I have," Stephen interjected. Clara shook her head.

"Not even your father." She took the rod from Max as he picked up the fish, holding it at his side.

"Mrs. Pennell is going to be well pleased with this fish. Pity you did not catch one as well today, Father."

Stephen messed up Max's hair before their son turned for the house, trying to run as fast as he could, the large fish in his hand an impediment to his speed. Stephen reached over, taking the rod from her and taking her hand.

"I'm sure I've caught a fish of that size. You're mistaken, my lady."

"Hmm," she said, "If you have it was before you gained approval to fish here from my father and I never saw it."

He shot a look at her, his eyes wide. "I never fished here before I was allowed and you well know it. I wouldn't dare bring the wrath of the Lady Clara Quinton upon my head."

She chuckled. "To think that you and I officially started in this very spot. I can still see you walking across the grounds with Father, asking him if you may fish in his river. I was so annoyed that you had dared come here, but then I was pleased too. I always enjoyed sparring with you. A little at least."

He pulled her to a stop, throwing the rod to the ground and hoisting her up against him. Her heart thrummed loudly in her ears and she reached up, clasping his face in her hands. How lucky she was he was hers. "I always enjoyed verbally sparring with you also, and everything else." He grinned.

Stephen leaned down and kissed her and yet again, in front of the gardeners, gamekeepers and staff alike, the Lady Clara Quinton and Mr. Grant once again showed a public display of affection and couldn't care less who viewed them doing so.

Certainly they did not.

# A DUKE'S WILD KISS

## Kiss the Wallflower, Book 5

*Miss Olivia Quinton is certain a marriage proposal is imminent, but her hopes are dashed when her gentleman admirer moves his attentions to another at a country house party. Disappointed by these turns of events and seeing the man for the fiend he is, Olivia hatches a plan of revenge. With the aid of Duke Hamlyn, she sets out to make her past love interest pay for his betrayal.*

*Jasper Abraham, Duke Hamlyn, did not think his Season would be taken up with helping a bedeviling chit in gaining her revenge. Everything would work out splendidly well if he hadn't already agreed to help his friend keep Olivia away from him during the house party and remaining Season.*

*Thrown together with opposite goals, Jasper cannot help but wonder why anyone would overthrow the delectable, sweet Olivia Quinton.*

*Playing her fake beau is no chore, and the more time he spends with her, the more he wants to do a lot more than flirt with the chit.*

*Unfortunately, when games are played, there can be only one winner, but perhaps in this folly, everyone will lose.*

# CHAPTER 1

*Kent 1810*

"Will you do it for me, Hamlyn? We're not far from Chidding Hall, and I need your assurance you will support me with this matter. I need to have your promise, as my friend, that you will help me."

Jasper Abraham, Duke Hamlyn, gaped at his friend, Marquess Oglemoore. Had the fellow gone mad! He shook his head as the blood rushed back into his brain. "Absolutely not. Should I court Miss Quinton, she'd believe me to be enamored of her and possibly want a declaration of love and marriage soon after. If you led her to believe you liked her in town last Season and you did not, then you need to be the one who cleans up after your mistakes. I will not do it for you."

"You owe me, Hamlyn. Did I not step in at Bath just last month and stop those laborers from giving you a good thrashing? Which, by the way, I'm still unsure that you did not deserve."

"Now see here, how is it my fault that one of the men's

sweethearts worked at the tavern and rented out her assets to those who could pay? I did not know she was betrothed."

"So you *did* sleep with her? I should have let them thrash you," Oglemoore said, raising his brow with a sarcastic tilt.

"I did no such thing. The woman seized my hand and placed it on her breast at the very moment her betrothed walked into the taproom. Had it been a bout of one-on-one, I would have had no qualms in thrashing the fool for allowing himself to be played so, but one on five and I drew the line." Jasper glared at his friend, disappointed. "What is more surprising to me is your seeking repayment of that service. I should have taken the bloodied nose and been done with it. I do not want to fool Miss Quinton in such a deceitful way. When she was in town last year, what I remember of her was a sweet, pleasant-looking woman. Are you sure you do not wish to court her instead of this Lady Athol Scott chit?"

"Absolutely certain. Miss Quinton is not for me. She's the niece of a duke, granddaughter of one, but other than the house she inherited from her father, and a notable portion, she has little else. Her cousin Lady Clara rules London society like the strict headmaster we had at Eton, and I'm not looking to be under her rule for the remainder of my days.

"I'm Marquess Oglemoore, my family has always married well. Lady Athol owns half of the Scottish lowlands. Imagine the hunting we can do if I marry her. No, Athol suits me very well."

"So, it's a love match, then?" Jasper said, his tone riddled with sarcasm.

Oglemoore's lips thinned into a disapproving line. "I do not love her, but I'm sure that will follow in time. I am fond of the chit, and so she will be my wife. But as for Miss Quinton, you must be the one to show more interest in her person. I need you to do this, truly. When she finds out that I'm courting someone else, she'll be right grieved. But if you, my handsome, English-titled friend show her there is more in the world than me, then she'll move on quick enough."

"And if she chooses me to be the man that she moves on with, what shall I do then? I do not want to be saddled with a wife. I have a mistress in town. A life." The horror of doing such a thing to an innocent woman did not sit well with Jasper, no matter who he had waiting for him back in London. He hated lies and deceit above most things. Oglemoore ought to know better. That he did not was no act of a gentleman.

"Please, my old friend. I'm begging you."

Jasper sighed, glaring across the carriage as it turned through the gates of Chidding Hall. "Very well, but this more than pays back my debt and then some. You owe me by quite a lot."

Oglemoore beamed, clapping his legs with his hands. "I knew I could count on you, my good friend. I shall gladly pay you back tenfold for this. Thank you."

Jasper wasn't so sure he would ever be repaid for acting the lovesick fool trying to turn a woman's eye toward him and off another. Even so, he would do it for his friend since he seemed so desperate. He could be Miss Quinton's friend, guide her away. There need not be anything romantic between them. If he followed that rule, all would be well and work out in the end.

"We're here," Oglemoore said, sliding toward the door.

Jasper picked up his top hat, slapping it onto his head. "Let the games begin," he said, throwing his friend a small grimace.

*Let the games begin indeed.*

OLIVIA SWALLOWED the bile that rose in her throat at hearing her closest friend declare that she hoped to marry Elliott Keating, Marquess Oglemoore.

"We were introduced at a ball in London. He's affable, and I enjoyed his company. I look forward to seeing him attend the house party," Athol said, a small smile playing about her lips.

The world spun around Olivia, and she clasped her stomach, taking a deep breath to try to stop her stomach contents from making an appearance.

"I had no idea you were even acquainted?" she stated, quite shocked by the fact. Lord Oglemoore was not only one of the most highly placed gentlemen in the *ton*, but he was also one of the most handsome. There was not a feminine heart in London that did not flutter in his presence.

Last Season Olivia had happened upon Lord Oglemoore as he'd stumbled out of the supper room after slipping on some barberry ices. She had awkwardly caught him, but instead of acting the assaulted debutante, she had laughed off the collision, and they had been friends ever since.

"Oh, it's all a bit of a shock to me too. We met at Almacks one Wednesday evening. He asked me to dance, and I agreed. I like him, and I do believe he likes me as well. Or," her friend said, biting her lip, "I hope he does, at least. The ladies speak highly of him, and he seems determined to find a wife. I merely hope he chooses me."

"Of course," Olivia said, her mind reeling. "As a gentleman, I'm sure he will not play you false. If he's shown an interest in you and you return favorably, this house party may end with a betrothal announcement."

Olivia smiled at her friend, whom she loved most dearly, but the idea that the one gentleman whom she'd believed to have wanted to court her was instead seemingly interested in Athol was indeed a bitter pill to swallow. How had she been so wrong to read his character and interest so incorrectly?

Athol chuckled. "I do hope so. I seem to have pinned all my hopes on him, even though I have many gentlemen in town who stated they were awaiting my return. But I like Lord Oglemoore best of them all. He will do for me, I believe."

Olivia stared at Athol, unsure what she was hearing was true. Athol was going to marry a man simply because of what? "I'm sorry, my dear, but why marry him if you only think him your best choice? Why not take your time? This is only your second Season. Find a gentleman who puts your heart in his hand and never lets it go."

Her friend shrugged, plopping a grape in her mouth. They were seated out on the terrace that overlooked the grounds of her cousin's estate, the day warm without a breath of wind in the air.

"If you haven't noticed, we are getting rather long in the tooth, Olivia dear. We're both from respectable families and will do well together. I never cared overly much for a marriage to be based on love. You know I've always been practical with those types of things."

Olivia nodded, looking out over the gardens, bewildered at her friend's words. If she did not love Lord Oglemoore, then why could she not leave him be? Leave him for her?

The sound of a carriage approaching caught her attention, and Olivia glanced to where the road leading into the estate became visible through the trees. A black, highly polished carriage flittered through the foliage—more guests she assumed.

Athol shot to her feet, checking her gown and hair. "This will be Lord Oglemoore now. He said he'd arrive today. I'm so thankful that Lady Clara was willing to invite him and his friend to stay for the house party too."

Olivia did not move, not sure if her legs would support her. What a fun party they would all make with the man she had pinned all her hopes upon and her best friend who was trying as hard as she might to gain an understanding with him. She inwardly groaned, wanting to vanish to her rooms instead of meeting the guests as she should.

"Come, Olivia. Let us go out to the front and welcome them."

Olivia nodded, following without a word. Athol strode ahead, every now and then stopping to call for Olivia to quicken her pace. They made the estate front just as the carriage rocked to a halt, a billow of dust and all.

Her cousin Lady Clara and her husband, Mr. Grant, were already waiting on the home's steps, a warm smile on their lips as they prepared to greet their guests. Clara met Olivia's gaze. Puzzlement crossed her features before she joined her on the graveled drive.

"Are you well, Olivia dear? You look somewhat pale." She reached out, touching her forehead. "You do not feel warm, is there something else that is bothering you?"

Besides the fact that her best friend wanted to marry the man she coveted as her husband, no everything was perfectly well. "It is nothing, I assure you. Perhaps I have had too much sun today."

A footman opened the carriage door, and Lord Oglemoore jumped out, clasping Mr. Grant's—Stephen to those who knew him well—hands in welcome. He then turned to Athol, who stood waiting close by. Pleasure crossed his features, and Olivia felt the devastation of his attachment to her friend to her core. He liked her, to his credit. More than she'd thought, considering Athol merely liked the fellow, not actually loved him. Even so, Lord Oglemoore smiled lovingly at her friend, and Olivia did not miss the blush that stole across her friend's cheeks.

The carriage dipped a second time, and another gentleman appeared in the door. Olivia glanced at the man who jumped out of the equipage, dismissing him when Lord Oglemoore spoke.

"How wonderful to be back here again. It has been too long, Lady Clara, since you've opened the house," he said, smiling at her cousin before his gaze met hers.

He stepped toward her but did not drop Athol's hand that sat upon his arm. "Miss Quinton. You are a welcome sight, to be sure. I hope you're well?"

Somehow in all the despondency that pumped through her veins, she remembered her manners and smiled. "I am well, Lord Oglemoore. It is good to see you again too."

Oglemoore gestured to the gentleman behind him, and for the first time, Olivia took in the other house guest. He was taller than his lordship, athletic in build and surprisingly handsome.

She frowned, feeling as if she'd met him before, but unable to place where.

He smiled in welcome, a contemplative look in his eye when his gaze landed on her.

"This is my friend, His Grace, the Duke of Hamlyn."

Stephen held out his hand to His Grace, shaking it. "It has been too long, Hamlyn. I'm glad you're able to make the trip to Kent."

"Thank you for having me stay and congratulations on your marriage," the duke said, in a honeyed, deep tone.

Olivia watched as the duke kissed her cousin's cheeks.

She turned for the doors, ready to go inside where she may be able to slip away for a moment or two to gather her wits. The house party loomed like a week of torture, and she wasn't so sure she wanted to be here anymore.

Her escape was blocked when Clara caught up to her, leading her into the drawing room where an array of refreshments and a light lunch were prepared.

"Where do you think you're disappearing to, my dear? You have guests whom you must help me with."

Olivia sighed, letting Clara lead her into the room. "I need to speak to you when you are free. It is imperative."

Clara glanced at her, her brow furrowed. "Of course. I knew something was troubling you. We shall speak as soon as we can."

"Thank you." Olivia blinked away the sting of tears as she watched Athol and Lord Oglemoore seat themselves together on the settee by the window that overlooked the river. The duke hovered near the unlit hearth, speaking to Stephen.

"I'll come to your room before dinner this evening, and we'll have a chat," Clara said, patting her hand in comfort.

"Thank you." Olivia seated herself on a single leather-backed chair, willing the time to go by fast. A shadow passed over her and she glanced up, only to meet the amused gaze of the duke. She raised one brow, contesting his inspection of her with one of her own. "Is something amiss, Your Grace? You're scrutinizing me as if I have a blemish on my nose." Her question was, she supposed, rather rude, but she was no longer in the mood to be congenial. When one's hope of happiness was stripped, one was allowed to be curt.

"I do believe we've met, Miss Quinton. Last Season, in fact," he answered, his lips catching Olivia's attention for a moment before she tore her gaze away.

She shrugged, not willing to admit she knew him as well. A passing acquaintance and nothing more. He certainly never asked her to dance, she remembered that all too well. "It is possible that our paths crossed, Your Grace. I've met many people over the last few years in London." Pity he had not deemed her worthy of his interest, for he was known as a most sought-after catch.

He kneeled beside her chair, his hand resting on the arm. Olivia glanced at it. Really, did the man have to invade her space as well as ask her questions about a Season she'd prefer to forget?

"I assumed when you did not return to London this year that you had married." A light blush stole across his cheeks. Olivia narrowed her eyes, undecided if she would let him get away with what he was implying, that she was still unwed, an old maid in the making.

"I did not think gentlemen cared whether women they hardly favored to know married or not." He glanced at her, an amused look she found annoying filling his eyes. Did the man have no shame?

"I merely was surprised that an intelligent and beautiful woman such as yourself had not been swooped off her feet and carried into the sunset. That is all."

Olivia shut her mouth with a snap and tore her gaze away from him. He did not need to be so forward as that. Nor did she like his light flirtation with her. She did not want it from the duke.

She wanted it from Lord Oglemoore. Not that that was a possibility since the gentleman had his whole purpose fixed on her best friend. "I have not found anything to tempt me to the altar, my lord."

"Is that so?" he stated, glancing at his friend and then back to her. Olivia refused to blush or break her gaze. To do so would give credence to what he was saying, and she would not give him that pleasure. He continued to stare, not giving an inch on their little challenge and her blush deepened, their fixation on each other growing awkward.

Stephen cleared his throat, coming to stand beside Olivia. "Everything well, my dear?" he asked her, touching her shoulder.

Olivia nodded, cursing that she had to look away before others noticed their frivolous game and made a comment.

"Of course. His Grace was just telling me how fond he is of your home and would like a tour," she lied.

Olivia stood and strode from the room before her cousin's husband asked if she would do the honors. Under no circumstance was she in the mood to play tour guide, and certainly not to a man who seemed amused by what was going on between her and Lord Oglemoore.

She strode toward the stairs, not caring she did not resemble the duke's granddaughter she was. She needed to reach the sanctity of her room. A place she could think and plan.

What that plan was, however, she was not certain just yet. Would she try to dissuade Athol into marrying Lord Oglemoore should he ask? Over the years, she'd certainly heard plenty of tales about the gentleman's antics both in London and Bath.

Some of which had made even herself blush a time or two, but after his kindness toward her last Season she had dismissed the stories as false.

Olivia made her room, closing and locking the door before she flopped onto the bed. How could this have happened? She had been so sure of his regard for her. Last Season, Lord Oglemoore sought her out, danced and took supper with her. The horrible thought crossed her mind that it was all for show, a game he enjoyed to play with unattached women.

She sighed, staring up at the wooden beams lining her bedroom ceiling. There were two choices she could make regarding this awful turn of events. She could wish them well and move on with her life. Have another Season and see if any offers were forthcoming.

To parade herself again would be a humiliation she doubted she could ever recover from, and she wasn't certain she had it in her to do again. To walk into a ball-room, night after night, and try to find love.

She swiped a tear from her cheek, annoyance thrumming through her. Athol deserved better than a man who would treat her friend or any woman with so little respect. What was stopping him from throwing Athol aside when someone better in his opinion came along? Nothing.

Olivia sat up, thinking of what could be done. He would pay for his callousness. She would show Athol he was unworthy of her during the week that he was here. Olivia chewed her bottom lip, frowning in thought. But how, that was the question, and one she would mull over before tomorrow.

# CHAPTER 2

Later that evening, Jasper sat before the hearth in the blue salon, sipping a whisky and thinking over Miss Olivia Quinton. He could not fathom why his friend Oglemoore had not courted the woman himself. She was a beautiful lady. In fact, he'd almost choked on his own tongue when they had been introduced for a second time. She had changed from the last time they had met. Her body had transformed into a generous feminine curve. Breasts that a man's hands hungered to knead. Hips one wanted to press against one's own. She would look absolutely stunning lying pliant and ready, wet and willing before him.

He adjusted his seat as footsteps sounded on the wooden passage leading to the salon.

"Ah, Hamlyn, just the man I wished to see. May I join you in a drink?" Oglemoore asked, striding into the room toward the decanter of whisky.

"Of course." Jasper observed the flames in the hearth as they licked at the wood, conflicted over his agreement with his friend to seduce Miss Quinton so as to make his life more palatable. If Oglemoore had shown more affection than he ought, then he needed to face the consequences of his actions and man up.

"What a day we've had. Thank you again for distracting Miss Quinton after dinner. I know she harbors feelings for me, but I'm hoping when she sees me with her friend, and you show a keen interest, her own emotional connection will wane."

Jasper sighed, rubbing the back of his neck, doubting Miss Quinton would do any such thing. She might be quite displeased to have been treated as a fool in London by Oglemoore. "She did not appear enthralled by my attempt to speak with her. It did not help that because I had not danced with her in London, I was seen as wanting. I cannot see how this plan of yours will work, Oglemoore. Miss Quinton has thorns, and they're aimed at my ass."

"I'm asking that you distract her from me. Marriage is not a requirement. You simply need to show her there are other options for her. She needs to see that whatever misapprehension she was living under regarding myself was misplaced."

Jasper narrowed his eyes, not understanding how his friend could not see that his interest in the chit could lead to the same problem Oglemoore now had with her.

"I do not understand you, Oglemoore. Why not marry Miss Quinton instead of Lady Athol? I confess," Jasper said, leaning back in his chair and folding one leg over the other. "She was not as I remembered her. Miss Quinton is far superior in appearances than I recalled."

"Hmm," Oglemoore said, frowning into his glass of whisky. "Which is exactly why she would not suit me. I'm a jealous sod. I dislike my paramours being ogled, nevertheless my wife. Miss Quinton is beautiful, I grant you, but Athol is more to my taste. She is rich, but not too handsome that she will be plucked from my arms by some fiend. You've seen how invidious I become when anyone compliments my paramour."

"You are not going to part ways with Heidi, then?" The idea repulsed Jasper. If a gentleman were going to marry, he ought to respect his wife enough to separate from his mistress. His parents had a loveless marriage, and he would not wish that on any wife or child.

Oglemoore's jaw clenched at his words. "Whoever ends up as my wife will not know that I have a mistress. Heidi is of no consequence to this discussion."

"I wish you well with that," Jasper said, knowing full well he wasn't ready for a wife or to lose his own mistress Lotty, and wouldn't ask anyone to be his wife until he was ready to. It had taken him some weeks to wear his mistress down, gain her trust. He didn't particularly want to lose the arrangement they had simply because his friend had tangled himself into a bind and needed saving. If Miss Quinton thought him in earnest to gain her affections, his life as a bachelor in London would be over.

"How am I to distract her from you when she does not want anything to do with me? Did you see her today? She all but bolted from the room at the mere mention of giving me a tour. If that does not show a woman determined not to be pursued by me, I'll eat my own gloves."

"Display some of that English charm I hear you possess. Miss Quinton will not be able to deny you her friendship. You merely have to distract her, not sleep with her."

Jasper sighed, a noose settling about his neck, threatening to choke him. This would not end well. Women, in general, always saw a man's attention for more than it may be. It gave them hope where there was not always hope to have. He liked Miss Quinton, and to play her a fool for a second time was not right. Nor could he allow his friend to marry a woman he did not want. That, too, would be unfair for Miss Quinton.

"I shall continue my friendship with her, but I shall not be seducing her or taking any privileges she may offer if she starts to believe she and I have a future together. I do not want to become embroiled in a scandal that sees my leg shackled to her. If I do, you can be guaranteed I shall not be the only one going down with the ship, Oglemoore. I shall be pulling you down under with me," he said, his tone severe.

Oglemoore glanced at him, all seriousness and joking wiped from his visage. "Thank you for your assistance, Hamlyn. Know that I do not want to hurt Miss Quinton any more than you do. I'm happy for you to be friends and nothing more so long as she stops wishing that she'll turn my head, and I'll offer to her instead."

Jasper raised his brow, wanting that to be true, and yet his unease would not dissipate. This could end badly for all of them.

OLIVIA SNUCK AWAY the next afternoon after lunch to her favorite location in the garden. An old oak sat before the river's edge, not far from her cousin's home, where she'd spent many hours lying on the grassy bank, reading, drawing, dreaming of a future whenever she visited here.

Her future after the last Season she'd hoped would include Lord Oglemoore, but that was not to be. He was not interested in her as he once had been, which in itself ought to vex her. The idea he'd used her poorly, teased her with the idea of them, hurt.

She caught sight of the man himself, walking with Athol and the duke. Together, His Grace was a striking man against Lord Oglemoore. Taller, broader across the shoulders, long, lean legs that looked well-toned from years of horse-riding. He was a handsome gentleman. No doubt turned the heads of many fine ladies. His buckskin breeches and black jacket fitted him to perfection, and he looked comfortable and at ease within himself. Sure of his own capabilities and situation.

She narrowed her eyes, thinking of a way to repay Lord Oglemoore's treatment. Of how she could show him what he'd overlooked by choosing another, even if that person was her best friend and someone she would not allow him to misuse either.

Olivia turned away, leaning upon the tree and watching the river's water idly float by. Her plan was not without merit, but she needed a gentleman willing to help her tease Lord Oglemoore into thinking he'd made a mistake.

"Good afternoon, Miss Quinton. What a lovely situation in which you have found yourself."

Olivia gasped, looking up to find His Grace staring down at her, a silly, lopsided smile on his lips. The scent of sandalwood and pine teased her senses. Heavens, he smelled nice for a man, as if he'd bathed in the forest just for her.

The thought of His Grace naked and lathing his skin in hot, scented water sent a frisson of longing through her. Her cheeks warmed.

"As you see," she said, turning to pick up her sketch pad and slapping it onto her lap. "Can I help you with anything, Your Grace?"

He sat beside her, leaning back on his elbows, continuing to admire the river. "I saw you just now, peeping from behind the oak." He gestured to her paper. "What are you drawing, may I ask?"

"Nothing of importance," she replied, closing her sketch pad. "Was there anything else that you wanted? Or do you simply intend to while away the afternoon in my presence?" Not that she minded his company, but now that she'd thought of her idea on how to make Lord Ogle-moore pay, she needed time to think about her plan. The duke, as handsome and nice as it was for him to be sitting beside her, made her mind less clear. She was unable to concentrate as much as she should.

Laughter lurked in his blue orbs, and he grinned. "Would that be so very bad if I wished to do exactly that?" he asked, meeting her gaze.

He truly did have lovely eyes. A darker, stormier shade of blue than Lord Oglemoore's. "Is there nothing more stimulating you could be doing than lying here with me? I do not have a chaperone. It's not seemly for you to be here."

His Grace glanced over his shoulder and then turned back to her, shrugging. The wickedness of his features told Olivia all she needed to know about this man. He was a consummate rake and well used to getting his own way.

"I can be seen from the house, and since I do not have you in my arms while I ravish that pretty, delectable mouth of yours, there will be no harm done."

Olivia stared at him, unable to believe he had said something so shocking. Ravish her pretty, delectable mouth? The idea of him kissing her, of pulling her hard against his chest... It would be wicked and thrilling to experience. And if Lord Oglemoore happened to see them...

"You cannot say such things to me, Your Grace." Yet, the thought he may stop at her chastisement was equally annoying. She was not so proud as to admit that while in London, she had enjoyed the attentions of Lord Oglemoore. That his consideration now seemed to be elsewhere was another point altogether. Having the duke admit he found her enticing was, in itself, a nice boost to her soul and helpful to her plan.

Olivia studied the man at her side a moment, his teasing grin firmly set on his delectable lips. If he were so bold to her, nothing was stopping her from doing the same. She was, after all, a duke's granddaughter. High enough on the peerage ladder that His Grace would not dare to slight her publicly at her words. "Your Grace, since you're quite willing to speak plainly, may I do also?"

He raised his brows, a curious light in his eyes. "Please, say whatever comes to mind, Miss Quinton."

"You may call me Olivia if you prefer."

Pleasure stole across his features before he said, "I would like that very much, Olivia. You, in turn, may call me Jasper or Hamlyn if that is more comfortable."

Jasper? The name suited him. It was nice to hear a name that was different from the norm. Not another boring Arthur or William. "I would like to have your assistance with a concern I'm having, but it is one that is quite personal and sensitive, if I'm honest."

He leaned his head on one hand, watching her keenly. At some point, he'd picked up a piece of straw and slipped it between his lips. The sight of his tongue flicking the tiny plant from side to side made her stomach flutter. The man was awfully distracting.

"Intriguing, Olivia. Do tell," he teased her, wickedness dancing in his eyes.

Olivia took a deep, fortifying breath to say what she must. This was for the best. Oglemoore must pay for his crime. "I need your assistance, Jasper. I need you to help me portray that we're courting, and possibly falling in love. I need you to do this with me to prove Lord Oglemoore for the fiend he is. I know, he is your friend, and I'm sorry for speaking ill of him, but he played me the fool last year and he shall not get away with it, or court my friend only to throw her aside as well. Will you help me with this?"

There, she had done it. Said the words she'd not thought to ever utter to a man, and not just any man, but one she hardly knew. But what better ally to help her with her revenge than his best friend? If one was to become jealous over affections, one must be in the mind's eye at all times. The duke was always about Lord Oglemoore. It was the perfect plan.

His tongue halted flicking the straw. He pulled it out, throwing it aside. "Let me understand this. You wish for me to court you to make Oglemoore jealous and therefore want you back, only this time you will tell him to go hang and in turn prove to your friend Lady Athol that she is better rid of his lordship and his fickle nature?"

She nodded. "Yes, that is exactly what I propose. Are you a willing participant, or do I need to find someone else?"

# CHAPTER 3

Bloody hell. He could not believe what Miss Quinton proposed. Had she really asked for him to help her torment Oglemoore? His friend had asked him to befriend her only two days ago, distract her from his courtship with Athol. Were the two of them playing some sort of game on him he wasn't aware of? What were the odds of both of them asking for such assistance?

What had he managed to get himself into now?

Her eagerness, her desire to right the wrong Oglemoore had bestowed upon her pulled at a place within him he'd not thought he had. He reached out, sliding a finger across her jaw, taking in the few freckles that sat across the bridge of her nose. Hell, she was pretty, sweet, and headstrong, a woman to be reckoned with and one who had asked for his assistance. He could not deny her, nor could he stop assisting Oglemoore. He would do as both asked and hoped he survived the ordeal.

One boon of helping Miss Quinton was that he could be near her person whenever he wished. After all, she was handsome, and someone had he taken the time to meet last Season, may have flirted with the idea of courting himself.

"What would it entail should I assist you?" he asked, sliding his thumb across her bottom lip. "Can I touch you as I am now?" Her lips were smooth and as soft as a feather. His body hardened at the idea of teasing his friend Oglemoore into imagining he'd made an error for his choice of bride. Of the stolen kisses Miss Quinton may now allow.

*This house party may not be such a bore after all...*

"Well, we can stroll about the house and gardens together. Always look as if we have important things to discuss, have our heads together, that sort of thing. Hand-holding, but only when Lord Oglemoore is about so he may catch us. You must stare at me adoringly and often."

He stared at her now, adoringly, and knew all too well it would not be an effort to pretend to like this woman. Not that he wanted to marry her or anyone, but to pretend, well, that was safe, was it not? They were deceiving everyone else, not themselves. It was the perfect way in which to satisfy both his promise to Oglemoore and Miss Quinton.

"Is that all I'm allowed? What about a stolen kiss or two? How I touched you just now? If we know Oglemoore will see it, what harm could that do, do you think?"

A pretty blush kissed her cheeks. He grinned, lying back on his arms to stare up at the sky through the dappled leaves of the oak above them. "I must admit that to kiss you would be no chore, Olivia."

He heard her small intake of breath. "We cannot kiss, Your Grace. That would be too scandalous," she said, her tone outraged, along with her features.

He chuckled. "Pity," he sighed. "I could teach you so you would be an expert by the time the gentlemen of the *ton* do come to their senses and offer for your hand. A man such as the marquess would know how to kiss a woman, and you should be prepared if you wish to marry."

"You think I'm terribly wicked for doing this to Ogle-moore, do you not?" she asked, a frown between her perfect brows. "My friend must come to her senses and see him for the fiend he is. I will not let him get her hopes up only to disappoint her as he has done to me."

He glanced at her and reached out to smooth the small line away. "If you believe this is truly a mistake and your friend is yet to find the man whom she will love with all her heart, then perhaps not so bad. But," he said, his hand dropping to his side, "should Oglemoore turn out to be a good match for your friend, and you hurt Athol through this scheme, then you risk losing more than you would gain."

She sighed, lifting up her knees to lean atop them. "No matter what I do, this I promise you, Your Grace. I shall not throw myself at your friend, no matter how he reacts to our flirting. I shall allow Athol to see that his affections are not honorable toward her and that she should not marry him. As for Athol's own affections, I believe they are not engaged. Not as one's emotions should be, I assume. I think, therefore, what I am doing is a service, not an injustice."

The sound of laughter caught their attention, and they both watched as Oglemoore and Athol strode together, arms linked, into the house.

Jasper took the opportunity to study Olivia. How was it that a woman such as herself had not been swooped up and carried down to the altar already? Was she so set upon Oglemoore that she'd failed to see who else was trying to gain her attention?

"We're quite hidden here under this oak, and even

though you can be seen from the house in this position, I do not think that is the case. Perhaps you ought to lean down and kiss me now, Olivia. We can start your kissing lessons early."

She gasped, staring at him, but the small, teasing light in her eyes told him she was intrigued. He sat up, placing his face as close to hers as he dared. "Have you ever kissed a man before?" he whispered, his attention dipping to her sweet, sensual lips.

"No," she murmured. The reply pleased him. He didn't want to think of her kissing anyone else, and certainly not Oglemoore. He did not know where that odd thought came from, and he pushed it aside for later evaluation.

"All you have to do is lean a fraction closer and touch your lips to mine." He reached out and caressed her hand, relishing the feel of her soft skin. "Kiss me, Olivia." Her gaze dipped to his lips, and he leaned closer still. So near now that he could almost taste her. "Use me to make Oglemoore pay for his crime." If this is what both Olivia and Oglemoore wanted, Jasper would serve them both well. He may not have always wanted the position he was placed in, but this turn of events was fortunate indeed.

He would enjoy everything she would give and be a good friend to both her and Oglemoore at the same time. It was indeed a perfect plan.

AT THE MENTION of the marquess, Olivia's decision to kiss the duke was made. She closed the small gap between them and pressed her mouth to his. For a moment, she did not move, simply kept her mouth shut and against his, feeling for the first time what a man's lips felt like. His were warm and so very soft. She had not expected that from him. Her mind whirled at the idea of kissing him whenever she liked, and she found herself quite excited about teasing Oglemoore over the next week with her new beau.

If she hoped for a ravishing kiss, she was utterly wrong. Hamlyn did none of those things. Oh no, he did something so much worse. His hands cradled her face, tipping her head to one side as his mouth explored hers in languorous, deep strokes that made her toes curl in her silk slippers.

He tasted of tea and strawberries. The kiss was unlike anything she'd ever experienced before. It was raw, new, and addicting. How many women had this rogue kissed to know how to make a woman purr?

Olivia pushed the unhelpful thought aside, not wanting to think about how many women he may have had in his life. Men, such as the duke, kissed many women. She wasn't a simpleton to believe she was his first.

*But maybe you could be his last…*

Heat pooled between her legs, a reaction that was new and wonderful. The idea of crawling onto his lap, of rubbing herself up against him to soothe the ache that thrummed at her core taunted her. This kiss stole her wits. Made her want things no well-bred young woman ought to want.

This kiss was dangerous. How unexpected and pleasant.

Olivia pulled back, staring at him, trying to right her addled mind. Any kiss she shared with the duke—Jasper, as he wanted her to call him—was not supposed to muddle her mind and distract her from her plan.

His Grace had one purpose and one purpose only. To make Oglemoore jealous, to make him show his true colors and nothing more.

Her mind whirled with thoughts, anything to diminish the fact she may have just experienced a kiss she would dream about for years to come. Long to do over again and again.

His Grace studied her, a curious look in his eyes.

"Do you think Oglemoore saw our kiss?" she said, tearing her gaze away from Hamlyn and looking back at the house where they'd seen Oglemoore and Athol last. Anywhere but the handsome face that tempted her more than it ought. More than Oglemoore ever had.

Oglemoore was nowhere to be seen, and a small part of her was thankful for it.

"I do not believe so."

Olivia glanced at Hamlyn, not missing his curt, annoyed tone. With a small shake of his head, he stood, brushing down his breeches. "Shall we return indoors, Miss Quinton?"

Unsure what his lordship's matter was, she shook her head, leaning back against the tree. "No, I shall remain here a while longer. Thank you again for your assistance, Your Grace. I look forward to seeing you at dinner this evening," she said, not giving voice to her concern toward his suddenly cool demeanor.

"Of course, good afternoon." He strode from her, back straight and hands fisted at his sides. She narrowed her eyes. Perhaps he had not liked kissing her as much as she enjoyed kissing him. He'd kissed many women, and this was a game after all.

Olivia picked up her sketch pad and pencil and started to draw the river, supposing it may all be in her imagination that he was rather put out. She would be a fool indeed if she thought his kisses meant anything more than their agreement.

She made a terrible error of judgment with Oglemoore. She would not make the same mistake with the duke.

# CHAPTER 4

"I saw you this afternoon sitting with Duke Hamlyn. Do tell me if he's showing an interest in you, Olivia. If you become attached to his grace, perhaps we can have a double wedding," Athol said, grinning across the bed from Olivia as they drank hot chocolate before retiring for the night.

Athol had stolen into her room after she had procured two cups of hot chocolate, and now it would seem that at least Athol had noticed her outing with the duke. Did that mean Lord Oglemoore had too?

"I was sketching the river, and he joined me, nothing more. Please do not read into his attentions any further than that."

"I will not. I promise," Athol said, finishing her cup of chocolate and placing it on the bedside cabinet. "I wanted to talk with you about something, and I want you to be honest with me."

"Of course," Olivia said without thought, wondering what it was Athol had to say. Perhaps Lord Oglemoore had asked her to be his wife already, and her plans on making him pay were lost already. The thought soured her hot chocolate on her tongue.

"Elliott mentioned he thought that you may have been upset with him upon his arrival. Say it isn't so. I need you both to be friends, to like each other if I'm to marry him."

Olivia choked on her drink and coughed. Did Lord Oglemoore suspect her past hopes toward him? Oh, how mortifying!

"What makes you think such a thing?" she asked, frowning, and in truth, not wishing to know how Athol, or Elliott—since her friend seemed to be on a first-name basis with Lord Oglemoore—would think such a thing. Only Hamlyn knew of her plan, and he would not dare tell anyone.

"I was having afternoon tea with Elliott today, and he mentioned it in conversation. I know he grew quite fond of you when you were in town last year, but I'm sure he was just being polite. It would not make sense that he is courting me now if he wanted you as his bride last Season." Athol giggled, but Olivia could hear the nervousness in her friend's tone. "Do you not agree?"

Athol was not the type of friend to believe words Olivia would state about Oglemoore, she needed to see with her own eyes what type of man he was. If she could make the marquess show what his true make up was, she was certain Athol would not marry him.

"Lord Oglemoore was one of the kindest, most honest gentlemen I met last year in town. I would hope he would not play any woman a fool. If he has asked you to be his bride, I'm certain that our friendship was nothing more than that…a benign friendship." Not that Olivia believed that for a moment. The fiend had used her, played her like a string on a harp, and had now seemingly moved on to greener pastures. Well, she would not allow it. He would pay, or she'd die trying to make it so.

Athol frowned, staring down at her clasped hands in her lap. "He has not asked me yet, but I expect him to any day. I am, after all, an heiress and an earl's daughter. Surely it is only a matter of days before he offers me his hand."

Olivia stared at her friend, unsure she'd ever heard her sound so desperate to have a husband. What had come over her? "Lord Oglemoore and I did spend time together in town, but I'm sure you do not have anything to worry about. It seems he has chosen you to be his wife, even if he has not yet voiced such declarations out loud." Olivia could not help but plant the seed of doubt in her friend's mind. She no longer trusted Oglemoore to be true, and Athol deserved much better than him. Marriage, after all, was a lifelong commitment. One did not want to make a mistake.

At her friend's worried frown, a pang of guilt pinched her conscience. She did not want them to be at odds over a gentleman, but Oglemoore had been overly familiar with her. What else was she to think but that he wanted to court her? Possibly marry her. His being here at her cousin's house party, she had thought, was proof of his attachment. The Quinton pride ran deep, and it wasn't in Olivia to simply leave things as they were and move on. She had thought her hunt for a husband over. She could not simply walk away and allow his lordship to get away with what he had done, nor could she allow Athol to marry such a man. A flippant, untrustworthy one.

Athol had said herself she had multiple gentlemen seeking her hand. Why did she want Oglemoore anyway? She did not love him.

"He will voice them soon, I feel. I think you shall find

before the house party comes to an end, I shall be happily betrothed to Lord Oglemoore."

Olivia smiled at her friend's words, not wishing to say any more on the matter. "What do you think of Duke Hamlyn?" she asked, the reminder of his kiss this afternoon still fresh in her mind. Of how her body had turned to liquid heat. He was simply the perfect vessel to make another man rue the day.

"He's so very handsome, Olivia. When Elliott introduced me for the first time, I imagined myself rather in love with him and somewhat mad at myself that I had allowed Oglemoore to believe I was in love with him more."

"He does have a pleasing face," Olivia conceded, not wanting to give too much away. It was not like their repartee was true and possibly the start of something between them.

"Pleasing face," Athol mocked. "I wager it's more than pleasing. Hamlyn's face is sculpted to precision. His eyes are the deepest shade of blue I've ever seen. As for his aristocratic, perfect nose and lips that were made for sin, I wager he's more than pleasing. That he's here in Kent and for a whole week, la, I'll wager the ladies in London are most displeased."

"That does not mean anything," Olivia said, watching the flames in the hearth. She already knew what those lips felt like, how they incited a need she'd not known she possessed. He was too handsome for his own good and had a sweet temperament that was equally charming. Not many gentlemen would help her taunt a fellow friend into believing they had chosen the wrong woman to marry.

"It means a great deal," Athol argued. "It means you may have a chance of winning him. He certainly looks at you a great deal. Why at dinner this evening, I often caught him watching you, listening to your every word. He appeared very much in awe of you, in fact."

Warmth filtered through her at the thought of the duke being interested in her outside her own scheme. Surely not. He was one of London's rogues. On top of that, she was sure she'd heard he had a longtime mistress set up in town.

"What did he look at me like?" she asked anyway, despite her own warnings to herself and the fact it didn't matter how he observed her. It was all a game anyway and not real life.

"We're both maids," Athol continued. "But the duke watched you this evening as a rake watches his prey. Contemplated all the naughty things you could do together if you were alone."

"Athol!" Olivia gaped, as her friend laughed and shrugged.

"It's true, no matter what you may say to the contrary. The next time you're around Hamlyn, I suggest you watch him, catch him yourself eyeing you, and then you will see what I say is true."

Olivia could not believe it was so, but what if it were? The duke certainly seemed put out this afternoon with her. Was he jealous? It was not possible! They had an agreement. She was seeing things where there was nothing to be seen at all. Even if the idea of the duke's interest in her was enticing and flattering notion to consider.

"I shall observe His Grace and get back to you on my findings. We shall discuss the matter at the end of the house party."

Athol slid off the bed, a mischievous grin on her lips. "A wager? Five pounds says he becomes an admirer of yours."

Olivia held out her hand, shaking her friend's. "That is

a wager I'm willing to take." And win, considering the
duke's attention on her this evening like a besotted fool was
merely part of his acting as if enamored of her already.
Poor Athol, she did not stand a chance at winning this bet.
The five pounds was hers for the taking.

Jasper thundered across the land at blistering speed, his mount well worth the thousand pounds he paid for the gelding he'd had sent for from London for the duration of the house party. The horse was fast, strong, and capable, and went a long way in distracting him from the alluring Miss Quinton back at Chidding Hall.

Oglemoore, he could see out the corner of his eye, could not keep up to his mount's speed. He laughed aloud, knowing how much that fact would annoy his friend. Jasper pulled on the reins, slowing to a walk.

"Ah, this is living, do you not agree?" Oglemoore said, pulling his mount up alongside Jasper.

He nodded, relishing the green, picturesque fields of the late Duke of Law's lands. "It is beautiful here. I can see why Lady Clara invited us all down to Kent for a well needed distraction during the Season."

"Yes, and speaking of distraction, how is your courting of Miss Quinton coming along? I can assume by the fact she's not been chasing me about the estate that it is going better than I planned."

Jasper thought about how he would reply. He was, in fact, working for both parties, but for different reasons. His friend Oglemoore to keep Miss Quinton from having designs on him, and Miss Quinton to make Oglemoore regret his choice of bride and to stop him from gaining her friend Athol. A muddle anyone could make an error performing.

Jasper hoped for both his friend's and Miss Quinton's sake he could be of assistance, but he was starting to doubt that he would. After his kiss with Olivia yesterday, his mind had been less clear on his conduct and the rules he'd promised to obey.

His own rules regarding his life and his decision not to yet look for a wife himself.

She was a handsome woman, intelligent, if not a little misguided by her past affection for a man who clearly sought his future elsewhere. "We are becoming better acquainted," he answered, not wanting to tell Oglemoore everything that had passed between them. "I shall keep her occupied enough that she will not trouble you while we're here."

Oglemoore grinned. "I knew I could count on you. There are few women who would not look for a diversion in your arms, a verified rake that you are. But keep in mind, I do not wish for you to seduce her. That would be unfair to Miss Quinton."

The whole of Oglemoore's plan seemed unfair to Jasper already, but with Miss Quinton having her own scheme, he could not see the harm in assisting them both. So long as neither found out.

"Tell me," he said, changing the subject, "what is new between you and Lady Athol? Are you certain you want to marry the chit now that you're spending more time with her?"

Oglemoore looked out over the land, a frown between his brow. "I believe so. She's a sensible woman and compliments me well. I kissed her the other evening and was quite pleased with the outcome."

Jasper stared at his friend. *Pleased with the outcome?* Whatever sort of reaction to a kiss was that? After he'd kissed Olivia, he'd all but lost his wits. He'd forgotten entirely his scheme with his friend and the one the lady herself had made him promise to follow. All he'd thought of afterward were her soft lips. Her sweet exhale when he'd deepened the embrace. He wanted to do it again with a need that was foreign to him. The idea of kissing Miss Quinton outdid his desire to see his mistress in town. And he received far more than kisses from his mistress. An odd reaction, no doubt.

"Was the kiss not as passionate as you would like?" Jasper asked, adjusting his grip on the reins.

Oglemoore shrugged. "It was pleasing, but," he sighed, running a hand through his hair, "Lady Athol is a hard nut to crack. I do not think she allows her emotions to come to the fore. I had hoped she would be more passionate when I kissed her for the first time, but she was not. I'm unsure of how to make her respond to me."

"Do you think her feelings are engaged?" Jasper certainly knew from Miss Quinton that she believed they were not. The thought that Olivia's scheme in making his friend regret his choice left a cold shiver to run down his spine. He didn't want her to be anyone's second choice, not even his friend's. Oglemoore no longer deserved her attachment. He'd chosen another, and he ought to live with that decision.

Miss Quinton deserved to be loved for the strong, amusing, competent woman she was. Not simply because his friend could not engage another woman's desire and make her fall at his feet as he would like.

"I shall continue to court her and hope for the best." Oglemoore waggled his brows, mischief in his gaze. "I can always fall back to Miss Quinton, I suppose. She will always be there waiting in the wings should Lady Athol turn out to be a cold fish."

Jasper schooled his features, disdain for his friend running hot through his veins. There was no way in hell he'd allow Miss Quinton back into Oglemoore's arms after how he just spoke. As for Lady Athol, Olivia was right, she too deserved better than Oglemoore. What was wrong with the man that he spoke in such a demeaning, unlikeable way toward women?

Marriage may not be a situation he wished to be involved in at present, but he did hope that when he decided to marry, he would desire his bride, want her in his bed, and beside him in all things. Oglemoore spoke of marriage with such aloofness that it turned his stomach.

They fell into an uncomfortable silence, at least on Jasper's part. Oglemoore did not seem to have noticed that his words were offensive. "Enough with all the talk of the ladies present, shall we go for a run? Stretch our horse's legs?" Oglemoore said, kicking his mount into a gallop and sprinting ahead.

Jasper let him gain some distance, content to canter behind and mull over his friendship with Oglemoore and his developing one with Miss Quinton. He liked her, and one truth he did know was she was not for his friend, and he'd ensure that at the end of the house party, that remained the case.

# CHAPTER 6

There was something seriously wrong with her. Olivia sat in the blue drawing room upstairs and watched as Lord Oglemoore and the duke played a game of piquet. For all her distress at having to watch Oglemoore court her friend, it was not his lordship who held her attention this day.

With a will of their own, her eyes kept flicking up from the book she read to Hamlyn. A small lock of hair kept falling over his brow, and he seemed to frown and bite his lip when he concentrated on his game.

She bit back a smile. He was simply the most adorable piquet player she'd ever beheld and from looking at his distress, not the best one either.

Her cousin Clara sat beside her on the settee, meeting Olivia's amused grin with one of her own. "Your attention is marked toward a certain gentleman guest. Is there something you would like to tell your favorite cousin?"

Olivia placed her book in her lap, shushing her friend and family member. "Of course not. You should not say such things, and out loud, mind you. Someone may hear."

"Hmm," Clara said, glancing at the table where the men sat. "You have a particular look that I always see on a fox before it lunges at a rabbit. Contemplation, deliberation, what the rabbit may taste like."

Olivia gasped, shushing her cousin. "Clara! You need to behave." She chuckled despite herself. "In any case, I did not know you've been hunting lately and knew how foxes look at rabbits."

Clara grinned. "Let me just admit to knowing the look well. I am married, after all." She paused, settling farther on the settee and moving nearer to Olivia. "Hamlyn is very handsome. He seems to only get better with age. Like a good red wine, I would say."

"Remember, you're married, my dear."

Clara glanced at her husband, who sat opposite them, reading a book. Her cousin's features softened, and love all but glowed from her eyes. "I'm not looking at anyone else, I promise you. But I am a woman, and I do see your regard. I thought your heart was set on Oglemoore. That was certainly what town gossip had to say."

Olivia swallowed the awful thought that she was being gossiped about in town and in part annoyed that society had picked up on their friendship that blossomed last year. It only proved yet again he had shown considerable attention toward her and ought to be ashamed of himself being here and courting her friend.

She glanced at Oglemoore and caught him watching her. She turned back to Clara, unsure what that look meant, and no longer caring what it did mean. "At this point in time, I doubt I shall ever marry. I will admit that Hamlyn has been friendly and affable toward me. We get along quite well." So well, in fact, that his kiss still made the blood in her veins pump fast. She'd not been able to get the moment out of her head. How the slight stubble on his jaw had scratched across her face. His soft lips, what his tongue had felt like stoking her own.

A shiver wracked her.

"I'm glad for it, cousin. I want to see you happy and settled, and Hamlyn will do as well as Oglemoore. More so, in fact, for he's richer and higher placed in society."

"Stop talking as the duke's daughter and seeing people for what they have and not who they are."

Clara laughed, taking no offense. "It is a hard lesson to unlearn, Olivia. And you're a duke's granddaughter, so the same as me. In any case, there is one thing that I wish to advise you of, caution you if I may, with Hamlyn."

"What is that?" she asked, eyeing his lordship for a second, or was it the third time since she sat down? A shiver of awareness thrummed through her at his dark, hooded gaze. He seemed to be listening to Oglemoore discuss the card game, but otherwise, his attention appeared solely fixed on her. She swallowed, unable to look away. Was he playing the besotted fool they had agreed to, or was there more behind the wicked, contemplating light in his eyes?

That Olivia could not answer, but she hoped it was both. That she wasn't so hideous and unweddable that she had to ask gentlemen to feign interest in her to make others take note.

"I adore Hamlyn, he is a good friend of the family and has been for some years now, but he is not without his faults."

His Grace had faults? Olivia doubted that very much. "Oh? What are his vices that you speak of?" she asked.

Clara lowered her voice to a whisper. "He has a mistress, Olivia. I feel I need to notify you of this should you look at him as a potential suitor. If he does offer marriage, at the end of my short house party or in London during the remainder of the Season, I need you to know this so you may put a stop to it before any vows are spoken."

Her stomach lurched, and she fought to school her features to one of indifference. So it was true. Hamlyn did have a lover. She closed her eyes a moment, ridding herself of the vision of them together. It was any wonder he kissed so well and knew how to make a woman dream with his devilishly handsome looks.

"I had heard a rumor, and will keep it in mind should anything progress."

"As you should," Clara continued. "He has had her for some years now. They are quite close from all accounts. Should you marry him, she must go. That is not negotiable in the contracts."

Olivia nodded. Even without her cousin's demands, such things could never stand. She would not marry a man who had a lover tucked away elsewhere. No marriage would stand a chance of being happy under such conditions. "Let me assure you, Clara, Hamlyn is being kind to me and nothing more. He has no intention of offering for my hand. We are friends." Disappointment stabbed at her at the truth of her words. She wanted the night over with and the sanctity of her room. "I'm going to retire. I shall see you in the morning." She stood. "Goodnight, everyone," she said to the room at large, slipping from the salon and making her way upstairs.

Not far from her room, footsteps sounded fast and determined behind her. A hand clasped her upper arm, whirling her about. Before she could say a word, Hamlyn took her lips. She stilled in his arms, shock rippling through her before other emotions took hold.

Pleasure. Need.

He was too delicious for words, even if she were capable of uttering any right at this moment.

His arm slipped about her waist, wrenching her against him. Her hands wrapped about his neck, her fingers tangling into the locks at his nape. His kiss was hot, deep, and wonderful. Her body burned, came alight like a flame. Unabashedly she pressed herself to him, the secret place between her legs undulating against his manhood that stood at attention.

He made a sound, half gasp, half groan. Did he enjoy her movements? Was this how men and women found pleasure? Was this what ladies of the night wanted every time they were in their lovers' arms?

He drew back, his breathing ragged, his eyes bright with need and something else she could not read. "Good-night, Olivia," he whispered, and then he was gone, striding away without a backward glance.

Olivia stared after him, her body not itself. Her fingers touched her lips, still tingling from his kiss. What was he doing? She glanced up and down the hall, seeing no one else about, certainly not Lord Oglemoore, whom she was supposed to be flaunting her newfound friendship with Hamlyn with.

Why would the duke kiss her so?

She smiled, biting her lip before turning for her room. Perhaps his attention toward her was not wholly schemed after all. A sweet idea to mull on while she went to sleep, and if there was one gentleman who was pleasant to reflect on, it was Hamlyn and his wickedly handsome face.

# CHAPTER 7

Olivia sat at the breakfast table the following morning, disappointment threatening to make her lose her composure.

"I am terribly sorry to have to bring our house party to an end," Clara continued, "but we must travel up to Scotland without delay."

"I hope there is nothing wrong, Stephen," Olivia stated, knowing how close Clara's husband was with both his sisters.

"A difficult pregnancy, and I must be there for Sophie. She needs her family around her at this time. Her sister-in-law is in Edinburgh, you see, and therefore we have been summoned."

"We are sorry that our few days here will come to an end," Oglemoore said, standing and placing his napkin down with a flourish on the polished table. "We shall depart forthwith and hope to see you all very soon in town."

Hamlyn met Olivia's gaze, and she could see the regret

in his eyes. He gave her a small bow. "Good morning to you all, and thank you for having us."

As the door to the dining room closed, leaving Olivia, Clara, and Stephen alone, as her friend Athol had opted to break her fast in her room, Olivia turned to her family, seeking answers. "Whatever has happened that has you racing to Scotland? I hope Lady Mackintosh is not in any danger?"

Clara reached out, taking Stephen's hand. "We have received word that there are complications with her second pregnancy. Nothing too serious, it is told, but it will be her last child. We need to be there for her. I'm sorry to have to cut our house party short, my dear."

Olivia shook her head, the house party be damned. "Lady Mackintosh comes before any silly house party. Do you wish for me to join you? I do not have to return to town."

"No, you should go and enjoy what is left of the Season. I will write to you and notify you of Sophie's progress and outcome. I'm certain we shall bestow good news on the birth of their child soon."

Olivia frowned. "If you're certain, I shall do as you ask, but you will be missed. Please give my love and good wishes to Lady Mackintosh and tell her that I pray for her every night."

"Thank you, dearest."

The remainder of the day was frantic. Trunks were packed, the house closed up, and by dusk, Olivia's carriage was rumbling into the streets of Mayfair. With both her parents long gone, she did not look forward to returning to the house on Grosvenor Square, the large, empty rooms, and quiet surroundings. Her companion, who had remained in London, stood at the door as the carriage rocked to a halt. A welcoming smile on her lips.

"Olivia, welcome home. I'm so pleased you've returned safely." She came down the steps, joining her. "I have taken the liberty of having your dinner ready. As soon as you're settled, I'll have it brought up to you."

"Thank you, Anna," Olivia said, entering the house. After Clara's marriage to Mr. Grant, she had grown closer with her companion Anna, and now they did most things together, going out to balls and parties. Anna, having lost her husband several years ago to a lung ailment, had sought employment.

"What a shame the house party has come to an end. When do you believe Lady Clara and Mr. Grant will return to town?"

"Not for several weeks, I would think." Olivia moved into the front drawing room, pulling off her gloves and bonnet. She sighed as she sat before the unlit hearth, pleased to be home. The night was warm, and already Olivia missed the clean and clear night skies over Kent. "I will see out the Season here alone, but we shall muddle along well enough. Athol will be in town next week. She had to travel back to her parents' house in Bath before coming here."

Anna seated herself across from Olivia, clasping her hands in her lap. "Were there any gentlemen at the house party who caught your eye? I understood Lord Oglemoore was present."

She sighed, leaning back in her chair. "Lord Oglemoore was present, but he showed scarce interest in me. More for my friend. There is nothing between myself and his lordship. He made that perfectly clear in Kent." The thought of his treatment made her tempered anger simmer to a boil. It was beyond time that the gentlemen within society who treated women like property suffered a set down or two. A good clip about the ears may help also.

"Well, now that you're back in town, perhaps he will explain himself. Seek you out and make amends. He was certainly showing considerable attention last year. I cannot see his lordship being so fickle as to treat you with so little respect as to cast you aside."

And yet, that is exactly what he had done. He had cast her aside in Kent and had made no pains to hide his affections for her friend.

"I shall enter society and finish the Season, but I think next year I shall return to Fox Hill. I feel at my age I'm no longer obligated to attend every year. And Fox Hill is my home, the estate my papa left me. I do not need a husband if I do not find one to my liking. I can become an old, unmarried maid and do well enough on my own."

Of course, she would seek out Hamlyn now that they were all returned and see if he would continue to help her. Oglemoore had been everything she'd wanted in a husband, but now he would rue the day he treated a duke's granddaughter with no respect.

The image of Hamlyn's handsome features fluttered in her mind and erased all thoughts of Oglemoore. If only the duke were more marriageable material. He was not. He had a longtime mistress for starters and one whom she doubted he was ready to part with. The idea of his lordship taking his pleasure with a nameless woman made her want to snarl. Not that it surprised her his lordship would seek a woman away from the *ton* for his pleasure. He showed no interest in marriage or searching for a wife when she'd crossed paths with him last year, and never had she heard a rumor he was courting anyone in particular.

The memory of his kiss before her room at Chidding Hall made her stomach flutter. What a shame he was off the market, and his kisses were all for show and nothing more.

Olivia frowned as a light knock sounded on the door, a footman entering with a tray laden with food.

"Ah, your dinner is here," Anna said, taking it from the servant.

Olivia picked at her meal, thinking on her musings of Oglemoore and Hamlyn. She had marked Oglemoore simply because he'd taken a keen interest in her. The idea that she had thrown herself before an uninterested gentleman was humiliating.

Olivia shook the disturbing thoughts aside. She would finish off the Season with the help of Hamlyn and have retribution. No longer would she seek out Oglemoore, or try to keep the friendship she thought they had.

One day she would like to marry, have children, a family to call her own. The man she married would be loving and loyal, not fickle and false.

"The Davenport ball is tomorrow evening, Olivia. Do you wish for me to send a note to her ladyship to tell her you will be attending now that you're back in town?"

"Yes, please, Anna. That would be best, I think." Olivia finished her meal and wished her companion goodnight. The Davenport ball was as good a place as any to start her next phase in her plan, and there was little doubt Hamlyn would be there.

A smile quirked her lips at the thought of seeing him again. It was pleasant having a friend who knew her secrets, her wishes. That he had not denied to help her or teased her mercilessly over her plan helped her estimation of him.

With Hamlyn on her arm, one never knew. Other gentlemen may show awareness, and Oglemoore would be nothing but a passing phase, an apparition of her past before she stepped into her future. A mistake one was wont to forget.

# CHAPTER 8

The Davenport ball was a crush. The multitude of scents, perfumes, powder, and sweat that mingled in the air not always pleasant. Laughter and chatter overrode the possibility of quiet conversation. The only lovely feature of the ball was the music and the skill of the orchestra hired for the evening.

Olivia stood alone at the side of the room, content to watch the *ton* at play, Anna not far from her side. Couples danced, people drank champagne in abundance—a ball resembling the madness and gaiety of a night at Covent Garden more than a Mayfair dance.

She had not seen Athol here this evening, and she could only assume she had not returned to town in time to attend.

A tall gentleman who towered half a head over most present started her way, his golden, wavy locks giving her a clue as to who he was. She bit back a smile, unable to stem the hope that swelled within her that Hamlyn was here and had not forgotten their plan. Had not forgotten her.

He came before her, his eyes twinkling in mirth and

pleasure. He bowed. "Miss Quinton. How pleased I am to see you here this evening."

She smiled up at him, giving him her hand. His lips brushed her silk glove, and the pit of her stomach fluttered. He was so handsome, and on seeing him yet again, she had to admit that perhaps he was even more handsome than Oglemoore. How had she not noticed him at a ball before now?

"I'm happy to see you too, Your Grace."

He pulled her toward the floor as the first strains of a waltz sounded. "Dance with me, Miss Quinton."

She chuckled, unable to refuse him and not wanting to if she were honest with herself. They made their way onto the floor, taking their places. Other couples stood about them, and with the crush of the night, it placed them closer than they ought to be.

The hem of her golden, silk gown touched his boots, and she was certain he could feel her heart pumping hard in her chest. His eyes raked her, taking in her dress, warming in appreciation. He swung them into the dance, and Olivia laughed, feeling as light as a feather in his arms.

"You look beautiful this evening, Miss Quinton. That gown is quite fetching."

She could not look away from his stormy, blue orbs. "You're very good at this game I have asked you to play, Your Grace. One would even think that sometimes you mean what you say, so proficient that you are."

He cocked his head to the side, pulling her close as he spun them at the end of the room. "What would you say if I were to admit to not playing your game? That what I say is heartfelt?"

"I would say you're lying, but I would enjoy the compliment in any case. A woman is never unhappy to be told she looks beautiful or fetching or something thereof."

His hand slipped lower on her back and pulled her ever so slightly closer to him. The breath in her lungs hitched, and her body liquified. Hamlyn made her feel things she'd never felt before. A simple touch, like the one on her back, should not be enough to discombobulate her, but it did.

She had not reacted so with Oglemoore, and the knowledge gave her pause. She had liked Oglemoore, they had got along well enough, but she'd never wanted to kiss his lordship as much as she longed to kiss Hamlyn right now.

Olivia tore her gaze away from his lips, which were slightly tilted in a knowing grin. She met his eyes, and the hunger she read in his blue orbs sent her pulse racing. "You know it as much as I do you're the most handsome woman here this evening. Are you so blind that you cannot see every married and unmarried gentleman ogling you, wanting you? Men, no matter what they may say to disavow my opinion, are tonight jealous that you're in my arms and not theirs."

Hamlyn gestured to a place somewhere over her shoulder, and he spun her, giving her the ability to see what he had. "Look, Oglemoore is no different. He has been glaring at us both these past few minutes. I think you may safely say that his lordship is jealous of our association."

Oglemoore who? Olivia no longer cared about what Hamlyn's friend thought or decided. All she could think of was being in this man's arms—his secure hold, his height, and devilishly handsome face that was hers to enjoy. Savor.

"My plan would not have worked had I not too had one of England's most fetching rogues on my arm, making everyone envious. Do you not see the young women who flutter their fans when you pass, their mothers discussing your assets and worthiness for their daughters? If I am making men jealous, you too are making women equally so."

His eyes narrowed. He closed the space farther between them, and the breath in her lungs hitched. He would not dare kiss her here. Hamlyn may be a rogue, but he was no fool.

"It is fortunate then for you that I have you in my arms and not anyone else." He threw her a wicked grin, his thumb making tiny circular motions against her back. "How do you wish to play this game now that we're back in London? I cannot steal you away here and kiss you. Ogle-moore will not be able to see."

The idea of Hamlyn kissing her made her yearn for him to do precisely that. It had been several days since she'd tasted those delicious lips that smiled down at her. Felt his hunger for her, to have more of what he could make her feel.

Her heart quickened, and she flexed her hand on his shoulder, reveling in the feel of his superfine coat beneath her palm. "You do not wish to kiss me in any case, Your Grace. You are a veritable tease, and you know it."

His chuckle was deep and laden with promise. "Would you care to walk with me and see if that is the case?" he whispered against her ear.

She shivered. What was this that he was doing to her? It was any wonder women fell at his feet, and he had kept his mistress so long. No sensible woman would want to lose a man as seductive and charming as Hamlyn.

"You would not dare. There is no point to us stealing away. It would serve no useful purpose with our plan."

He shrugged, maneuvering them close to the side of the ballroom floor. "No useful purpose, you are correct, but a pleasurable one when all told. Shall we?" He spun them to a stop, stepping back and holding out his arm for her to take.

Without thought, Olivia placed her hand on his arm and let him lead her out of the ballroom. They stepped outside onto the large, flagstone terrace. Other couples mingled out-of-doors, groups of guests spoke and drank champagne under the light of the full moon and lanterns that were hung from the wisteria growing on the trellis above.

After the cloying, overwhelming scent of indoors, the purple flower's sweet perfume was refreshing. They strolled down the terrace, speaking to guests who turned toward them.

Hamlyn kept his hand atop hers, unfazed if his marked attention was noted. A footman passed them two champagne flutes, and His Grace handed her one, clinking the glass rims together.

"To the Season. May you gain what you're looking for, my sweet Miss Quinton, and have a happy heart."

She tipped her glass against his, unable to hold the smile his words brought forth on her lips. "You know, Your Grace, you can be quite the flatterer and a sweet man when you want to be. You speak of me and my unmarried state, but what of yours? You're what, one and thirty from what I hear? Do you not think a wife ought to be in your life sooner rather than later?"

He shrugged, sipping his drink. "Are you applying for the position, Olivia?"

Since the day of their kiss, he had not used her name, and to hear it on his lips now sent her wits to spiral. How lovely it sounded coming from him. She would never get sick of hearing it, she was sure.

"No, of course not, and you should stop your teasing.

We're supposed to be tricking other people of our acquaintance, not ourselves."

"Hmm," he answered noncommittedly. "Very well, you are right. I'm not searching for a bride as yet, but that is not to say I shall never marry. I'm certain there is someone out in the world who will pique my interest, and I shall court her."

A pang of jealousy, strong and unexpected, tore through Olivia. She did not want to think of Hamlyn courting another woman and one he would promise to love and cherish for all time. It was almost as bad as His Grace having a lover tucked away in town.

"Ah, yes, but what will your mistress think if you start to court a woman? I should imagine she will be terribly displeased to lose your protection," she said, unable to hold back the words a moment longer. And wanting desperately at the same time for him to deny her claim.

# CHAPTER 9

Jasper sucked in his champagne and understandably choked. He coughed, his mind reeling at the knowledge that Miss Quinton, Olivia, knew he had a mistress. How on earth had the woman found out?

"That, my dear, is a conversation subject decidedly off-limits."

"What a shame?" She grinned, the gesture not reaching her eyes. She sipped her wine. "I know that if I were your lover, I would be terribly upset to lose you. There is something unique about you, Hamlyn, that I do not even think you're aware of."

"Really?" he asked, curious, the idea of having her as his lover an image he'd thought of quite a lot these past days. "Do explain, my dear."

"You're likable. Honest and trustworthy. Both men and women of our social sphere know this of you. It is why I trusted you with my plan to make Oglemoore madly in love with me again just to spite him. I know you will not abuse my trust in you and tell anyone of what we've spoken. I think you're a good person. A good friend to have. Your mistress knows you are not violent and would not mistreat her, so yes, I think she would miss you terribly should you marry and leave her to find a wife."

Jasper cleared his throat. "We should not be talking about my mistress." He took another long swallow of his champagne. "It isn't appropriate."

"Neither were our two kisses in Kent, but they still happened." She paused, staring up at him, her eyes narrowing as her gaze flittered over his features. "Would it be so terribly crass of me to admit that I would like to kiss you again?"

An ardent, uncontrollable need thrummed through him at Olivia's words. He glanced at the many people who surrounded them. He could not kiss her here, even though he longed to. He took her hand, pulling her toward the steps that led down to the lawn.

As idly and unhurried as he could appear, Jasper led Olivia deeper into the gardens. The Davenport's London estate backed onto a small, wooded area if his memory served him correctly. And he wanted them to be as far away from prying eyes as they could be.

All thoughts of showing his affection, his interest to the *ton* at large fell away. Jasper wanted Olivia alone, all his for a small piece of the night. The idea of Oglemoore seeing them no longer mattered, nor did her request to make his friend green-eyed.

Oglemoore could go hang. The thought of Olivia kissing his friend as he was about to kiss her heated his temper. He fisted his hand at his side, forcing the troubling thought aside. Oglemoore would not have her, not now and certainly not after he had discarded her without a second thought.

Who in their right thinking would not want Olivia in their arms? She was perfection, sweet and playful, not to mention absolutely stunning. He had seen how men devoured her this evening in her red, silk gown with gold beading across the bodice.

He'd almost swallowed his tongue at the sight of her. So beautiful, alluring, and unattached. Untouched by anyone. Never married or sullied by another man's hand. Simply perfect.

The need to have her in his arms, to taste her sweet lips once again, was overwhelming. He'd carved a path through the abundance of guests, needing to be by her side. He'd left Oglemoore gaping after him, barely saying good evening in his haste to be beside her.

His reaction to Olivia did send a small tremor of fear through his mind. He'd never behaved in such a way toward a woman. Not even his past lovers had he singled out as much as he had Olivia.

Was there more happening between them besides a deal, a prank on his friend to make him covetous? Was this more than his promise to Oglemoore that he'd keep Olivia distracted so he may court Athol and ask her to be his wife.

They came to the end of the garden, only dappled light from the terrace and the mansion behind them reached them here. He turned, gazing down at her.

Their eyes met. Held. Time stood still, his body thrummed with expectation and need.

"We're quite alone now, Hamlyn. It is highly doubtful Oglemoore will see your attention toward me out here in the bushes," she teased, amusement in her eyes.

He reached out, clasping her side and pulling her against him. She did not fight him, obliged his request. Her hands fluttered against his chest, and he wondered if she could feel his heart beating fast beneath his ribs.

It felt as though his organ would burst free from his body. The intoxicating scent of jasmine wafted in the air, taunting him further. He leaned forward, kissing her cheek, her jaw, until he found the lobe of her ear.

Her inhale of breath spurred him further. Her hands slid up his chest to settle and squeeze his shoulders.

"You smell good enough to eat, Olivia."

She shivered in his arms, and now all he could think about was eating her in truth, of lifting her siren-red gown to her waist, laying her over the nearby stone bench, and taking his fill. Bringing her to climax on his face, reveling in her sighs and begging as he made her come.

*Holy fuck, he was in trouble.*

He kissed her throat and groaned when she clasped his jaw in her hands, bringing his mouth back to hers and kissing him. God damn it, yes. This is what he wanted. Her, in his arms, kissing him with as much desire and need that catapulted through his body.

Her mouth fused with his, her tongue tangling with his own. The kiss was not sweet. It was hard, frantic, and had an edge of demand to it. It took ownership of him, and he was at a loss as to how to bring his senses back from spiraling.

He reached down, sliding his hand over one ass cheek that he declared the most perfectly taut piece of backside he'd ever held. He kneaded her thigh, lifting it about his hip, and pushed himself against her.

She gasped through the kiss, and he felt her undulate, taking what she could of him in this position. His cock, hard, grew to attention when she pressed herself to him.

Olivia mewled some unintelligible sound, but he understood her completely. He was as mad and as hot for her as she was him. All thoughts of his friend, of his plan to keep Olivia respectively occupied vanished.

Never in his life had he ever behaved without so much as a care when around an unmarried woman. He'd had many affairs, yes, but the women were widows, unhappy in their marriages, or were from the *demimonde*. Never the *beau monde*.

He did not need this complication in his life, but also he could not, would not, let Olivia go from his clasp. Heat rushed to his groin, and he knew he could spill in his breeches if they continued what they were doing.

Olivia seemed to have lost all thought too. She rubbed against him like a kitten seeking a pet. Her breath mingled with his, and he knew she wasn't far, could climax here and now in the gardens at a *ton* ball.

Jasper broke the kiss, let go of her leg, and stepped back. She stumbled before righting herself, staring up at him. Her eyes were as glassy as the moon, twinkling up at him like two bright stars that had found their purpose in the sky.

God damn it, he wanted to be her universe. He wanted to do whatever she asked him to. But he could not seduce her. Take her here and now in the garden like some rutting beast.

"Why did you stop?" Her question was breathless, and somewhat uneven.

It killed him to hear the need in her tone. He understood better than she would ever imagine what she was going through. However, there was one thing she would never know, and that was how close she came to being tupped in the outdoors at a grand London ball where anyone may be watching.

"If I do not stop now, there will be no turning back. It is not the deal we made, Olivia. We must try to remember that the next time we embark on kisses in darkened gardens where no Oglemoore will view my regard."

His words acted just as he wished, and like a bucket of

cold water had been poured over her head, she stepped back, busying herself with righting her gown.

"You're right, of course. I'm so sorry." She laughed, and he did not miss the nervousness in the gesture. "You're very good at what you do, Hamlyn. You made me forget myself."

He had forgotten himself too. Utterly reprehensible actions he could not allow to happen again. He would show interest, court, and flirt with her in public, but he could not steal her away, be alone with her unless he wanted her for himself.

And he did not want Olivia, as precious and sweet as she was.

Truly he did not, he reminded himself.

He was not ready for a wife. His father had not married until his forties. He was one and thirty, too young to settle down to only one woman for the rest of his days.

She threw him a small, brittle smile, and a punch to the gut would have been less sharp. He swallowed, taking her hand and pulling her back toward the ball. Jasper did not look at her again, not even when he deposited her beside Anna, her companion, and bid them both goodnight.

Walking from the ball, he rolled his shoulders, feeling the burn of Olivia's gaze on his back. He was her friend, helping her make Oglemoore pay for his base treatment of her. What he needed was a good hard shag with his mistress.

Summoning his carriage, he tapped his feet, unease and annoyance thrumming through his veins. Charlotte would soothe his soul and scratch his itch. He climbed into the equipage, calling for Seymour street and forced himself not to look back at Davenport house.

# CHAPTER 10

Three nights passed, and Olivia had not seen Hamlyn for as many days. Where was he? After their third kiss, she had watched him stride from the ball with a feeling of unease and uncertainty running down her spine.

She had not wanted him to leave and nor did she understand what had actually transpired between them. All she did know was she wanted to kiss him again and again. To have him hold her in his arms, tease her senseless and make her crave.

Never in her life had she wanted to act unlike the lady she had been brought up to be. She wanted him to touch her where she ached. To feel his large, erect manhood press against her sex. Take her as a man would take a woman, fill her and inflame her as much as she was already.

Oh dear, she had turned into someone she could not recognize.

Had he mentioned wanting her in that way, asking if she would permit him such liberty, Olivia was certain she would have allowed him to make love to her.

She'd been all but ready to lie on the grassy lawn and give him what they both wanted.

Her friend, having returned from Bath, stood beside her, sipping her ratafia. "I'm not certain that I want Oglemoore as my husband any longer. I went to the pump rooms while I was home in Bath, and I met with Lord Dormer. How handsome and accommodating he is. And," she said, pointing across the room, "do you see he too has returned to London? I think he is back to court me."

Olivia glanced in the direction of Lord Dormer, an earl from Derbyshire, and noted him nodding in welcome to her friend. "Is he not looking for an heiress? I thought I heard it said that his pockets are for let."

"They may be, but I'm more than capable of fixing his currency issue." Athol grinned. "He is handsome, do not you think?"

Olivia frowned. "What about Oglemoore? The last time we spoke, you were quite determined to have him as your husband, and you kissed him."

"That was in Kent, Olivia. Do keep up."

Taken aback, Olivia stared at her friend, wondering who she was or had become in the last few months. She turned, sipping her wine and watching the dancers who were partaking in a minuet. Across the room, she could see Lord Oglemoore talking with a group of gentlemen, his attention sometimes stealing over to where they both stood.

Athol, seemingly noting his lordship's notice, mumbled something about needing to go to the retiring room and disappeared into the throng. Oglemoore watched Athol leave, his eyes following her out of the room. Olivia had thought he would follow her, but he did not. Instead, he excused himself from his conversation and started toward her.

Olivia watched him, again agreeing with herself that

Oglemoore was a handsome gentleman, but now there were a few minuscule things she noticed that she had not before. He was shorter than Hamlyn, less refined, and had a pettiness about him she had not thought him capable of.

What man courted a woman for a Season, only to never offer for her? That was certainly how he'd treated her last year. His fixation on Athol at her cousin's house party made his conduct even worse.

"Miss Quinton," he said, taking her hand and kissing it. Where once Olivia would have reacted to his touch, to his presence, now she was merely bored. He bored her, and that in itself was telling.

"How nice to see you again. I see you returned to London safe and sound. Are you enjoying the ball this evening?"

She smiled, glancing about the room. "I am, my lord. Very much so." She gestured to where Athol had departed. "I'm sorry you just missed Lady Athol. She will be most displeased to have missed you."

He nodded, coming to stand beside her. "I shall, catch up with Lady Athol in good time, but it is you I wanted to seek out. Would you care to dance with me? I believe there is to be a waltz soon."

Olivia started at his request, not the least interested in taking a turn about the dancefloor in his arms. He continued to stare at her, seeking an answer, and she had no option but to concede.

"Of course, my lord. I would like that very much."

He smiled, and for a moment, neither of them spoke. Olivia fought to think of something to say. A conversation starter or the latest gossip going about London. Anything to halt the plainly obvious fact they had nothing to discuss.

"My friend, His Grace, the Duke of Hamlyn danced

with you the other evening. I hope I shall too bring such joy to your night as he seemed to achieve."

Olivia stilled at his lordship's words. Did Oglemoore mean the waltz she and Hamlyn had shared or their kiss, that to this day made her toes curl up in her silk slippers? "The duke dances well."

Oglemoore chuckled. "Well, of course, he does, my dear. He has had the best dancing masters to teach him during his youth. A marquess I may be, but I still hope to do our dance justice this evening."

"I'm sure you shall, my lord. It is only a waltz, after all." She studied his profile as he sipped his wine. What was he up to? He had not sought her out at her cousin's house party. In fact, for a time there, Olivia was certain she had the pox or some other type of illness that would make her unpalatable to his lordship.

His interest in her yet again, hot and cold, was like a season gone topsy-turvy. Had her marked interest in the duke made Lord Oglemoore see her in a new light? Did he wish to court her again over her friend, who seemed less than interested in the marquess? She hoped that was the case so she could stomp on his emotions like he did her.

"I see Hamlyn has arrived. The ladies will be pleased," Oglemoore professed, a small smile playing on his lips.

At least his friendship with the duke did not seem affected even after Hamlyn played her game of making Oglemoore jealous. Olivia glanced over to where the duke was giving his regards to the host and hostess, bowing over her ladyship's hands.

"You've been friends with the duke for many years. How was it that you became acquainted?" She had not asked before, and they were an unlikely pair, having such different personalities.

"Hamlyn saved me from a bloody nose at Eton. I was

not much liked for whatever reason. He stopped the Earl of Dormer as he is now from giving me a thorough thrashing for merely bumping into him during a change of class. We have been friends ever since."

So Hamlyn was also an honorable man and loyal. She liked him even more now knowing that about him. She glanced over to where she saw him last and caught him talking to Lady Graham and The Duchess of Carlton. Hamlyn took a sip of his brandy, and his eyes met hers over the rim of his glass.

From across the room, Olivia felt the reaction to his gaze. It smashed into her like a thousand horses toppling her to the ground. The glance was filled with promise, questions she was unsure she had the answers to.

After their kiss the other evening, something had changed between them. Certainly, the presence of Oglemoore at her side was not having the same response she had last year. In fact, he may not even be standing beside her for all she cared about the matter.

Was she a terrible person changing her mind so quickly on whom she wanted for a husband? She had been determined to marry Oglemoore. But his denial of her, his treatment in Kent had put paid to that thought. She did want him to regret his choice, but she would no longer entertain the idea of marrying him herself.

Oh no. And while she may not marry Hamlyn either, so long as she continued receiving his delicious kisses, she would be well pleased.

"The duke is a good man. You are fortunate to have him as your friend."

The strains of the waltz sounded, and Oglemoore bowed before her. "My dance, Miss Quinton."

She allowed him to lead her onto the floor and take their places. The music started, and then they were gliding about the room, another uncomfortable silence descending between them. What was wrong with her that she could not keep up a conversation with the man? Had her kissing Hamlyn stripped her of her wits when it came to other men?

Refusing to speak of matters that were wont to bore one to death, Olivia elected to remain silent and simply to enjoy the glide and steps of the dance. Oglemoore was well versed as a dance partner, but she may have been dancing with Athol for all the influence it caused in her.

No shivers of delight, no hunger for a man's lips to take hers, no desire to hear his voice whisper sweet words against the whorl of her ear.

They spun and moved beside and around the other couples, and all the time not a word was said. As the dance came to an end, Oglemoore swept her to a stop, smiling over her hand. "Thank you for the wonderful dance, Miss Quinton. I hope we shall partner again this evening."

Olivia thanked him, stepping off the floor only to run directly into a wall of muscle. She stumbled, and a pair of strong arms wrapped about hers, holding her steady.

"Did you enjoy your dance, Miss Quinton?"

*Hamlyn.*

His voice sent her nerves to jump, and she steadied her feet. She met his gaze, and had she hoped to see pleasure written across his features, she would be sadly disappointed. She schooled her emotions, wondering whatever she could have done to vex him.

"I hope I did not hurt you just then, Your Grace. I was not watching where I was going."

He humphed out a disgruntled breath before holding out his arm for her to take. She did not dare refuse him. He strode to the side of the room, away from the ballroom floor. "I suppose you were otherwise occupied dancing with

Oglemoore. Our newfound friendship seems to be having the effect that you wished. He is taking an interest."

Hamlyn stopped and flicked his chin in a direction across the room. Olivia looked to where he pointed, only to see Oglemoore watching them, a contemplative look in his eyes.

"Perhaps it is working," she admitted, not wanting to have Hamlyn leave her so soon should he think his work to gain her a husband served. That was no longer the case, not if she were honest.

Oglemoore was not honorable, nor likable now that she knew him better. Hamlyn, on the other hand, was a catch for any woman in England.

"How many more nights do you think you will need my help in securing him? Mayhap I ought to lean close to your side, like this," he said, dipping his head, the breath of his words kissing her neck. "So he shall think we're speaking secretively."

Olivia closed her eyes, reveling in his nearness. Having him with her again after three days was too long. She turned her head, placing her lips within a breath from his. His eyes dipped to her lips. Need thrummed between them.

Her stomach flipped, and for the life of her, she could not look away. "Where have you been these last days? I had wondered if you had changed your mind in helping me." Not that she wanted him to help her in that sense any longer. Oh no, now she wanted Hamlyn close to her for another selfish reason altogether.

Now she wanted Hamlyn by her side so she might have a chance with him. The man she had thought to use for her own means.

"I am not incensed," he replied, stepping back and giving them space.

Olivia looked about and noted a few eyes upon them, Oglemoore's too. "Yes, you are, or you would not be so curt with your answers. Is there something the matter? Has something happened that you're now so put out with me?"

A muscle worked in his jaw, and she could see he was fighting to voice what was running through his mind. Dare she hope Hamlyn was no longer interested in making Oglemoore jealous any more than she was? Dare she hope he too was fighting the blossoming feelings that she herself was having?

"I have been busy elsewhere, that is why you have not seen me."

Olivia stared at him, not believing that for a moment. "Is that the truth?"

Hamlyn sighed, a muscle working in his jaw. "Oglemoore mentioned at Whites the day after the Davenport ball he had noted our dance and stroll on the terrace. I hoped that it would be enough for him to figure out who he wanted to marry. That I come here tonight and find you dancing with his lordship, hanging off his every word, I suspect my deliberations are right?"

They were not right, and nor was she hanging off Oglemoore's every word. She could not care a hoot what the marquess had to say. In fact, they had hardly spoken at all. "I think I shall need your assistance for a while longer, Hamlyn. Oglemoore spoke of Lady Athol, and so I do not think he's turned his attention back to me as yet," she lied.

Olivia, unsure how to react to Hamlyn's strange mood, fought to find the words to keep him from storming off yet again. His disagreeable nature this evening may not have anything to do with her. May, in fact, have something to do with his mistress or some other matter.

The thought made her blood run cold, and she fought not to glare at the guests in the room.

"So, I'm to help you still?" Hamlyn ran a hand through his hair, leaving it on end. "How much longer shall you need me to act the besotted fool? I'm not one to play such a character ever."

Olivia's attempt to remain cordial gave way to irritation. She looked up at him, pinning him with a warning stare until he met her eyes. "You agreed to help me. Stop acting like a jealous fool."

"I am not jealous, madam."

She scoffed. "Then why are you talking to me as if you're angry with me for dancing with Oglemoore? As if you do not want to see me with him. That was the deal, was it not?"

"Damn it, yes, that was the deal," he seethed, taking her hand and pulling her from the room.

# CHAPTER 11

Yes, God damn it all to hell it was the deal. And one he, after having arrived tonight, wanted to discard. Along with Oglemoore. He could bugger off as well.

Seeing Oglemoore clutching her and smirking as he danced with Olivia sent his temper ricocheting to heights he'd never experienced. Olivia was his friend, he reminded himself. He was the one who offered to help her tease Oglemoore into proposing marriage so she may spurn him in return. Instead, kissing her three times now had made his mind more muddled and unclear than it ever had been in his life.

Today, in fact, he'd gone to his see his mistress. He'd intended to spend the day shagging, taking her in as many ways as he could possibly think. Anything to clear his mind of a particular dark-haired goddess. Yet, instead, he had spent the time discussing the end to their understanding. The pension he would gift her that would see her settled comfortably for the rest of her days. Charlotte had been good to him, and he wanted to ensure she did not have to work or find a new protector if she did not choose to.

Now, at tonight's ball, without having fucked his afternoon away, he found his blood pumping hot and fast. Seeing Olivia in Oglemoore's arms had sparked his ire, and he could not seem to rein it in.

She was not for him. He did not want a wife. His reaction to seeing her be courted by another was preposterous. He needed to get a grip on himself.

"Yes," he ground out, "that was the deal. I would therefore appreciate it if you could hurry the hell up and make him offer for you before I lose my patience."

The moment he said the words, he wished he could pull them back. Shock registered on her face, and her eyes filled with unshed tears. Oh, God damn it. Now he'd made her cry.

In an instant, Jasper's annoyance and hurt—yes, it was hurt that he was also feeling—dissipated. He pulled her along the darkened passage farther from the ball and out of sight of the guests.

The muffled sounds of a quadrille played as he walked her along the deserted hall, far enough away from the door that they would not be overheard. "I'm sorry, Olivia. I did not mean what I said."

She tugged her arm free. Fear curled in his gut that he may have lost her friendship, acting like a cad. He liked her, more than he ever thought he would when he'd accepted her proposition.

"How dare you chastise me. You agreed to my scheme. I did not force you."

He ground his teeth, hating the idea of Oglemoore marrying the woman standing before him, wiping her cheeks with the back of her hand. He was a bastard, and he deserved to go to hell talking to her as he had done.

*Fool.*

"I do not understand the attraction you had for him, my friend or no. He chose another, played you a fool. Do you not want a marriage full of desire and love? An all-encompassing union you cannot get enough of? One that has respect above anything else?"

She sniffed, meeting his gaze. "Of course I do, and I will not accept anyone's offer of marriage unless I have all those things. I want Oglemoore to pay for his treatment of me, nothing more. He has not learned his lesson yet, I think."

Her words sent a frisson of hope to course through his blood. So, she wasn't so set on Oglemoore that she would dismiss *him* out of hand.

Jasper stilled at his own thoughts. Dismiss him? What on earth was wrong with him? He did not want a wife. If Olivia did not stand before him, he'd smack his own self about the ears.

He pulled her into his arms, running his hands over her back, giving comfort. "I did not mean what I said, Olivia," he whispered against her neck. Her slight nod of acceptance tore at his heart, and he kissed her shoulder.

Hell, she smelled divine, clean. Like a room full of hothouse flowers. They stood so close he could feel her chest rise and fall against his. The slight shiver that stole through her when his lips brushed her skin. Unsated, he took the small lobe of her ear into his mouth and suckled it.

Thankfully she wore no earrings, and it allowed him to tease her, kiss her as much as he wanted.

"You should not be kissing me, Jasper. This is against the rules we've just been arguing about, is it not? Your demand for our fake liaison to be over."

Oh yes, he wanted it over with, but not for the reasons

she thought. He wanted her for himself. Having her in his arms again, having spent the past three days thinking of no one but Miss Olivia Quinton told him there was something peculiar about his attachment to the chit.

He knew what that regard was now. He no longer wanted to help his friend keep her away from him, so he may win Lady Athol Scott's affections. Oh no, holding Olivia now told Jasper that he wanted her in his bed.

The thought of her marrying another, being courted by anyone else, was like a stake to the heart, and he would not allow it to occur.

She pulled back, looking up to meet his gaze. "If you do not wish to continue with my plan, I understand. It does not mean that we cannot remain friends."

Friends? Oh no, no, no, that would never do. He wanted to be her lover and nothing less. "No more talking, Olivia." He dragged her against him, holding her face in his hands. "Kiss me," he begged, brushing his lips against hers. "Just kiss me and erase the memory of me seeing you in Oglemoore's arms."

She gasped, kissing him back. Her arms wrapped about his neck as her mouth slammed against his. It was hot, delicious, and hard. His blood pumped fast in his veins. He bent down, clasping her thighs and picking her up. She understood his motive and hooked her feet about his back. Her core pressed against his cock, hard and aching in his breeches.

Jasper closed the few steps to the wall and pushed her up against the silk wallpaper. She moaned through the kiss as he used the extra support to thrust against her heat. Stars burst behind his eyes, and he wanted to flick open his breeches, free his cock, and sheath himself in her warmth.

She moaned, pressing against him. "You make me want things I do not understand."

Oh, God almighty, she made him want things he never thought to want or need too. "As do you," he admitted, kissing her yet again, determined this time not to leave her longing for more, but to ensure she found pleasure from him and him only.

# CHAPTER 12

O livia was not herself, nor did she care where she was. Music continued to play somewhere in the house, laughter and clinking of glasses and plates sounded, but she pushed it all to the side, focusing on the man in her arms.

Concentrating on what that particular man was doing to her.

Her body burned, ebbed, and flowed with a need she could not sate. He was doing something to her, but what that was she could not fathom.

She clutched at his shoulders, scoring her nails into his skin as a tremble teased her most sensitive flesh. "I want more, Jasper. Please, help me."

He mumbled words that no well-bred woman ought to be privy to, and then she was standing again on her silk slippers, Jasper breathing ragged and hard before her. He looked like a wild man, unkempt and completely disheveled.

Olivia ran her hand through his hair, pulling it to bring

him close for a kiss. "You are too handsome for your own good. Do you know that?"

His eyes burned into hers, and a wicked light shone back at her through his blue orbs. "The same could be said of you, Olivia."

And then she felt it, his hand, sliding up her leg and pooling her gown at her waist. He slipped his fingers between her legs, brushing his hand across her mons. She ought to feel embarrassed at his touch, push him away, mortified he dare touch her *there*, but she could not bring herself to care.

His fingers softly rolled a particular place, and her legs threatened to buckle. Olivia rested her head against the wall and gave in to his touch. What was he doing to her?

Bliss, utter, decadent pleasure rolled through her as he worked his magic touch against her flesh. Like a wanton she had not known she was, she parted her legs, giving him admittance.

"That's it, my darling. Open for me. Let me touch you."

Oh, she'd let him touch her as much as he liked if this is what he made her feel. Like her body was not her own. Taunting and teasing her toward a pinnacle she imagined quite wonderful, but wasn't for sure certain.

He kissed her, deep and long, all the while his touch never abated. He overwhelmed her, and she clutched at him, her only means of grounding, and then it happened. With each stroke of his hand, pleasure rocked through her body, thrumming at her core and bursting into light.

Olivia gasped his name, riding his hand like a woman outside of herself. All she knew was that she wanted more of what he had given her. Was not ready for this to end.

Where had Hamlyn been all her life, and why on earth had she taken so long to find him?

She slumped against the wall and knew she had a silly, self-satisfied smile on her lips. Olivia did not care. Jasper kissed her neck while he righted her gown.

"You're so beautiful. I shall never forget you coming apart in my hands, Olivia. You're truly magnificent."

Olivia opened her eyes, leaning forward to wrap her arms tighter about his neck. "I had no idea that such a thing was possible between a man and a woman. Can I do something similar to you to bring you joy?"

His eyes scorched her at her words, and she knew the answer to her question before he replied. "Oh yes, you certainly can, but not here. I should not have touched you in such a public place where anyone could have come across us. It was foolhardy of me."

She grinned, brushing her lips against his. "But so very worth it." And now that she'd done this once, she would do it again. Something told her there was more to know and enjoy in a man's arms, and she couldn't wait to find out what.

THE FOLLOWING evening Jasper stood beside Oglemoore and fought to keep his patience with his friend. The man was becoming a menace, and not only that, a gentleman who he doubted knew his own mind.

"I thought you were going to ask Lady Athol for her hand in marriage? You're now saying that you're unsure who you want to be your wife?"

Oglemoore shrugged, sipping his wine. "Lady Athol, rumor has it, has been seen taking the air in Hyde Park with Lord Dormer. You know the fellow, the one who wanted to bloody my nose back at Eton." He shook his head, his lips thinning into a displeased line. "I'm unsure what her feelings are toward me now that we're both back in London."

Jasper schooled his features and bit back the words of telling his friend that karma was an unfortunate mistress and one that Oglemoore had obviously suffered from. He'd played Olivia last Season, threw her aside for her friend, and now had the same happen to him. Jasper ought to feel sorry for him, but he could not. After treating Olivia with so little respect, he could not help but be glad Oglemoore had missed out on both the women.

"I think you should stop our game with Miss Quinton. That will allow me the opportunity to court her during the last weeks of the Season. I'm certain she will be amenable to my interest, and should I ask her, I think she will marry me."

Jasper massaged his temple, trying to stop the incessant ache that thumped there. "You no longer want me to distract Miss Quinton away from you as I have been these last few weeks. What if someone else catches your interest in town, and you throw her over yet again? I do not think you should court Miss Quinton a second time."

Oglemoore gaped at him, clearly affronted. "And whyever not? She is not engaged or attached. You do not see her in a romantic light. The only reason you speak to her at all is because of my bidding. Do not tell me you've grown a conscience since I asked you to help me. That is unlike you, Hamlyn."

It may have been what he was like before he'd grown to know Olivia, but the thought of her being hurt for a second time by Oglemoore would not do. He would not allow his friend to play Olivia the fool no matter how many years they had known each other.

"Miss Quinton deserves better than being your second or third choice. Move on and find another to marry."

Oglemoore frowned, sensing Jasper's ire, which was simmering to a boil. "I will not play her a fool again. I promise you that, my friend." Oglemoore clapped him on the back as if all were forgiven, and Hamlyn was merely playing a protective father. He was not. In no way would he allow Oglemoore to change his mind on a whim and think everything was perfectly well.

"I see Weston has arrived. I need to speak to him about his gelding he means to auction at Tattersalls. I may be interested in him if the price is right," Elliott said as he moved away.

Jasper watched as his friend moved off into the throng of guests. He narrowed his eyes, not caring for his words or his plans for Olivia. Jasper may have started out keeping Olivia distracted enough that she would not grow too upset about Oglemoore's attention toward her friend, but things had changed now. They were close, most certainly friends, even more than that.

He spied her across the room, smiling and chatting with the Duchess of Carlton. Oglemoore moved past her, certainly within her notice, and she did not glance his way or proceed to wish him a pleasant evening. Had Jasper been a betting man, he would have laid money she had not noticed his friend at all.

The thought pleased him, and he finished the last of his drink, a quiet calm settling over him that Olivia would not be so foolish as to allow Oglemoore another chance at winning her hand. Surely his time with her, even if she thought that time false due to their understanding, would make her see that not all men were the same. That there were men in the world who would like her for who she was, her kindness, sweet nature, pleasant self... Not simply because she was available, and it was time for the gentleman to choose a bride.

Olivia deserved to have a marriage of love. Anything less would be a waste of her life.

Later that night, he caught up to her as she was entering the supper room, thankfully on her own. He sidled up to her, dipping his head to ensure privacy. "Would you care to take supper with me, Miss Quinton?" he asked, reveling in the pleasure that bloomed on her handsome features.

"Of course," she gushed, coming to a stop behind the line of guests already waiting to choose their meal. "I did not know you were going to be here this evening. Did I not hear that you best Lord Lindhurst in a sparring match at Gentleman Jacksons, and he still has not forgiven you?"

Jasper laughed, remembering the day well. "Ladies are not supposed to know details such as those. Who told you?"

She shrugged, taking a plate from a footman and studying the selection of food laid out before them. "I forget who relayed the gossip, but he is, from what I understand, still quite put out. I'm surprised they allowed you entry."

"I'm the Duke of Hamlyn, there are few who would not admit me." Jasper picked up two crab cakes and a lobster tail. "He has asked for a rematch, and perhaps I shall let him win that bout, merely to keep the peace."

She turned with a plate laden with her selections. "That is very kind of you. I doubt I would be so charitable. I dislike losing as well, you know."

They made their way over to a table for two, seating themselves. "Is that why you asked me to help you with Oglemoore? Simply because you wanted revenge so desperately?"

She threw him a sheepish look. "In part, it was wrong

of him to court me only to throw me aside when he deemed me not actually what he wanted. However, I do think that our ruse has paid off. He was questioning me at last night's ball, similarly to how he was toward me last year. I cannot help but think that Athol's disinterest in him since her return to town and your marked attentions toward me have reminded Oglemoore what he's thrown aside." She chuckled. "The poor man is wasting his time with me, I'm happy to report."

Jasper chewed his lobster, taking his time to cool his annoyance at Oglemoore's renewed attentions. "For what it is worth, I do believe you can do better than Oglemoore. He is my friend, yes, but even I am not blind to his faults. He should not have treated you the way he has. I'm sorry he hurt you."

A smile touched the corners of her lips. Her gaze bored into him, and he hoped it was interest for him he read in her eyes and not Oglemoore.

Heat licked his skin, and he had the overwhelming desire to reach out, touch her, anywhere, her hand, her cheek, a lock of hair, just so long as he was touching her.

"I no longer want Oglemoore, Jasper," she whispered, holding his gaze.

He took a calming breath, his heart pounding. What did that mean? "May I escort you home this evening?" To ask such a question was scandalous. He ought not, but nor did he want to leave her side. Jasper told himself it was to ensure she arrived home safely. She had no living parents and a questionable chaperone, so a gentleman ought to step up at times.

"That is kind of you, but you need not do that. I can catch a hackney home. It is not far in any case." She smiled, taking a sip of her champagne. "I could probably walk from here, all told."

He shook his head. "No, I could not allow that." Just the thought of her walking home sent a chill down his spine.

"When did you wish to depart?" she asked. "I am ready to leave whenever you are."

His body tightened at the thought of having her alone in his carriage. Five minutes or five hours, he would take whatever he could. "When you've finished your meal, we can leave. I'm at your service."

She raised her brows. "How delightful that sounds. I shall hold you to that, Your Grace."

He almost groaned. *Oh, please do.*

They finished their meal and separately made their goodbyes to their hosts, before coming together on the front steps of the London home. His black carriage, pulled by two gray mares, rolled to a stop not long after.

A footman opened the door, and Jasper helped her up into the carriage. He called out the address before joining her. He sat opposite, waiting for the carriage to lurch forward before closing the blinds. If he had minutes only, he wanted to make full use of them.

Her eyes glistened in the dark, and it was only every now and then when they passed a street lamp that he saw her pretty face. He untied the blinds, letting them down.

"Why the privacy? Are you planning something, Your Grace?"

He opened the small portal near the driver's chair and told his man to drive about Mayfair. "If I were," he said, turning back to face her, "would you think bad of me?"

She shook her head, a small curl bounced across her shoulder. "No," she whispered, her attention snapping to his lips. She bit her own, and his body roared with need. Although uncertain what was happening between them, the game they started to play had morphed into something so much different.

*So much more.*

# CHAPTER 13

The carriage rumbled down the street, the driver taking pains not to take the corners too sharp. Olivia did not feel like herself. The look in Jasper's eyes left her feeling as if there was something in the air, something about to happen.

*Between them.*

For herself, she wanted Jasper to take her in his arms, to touch her, kiss her, be with her as he was the other night at the ball. His steely gaze did not shift from her person, and by the time he did speak, she was squirming on the leather squabs.

"Thank you for letting me take you home this evening, Olivia. I will admit to wanting to be alone with you all evening."

Olivia bit her lip, having watched him all evening, wanting to be alone just as they were now. Never had she wanted to be with anyone as much as she had wanted to be with Jasper. Oglemoore was nothing but a figment of her past imagination.

She patted the seat at her side and smiled as he came

to sit beside her without a word. Her breathing increased, and she all but sizzled with a longing for him to touch her. Unable to wait a moment longer, she closed the space between them, taking his lips in a searing kiss and giving herself what she'd coveted since supper.

He kissed her back, clasping her face and tipping her head to deepen the kiss. His hands moved over her body, where she could not say until they clasped her breast. She sighed, loving his touch. He kneaded one, rolling the nipple between his fingers.

Olivia pushed herself into his hands. This was what it was like to be adored, to be wanted. She could get used to being with a man in such a way, and not just any man, but Jasper.

"You drive me to distraction," he gasped, kissing her jaw, her neck, swift nibbles toward her ear.

"I want to feel you. Let me touch you, Jasper," she whispered. He slipped the bodice of her gown down, taking a moment to admire her. His eyes burned a path across her body before he dipped his head and paid homage to one nipple.

His tongue was beyond intoxicating. He lathed, kissed, and teased her pebbled flesh, liquid heat pooling at her core.

"You want to touch me, Olivia? Be my guest," he replied, not moving from her breast.

She slipped her hands down his taut, muscular stomach, reveling in the feel of his perfect physique. Her hand dipped lower still. At the top of his breeches, the bulging shaft of his manhood, erect and ready, pressed against the pants.

He felt well endowed, not that she had anything to compare him to, but surely not many men stood to attention in such a way. Swallowing her nerves, she slid her hand over his length, basking in his moan when she squeezed him through the fabric.

He was wide and long and as hard as steel. "I want to see you."

He released her breast with a pop. Already she missed his kisses on her skin, but she wanted to know more about him, see what she could do to him to bring him pleasure. As much as he had brought to her only last evening.

Olivia pushed him back against the squabs, fixing her gown before turning her attention to the buttons at the front of his breeches. He sat back, kept his hands on the carriage seat, and allowed her to do as she willed.

With a patience she did not think herself capable of right at this moment, she worked the buttons free. Her eyes widened at the sight of his impressive manhood.

She ran her finger along his length, following the rigid, blue vein that stood out. "So soft." Olivia licked her lips as a bead of pearly white liquid formed at the end. Thoughts of what he would taste like bombarded her mind. Images of her taking his rigid length and slipping it into her mouth.

She wrapped her hand around his manhood and stroked. He moaned, closing his eyes, his hands fisting against the edge of the seat.

"You're killing me, Olivia," he groaned, his whole body taut and still.

Without a whit of trepidation, she bent over him, taking him in her mouth, wanting to taste him, feel and give him pleasure. One hand fisted in her hair, guiding, pulling her up only to push her back down.

She liked his command, and she enjoyed the power she had over him like this. He bucked under her, his quick intake of air bolstered her attempt to please him. To make love to him with her mouth.

He tasted of salt, of musk, and man, a delicious combination. He pumped into her, taking his pleasure, and she did not pull away. There was something uniquely erotic about giving another pleasure while taking none. Even though having Jasper in her mouth made her hot and needy.

"Enough," he gasped, pulling her from him. "My turn, my darling."

Somehow in the small space of the carriage, he carried her to the other seat, laying her down. He rucked up her dress to pool about her waist, and then he was on his knees before her, his eyes glowing with wicked intent.

Olivia gave herself over to the sensation of him kissing her *there*. She no longer cared what sounds she made, or Jasper's moans that mingled with hers. He kissed her, flicked and teased her flesh until she was writhing in unabashed need. Oh, yes, this is what she wanted. This, his mouth, his delicious tongue that she was certain was magic.

It wasn't, of course, it was simply Jasper.


JASPER WORKED his cock with his hand as he fucked Olivia with his tongue. He could not get enough. He was close, so close, yet he would not spend until she found her own release.

He teased her nubbin, licked, and suckled her tiny erect button. Her fingers tightened on his hair. Pain tore through his skull, adding to the pleasure as the first contractions spasmed from her cunny.

Jasper let himself go, stroking his cock painfully fast. They came together, and he moaned against her flesh, licking and kissing her as she rode his face to fulfillment.

For a time, he stayed where he was, resting between her

legs as he gathered his breath. Her wet, glistening cunny teased him still, and before he moved, he took one last opportunity to taste her sweet self.

She groaned, her fingers sliding over his face to tip up his jaw to look at her. "You're a wicked duke, Jasper."

He grinned, helping her to sit before he moved back to his seat. His cock, still semi-hard, took a little maneuvering to get back in his breeches. Buttoned back up, he looked across the carriage and met her interested gaze.

"I would like to see that as well one day."

"See what?" he asked, moving to sit beside her and pull her into his arms. She lay on his shoulder, the carriage lulling them both after their exertions.

"I would like to see you take yourself in hand and climax. Will you show me sometime?" she asked, looking up at him.

Her beauty, rather disheveled, cheeks rosy from their escapades made his chest ache. "I will show you, yes. So long as you do the same?"

Her eyes widened, and she sat up. "Is that possible? Can I find such pleasure myself?"

He groaned, the idea of her experimenting when she returned home almost too much for his hot-blooded self. "You can, of course. It is the same for men and women. You are not told these delights by your mother, but they are as true as you and I sitting here, spent and sated."

A wicked glint entered her eyes, and he knew she would touch herself. Maybe not tonight, but soon. His cock hardened at the thought.

"I can agree to those terms. When can I see you again?" she asked, her hand idly running over his stomach, playing with his coat button.

"I'm to attend the Cavendish's dinner tomorrow

evening. Come to my home under cover of darkness. I can meet you at the mews if you prefer?"

Olivia took only moments to think over his words before she nodded, resting back in the crook of his arm. "I will join you at midnight."

He kissed the top of her head, the hours until he saw her again already too far away. "I look forward to your company."

"As I, you," she replied. Her response ought to scare him, but it did not. If anything, it hammered home just how much she'd come to mean to him. How much he longed to be in her company and no one else's. Their game's stakes had changed, heightened, and he was power-less to stop it and nor did he wish to.

That, however, did give him pause. What did that mean, and where would this newfound obsession for them both lead? Jasper adjusted his hold on her. He supposed they would find out, and soon enough. Tomorrow night, in fact.

# CHAPTER 14

The following evening Olivia snuck out of her townhouse and made her way on foot to Jasper's home. She turned down the darkened alley beside his house, seeing the lights of the mews at the back of the estate. A shadowy figure of a man waited near the garden gate, and her steps slowed as she tried to make him out.

Trepidation marred her every step with the knowledge of what they would do this evening. Her being at the duke's home meant one thing and one thing only. When he had asked her to come, Olivia knew what he was asking of her, and she was powerless to say no.

She wanted to be with him in all ways. To have him make love to her, take her and make her his, even if for only one night. Although she was unaware of what her being here meant regarding their future, she did know she would never regret her choice.

He stepped from the gate, and the moonlight illuminated his handsome features. Her stomach did a flip, and she grinned, excitement thrumming through her blood.

Tonight would be fixed in her mind for the remainder of her days.

At the age of seven and twenty, she was more than ready to be tupped. If she did end her days as a spinster, at least she would have this one night in his arms.

"Olivia," he whispered as she came up to him. He hoisted her in his arms and kissed her soundly. The fleeting embrace was not enough and only teased her for what was to come. She shivered, reveling in all that he gave her and clutching him close, having missed him since she'd seen him last evening.

"Come, I have champagne and oysters prepared in my room. We shall have a feast before I feast on you."

She let out a breath, already feeling the thrum of need he brought forth in her. "I would not think you would want any more food. How was your dinner at the Cavendish's?"

"Uneventful and the food unfortunately tasteless, although I do believe that was because my mind was occupied elsewhere."

He led her through the gardens, slipping them into the house by the terrace doors. Without being seen, they climbed the main staircase, making their way toward the ducal suite. Olivia had not known what to expect from Jasper's home, but she was surprised at the light, homey, and well-appointed rooms that encompassed the home.

The walls were adorned with light wallpapers and family portraits. There were flowers arranged throughout the common areas and the home smelled of springtime. His hand tightened on hers as they came to a set of double doors. He turned to her, meeting her gaze. "Are you sure, Olivia? There is no turning back from here."

She hoped he was correct in that estimation. Olivia reached for the door handle and opened the door herself, pushing it wide. Without a word, she pulled him into the room, locking them away from the world, his staff, society's expectations, everyone.

To hell with all that nonsense. Tonight, she would sleep with a man, give her whole mind and body to pleasure, and the consequences be damned. She'd worry about them tomorrow.

They stared at each other. The tension in the air wrapped about her, expectation and need riding hard on her heels. She stepped into his arms, taking his lips.

He wrapped his arms about her, reaching down to her bottom and hoisting her up in his arms. His steps ate the short distance to his bed. He kneeled on the mattress, laying her down. Olivia calmed her breathing as he rolled her onto her stomach, his hands running up along her legs, kneading her bottom before unbuttoning her dress.

"Jasper," she gasped as he kissed her neck, his fingers frantically working the laces of her corset, and then she was on her back again. With a wicked light in his eyes, he pulled her dress from her, her corset and shift gone.

His eyes darkened with need, and she squirmed, her breathing ragged as he simply took his fill, his eyes running hungrily over her naked form.

"So beautiful." He lifted her foot, sliding his hand along her silk stocking, only to pull it slowly off. She shivered at his touch, his ability to quicken and slow their undressing.

Olivia reached up, pulling at the knot on his cravat. "Now it's my turn."

"Not yet," he teased, standing and stripping without shame. His jacket, waistcoat, and shirt discarded on the floor. In his haste, a button flittered to the floor, his breeches wrenched down without heed to pool at his feet.

Olivia felt her mouth open at the sight of him naked. She'd never seen a man in such a state before, and certainly, this man, who stood before her, was the epitome of absolute beauty.

Rippled muscles stole across his abdomen, a light sprinkling of hair on his chest. His manhood was erect and large. Heat stole between her legs wet and aching.

She bit her lip, wanting him inside her. The need that thrummed through her stole any trepidation she had at being with a man for the first time. He would not hurt her. He would only bring her pleasure.

Olivia reached for him, and then he was there, over her, kissing her into blissful oblivion. His manhood teased her aching flesh, and she could not wait. She had spent years hoping, wanting a husband, a lover. The time for respite was over.

Olivia reached down and took him in hand, taking the opportunity to feel him again, tease and stroke his flesh. She placed him at her entrance, liking the way he felt there.

"I do not want to wait any longer, Jasper."

He stared down at her, almost nose to nose. "Tell me to fuck you. I want to hear you say it."

She sobbed, not wanting to play such a game and unsure of what the word he wanted her to state meant, but she could gather the significance of it. Olivia wrapped her arms around his back, scoring her nails down his spine.

"Fuck me, Jasper." She gasped as he thrust into her. Sensation swamped her, stinging pain, yes, but also fulfillment, pleasure, an ache that wanted to be pet and teased until satisfied.

He moaned her name, kissing her. Olivia lifted her legs, wrapping them about his back as the small hurt subsided, and then there was nothing but pleasure, satisfaction left in its place. She moved with him, pushed, and strove to reach the pinnacle he'd given her every other time they had been together.

This, however, making love, was different. It was coarser, harder, felt as though she would split in two if he did not make her come.

"Jasper," she gasped when he pulled out, flipping her onto her stomach and hoisting her bottom into the air.

"Stay like that," he commanded, pushing on her back when she went to sit up. "Trust me."

A shiver stole down her spine as he bent over her, kissing her neck and spine. And then he was there again, entering her from behind, filling and inflaming her more than she thought she could bear. She moaned as his deeper penetration teased a special little place inside.

She was going to die from the pleasure of it all. However would she live without this, without Jasper, when their game was over? She knew she could not.

JASPER THRUST into Olivia with a desperate need he'd never felt before. He wanted to fuck her in every way he knew. She rode his deep, long strokes, fought for her own pleasure, and he'd almost spilled his seed multiple times as her hot, tight cunny wrapped about him like a glove.

The slap of skin on skin was music to his ears. His balls tightened, pulled up hard against his cock, and he knew he was close. Olivia's muffled moans into his bedding told him she was as well. He increased his pace, hard, deep thrusts, and then she was there, grappling for purpose on the bedding, moaning his name as she convulsed around him.

"Fuck, Olivia," he panted, letting himself go. He pulled out, spilling his seed over her ass and up her back, using her sweet cheeks to drain him of his pleasure.

He collapsed beside her, and she turned, grinning over to him, a self-satisfied smile on her lips.

"That was utterly wonderful," she sighed, shuffling over to lie in his arms.

He pulled her close, dropping a kiss on her nose. "Let me catch my breath, and we'll go again."

She slid up against him like a purring cat. "You can do that again? I fear I shall never leave your bed, should you be so clever."

He chuckled, rolling her onto her back and settling between her legs. His cock twitched, working its way to being hard yet again. "Oh, yes, I can do that again and more. Just you wait and see."

"Mmm," she replied, wrapping her legs about his back. "I like the sound of that."

Jasper groaned when she pushed her wet heat against his cock, making him see stars. He liked the sound of it as well as he thrust inside her a second time in as many minutes, losing himself in her and not caring if he never found himself ever again.

# CHAPTER 15

O ne week later, Olivia sat with Athol in her front drawing room that overlooked Grosvenor square. Her friend all but bounced in her chair, excited with some news she wanted to impart. What that news was, however, Olivia had yet to determine as she'd not stopped fluttering about and ensuring everything was perfect before she told her.

"Athol, tell me this news. We're alone now, and you have tea and biscuits just as you asked."

Athol beamed at her from her seat. "It is the best news, Olivia dear. I am engaged. Lord Berry has offered me his hand, and I have accepted him."

Olivia remembered to smile. At the same time, she tried to hide her shock. "I did not know Lord Berry had taken such a keen interest in you. I thought you had spent time with Lord Dormer when you were in Bath, and do not forget Lord Oglemoore."

A light blush rose on her friend's cheeks before she waved Olivia's questions aside. "Oglemoore has been long over, and Lord Dormer offered to Miss Wilkins last week.

Where have you been, Olivia dear? Surely you heard that news during one of your nights out."

Olivia sipped her tea, having missed all of this news. The past week had been spent sneaking over to Hamlyn's home, spending countless hours in his arms and bed. Enjoying every kiss and touch he bestowed on her. He was a magnificent lover and one she would struggle to walk away from, now that she'd tasted what being with a man like him was like.

"Olivia, did you hear me? Are you ill? You're splotchy and red," Athol said, placing down her half-eaten biscuit on the small table before them.

"I'm quite well, the day is warmer than I dressed for."

"Well, are you not pleased for me? I am the happiest woman in the world."

Olivia smiled. "Of course I'm happy for you, dearest, I'm just startled, that is all. I have not heard of Lord Berry's affections toward you before this day. Are you certain he is the gentleman for you?"

Athol started at her words, a small frown between her brows. "Of course, he is for me. Are you not happy for me? I know that you have not found a gentleman to marry this Season, but I would have thought as my best friend you would be pleased for me, not jealous."

Olivia stuttered to form a reply. "Athol, that is unfair. Of course I'm happy for you, but you must admit that you've flitted about from Oglemoore to Dormer and now Lord Berry. It does leave one somewhat turned about."

"I thought you would be pleased." Athol stood, hastily pulling on her gloves. "It leaves Oglemoore free for you now, as you've always wanted. You may think I did not know that you preferred him. And certainly after your disappointment, which you hid unwell in Kent, told me that was the case. You may marry him now, and all will be well." Athol walked to the door before turning to face her. "That's if the marquess chooses you to be his wife."

Olivia stood, biting back the tears that threatened at her friend's harsh words. "It is no lie I thought Oglemoore was courting me last Season, and when I heard of him joining Clara's house party, I did hold a small hope that perhaps he would offer for my hand if his feelings were still engaged. But it has been many weeks now that I have not sought his company or his offer. I want nothing at all from Lord Oglemoore just as you do not."

"So you *are* angry and upset with me because he chose me over you, and that is why you cannot be happy for Berry and me. I shall take my leave of you, Olivia, and wish you a good day."

Olivia watched as her friend flounced from the room without a backward glance or apology. She slumped down onto her settee, lost for words. What had just happened? She had not meant to criticize her friend's choice, but to ensure she was happy with her decision. Marriage was forever, after all. It was not a decision one ought to make lightly.

A knock sounded on the door, and she gasped, glancing up to see Mary, the Duchess of Carlton, smiling in greeting. "I hope I'm not interrupting you, Olivia. I thought I would call by. I'm out and about making calls, and I saw Lady Athol leave rather suddenly, and I wanted to make sure everything was well."

Olivia stood, going to the duchess, and pulling her into the room. "You're always most welcome, Mary. Come, we shall have tea."

They settled down on the leather settee, the duchess studying her most peculiarly. "What happened between you and Lady Athol? You seem out of sorts to me."

Olivia sighed, handing the duchess a cup of tea. She

rubbed her forehead, a slight ache across her brow. "She is recently engaged to Lord Berry, and I merely asked if she was happy with her choice. She's been so unsettled, allowing different men to court her that it is hard to keep up. She accused me of being jealous."

"And are you jealous, my dear?" the duchess asked, meeting her gaze over the rim of her teacup.

"Of course not," Olivia denied. "I am truly happy for Athol, but only several weeks ago she was kissing Lord Oglemoore. One week ago, she was being courted by Lord Dormer. One must admit to being skeptical of her decision making."

The duchess chuckled, setting down her teacup. "Let her have her choice. If she chooses worse than you would have picked for her, that is her own doing. And talking of gentlemen admirers, what is new with you, Olivia? How is the Season progressing?"

Excitement thrummed through her, and she shivered at the thought of Jasper. His touch, his kisses, his body that made her burn and come apart into a thousand stars. She would not see him tonight for they were attending different events, but tomorrow she would, and she was already counting down the time until they assembled.

"The Season has been quite diverting this year. What with Clara's house party to break up the time, and with only a few weeks left in town, I have enjoyed myself immensely."

The duchess nodded, a small smile playing about her mouth as if she knew something Olivia did not. "I have noticed Hamlyn is spending a great deal of time with you lately. To me, he seems quite taken with you, my dear."

Did he? She schooled her features, not wanting to burst out into childish laughter at the idea he liked her as much as she was starting to fear she liked him. They had not discussed their original deal for several days now.

Would Jasper pull away from her if she raised the possibility that her request of him had gone too far? That for her, spending time with him, getting to know him in all ways, not just the façade he portrayed to the *ton*, but the man behind the door when they were alone and private, had made her heart his. Or would he declare, as she hoped, undying love for her and ask her to be his wife?

She was not certain what she would do should he still be playing her game and had no emotional attachment to her at all.

"The duke and I have become friends, yes, but I'm uncertain of his intentions toward me. He has certainly not asked me to be his wife."

"Do you think he may?" Mary asked, a contemplative look on her pretty face.

Olivia shrugged, wishing with all her heart he would. "I do not know. That is yet to be seen."

"Hmm," the duchess said, her eyes narrowing. "I heard that he has parted ways with his mistress, and with his considerable attention toward you, which has not gone unnoticed in town, I wondered if there was something between you or if not, perhaps will be very soon."

*He had parted ways with his mistress?*

Olivia did not know how to answer such a statement, and for the duchess to bring up a duke's lover was far from appropriate. Not that Olivia could say much on the subject of appropriateness after what she had been taking part in the last week. Nights of debauchery and utter unadulterated pleasure.

"I do not know anything about the duke's private life, Your Grace. But if he does choose me to be his wife, of course I would hope he would part ways with his mistress. I would expect nothing less."

"Of course you wouldn't, my dear. Just know that should you need any advice or guidance, I am in town and here to help you until your cousin returns."

"Thank you," Olivia said, seeing the duchess off only a few minutes later. She slumped against the front door after her two visitors for the day, both of whom brought up issues that were taxing and hard to discuss.

The duchess was right however, she needed to know where this love affair with Jasper was heading, if anywhere at all. She could not remain his lover forever, the risk was too high. And she was an unmarried woman, she didn't even have the cover of being a widow to protect her. Should the *ton* find out about their escapades, she would be ruined forever and her marriage chances along with it.

They needed to end the affair or marry. Those were the only two options. Olivia pushed off from the door, heading upstairs to bathe and prepare for the ball. At least tonight, she could dance and enjoy her time in the *ton* and not worry about talking about such matters with Jasper. Their conversation would keep for another day until she saw him again. A small reprieve this day at least.

# CHAPTER 16

The widow Lady Craven's ball was a crush, but thankfully the late Earl Mayfair's home was generous enough to host such an event.

As expected, Olivia had not seen Jasper here this evening, and yet she had seen Oglemoore, moving about the room and talking to acquaintances since his arrival, not an hour before.

The Duchess of Carlton was also in attendance and had raised her glass of champagne in salute when they had spied each other across the room.

Olivia stood speaking with some friends when Oglemoore appeared before her, dipping into a bow. "Miss Quinton, how well you look this evening. Will you do me the honor of dancing with me?"

She smiled, offering her his hand out of politeness. Certainly her interest in the man had long ceased. In fact, as she placed her hand into his, she had to wonder what she ever saw in the gentleman. He had nothing on Hamlyn, who was amusing, kind, and sweet. Oglemoore had proven himself to be flippant, and after his treatment of her in Kent, she ought not to give him the time of day. Athol was fortunate to be rid of him, truth be said. There was something about the man that left Olivia knowing he would not be faithful or a true husband to any wife. She doubted he would part with his mistress if he chose to marry.

His lordship stumbled with the steps, and she shot a look at him. "Are you well, my lord?" she asked, moving forward with the dance.

"Of course." He chuckled.

She studied him a moment and noticed for the first time his glassy, unclear eyes. Was he foxed?

"A misstep, nothing more," he continued.

They resumed the dance, Oglemoore making so many errors they caught the eye of some of the guests. Not willing to be gossiped or mocked, Olivia falsely tripped and, feigning a sore foot, allowed Oglemoore to escort her from the floor.

A footman went to pass them, and his lordship reached out, snapping up two flutes of champagne, handing her one.

"Tell me, my lord, what are your plans once the Season comes to an end? Are you for Surrey?"

He finished his drink with barely a breath, and Olivia stared at his empty glass. The dance was not so taxing that one drank to such an extreme. "I'm not certain as yet. Everything is to be appointed." His slow, standoffish drawl piqued her interest.

"Is something the matter, my lord? You seem offended."

He started to laugh. Cackle would be a better term to describe his mirth. Other guests glanced in their direction before moving away from them. Olivia felt the kiss of heat on her cheeks.

"Nothing is the matter, my dear. Nothing at all, except…" He smiled, his mirth not reaching his eyes. "I do wonder what you're playing at, my dear. What you hope to achieve."

"Pardon me?" she asked, lowering her voice, not wanting anyone else to hear his accusations.

"Pardon you indeed," he replied, hiccupping. "I know you wanted me to marry you, had your heart set on an alliance with my family. I also know that out of spite, you turned Athol away from my suit, and now she is lost to me forever."

"I never did such a thing," she stated, her voice stern. "How dare you accuse me of such a thing."

"Athol told me herself. Tonight, in fact, stated that she has chosen another because you did not approve. How could you?"

Hurt spiked through her heart at her friend's lie. Why would Athol say such a thing? "I never turned Lady Athol from your suit. That she chose Lord Berry is perhaps more to your inability to ask her for her hand than anything I have done."

"You don't say?" he stuttered, stumbling toward her. "Well, I have some news for you, Miss Quinton. I have seen you these past weeks since Kent throwing yourself at Hamlyn. Flaunting your assets so to turn his head, but it is all a ruse, you know. He is not interested in you at all."

Olivia stilled, swallowing the bile that rose in her throat at his words. A ruse? Fear curled about her heart, and she looked around, not wanting to cause a scene. "I do not understand what you're saying. If you'll excuse me."

"I will not," he said, clasping her arm and holding her in place when she went to flee. "I knew you wanted me as your husband. I made a judgment of error last year in seeking you out to be my bride. I did not find you attractive as a husband should find his wife, and therefore I cooled my friendship with you once I realized my mistake. I asked Hamlyn on our way to Kent to keep you occupied and out of my way so I may court your friend. He readily agreed to keep you distracted. You were only ever a game, my dear. I hope you did not get your hopes up too much. I would hate for us both to have lost in love this year." Oglemoore smiled as if he were doing her a great service.

"You lie," she said, not able to imagine all that she'd shared with Jasper to be false. He could not act so heartlessly. Not even a rogue like he was.

Olivia stumbled back, catching herself on a nearby guest. She thanked them before fleeing, fighting her way through the throng of guests to the door. She could not stay here, did not want to listen to any more of Oglemoore's cruel words.

*Jasper had only shown an interest in her at his friend's behest?*

Oh dear heavens, she'd made a fool of herself. She had also made a fool of herself to Hamlyn. He knew of her plan to make Oglemoore jealous, and all the while, he was keeping her engaged for Oglemoore?

*How could he?*

Her vision blurred, her stomach roiled. Blindly she ran out onto the footpath, calling for the first hackney she spied, yelling out the direction to home. She had to leave London. Hide and never come back after this. The people at the ball would have heard Oglemoore and his cruel, mocking words. By tomorrow she would be the latest *on dit*.

She would never forgive Jasper for this. At least she had been truthful in her plan, and although she schemed to make Oglemoore jealous, she never intended to play anyone the fool as they had her.

The bastards had not done the same.

Jᴀꜱᴘᴇʀ ꜱɪᴘᴘᴇᴅ his coffee in Whites the following morning, reading *The Times* and thinking of tonight when he would see Olivia again. Yesterday he'd taken the time to go to the jeweler to have the ring his father had given his mother upon their engagement cleaned and polished.

Tonight he would offer Olivia his hand and his heart and hope like hell she would accept him. Their game, their original scheme to make Oglemoore jealous had not worked. Even though it was a lot of fun, it had changed, grown into something so much more than a game.

He adored her. Wanted her to be by his side for the rest of his life. His partner and wife. His love.

A hand came down over his paper, ripping it away. Marquess Graham glared at him, taking a seat across from him without a word.

"Graham, whatever do I owe the pleasure?" he asked, straightening his paper and wondering why he'd gained the ire of one of his friends.

"Indeed," Graham drawled, his mouth set into a displeased line. "Have you looked around you this morning, Hamlyn? Have you noticed anything different in your world?"

Jasper laid the paper on his knee and glanced about the room. The older gentlemen sat and ate their breakfast, drinking their coffee without a by your leave, while the younger men superstitiously glanced at him, raised their brows, and smirked.

He frowned, dread coiling in his gut. Whatever had he done now?

"You need to call out Oglemoore for making a fool of a woman who is practically family to me last evening. She was belittled and mocked and is now the laughing stock of London."

"What?" Jasper bolted upright. "What did he do to Olivia?"

Graham's jaw clenched. "Well, at least I'm glad to know that you assumed it to be Olivia who had been harmed." He paused. "Oglemoore, well in his cups last night, declared to anyone within hearing distance of his booming mouth that you had courted Miss Quinton only to keep her occupied and out of his hair. Made her sound like a besotted idiot toward the fool and a game for you and Oglemoore. How could you do that to her? She does not deserve such treatment."

*Fuck!*

Panic seized him, and for a moment, he could not speak. Could not think straight. "He said that to her?"

"Of course, and other things too. Cruel words that have seen her flee London. She will not return this Season, and you need to make this right. You have been seen on multiple occasions in her presence, dancing and paying attention to her every word. You will offer her your hand and declare Oglemoore a liar. Friend or not, I will not have Miss Quinton come out of this game you decided to play being the one to lose. You will be her husband, and she will save her reputation and pride. I do not care if you wish to marry her or not. That is what you will do."

Jasper would not normally take such a set down, such rules from anyone, but in this case, he would. He had already decided to offer for Olivia. He would not let her down in this. Face this scandal alone. "I will go to her and make things right." He would first find Oglemoore and give him a good dose of reality and possibly a fist to his nose.

How dare he tell Olivia of his plans? Why would Ogle-moore have wanted to hurt her so?

He stood, throwing the paper onto the chair and striding from the room. His carriage waited outside the club, and he called out Oglemoore's address. Anger thrummed through him at his friend's treatment of her. The bastard would not come out of this smelling like a rose. He would make sure of it.

A few minutes later, the carriage rolled to a halt before the modest townhouse. Jasper took the stairs at the front of the house two at a time. He did not wait for the door to be opened, trying the handle himself and finding it unlocked.

The house was dark, the curtains yet to be opened even at this late time in the morning. A footman skidded to a halt in the foyer. "Your Grace, Lord Oglemoore has not yet risen today. Would you like to leave a message for his lordship?"

Jasper started up the stairs, ignoring the servant's calls for him to stop. "I shall wake him myself. No need to trouble yourself," he called out over his shoulder. The house was smaller than his own, and it did not take him long to find Oglemoore's room since his door was ajar, and there was a decidedly loud snore emanating from the space that reeked of sweat and spirits.

"Oglemoore," he yelled, slamming the door wide.

Oglemoore stuttered awake, sitting up. His once-friend blinked, his eyes narrowed as he tried to focus on one point. "Hamlyn?"

"Get up," he commanded, waiting for Oglemoore to slip from the bed. The man, still clearly foxed, stumbled before righting himself.

"Why do I have to get out of bed?" He glanced at the clock on the mantle. "It's not half past ten. A bit early for callers surely."

Jasper walked over to him, shaking his head. "This is not a pleasant visit between friends. I just did not want to belt you in the nose when you could not fall back on your ass." He pulled his arm back, made a fist, and cracked his friend in the nose. A satisfying thwack rent the air.

Oglemoore flew backward, falling onto his back, holding his nose and groaning.

Jasper rubbed the bones on his knuckles, a small cut on his skin from his assault. "How dare you treat Miss Quinton with so little respect. I shall never forgive you for being so cruel."

Oglemoore sat up, pinching the bridge of his nose to stop it bleeding. "I'm cruel? She turned Lady Athol away from me, and now I have no one. She was spiteful and did it to pay me back for not choosing her."

Jasper shook his head, striding to the door before turning to face his old friend. "You're a fool. Anyone with a brain could see that Lady Athol is as fickle as they come. She never cared for you, you idiot, but Miss Quinton did. A foolish mistake on her part, and now you'll be lucky to have her as a friend. What you did last evening crossed a line."

Oglemoore struggled to stand, swiping at his nose to wipe the blood from his face. "What does it matter to you? You were only pretending to help me. You're just as complicit in my hurting of her as I am."

"I'm to Kent now to talk to her. Apologize on both our behalf and hope that my friendship with her can be saved."

Oglemoore scoffed. "Do not tell me you have fallen for the chit. She may be rich and handsome enough, but is she worth losing our friendship over? If you chase her down, do not include me in your apology. I care nothing for her now that she has ensured the woman I intended to marry is lost to me."

"Olivia never did anything of the kind. You're just as blind as Lady Athol. Always looking for something you believe to be better, more handsome, more flirtatious, rich, or higher on the social rank. Nothing will ever be enough for either of you. It is just a shame you did not win Lady Athol, for you would have made both your lives a living hell."

Jasper strode from the room, ignoring the startled faces of Oglemoore's staff as he passed them by.

He slammed the front door to the townhouse, closing that part of his life along with it. His friendship with Oglemoore was over, and now he had to find Olivia and see if he could win back her trust and, dare he say it, affections.

Jasper called for home. He would win her back, earn her trust and forgiveness. They were suited in all ways. She made him laugh, love, and play with the utmost pleasure. He could not live his life without her in it. His future would be a bleak landscape should she refuse him. A missed opportunity that in time they both would regret, he was certain of it.

# CHAPTER 17

Olivia arrived at her estate and told her staff to inform all visitors she was not at home. She had been at her house for three days, and still the humiliation, the devastation that Lord Oglemoore's words brought forth in her were enough to make her cry.

Perhaps her playing a small trick on Oglemoore had forced karma to make an appearance. Still, the fact Jasper had been in on Oglemoore's scheme hurt. She had thought herself in love with the man.

There was nothing else left to say on the matter. She had fallen in love with him the moment she gave herself to him at his home. Never would she have been so careless unless a small part of her believed Jasper loved her in return and would make her his wife.

How desperate everyone must think her. What a pathetic human being. No doubt all of London was having a jolly good laugh at her expense right at this moment.

She stepped off the terrace in the twilight, walking out onto the lawns and toward the lake just visible through the trees. The water always brought on a calming effect, and she needed that more than anything right now.

"Olivia?"

She gasped, turning to face Hamlyn, who strode toward her, his steps as determined as the look on his face. What was he doing here?

"Leave, Your Grace. You're not welcome here," she said, marching back toward the lake and ignoring his calls for her to stop. She would never stop being angry at him. What he had done had made her look the fool. All this time, he knew of her plan while working for his friend. She cringed, her stomach threatening to bring up her dinner at the thought of it all.

"Stop. Olivia, wait."

She heard him running, and she took a calming breath, not wanting to listen to a word from him. Never again did she even want to see his two-faced mouth.

He caught up to her, clasping her hand to pull her to a stop. She wrenched free, startling him. "Do not touch me, Hamlyn. Do not ever touch me again."

The pain etched on his face pulled at the place her heart once beat, but she thrust it aside. Reminded herself what he'd done. What he and Oglemoore had schemed.

"I'm sorry. I'm so sorry, Olivia. Oglemoore was wrong to tell you what he did. His scheme was never meant to hurt you, merely let you down gently without him having to tell you outright that he did not want to offer marriage."

His words hurt, stung, and she crossed her arms over her chest. "How hard is it to be honest? I'm a grown woman, I can listen to a great many things and not get emotional."

"I know that," he said, tipping his head to one side, willing her to forgive him with his sad, worried frown, but she would not. She'd been humiliated in front of the *ton*. There was no forgiveness for such a slight.

"Oglemoore should have told you the truth. Hell, I should have told you the truth, but when you asked me to tease him into thinking he'd made a mistake, I decided another path. I enjoyed spending time with you, and if you found out Oglemoore was indeed courting another, and the game was over, I feared you would push me aside. I did not want to lose you."

"You did not want to stop tupping me is what you ought to be saying. Well," she said, starting for the pond once more, "you will not be touching me again ever, so I hope your game with Oglemoore was worth your time."

"Damn it, Olivia, listen to me." He clasped her arm, pulling her around. "I saw no harm in doing either Oglemoore's bidding or yours. When you seemed to lose interest in Oglemoore I thought it a blessing that perhaps you liked me more than your own game. My courting of you may have started at the behest of my friend, but it is not why I continued once we returned to London. I wanted to be with you. I enjoyed your conversation and wit. At someplace along the way, I wanted you for myself."

Olivia stepped back. He wanted her for himself? "Pardon?"

"I'm in love with you, Olivia. I traveled here as soon as I found out what had occurred in London. Since yesterday morning, after being denied entry for the second day in a row, I have been hiding in your woods. I hoped to catch you in the garden, and it wasn't until tonight that my luck changed."

Olivia watched as Jasper's lips moved, explained how he came to be here, but her mind had halted thought at the five words he just admitted. He was in love with her?

"You're in love with me?" she repeated, hating to sound so arrested.

He sighed, running a hand through his hair, stepping closer. "I am utterly, absolutely, wholeheartedly in love with you." He rummaged in his coat pocket, pulling out a small blue velvet box. "I had planned on giving this to you the night we were to meet again, but I suppose now is as good a time as any." He opened it, and she gasped, stepping back.

A diamond circled by dark-green emeralds twinkled up at her in the twilight. She met Jasper's gaze, unable to fathom what was happening. She was angry with him, she reminded herself. Had promised all sorts of retribution against his person, some of which may have involved torture. His asking to marry her had not been in her mind.

"Marry me, Olivia. I adore and love you so very much. You have my heart, and I do not want to be parted from you again. Please tell me you'll be mine."

Not quite ready to forgive him, she crossed her arms to stop herself from reaching for the stunning ring. "If you marry me, you do know that you'll be the butt of all jokes in town for marrying a woman who is the latest *on dit*. Are you proposing to save my reputation? Because I'd rather not have you if that is all my marriage will be, another falsehood."

"No." He reached for her, wrapping her in his arms. For a moment, Olivia thought about trying to escape his grip, but then, being in his arms again was a comfort that she'd missed these past three days. "While I do care about what people think of you, I also do not care what they think of my proposing. I know that I'm asking because I want you and no one else. Oglemoore is right at this moment sporting my opinion of him on his face, and I want you to show what I think of you on your finger. I'm the Duke of Hamlyn, no one would dare speak a word of Oglemoore's ploy against you from this day forward."

She narrowed her eyes, and yet, at his words, a little of her ire left her. "The *ton* will laugh at me, behind my back. I cannot return to London."

"I will blacken everyone's nose should they dare speak a word of Oglemoore's scheme."

Olivia debated hating him still, but at his earnestness, his soulful eyes, she could not. She reached up, wrapping her arms about his neck. Oh, how she had missed him. The thought that he was lost to her had broken her soul in two, never to be the same again.

"Are you telling me that Lord Oglemoore is donning a broken nose?"

He grinned, kissing her own nose. "And perhaps a couple of black eyes."

Olivia chuckled, and Jasper stepped back, lifting the velvet case yet again before her. "Will you marry me, my love? I promise you this is no lark. I want you to be my wife, my duchess, my lover and friend. Be mine?" he asked her, taking the ring out and holding it before her.

Olivia bit her lip, hope, love, and relief pouring through her like a balm. She held out her hand, smiling. "Yes, I will marry you, Jasper."

His smile lit up the twilight, and he slipped the ring on. It was heavy and so beautiful. Olivia stared at it a moment, unable to comprehend she was engaged. And not only engaged to be married, but to a man whom she loved so much that at times the emotion had almost overwhelmed her.

He wrenched her into his arms, spinning and kissing her. She clung to him, taking his lips, having missed him so very much. The idea of not being with him as they now were had torn her in two, and she had wondered if she would survive the heartbreak.

"I need you. Please tell me I can escort you back to the house?" he asked, his voice a gravelly, deep growl that promised unfettered pleasure.

"You may," she said after he set her down. She pulled him toward the house at almost a run.


OLIVIA TOOK Jasper directly to her room, shutting and locking the door on anyone who may disturb them. They stripped before the bed, only stopping to help the other with ties or clips they could not handle themselves before falling onto the mattress.

Jasper kissed her deep and long, relief pouring through him that she was his. That she had agreed to marry him and be his from this day forward. He would never allow anyone to insult or harm her again. He'd been a fool to have allowed his friend his stupid scheme. When he had the chance, he should have told Oglemoore to man up and be honest with Olivia.

Her legs wrapped about his waist and, unable to wait a moment longer, he took her, thrust deep into her welcoming heat, and made them one.

"Oh, Jasper. I have missed you," she gasped, throwing her head against the bedding as he took her with long, hard strokes.

"I missed you." He breathed in her delicious scent of jasmine and another that was wholly her. To think he could have lost the love in his arms through his own foolish actions left him grappling for purpose.

He would never hurt her again or embarrass her in such a way.

He took her lips, kissing her and slowing his strokes,

wanting to make tonight last, take their time in making love, enjoy the other without time restraints. He would stay here forever if he didn't want to get her down an aisle within the week.

She shifted beneath him, seeking her own pleasure, and he saw stars. Damn it, she made him want to lose control, to let her use him for her own means. Jasper reached down, clasped her ass and rolled, pulling her to sit atop him.

Olivia stared down at him, her eyes wide with uncertainty. "This is just another way in which to make love, my darling. Use me at your will," he offered, folding his arms behind his head.

She slid down on him, her exhale of breath making his cock harden to rock. She soon fell into a steady rhythm. Jasper breathed deep, steeling himself not to come. Her breasts swung before him, and she clutched at his chest, rising and falling with abandonment as she sought release.

"You're so damn beautiful," he gasped, reaching for her hips and helping her fuck him.

She moaned, throwing her head back, her long, dark locks tickling his balls. She convulsed around his cock, pulling him into such a strong, pleasurable orgasm that his moans intertwined with hers.

Her rocking upon him dragged his release out for longer than he thought possible. He could hardly wait until he took her again. She was an addiction he would forever crave.

She slumped over him, their bodies still engaged, and gasped for air. "Oh, Jasper. How lucky am I that I can have you in this way whenever I please?" She waved her ring before his face. "Tell me, when can we be married?"

"Return to London, and we shall be married by special

license by the week's end. I cannot be without you in my life or bed another night."

"Mmm," she said, placing light kisses across his chest. "Yes, I agree. I do not want to not be there either." She grinned down at him, and his heart thumped hard. "I love you too. Just in case I had not said so already."

He pulled her close, rolling to lay over her. "I'm glad to hear you say it, my love. I would hate to be the only one here in love."

She reached up, clasping his jaw. "You're not alone, and nor will you ever be alone again."

"Perfect." He kissed her soundly, catapulting them into pleasure a second time in as many minutes. The night was young, and there was more indulgence to be had, both in each other's arms and with each other's company—the unspoiled way to end the day.

# EPILOGUE

*One year later*

True to his word, Jasper married her before the week was out in a small church in London. The Marquess and Marchioness Graham, along with the Duke and Duchess of Carlton, their only witnesses.

Twelve months on and Olivia still had to pinch herself every now and then to remind herself she was indeed married to Jasper, the Duke of Hamlyn, and absolutely, utterly in love with the man.

As promised, the *ton* did not dare gossip about her. Anyway, the *ton* had more than enough fodder to keep them busy after her friend Lady Athol married Lord Berry only to run away with Lord Oglemoore to the continent a month later. London had talked of nothing else, and Olivia had not heard from Athol since the day they argued.

All she could hope was that her friend was happy and not regretting her choice, which seemed to change as much as the days of the week.

Now back in the country after a whirlwind Season,

Olivia was glad to be at the ducal estate for the winter. Over the past weeks, she had grown severely tired and lethargic in the mornings, her stomach roiling at the oddest smells.

So much so she had sought out her doctor in town, only to have confirmed her most dearly wished-for dream. She was pregnant, and they were going to have a baby.

Olivia strode into the ducal suite, locking the door behind her when she heard the splashing of the bath. Striding into their bathing suite, Olivia made short work of her clothes, the amused, naughty light in Jasper's eyes telling her he did not mind that she was about to join him.

She stepped into the copper tub that sat before a fire, ignoring the bit of water that splashed over the sides. "Good evening, Your Grace. I have missed you today," she said, moving onto his lap, sliding her hands up his chest.

His own clasped her waist, moving her to straddle his legs. "Hmm, I have missed you as well," he said, kissing her lips, her cheek, her neck before nibbling on her ear. She shivered.

"I need to talk to you about something," she managed to say as he continued to tease her.

"Hmm, you do?" he said, his hand coming about to clasp her breast, kneading it. She gasped when his fingers rolled her nipple. "Does that feel good, wife?" he asked.

"Yes, you know it does, but let me talk first, and then we can play. I want to tell you something."

He leaned back, meeting her gaze. "What is it? Is something wrong?"

"Nothing is wrong, but there is something." She shook her head, wanting to dispel his unease. "Everything is absolutely fine. But you know how I have been so very tired of late, somewhat low-spirited and ill."

"Yes," he answered cautiously. "I have noticed," he admitted, his hands idly running over her back.

"Well, I know what has been ailing me of late."

Jasper frowned, his ministrations on her skin halting. "What is it? Should I be concerned?"

She shook her head, swallowing past the lump in her throat. So many months they had tried for a baby, and each time she bled, she had felt the stab of disappointment, the loss of a small part of them that she so desperately wanted.

"No, not worried. I think you'll be happy." She blinked back tears, and Jasper's frown deepened.

"Tell me, Olivia. You're scaring me now," he demanded.

She ran her hands over his jaw, reveling in the feel of the stubble there. "I'm pregnant, Jasper. We're going to have a child."

His eyes widened, his mouth moved, and yet nothing came out. It was a first for him. He normally had so much to say. "You're *enceinte*? Oh my, darling. You scared me half to death."

She laughed as he pulled her into his arms, more water sloshing to the floor. "My darling, darling wife. How happy I am. And are you sure," he said, reaching for her stomach and laying his palm over her there, "that you are well, and nothing is wrong?"

She shook her head. "The doctor suggested rest and healthy eating, no lifting of anything too heavy. Other than that, there is nothing to report."

He kissed her, long and slow, and her stomach fluttered. "I adore you so much. You will want for nothing, pregnant or not. I shall wait on you hand and foot."

She laughed, having lived with him for a year now, there was scant she ever had to do. He pampered, loved, and spoiled her beyond what was necessary at times. Now that she was having his baby, she knew he would only grow worse with his mollycoddling, but she would allow him his way. If it made him feel better, what harm did it do?

"I had started to worry that we may not be able to have children. I hope it's a boy, Jasper," she said, covering his hands on her stomach with hers.

"Whatever it is, I just hope that you are well, along with the baby. That is all that matters."

And seven and a half months later, Olivia did give birth safely. To a girl and a boy, and the duke was yet again in awe of his wife and spoiled her appropriately for the remainder of their days.

As he should.

# TO KISS A HIGHLAND ROSE

## Kiss the Wallflower, Book 6

*Determined to put a troubled Season behind her, Lady Elizabeth Mackintosh eschewed the London social whirl to enjoy Edinburgh—the joie de vivre she hadn't realized was missing. When a handsome English Earl arrives and sets everyone's hearts aflutter, all the better.*

*Sebastian Denholm, Lord Hastings will endure a Scottish Season if it means he can seduce Lady Elizabeth Mackintosh. Coveting an estate she owns, marriage is the simplest way to acquire it. Shockingly, the courtship is enjoyable when Lady Elizabeth reveals herself as one of the most beautiful, intelligent women he's ever met.*

*But when marriage binds Sebastian and Elizabeth together, Sebastian's real reason for their union threatens to rip them apart. One English Earl finds there is nothing more fearsome than a Scottish lass who's been played the fool twice.*

# CHAPTER 1

*Edinburgh – 1810*

The first week of the Scottish Season was a crush and wonderful all at the same time. Lady Elizabeth Mackintosh admitted that being back within Scotland's society's bosom with all the scandalous goings-on was just what she needed. It had been two years since she'd traveled away from her brother's estate, taking part in the gaiety with her friends. Two women she loved dearly and who were forever reminding her of what she was missing. With a bountiful glass of chilled champagne in her hand, she inwardly toasted her unmarried friend, Lady Julia Tarrant, for making her attend tonight. The weeks to come were sure to be filled with laughter, fun, and perhaps marriage, if she were lucky enough to find a suitable husband.

God knows, she was well and truly old enough to find one.

The sound of a minuet filled the room, a collective murmur of gasps and chatter as couples made their way out onto the floor. Elizabeth watched the throng of guests, one of them her good friend, Lady Georgina Dalton, a widow, who seemed exceedingly happy with the man holding her in his arms and moving her through the steps of the dance. He was dashing, rakish even, if the wicked gleam in the gentleman's eyes was any indication.

Married twice and sadly widowed the same number, Georgina would have to be congratulated on having another man fall at her feet and so early in the Season. Now, if only introductions could be made for her with a suitable gentleman who piqued her interest, the night would be perfect indeed.

"Well, well, well, would ye look at that fine specimen of a gentleman? Too delicious to be English, dinna ye not think?" said her friend Julia, her gaze fixed on the man across the room.

Elizabeth laughed, taking her arm. Julia, Georgina, and Elizabeth had their Season in London the same year and had formed a close bond ever since. Of course, this was helped by the fact they were all Scottish by birth, heiresses, or had inherited their family's estates.

"Georgina certainly seems smitten by him. He's too dark-haired to be Scottish. Maybe Spanish, he certainly has eyelashes long enough to be European."

Julia nodded slowly. "Yes, and everyone knows a person's nationality can be guessed by how long one's eyelashes are," she teased.

Elizabeth grinned, not missing the sarcasm in her friend's tone. "Of course they can, silly. Did ye not know?" The gentleman in question glanced their way, and Elizabeth quickly looked elsewhere, not wanting to be caught ogling him like a debutante. But what were friends to do when one was dancing with such a dashing gentleman? One must look and admire.

Julia sighed. "Well, it seems the Spanish fox has caught

his hare for the evening, and ye must agree, Georgina does seem taken with the gentleman."

"Ye said Georgina was very taken with another such gentleman last evening. I no longer hold any sway with yer words. You're a terrible tease." Elizabeth smiled, taking a sip of her champagne. "And what about you? Is there no one here tonight that has caught yer attention? Ye cannot remain unmarried forever. There must be a man somewhere in Scotland who's perfect for our Julia."

"No one here, I'm afraid, who is exciting enough to marry, but the Season is young and there are many more nights before us. Perhaps my luck may change. And let's not forget, my aunts have threatened to travel here should I not become betrothed before returning home, so I must find someone. If at all possible, I would prefer someone ancient, who'll pass away within the first year of marriage, and I'll not have to bother with husbands after that."

Elizabeth laughed, having forgotten Julia was constantly trying to calm and beguile her two aging aunts. They thought their charge needed their help in all things, including gaining a husband. "So true. I shall look about and see who's elderly enough to be suitable."

They both were quiet for a moment, watching the play of guests, when a pricking of awareness slid down Elizabeth's back. She gazed about the room, wondering what it was that had a shiver steal over her. "Should we move away from the windows? I think there's a draft here."

Julia nodded, and taking Elizabeth's arm, they headed to the opposite side of the ballroom. After a few moments at their new locale, the sense that someone was watching her wouldn't abate.

A gentleman bowed before them and asked Julia to dance. Her friend agreed, casting a grin over her shoulder as she walked off.

"Good evening, Lady Elizabeth."

The deep, English baritone sent a kaleidoscope of emotions to soar through her. Without looking at his face, she knew the man would be devilishly handsome, could curl her toes in her silk slippers.

"Do I know ye, my lord? I do not believe we've been introduced."

"That's because we have not. I'm Sebastian Denholm, Lord Hastings. It's a pleasure to have your acquaintance, my lady," he said, bowing before her with more deference than was needed.

The English earl everyone one was talking about this Season here in Edinburgh. A rakehell from London, rumored to be carousing in Scotland for new skirts to lift. Or so it was said.

"And ye know who I am? How is that so, my lord?"

He leaned conspiringly close. "Doesn't everyone know who you are?"

Elizabeth started at his reply, knowing too well what he hinted. It was no secret in the society they graced that she was known to be unlucky in love. Two years ago, she had set off for London to enjoy another Season. Her brother happily settled, she had stupidly thought she too might find such companionship.

How wrong she had been. In London, one by one, her friends had married around her. They were courted and whisked down the aisle before she had time to change her gown. Not her, however. She had been the good-luck charm for those looking to wed. Lucky Lizzie people started to term her.

Unlucky more like.

"I beg yer pardon, but I do not understand yer meaning." She would not let him throw her disastrous past Season in her face. No matter how handsome he may be.

"I remember you from town. London deemed you a good-luck charm for debutantes looking to marry. I see you have not been caught by such inducement yet, my lady."

Heat suffused her face. So he had heard of her. She'd fought hard to forget the many young women who befriended her so they could find husbands. It was the oddest situation and one reason she was attending this year's Season in Scotland. Even so, it did not look like she could escape those who attended from southern locales and who remembered. "How gentlemanly of ye to remind me of the title. Is that why you're speaking to me now? Do you hope that your nearness to me will equate to ye falling in love and marrying?"

He grinned down at her. "On the contrary. I have no interest in marriage to any of these chits."

Elizabeth fought to close her mouth, sure she was gaping at him. Did he mean that being by her rendered him safe? Was she so inept at finding a husband that the *gentlemen* now thought her a secure woman to be around, so long as other women did not hover close by? How absurd! Not to mention humiliating.

She turned, facing him. "Let me assure ye, my lord, that being by me does not make ye safe from marriage. I'm sure since I'm Lucky Lizzie, the charm would also work on the men who flock to my side. Ye would be no different."

"Do many men flock to your side, my lady? Or am I the only one?"

She narrowed her eyes on him, unsure where his questions were leading, if at all anywhere. Why was he near her if he was not interested? He seemed to be playing with words and her to an extent. She did not like it. "Ye are beside me, are ye not? I'm certain you will not be the last to grace my side this evening."

"I sought you out not to tease you, my lady, and I do

apologize for bringing up your London Season. I merely wished to introduce myself and inform you of some news that I'm sure you will be well aware of soon enough."

"Really? What is this news ye wish for me to know?" Vaguely she remembered his lordship from town, a rake who enjoyed the *demimonde* and widows more than the debutantes. Handsome as sin, rich and wealthy like many of her acquaintance, but always the same. Men who looked for the next thrill, the next piece of skirt they could hoist. Not marriageable by any length. No matter what anyone said, rakes did not make the best husbands.

"You inherited Halligale, I understand."

"I did," she replied, saying nothing further. Her brother had gifted it not long after his marriage to Miss Sophie Grant. He had wanted her to have a home close to him, but that was hers. That it came with an abundance of land was equally generous. Her brother was simply the best person she knew.

"So, we're neighbors. I'm at Bragdon Manor," he continued.

She stared at him a moment, having not known that. If Lord Hastings was a Bragdon, he was closer to her than her brother was at Moy Castle. "I did not know ye had inherited."

Pain crossed his lordship's face, and the teasing light dimmed in his eyes. "I inherited the estate after my brother passed two years ago."

"I'm sorry for yer loss," she said, automatically reaching out and touching his arm. The moment she did, she knew it for the mistake it was. Shock rippled up her arm, a bolt of some kind she'd never experienced before. Elizabeth stepped back, breaking her hold.

"Thank you. My brother was a good man, if not ruled by vices that others sought to their advantage." His lordship seemed to shake off his melancholy and turned, watching her. He had dark eyes, almost gray, the blue so stormy. A handsome man and one who knew that fact well.

"We shall see each other often then," she said, sipping her champagne and willing her heart to stop beating fast in her chest. He was merely a man. A gentleman like no other. There was no reason her stomach would be all aflutter with him at her side.

He picked up her hand, kissing her gloved fingers. His eyes held hers, and again her skin prickled in awareness.

*Oh, dear.*

"I have traveled from England, Lady Elizabeth. I intend to see you as much as you will allow." With a wicked grin, he turned and strode off into the throng of guests, leaving her to watch him. Her gaze slid over his back before dipping lower. Well, it was not merely his eyes that were handsome, and what did he mean by his words? For the first time since her debut ball, excitement fluttered in her soul. Finally, perhaps this year, she would find love and have a marriage as strong and as sweet as her brother had found.

Maybe rakes did make the best husbands after all.

SEBASTIAN HEADED toward the card room to seek out his closest friend Rawden, Lord Bridgman, who'd accompanied him to Scotland. Bridgman had readily agreed to travel north, as the timing suited him perfectly well since he also had some business to attend while in the country.

He found Rawden just as he was leaving a game of Loo and looking mightily pleased with himself.

"How was your evening, my good friend? I saw you speaking to Lady Elizabeth Mackintosh. Did she confirm what you suspected, that she has indeed inherited Halligale?"

Sebastian looked back to where he'd left Lady Elizabeth, but could no longer locate her in the crowd. "Yes, I spoke to her, and unfortunately, she has inherited the estate. I need to find a way to make her sell it back to me, or I suppose I could always take Laird Mackintosh to court and fight him over his unlawful acquiring of the lands."

Rawden raised his brow disbelievingly. "That would be a feat made for giants. He's Scottish, and the land is in Scotland. If you think the Scots will find the acquiring of Halligale unlawful, you have rocks in your head. You'd be best to marry the chit and acquire it back that way."

The comment from Rawden was off the cuff, meant as a lark, but Sebastian stilled, thinking over the fact. If he married her, he would get back his ancestral Scottish estate that had been in his family for hundreds of years. That his brother, the dead lout, had lost in a game of cards. It would be nothing but a mere inconvenience to him should he marry the woman who now owned it. She could stay in Scotland, and he could return to England, visiting Halligale whenever he chose. The idea had merit.

"She is handsome and seems to have wit. Maybe I will court her."

Rawden shrugged, taking two glasses of wine from a passing servant before handing him one. "To be married, though. I'm not sure you're ready for such a step. And anyway, I thought you liked the widow Lady Clifford. You were certainly cozy with her at her mask in London, which I may remind you everyone noted."

Sebastian groaned, knowing what a colossal mistake that had been. He'd been so far in his cups he'd not known what the hell he was doing. One moment he was dancing with Maria, and the next, he had her in a shadowed corner with his hands in places they ought not to be.

"Do not remind me of my past mistakes."

"So, I should not remind you then that she's here and heading your way?" Rawden sipped his drink, laughter in his eyes.

Sebastian whirled about, panic seizing him. Maria was here! He took in the guests, only to see no one at all. Rawden laughed, doubling over, and Sebastian had the ultimate urge to kick him up the ass. "You think that is amusing. You're a bastard."

Rawden wiped at his eyes, laughing still and causing a bit of a spectacle of them. "I'm sorry, my friend. I could not help myself."

"Hmm," Sebastian said, sipping his drink and glancing yet again across the sea of heads to ensure Lady Clifford was not, in fact, in Scotland and could not get him in her clasp yet again.

"Lady Elizabeth is handsome, I will give her that. Do not be too hard on the chit. She probably does not know her brother won the estate in a game of cards."

"I never intended to be hard on her, but marrying her would certainly be cheaper than suing Mackintosh, and would be more pleasant for everyone. Why make war when you can make love with a woman like her?" He caught her moving through the guests, talking with another lady. Lady Elizabeth was tall, curved in all the right places, and with a bosom that would fit in his hands quite nicely. A well-developed lady, not some gangly, giggling debutante with no padding on her bones. Much more satisfying on one's palate.

Her laugh when it carried to him was carefree and without caution, bountiful and heartfelt. He liked the sound of it, and seducing her, marrying her, could make his few weeks in Scotland much more pleasant. Her brother may not like his sister's turn of events. Sebastian and Laird Mackintosh had already had terse words through correspondence over his acquiring of Halligale, but then, if his sister was in love, married even, what could Laird Mackintosh do about it?

*Nothing.*

"I'm glad to hear it," Rawden said, downing his drink. "Now, where are we off to next? Edinburgh is much like London. There is more than one ball a night to attend."

Sebastian laughed and started toward the house's foyer, all for experiencing what this ancient city had to offer that London did not. "Yes, of course, we have invitations for two other events this evening." And many more ladies to meet and flatter before he settled down to court Lady Elizabeth. With any luck, none of them would have emerald eyes and hair that blazed with a fire as bright as the sun itself.

# CHAPTER 2

"You're killing the flowers, my dear. Please, move away before the roses become headless along with leafless." Julia stated, walking past, before slumping onto the settee and throwing her an amused glance.

Elizabeth sighed, glancing down at the roses she had been arranging. Her friend was right, the floral arrangement was well on the way to being atrocious. "We're for the Fishers' ball this evening, are we not?" she asked, sitting opposite Julia and giving up on her arrangement. The maids would do a better job in any case, she had no touch for decoration.

"We certainly are." Julia crossed her legs and met her gaze. "Are you still attending this evening? Or are you asking me about the ball as a means of telling me you've changed your mind?"

"Oh no, I'll be attending. I ran into Miss Wilson in the milliners this morning and she was all aflutter over Lord Hastings and his friend Lord Bridgman, who have arrived in Edinburgh for the Season it would seem. When I told

Mrs. Wilson I had met Lord Hastings at the ball the other evening, she was beyond excitable and exclaiming that I must introduce his lordship to Emily. I do believe poor Emily was quite embarrassed by the whole conversation."

"I saw you talking with Lord Hastings the other evening. What did you think of the gentleman? His lordship and his friend, Rawden his name is rumored to be, are both too handsome for their own good."

Heat stole up Elizabeth's cheeks thinking of Lord Hastings' last words to her. That he wished to see her often. "He was very polite and kind. His downfall is that he's English, but since I have had an English sister-in-law these past few years, I have become used to their ways and I do not find them so very different to us."

Julia scoffed. "You make the English sound like they come from another planet!" She laughed.

Elizabeth chuckled. "Well, they almost do, do they not?"

Julia sighed, leaning back into the settee. "You're young and healthy, an heiress with an estate all your own. Lord Hastings would be lucky indeed if he captured your love. But the Season is young and there are many such gentleman as he. Do not set your cap on him too soon, cast your eye across everyone who's traveled north and decide if anyone else may suit you better."

Elizabeth raised her brow. Her friend had a point and she was right. The Season was young and there were many more balls to enjoy yet. "You know you're starting to sound quite intelligent. I think I shall do as you say."

Her friend smiled triumphally. "How many years have I been telling you so, but you have not believed me? If you follow my advice, you shall never go astray. And if Lord Hastings is genuinely interested in ye, he will not be put off should ye dance or be played court to by others. He will simply be all the more determined."

The idea of his lordship being determined to win her made her feel all tingly and excited. His dark, hooded eyes the other night she could happily fall into and never escape. So handsome, and that he had opted for a Scottish Season this year did say a lot about his intellect. He was obviously smart on that score. The London Season was overrated.

Julia picked up a cushion and held it atop her lap, playing with the multitude of tassels along its side. "What do ye make of Lord Bridgman? He's an interesting character, do ye not agree?"

Her friend's interest in the man was not missed and Elizabeth bit back a grin. "I dinna meet his lordship, but he seemed pleasant enough when I did spot him about the room. He certainly is what they say of him…handsome."

"I think I shall pursue him and see what comes of it. And if I keep his lordship occupied, it will enable you to get to know Lord Hastings better before ye make your choice." Julia grinned. "It is simply the perfect plan."

"It seems you have everything all worked out perfectly well, but I have not even decided if I want to seek his interest. You, however, may court Lord Bridgman if ye choose."

Julia held up her hands in defeat. "Very well, do as ye must, but I think ye should at least see if you suit. It is not often such a stunning pair of men enter our small society. We must make the most of it when we can."

The door swung open and in walked Georgina, a maid carrying a tray of tea and biscuits close on her heels.

"Good morning, my dears. I hope you all slept well."

At the benign question, something that Georgina was not known for, Elizabeth considered her friend. "What has happened, Georgina? It is not like you to care." She grinned, pouring herself a cup of tea.

"I've decided to hold a masquerade and you're both invited." Georgina picked up a biscuit, taking a generous bite.

"We live with you, Georgina. I think our invitation was always going to be delivered," Julia said, shaking her head.

"We shall invite everyone in Edinburgh for the Season, and it'll be the ball of the year. You may invite Lord Hastings, Elizabeth darling. He seemed quite taken with you the other evening."

She groaned. Julia choked on her tea, tried and failed miserably to mask it with a cough.

"I have just spent the last ten minutes explaining to Julia why I shall leave my options open. He spoke to me once. That does not mean he's the least interested in getting under my skirts."

Georgina grinned. "I do adore that I'm rubbing off on you, Elizabeth darling."

Elizabeth took a sip of tea, better that than to scream at her friend's teasing ways.

"You shall invite Lord Hastings, but please do not think there is anything between us. I spoke to him once." She took a calming breath, not wanting to discuss the Englishman anymore. Surely there were other more interesting subjects to talk about than him. Even if the memory of him was amusing and somewhat wicked with his parting words.

Georgina, sensing Elizabeth's annoyance, thankfully changed the subject. "Well, I had the most delightful dance with Lord Fairfax the other evening. He owns half of the Highlands. I think I may let him pursue me. Did you see him, girls? He was most handsome, was he not?"

Julia nodded, her eyes bright with excitement. "Oh yes,

he was an interesting gentleman. He was certainly charmed by *your* charms, is what I noticed most."

Georgina threw a grape at Julia, who picked it up off her skirt and plopped it in her mouth. "I think I shall let him kiss me at the mask. I'm sure he will try."

"You have just come out of mourning. Do you really wish for another husband so soon? If you marry before me yet again, I shall be forever termed the friend who cannot find a husband for herself. People will think that you being around me has enabled men to fall in love with you as they did in England. The good-luck love charm. I'll be mortified," Elizabeth declared, already hearing the whispers and tattle that would travel from Scotland all the way to Almacks in London.

"I promise ye, my dear, that I shall not marry again until you are safely in the arms of the man you'll love forever and a day. But that doesn't mean I cannot have restrained fun this Season. I'm a widow, after all. As long as I'm discreet," Georgina said, a wicked glint in her eyes.

"Well, I for one am going to enjoy my time here, as we all should. And we shall help ye in choosing a fine, sweet man who will love you as much as we love you, Elizabeth. He is out there, you know. And one can never say that Lord Hastings is not that man. If he seeks you out again, you must help him on with your regard. If he senses your interest, then you may be able to secure his affections."

Elizabeth slumped back in her chair, feeling drained and tired from all the work she had before her already, and it was still the first week of the Scottish Season. "My brother would skin me alive if he heard I was acting fast up in Edinburgh. With Sophie expecting, the last thing he needs is for a salacious rumor that his sister has turned rogue when it comes to finding a husband, and then traveling all the way up here to drag me home."

"He will do no such thing. He is too distracted to take any notice of what we're all up to in Edinburgh. The first he shall hear of anything will be your betrothal." Julia set down her cup and clapped her hands, gaining their attention. "Now, my dears, about this ball. What should the theme be, do ye think?"

"Well," Georgina said, "we could allow the guests to choose, but maybe notable characters throughout history. Thoughts?"

Julia nodded. "Oh yes, I shall go as Cleopatra."

"Heloise will do well for me. I'm as doomed in love as she is." Elizabeth was half-joking when she nominated her costume, even so, a small part of her reminded her that just because what all of London believed her to be before she left, a luck charm for her friends, but unlucky herself, did not make it true. This Season she could either let the past dictate her future or she could clasp the fun on offer here in the capital and enjoy herself to the fullest. Living with Georgina allowed more freedom than she'd ever had before. Her friend being a widow enabled her to act as a chaperone too. They could come and go as they pleased, sleep all day and dance all night if they wanted. What more could she ask for?

Julia and Georgina both barked out a laugh, their eyes brimming with unshed tears of mirth. "Oh my dear, you are not going as Heloise. I shall not allow it. No, you shall go as Peitho, the goddess of love and seduction, for that is who ye are and will be not just for this ball, but for the Season. No more lucky charm for others, my dear. It is time ye were the lucky charm for yourself."

Georgina grinned, nodding. "Peitho it is. Now, we must head down to the dressmaker and have her make our gowns. We must look the best since we're hosting. Oh, what fun we shall have."

"What hearts we shall steal," Julia continued.

"And what kisses we shall enjoy," Elizabeth finished, smiling and thinking that perhaps, this year, things would be different. She was with two women who were her true friends and had her back at every turn. They would not see her wronged and she would not be a wallflower this year, nor ever again.

# CHAPTER 3

"If you stare at the doors any longer, people will start to think you are a simpleton."

Sebastian tore his gaze away from Sir Fisher's entrance and concentrated instead on the gathered throng of guests. To his surprise, there were many from London. Even a few ladies who had debuted last Season but would seem to not have found a match were present.

"I do not know why Lady Elizabeth is so late this evening. I cannot make her fall in love with me if she is not here." Sebastian said, his tone gruffer than it ought to be, considering Rawden was trying to stop him from looking like a besotted fool, which he was not. Far from it, no matter how tempting Lady Elizabeth was to the eye, she was a means to an end. His way of gaining back a family estate that should never have been lost.

"Your fascination with the doors was gathering interest, and we can't have that." Rawden chuckled, and Sebastian ground his teeth. "But never fear, my friend, the woman who shall be yours has arrived. How fortunate for you both."

Sebastian glared at Rawden, not missing the sarcasm in his tone before. As casually as he could muster, he cast his attention toward the doors. The breath in his lungs seized, his skin prickled. Never had he ever seen someone as beautiful as the woman London had dubbed Lucky Lizzie.

How had the men of his acquaintance not seen her beauty? He swallowed hard, tempering the desire that rose within him at the sight of her.

"What are your plans with Lady Elizabeth? How will you go about courting her without her hearing that your family once owned Halligale? If she hears such a thing, she will be suspicious of you. The chit does not come across as a simpleton that one can fool."

She was not. Even from the short time they had spent together at the last ball, Sebastian gathered such a truth. "I can only hope she does not. I will tell her, of course, one day, but not until we're wed."

Rawden threw him a disbelieving look. "You are very sure of your charms. What if she is not interested? What shall you do then?"

"There is nothing I can do." He shrugged, hoping that was not the case. He'd always been popular with the opposite sex, never went without when it came to pleasures of the flesh. He cast his eye back to where Lady Elizabeth and her friends made their way through the gathered guests, speaking to those they knew. No, she would be no different, and from the rosy blush that had crossed her features upon their introduction, she would be an easy conquest. "I'm certain she will not be troublesome."

Rawden chuckled, sipping his wine. "I disagree. I think she shall be harder to crack than you think. These Scottish lasses have sturdier backbones than our English flowers. You do know that their national flower is a Thistle. That should give you a little indication of their prickliness."

Sebastian choked on his wine, laughing at his friend's words. "I consider myself duly warned." He cleared his throat, watching Lady Elizabeth as they came to stand across from them in the room. Her gown was deep purple, almost black, and shimmered under the candlelight as if it had a fine, sheer fabric over the top of the silky material. The color set off her green eyes and pink, kissable lips. His body hummed with the thought of her in his arms. He loved the chase, and she was a worthy and desirable woman to catch.

"Before Lady Elizabeth catches you ogling her like the besotted fool, all but drooling down your chin, care for a game of cards? I have a desire to procure some good, Scottish blunt. The night is young, and you have time to court your lady later in the evening."

"Lead the way," Sebastian said, distracted somewhat by the popinjay leading Elizabeth out onto the dance floor. The fop was a short man, and barely came up to Elizabeth's chin. He would never do for such a striking woman. He narrowed his eyes. Surely that wasn't the type of gentleman Elizabeth wished to be coupled with for the remainder of her life.

Rawden clapped him on the shoulder and laughed. "Stop, Sebastian. You'll scare her away before you have a chance to win her."

Sebastian harrumphed, supposing that may be true.

They paused inside the card room doors, taking in the gentlemen who were already playing. A footman brought over a tray of whisky, the delectable amber liquid just what Sebastian needed.

"Oh, before I forget. I have news, and some I think you'll be pleased with."

"What is it?" Sebastian asked, taking a healthy swallow of his drink.

"This afternoon, we received an invitation from Lady Georgina Dalton to her masquerade ball. The woman your conquest is living with for the Season. There is one hitch. The ball is being held at Lady Dalton's home out of Edinburgh. The estate is quite large from all accounts, and she has opened her home for her guests to stay a day or two afterward if they wish before returning to town."

A mask? How fortunate for such a ball to be held. One always enjoyed such entertainments where they had an edge of secrecy—a place for clandestine rendezvous. "When is it?" he asked, hoping it was soon. The more time he had with Lady Elizabeth, the better his outcome in winning her would be.

"The week after next," Rawden replied.

Rawden gestured to a table that two gentlemen stood up from, leaving the remaining players short. "Care for a game of whist? Let us show these Scottish lads how real men play cards."

"After you," Sebastian said, not quite sure his friend had picked the worst-playing gentlemen in the room, the size of their winnings putting paid to that notion.

"I'll deal," Rawden declared, introducing them to the other two players.

Sebastian sat, played without much thought while his mind debated how to court Lady Elizabeth. He needed to come across as genuine in his regard. He'd never had to act a lovesick fool before, and it would be new, if not somewhat degrading, to do so. Even so, his marrying her was for the best. It meant that Halligale was once again in his family, to be inherited by the future Earls of Hastings.

It was an unfortunate necessity and one he would not fail at. The estate would not be long in Mackintosh hands. Not after this Season, at least.

By the time Elizabeth arrived at Georgina's estate for the masquerade ball, the preparations were in full swing. Maids ran from room to room, up and down stairs, setting up the ball and the guest rooms. The footmen looked frayed from their endless chores and orders. Standing in the foyer, she pulled off her gloves, not missing the unmistakable sound of Georgina emitting orders from the front parlor. Julia, who traveled with Elizabeth to the estate, rolled her eyes just as Georgina strode into the foyer.

"La, you're here." Georgina handed them both a piece of parchment, pointing at it. "Here are yer chores to do before the guests arrive tomorrow. Do let me know if ye have any questions."

Julia looked over the parchment. She frowned before scrunching up the note in her hand. "Georgina," she said, leading them toward a private sitting room across the hall from the library. "What possessed ye to be so stringent with everyone who's staying here? Ye cannot possibly think we want to do these activities in the short amount of time we're here. I think the ball is adequate enough to keep the guests occupied."

Georgina gaped at Julia as if she'd sprouted two heads.

Elizabeth quelled her smile. "Julia, you're mean. All Georgina wants to do is ensure everyone has a lovely time." She patted her friend's hand, noting Georgina had yet to find her voice.

Julia unfolded the scrunched-up list. "I cannot swim, and yet I'm supposed to be boating out on the loch. Are ye trying to kill your guests with drowning as well as boredom?"

"These suggestions were merely that, a suggestion. I

only wanted my guests to know they have plenty of things to occupy their time here. I will not be out on the lawn each morning blowing a whistle and making ye all stand in line if that's what ye think."

Elizabeth grinned, imagining such a scene. "Of course, you won't be, and we never thought ye would. Julia's just in a mood because her aunts are on their way to watch her every move."

"I don't know why they have come. Georgina is a widow, adequate chaperonage for anyone."

Georgina stood and rang the bell for tea. "Not to mention my father has arrived to watch over all of us too. He's come back from London specially. I think he believes I'm still in pigtails." Georgina frowned. "Why did yer aunts insist on coming? They never have before."

Julia sighed. "To be nosy, I would imagine. They have heard the two Englishmen are going to be present and insisted they join the mask."

"I'm sure yer father can be persuaded to keep Julia's aunts occupied. They are of a similar age in any case," Elizabeth said.

"True," Georgina sat just as a knock sounded on the door before a footman brought in a tray of tea.

"Do ye really think people will have time for such games and diversions? They'll arrive, prepare for the ball the following day, and some will travel back to Edinburgh the day after. Must we prepare these events as well? We'll have enough to do with ensuring the ballroom, the food, and the house are ready for so many guests as it is," Julia pleaded.

"I just wanted options." Georgina looked down at her hands, a small frown between her brow.

"It is to yer credit that ye want everyone to have a

wonderful time, and they will. The mask is going to be a major success, the ball of the Season. You do not need anything else pulling your guests from what they have traveled here to enjoy." Elizabeth reached out, patting Georgina's hands.

Julia sighed, coming over to sit beside Georgina. "I'm sorry, dearest, for being curt. I'm tired from my travels, that is all. If ye truly want yer guests to do other things at the estate, then we shall, of course, help ye prepare."

Georgina's lips lifted into a small smile. "It's quite alright. I can see that I've been overzealous with my planning. The ball is enough. You're quite right."

"Now, do tell us who else is to arrive." Elizabeth settled back in her chair, relieved that her friends were back to being polite to one another.

"Most of our acquaintances from town, the two Englishmen, of course," Georgina said, throwing a pointed stare at her. "Just about everyone we know, but the house is large enough, the staff has been run off their feet this past week. It's been bedlam here, or so I've been told."

"I cannot wait to dance. My costume of Cleopatra is simply divine," Julia said, pouring herself a cup of tea.

Elizabeth listened as her friends discussed their gowns, how they would do their hair, and who they wished to dance with. The mask was certain to be a success, a night of dancing, of mystery and intrigue. She had not attended a masked ball since her first Season in London, and it would be nice to have one here in Scotland.

The idea that this time tomorrow they would be preparing for a ball sent a thrill up her spine. That Lord Hastings would soon be here was a welcome thought. Would he ask her to dance? Or would he stride off yet again without a backward glance as he had done previously?

Would she dance with him if he did ask? She would, of course. If only to see if her heart fluttered in his presence. Or determine that it was merely an odd reaction toward him upon their first introduction.

Time would reveal all, she supposed, at the masked ball.

# CHAPTER 4

Sebastian knocked Rawden's leg, smiled as his friend, whose face was squashed up against the carriage window, stuttered awake and wiped the dribble from his mouth. "I do so enjoy watching you wash the window with your own drool." He laughed as Rawden mumbled unintelligible words before sitting up and trying to wake.

"Are we here then? A ghastly long trip, was it not?"

"We're four hours from Edinburgh. I hardly think it's worthy of the word ghastly. And cheer up, Rawden, for we have arrived." The carriage lurched sideways as they passed through the gates of Lady Georgina's estate. Sebastian could see the house nestled in the valley below, small lines of smoke billowing from the numerous chimneys.

"I wonder if the prickly Lady Julia Tarrant will be there. It should make the ball more amusing with such women to spar with. Not to mention Lady Georgina is soft on the eyes."

Sebastian raised his brow. "Do behave. We do not need to be escorted off the property and sent back to the capital with our tails between our legs before I have a chance with

Lady Elizabeth. I have a property to get back. I can't have you causing any more trouble than I will myself should she find out my motives."

"I am your friend, and I support you in all that you do, but are you not the least bit unsettled by this plan? If you court her, win her heart, she will think you're genuine in your regard of her, which as much as you like her, possibly find her attractive, you will be marrying her for her land." Rawden fixed his cravat, and Sebastian turned to look back outside the carriage window, thinking on his friend's words. "Think of it this way," Rawden continued. "Had your brother not lost the estate, would you be in Scotland chasing Lady Elizabeth's skirts? I think not. You would have traveled up north for hunting and not much else."

Sebastian pushed away the guilt that pricked at his conscience. It may seem underhanded, ungentlemanly to court a woman for what she would bring to the marriage, but he had little choice. Halligale had been his home for a great deal of his childhood. Where his Scottish mother raised her two boys. Most of his fondest memories were swimming in the loch or running through the grounds, the heather, everything that made Scotland what it is. He loved the home, and so if he had to marry a woman he liked very much and not much else to gain it back, he would.

"First, shall I remind you that this was your idea? I had not thought of that option myself until you said so. But sleep soundly, I will treat Lady Elizabeth with respect. I shall not have a mistress, and she'll want for nothing. She never needs to know that our marriage was brought about by the estate she now owns."

The carriage rocked to a halt, and Sebastian waited for the footman, who hurried from the front steps to assist them alight.

He climbed down, looking up at the large castle that

had been built on to at some point. That Lady Georgina was accommodating some of the guests at her ball became perfectly clear. The house was well equipped to house many guests.

"Marvelous," Rawden said, coming to stand beside him. "If I was not so taken with Lady Tarrant, I may try for Lady Georgina instead if this is the home that she brings to the marriage."

Sebastian glared at Rawden and his comment that did not pass his notice.

A willowy figure exited the main doors to the house. Sebastian met the deep-green depths of Lady Elizabeth's eyes, his sole reason for attending. She was dressed in an afternoon gown, a lighter shade of her eyes. The small cardigan over her shoulders accentuated her bosom, and he was reminded of how well-endowed and pretty the woman was.

"Lady Elizabeth, how lovely to see you again." Sebastian came up to her, taking in her flushed cheeks. Did his arrival cause her pinked complexion? Perhaps his winning of her heart would be easier than he thought.

"And you, Lord Hastings," Elizabeth replied, smiling in welcome.

There was a rustle of skirts before Lady Georgina stepped outside, coming toward him and Rawden with outstretched hands.

"Welcome to Teebrook, Lord Hastings, Lord Bridgman. I hope yer journey north wasn't too tiring?"

"Not at all," Sebastian said, bowing over his hostess's hand. "I had good company, and so the time passed quickly. And we were eager to see your home and meet with you all again."

Georgina smiled, and Sebastian had to agree the woman was quite pretty, but not as pretty as Elizabeth.

"Thank ye so much, we are looking forward to the ball also. I hope ye have an enjoyable stay here."

Sebastian stepped back and gestured to his friend, whose gaze was fixed on Lady Georgina. "May I present Lord Rawden Bridgman, second son to the Duke of Albury?"

"We're honored," she said, dipping into a perfect curtsy, laughter alighting her eyes. "Would you like a cup of tea, or perhaps you'd prefer to settle in before dinner this evening? Luncheon has been laid out in the breakfast room if you're hungry after your travels."

"If a servant could show us to our rooms, that would be preferable, I think. We'll come down soon and break our fast."

Georgina waved a footman over, and soon Sebastian and Rawden followed the man who carried his luggage inside. The foyer was monstrous, a double oak staircase leading to the first floor. Guests already arrived wished them good afternoon, smiling in welcome while going about the house. Paintings adorned the walls, rugs littered the floors, a means of keeping the house warm in winter, he supposed. Candles burned from the sconces and upon hallway furniture, keeping the darkened halls at bay. Rawden was deposited in a room first before the servant showed Sebastian to his.

The suite was generous. A large, four-poster bed with tartan curtains sat against a dark wood-paneled wall. A fire burned bright in the grate and a daybed sat just off to the side of it, along with a single chair in deep-green leather. The room evoked a masculine feel, and Sebastian thought it quite acceptable. What a shame they would not be here long.

"Would you like me to send up the manservant assigned to you to unpack, my lord?"

Sebastian nodded, walking to the windows and to the view that captured his attention. Halligale did not even have such a beautiful view. The start of the Highlands in the distance was certainly impressive.

"And hot water, if you please," he added when the servant went to leave. "I need to bathe."

"Of course, my lord."

Sebastian worked his cravat free, throwing it aside. He should have brought his valet, Wilson, but staying here two nights, he did not think it necessary. He would have the servant unpack his things and set everything out for tomorrow night's mask.

He had opted for no costume, preferring a black, superfine suit. He did, however, have a mask that covered up much of his face. The evening was set to be one the Edinburgh society would not forget, and he, for one, hoped it was one that Lady Elizabeth did not forget either.

⚜

AFTER BATHING, Sebastian fell promptly asleep, and it was only when the servant from earlier woke him for dinner did he realize how late it was. Dressing quickly and hearing the dinner gong sound deep in the house, Sebastian strode down the hall, looking forward to the evening ahead.

He fiddled with his waistcoat and did not hear the door to another room open or see the woman who barreled into him at a force that sent him reeling. His arms instinctively reached out to stop her from falling. It did not work, she propelled him back, and they both went down, the delectable, supple Lady Elizabeth's body finding its home atop his.

"In a hurry for dinner, my lady?" She scrambled off him, her eyes wide with horror.

"I do apologize, my lord." Elizabeth stood, adjusting her gown, which he just now noticed. For dinner, she wore a deep, satin red, her lips glistening with a touch of rouge. The breath in his lungs seized, and for a moment, he merely stared at her. He knew she had red locks, but tonight, coiled up high, her fierce, green eyes and gown made her appear the most delectable Scottish lass he'd ever beheld.

*Damn it, she is beautiful.*

"I should have been watching where I was going. I'm normally quite punctual, and when I heard the dinner gong, and I wasn't already downstairs, I hurried. I am so sorry for not only running into ye, but…"

Sebastian waved her concerns aside as he dusted down his clothing. "It was my fault. I should have been paying attention to my steps ahead instead of adjusting my waistcoat."

She blushed prettily but nodded. "Of course. Shall we go downstairs together then?"

"It would be my pleasure." Their short walk to the dining room was not nearly long enough. Now that he was with Lady Elizabeth, he did not want to part from her or share her time with others. His courting required him to be with her, and preferably alone, or at least apart from the other guests.

How else would he ever get to kiss those delectable lips?

By the time they entered the dining room, the other guests were taking their seats. Sebastian led Lady Elizabeth to her chair, throwing her a small smile before moving on to where the hostess had him placed, which fortunately was directly beside her.

"How fortunate for us that we're to be dinner companions." Sebastian sat, placing a napkin across his knee.

Elizabeth smiled in agreement. "How are you finding

Edinburgh? Are you enjoying our Season here in Scotland?"

"I am, very much so. Your company in particular." Sebastian held her gaze for longer than he should and was pleased to see her blush. Oh yes, she was already a little in love with him. It would be no chore to win her hand and his house at the same time.

ELIZABETH TURNED her attention to the kale brose soup, rich with color, and smelling of vegetables and broth laid before her, wondering why Lord Hastings would say something so inappropriate. He enjoyed her company, that was all very well, but he should not have told her in such a forward manner. Whatever had come over the man?

While she did not mind his company, she was also wary. His particular attention did not make sense. She was known as Lucky Lizzie. Gaining husbands for others, somehow her gift. While he may think himself safe from her because he was male and not female, that did not ring true at all. Not if all the admiring glances directed at him were any indication.

She studied him as he took a sip from his wine, and her stomach fluttered anyway. He was awfully handsome. It was no surprise women flocked to him, that all of Edinburgh was aflutter with his presence in the city this year.

"I am most disappointed that I did not meet you when you were in London last. Promise me at tomorrow night's mask that you will save the waltz for me."

"Of course, if that is what ye wish. I have not been asked to save any dances yet, so I shall write your name on my dance card when I retire for the night." Elizabeth turned back to her meal. If she concentrated on the soup, the man beside her would surely be less diverting. The idea that he may be singling her out due to interest was not something she had considered before. She had been so unlucky in the past that she now automatically assumed no one would find her handsome.

That his lordship seemed genuine in his focus on her was a welcome diversion. A pleasant change from how her Seasons had traveled in the past.

The tapping of a crystal glass caught her attention, and she looked up to see Georgina's father, Earl Cathcourt, standing at the head of the table and smiling down at everyone. He was a jovial-looking gentleman and known for his kindness toward others. "Ladies and gentlemen, let me welcome ye all to Teebrook. My daughter and I hope yer stay here is enjoyable and memorable too."

The ladies about the table smiled in sweet agreement while the men nodded. It amused Elizabeth to note that the two women most interested in Lord Cathcourt's words were Julia's elderly aunts. Maybe Georgina's father would be able to distract the sisters for the ball's duration and allow Julia to enjoy herself without chastisement.

"Georgina." The earl gestured to his daughter. "You wished to say a few words."

"I did. Thank ye, father." Georgina stood. "I too wished to welcome ye and thank ye for traveling here at such short notice. The masked ball is sure to be a magical evening, and we hope you all enjoy your short stay here. After dinner this evening, there will be music, cards, and if anyone is inclined, dancing in the green drawing room, which for those who have not toured the house as yet, is the original castle's great hall."

A muffled, excited chatter sounded about the table, and Elizabeth had to admit the short house party here was exciting, made one almost not want to return to Edinburgh.

"I hope you all have a lovely stay and will come back to see us all very soon." Georgina sat, smiling at the guests.

Lord Cathcourt raised his glass in toast of his daughter's speech. Elizabeth raised hers, turned to see Lord Hastings watching her, a small smile playing about his mouth.

"To masked balls, my lady," he said, tapping his glass against hers.

"Of course," Elizabeth replied, unsure how to react to a man who looked at her as if he would like to devour her, just as a wolf would a rabbit. This being courted was a whole new experience for her. When in London, she supposed her Scottishness had gone against her. With fiery red hair and freckles across her nose, she was under no illusion she was not as perfect as the English liked their ladies. She was a little rough about the edges, opinionated, and her hair often did whatever it wished. Did Lord Hastings not mind her quirks? How diverting if he did not.

How alluring.

# CHAPTER 5

Elizabeth, along with Julia and Georgina, came downstairs and walked through the ballroom before the other guests were due to arrive. Many of those in attendance stayed at the castle, while some from nearby properties would come within the hour.

The room was everything one could wish for a masked ball. Seductive, secretive, and decadent. Hundreds of tallow candles burned in the chandeliers above their heads. Flowers and sheer, black fabric looped across the ceiling, making the room appear smaller and more wicked to the eye. Some of the large, porcelain sculptures were brought in to give the appearance of grandeur, miniature crowns placed atop their heads to mark them as royal statues.

There was gold everywhere, and in the short amount of time that Georgina had to prepare for this ball, Elizabeth wasn't sure how she had been able to pull it off so well, but she had. The space was magnificent. The orchestra too was dressed in black-and-gold livery, as well as the footmen serving at the ball.

"This is amazing, Georgina. Tonight is certainly going to be the place to be and talked about for the remainder of the Season." Elizabeth clasped Georgina's hands, squeezing them. "How clever ye are."

Julia smiled, turning in a circle to take it all in. "I'm in awe, truly. Tonight is going to be so pleasurable. I can hardly wait."

"I'm glad ye like it," Georgina said, walking toward the orchestra and telling them that they may commence. "I wanted it to be magical, and I think I have succeeded." She turned back to them. "Ye both look striking. Lord Hastings and Lord Bridgman will not know what has hit them when they see ye two."

Julie blushed, and Elizabeth glanced down at her gown. As her friends had decreed, she was dressed as Peitho, the goddess of love and seduction. The robes she wore were certainly seductive, and when she'd first viewed the gown, a shiver of caution had run through her at how risqué it appeared.

Her face was covered with a golden mask, disguised with paste diamonds. Elizabeth had painted her lips a deep red, and for the first time in all her life, she did not feel herself. The gown of black-and-gold silk left her feeling bold and seductive, just like the goddess, she supposed.

Georgiana joined her father as he entered the room and took their places near the door to welcome the guests who had started to trickle in. Elizabeth and Julia moved over by the terrace doors, pushed wide this evening to allow the guests to stroll on the terrace and gardens beyond.

"You look beautiful, Julia. Do you think you shall know Lord Bridgman when he arrives? For all that you deny the insinuation, I know that you like him."

Julia smiled, her eyes twinkling behind her black mask.

"I do like him, and I like teasing him even more. I think I shall know him. He let it slip that he's coming as King Henry the 8th. The robes themselves, Tudor in design, will give him away if his features do not."

"Do you think there may be something between you beyond the Scottish Season?" Elizabeth asked, curious at her friend's thoughts. Julia was more private than she and Georgina were, not with her opinions, but certainly regarding her thoughts on love.

"Perhaps," she said, shrugging. "We shall have to see if Lord Bridgman's kisses are as wicked as his words have been. Until then, I will not make a decision."

Elizabeth chuckled, sipping her champagne. "I like Lord Hastings, more than I thought I would like an Englishman. The way he looks at me sometimes." Her heart beat fast at the memory of the look in his eye at last night's dinner. Determined came to mind, along with want. "I think I should like to kiss him too to decide on his suitability to me."

Julia laughed as more people flocked into the room. They spoke to anyone who came over to them, wishing them a pleasant evening, and it wasn't before too long the room was bursting at the seams with guests. The dancing had commenced, and the loud hum of conversations rent it almost impossible to hear each other speak.

The thought of seeing Lord Hastings again made nerves skitter across her skin. No man had ever made her feel such emotion, and while she liked the idea of his flirting with her, she could not help but worry that it wasn't genuine. She had been so unlucky in the past for herself that she could not shake the fear that it would be the same with his lordship. That another woman would waltz by and take his attention, and she would be forgotten in the crowd.

"Lord Hastings is headed this way, Elizabeth. I think

that is him over by the Grecian statue." Julia nodded in the direction she meant, and Elizabeth turned to see if she was correct.

The breath in her lungs seized. Her mind scrambled for words. He was dressed in classic black, a long, dark domino over his shoulders and a mask covering half his face, leaving half his lips and one eye visible.

He swooped into a bow before them, a teasing grin on his lips. "Lady Elizabeth, Lady Julia, you both look remarkably beautiful." His lordship turned to Elizabeth, his attention stealing over every part of her like a physical caress. She breathed deep, scrambling to regain her wits.

What on earth was wrong with her? Was she so desperate for a husband that she saw interest where there was no interest to be seen? Dear heavens, how pitiful if that were true.

"I hope you have not forgotten our dance, my lady." He clasped her hand, kissing the top of her gold silk gloves. His eyes meeting hers as his lips touched.

"I have not forgotten, my lord," she managed, ignoring the nervous wabble in her voice.

He smiled and came to stand beside her. Lord Bridgman was not far behind his friend, and he soon swooped Julia into his arms and out onto the dance floor for a Scottish reel.

"I knew it was you the moment I came into the room. I think I could pick you out of a crowd anywhere."

Elizabeth chuckled, shaking her head. "Really, my lord? Is my costume so very bad to pick me out of a crowd so easily?"

He reached out, picking up a loose curl and sliding it through his fingers. Her heart stilled, her mind imagining his hands caressing other parts of her just so.

"Your hair, you see. Such a beautiful, rich red, makes one want to run their fingers through it to see if it singes one's skin."

Elizabeth couldn't form words. No one had ever said her hair was lovely. And yet the way Lord Hastings was looking at her right at this moment, she could almost believe he was earnest.

"You're in Scotland. There are many of us with such colored hair. I think you're flirting with me, my lord." And she loved that he was. Never before had anyone shown her such interest. The gentlemen who visited her childhood home, Moy Castle, always were wary of her brother's presence. The laird's sister was someone to be polite to, but never look at beyond friendship.

Her brother had a way of scaring off most suitors if he thought they were too forward. Her time in London had been tarnished by the nickname she coined. Men stayed away from her for fear of being married off to the women who flocked to her side. She had been glad when she returned home to Moy.

"Perhaps I am. Would it be so bad if I was?"

His eyes twinkled behind his black mask, watching, taking in her every word, her every reaction to him. He was enthralling, made her want things she'd never thought she did before. His lips lifted into a knowing smile, and she had the overwhelming desire to touch her lips to his. To see for herself if his lips were as soft as they appeared.

She inwardly sighed, knowing he would be an excellent kisser. Along with that thought was the disturbing one that other women had enjoyed being in his arms. Women he'd seduced just as he was trying to seduce her. Vixens all.

"It may not be so bad, even if you are English."

He clasped his chest in wounded dramatics. "Do not

injure me, Lady Elizabeth. I shall never survive the pain of your rejection."

The strains of a waltz sounded, and she set down her glass of champagne, reaching for Lord Hasting's hand. "Time to dance, my lord. Ye can flatter me on the ballroom floor."

# CHAPTER 6

Sebastian smiled, clasped Lady Elizabeth's hand tight as he led her out onto the floor. He pulled her into his arms, holding her close and losing himself in her bright, green eyes. When she wanted to be, she could be quite amusing, more than he thought she would be after their first meeting.

Her hand fit snugly in his, her body perfectly aligned to his height. Dancing with her for the first time made him realize she was quite the perfect height. The idea of seeing her long legs, untying her silk stockings, and sliding them off her satin skin, had him taking a deep, calming breath.

"You mentioned that we're now neighbors, my lord. Have you had Bragdon Manor for long, or is it a recent acquirement?"

"Two years or so. It was the property my brother left me after his death. I should not be the Earl Hastings, you see. I was the second son." Sebastian stopped himself from saying more or revealing that his brother had wanted him to have Bragdon Manor that sat beside Halligale, the estate that Lady Elizabeth now owned.

"Yer brother sounds like a good man to give ye such an impressive estate. I've always admired Bragdon Manor. I would like to see it one day if ye would not mind a visitor."

"I would not mind at all." He pulled her into a quick spin, laughing when she chuckled at his antics. "Tell me, Lady Elizabeth. You say that your brother gave you Halligale. Was the estate always in your family?" he queried, trying to find out how much she knew of the acquirement of the estate.

She shook her head, staring over his shoulder in thought before her eyes met his. "No, it is a new property my brother purchased two years or so ago, I believe. I do adore it, however. Two centuries ago, it was my great-great-grandmother's home on my mother's side. It is nice to have it back in the family."

"Really?" Sebastian said, having not known that tidbit of information. So both he and Elizabeth had an emotional connection to the estate. It made what he was trying to do, ensure a marriage between them, somewhat less brutal, considering he did not love the woman in his arms. That they both loved the estate tempered his guilt to a point. The house should be both of theirs, a home they both should be able to enjoy, not just Elizabeth.

"Did your brother purchase the estate?"

She bit her lip, and he had the distinct impression she was trying to think of something to say other than the truth. "He acquired it when in London, I believe. I do not know the particulars." She met his gaze, studying him a moment. "You're much interested in Halligale, my lord. Why?" she asked bluntly, taking him off guard.

He shook his head, looking beyond her shoulder to watch the dancers about them. "I'm merely curious about my neighbors, that is all." He did not say anything further for fear of saying something that may cause her to suspect him. To win her affections, he needed to be everything she wanted in a husband—caring, flirtatious, enamored. If she found out his sole reason for marrying her was to gain back his childhood home, she would run for the Highlands, and he'd never see her again.

"Perhaps when I visit Bragdon Manor, you may come and see me at Halligale, and your curiosity regarding the estate will be sated." Her fingers slid closer to his nape, and heat licked his skin. The music wound around them, and he took his eyes off the other dancers, turning his attention back to her. She would be a sweet bride to win, and it would be no trouble having her in his bed. He'd enjoy her beneath him, on top of him, before him…

Sebastian swallowed. "You're staring at me, Lady Elizabeth. Do I offend you in some way?" he asked, needing to rein in his wayward thoughts.

"I'm just curious, that is all. Yer are one of the most talked-about gentlemen in Scotland this year. So many are pleased ye have joined our small set of society and are partaking in the Season here. I merely wish to know what would bring an earl, an eligible peer many young debutantes would like to dance with, all the way to Scotland. It is out of the ordinary, I must say."

"Do not tell me that you want me to leave, my lady. Are you so sick of me already?" He was teasing her, but the questions regarding his motivations were strictly off-limits. She did not need to know anything, and if he was careful, she never would.

"I do not know you well enough to know if I wish for you to leave or not, but it is nice having more than our usual set in town."

"It is pleasant being here," he returned, spinning her to a stop as the waltz came to an end. He walked her back to where Lady Julia stood speaking with Lady Georgina.

Sebastian bent over Lady Elizabeth's hand, kissing it. "I look forward to dancing with you again soon," he said, turning to search out Rawden.

As much as he would like, he could not spend the entire night with Lady Elizabeth in his arms. He would play the appropriate gentleman and dance with others, but he would seek her out in the later hours. To win one's heart, one must be determined, or so he'd heard matrons of the *ton* tell their charges the few times he'd bothered listening in on their conversations.

He spied Rawden drinking whisky near the terrace doors. Joining him, he procured his own glass of wine from a passing footman. "The ball is going well. How is your chasing of Lady Julia going? You seem quite enamored of her."

Rawden grinned, saluting with his drink. "Very well, thank you. I may even steal a kiss later this evening if I can maneuver her into the gardens."

"Hmm, I wish you well with that." The idea did have merit, and he glanced back to where he'd left Lady Elizabeth, thinking of trying a similar move. Would she be a willing participant in a kiss? If he wished to marry her, he ought to find out if there was any sexual awakening on his part when he kissed her. Certainly, each time he touched her, he was loath to set her aside. A marriage by his estimation would work between them.

"You ought to try it yourself, Hastings. From what I hear, Lady Elizabeth is quite the catch in Scotland, no matter her disastrous Season in London. Did you know that her sister-in-law is the sister to Marchioness Graham and sister to Mr. Stephen Grant, who married Lady Clara Quinton, the Duke of Law's only daughter?"

Sebastian frowned, having quite forgotten the connections Lady Elizabeth had to high society in England. All the more reason she and her extended family never found out why he wished to marry her. Not until the deed was done, at least. They would loathe him for all eternity, tricking their Elizabeth into being his wife, but that wouldn't matter to him, not once he owned Halligale again.

"I had forgotten, you're right."

"Are you still going to continue on with your plan? The moment he finds out that you are courting his sister, her brother is sure to put a stop to it. He will see straight through your interest for what it is. A means of getting back the property he won from your brother at cards. I would suggest, as your friend," Rawden said, crossing his heart with his hand, "to give up the chase. For as much as she's beautiful, witty, and eligible, you will only cause her pain if you trick her into marriage."

Sebastian frowned, turning to Rawden. "Whose side are you on? Are you not supposed to be my friend? Have my back?"

Rawden glared back in turn. "I am your friend, and that is why I caution you on this. If you stop, no one will be hurt, and no Scottish lairds will be out for English blood."

He shrugged. "I like a good sword fight every now and then, and Mackintosh's underhanded ways of winning Halligale from my brother need attending to in any case. I may have to ensure there is no way of her refusing me. I shall have Halligale back then."

Rawden gaped. "You would ruin her to get your way?"

"Others have done it before me." Sebastian looked back to where Elizabeth stood, smiling with her friends, her lips a deep, rosy red that made his blood pump fast in his veins. No, he could not ruin her to get his own way, no matter how much easier that path would be. He wanted her to choose him because she wanted him above anyone else. Not because he had seduced her and they were caught.

"Do stop glaring at me, Rawden. I shall not seduce her. Disregard my earlier comment. I was an ass."

Seemingly satisfied, Rawden nodded, changing the subject to the events that awaited them in Edinburgh on their return. "So from all accounts, we're quite the popular gentlemen this year."

"I had heard," Sebastian said, spying Lady Elizabeth and her friend Lady Julia slipping from the ball through the terrace doors. "Come, we'll gain some fresh Scottish air. The night is surprisingly warm, and it will revitalize us for the late night we're to have."

Rawden agreed, and they walked from the room, stepping out onto the large, stone terrace that overlooked the grounds. There were just as many people out on the terrace as there seemed to be indoors. It made it almost impossible to spy where his quarry had disappeared to.

"She came outside, did she not?" Rawden asked, his tone bored.

"Yes." Sebastian chuckled, pushing ahead. "Come, she left with Lady Julia. Mayhap you can persuade her to dance with you and give me additional time with Lady Elizabeth."

Rawden sighed. "If we must. Lead on."

# CHAPTER 7

I t took Sebastian several minutes to find Lady Elizabeth and Lady Julia, but eventually he spotted them out on the manicured lawn. Lit lanterns hung from tree to tree, lighting the space. She was talking to a tall Scotsman, and when she reached up, kissing the man's cheeks, a spike of jealous rage tore through him.

Who was this bastard who dared touch her? The man hugged her back, smiling broadly.

*Shit, she has a beau?*

She turned and spotted him, and her smile widened. "Lord Hastings. Lord Bridgman." She gestured for them to join them. He did so, ignoring the fact his face would not mold into a smile. It seemed stuck at a glower.

"This is an old family friend, Angus, Laird Campbell. He is my brother's best friend since childhood." The fellow clasped Elizabeth's hand, placing it on his arm. He nodded to Sebastian.

"'Tis a pleasure to meet ye, Lord Hastings. I hope ye have been having a lovely time in Scotland."

Sebastian studied them both, wondering if there was

something between them that he was not aware of. Had the man traveled here to be near Elizabeth? To spend time with her away from the madness that was Edinburgh's Season? Did their friendship go beyond platonic?

"We are, thank you. It has been most enjoyable."

The man smiled between them, and for an awkward moment, Sebastian wasn't sure what to say. How to bridge the silence.

Elizabeth gestured to him. "Lord Hastings is going to be my neighbor, Angus. Since meeting his lordship, I have found out that he owns Bragdon Manor beside Halligale. We shall see him often, I think."

"Oh, 'tis a fine estate that one," Laird Campbell said. "When Elizabeth's brother, Laird Mackintosh, came into the estate next to the one ye own, we viewed the property from the boundary. But I imagine ye have others in England?"

"I do, yes, two in fact. Wellsworth Abbey near Netherfield, Nottinghamshire, and a townhouse in London on Grosvenor Square." Not that he would see either of those estates for several months, not if he wished to win the woman currently holding and smiling up at Laird Campbell with something akin to adoration.

Sebastian disliked seeing her so attached to another, and he couldn't fully explain as to why. He knew he wanted her to be his wife. He had to gain back his childhood home, the house where his mother had been born and raised, where he had spent so much time as a boy with his brother before life, and vice, changed him forever. And not for the better.

But why was he feeling so uncomfortable, so annoyed at her holding the laird's arm? He wasn't the jealous type. Seeing a woman he thought to court, or one he may have been seeking out had never before raised such ire, such annoyance in him.

Sebastian swallowed, running a hand through his hair. He looked back to her and found her watching him, a curious light in her eyes.

"Lady Julia, will you dance with me?" he absently heard Rawden ask, having forgotten his friend altogether. She agreed and left the three of them alone.

Just as he was about to leave, Laird Campbell waved and hollered to a gentleman behind Sebastian. "I do apologize, but I will leave ye now. I will meet you indoors, Elizabeth, and we shall have our dance."

Sebastian nodded his farewell as the man brushed past him, leaving them alone. At last, he had Elizabeth to himself.

"You are fond of the Laird Campbell. I hope I am not keeping you from him."

She raised her chin. The action accentuated her lush lips, still glistening with rouge. "Not at all, my lord. I have known Angus since I was a child. He's more like a brother to me than anything else."

Relief poured through him. She was not lost to him, not yet at least. Not unless she refused his suit and his offer of marriage that he would bestow on her when the time was right. "The gardens are most beautiful this evening. Would you care to stroll about them?"

"If you like," she said, moving off.

Sebastian followed, quickly coming up to amble beside her. "What a shame we're for home tomorrow. I would have liked to have seen more of this grand estate. I do not think I've seen anything more beautiful in all my travels to Scotland."

Lady Elizabeth glanced at the home, towering behind them. "It is picturesque and distinctive. Georgina, Lady

Dalton, inherited it after the death of her husband. She loves it, of course, but ye have not seen anything so beautiful until ye have seen my brother's estate and my childhood home, Moy Castle."

"Is the house as grand?" he asked, wanting to keep her talking with him for as long as he could.

"'Tis a castle, with turrets and numerous halls, a great hall that we still use frequently today and a loch of course. No Scottish estate is complete without a loch."

He chuckled. "I couldn't agree more. I hope to see it one day."

She met his eyes and held his attention. For the life of him, Sebastian could not look away. Somehow in the time they had been strolling, they had walked down an abandoned garden path, placing them out of view of the house and terrace.

Music drifted through the trees, and even though no lanterns hung here, he could still make out Elizabeth's pretty face from the moonlight above. She stopped, turning to face him before she reached up and pulled off her mask.

"Ah, that is better. 'Tis so hot under these things."

He ripped his own mask off, glad to be free of it. "I prefer to see you just as you are in any case." He took a step closer to her. "Do you know how stunning you are, Lady Elizabeth?"

She raised one brow, and he could see she was skeptical of his words.

"You do not believe me?"

One shoulder lifted in a delicate shrug. "I have not been the most sought-after lady in either England or Scotland. Do ye not see why I would be wary of such flattery?"

"Because of the name you were called in town. Lucky Lizzie, wasn't it?"

She flinched at the reminder. "It is partly because of

that, but also that I have not known ye for long and ye may flatter every woman ye meet in such a way. I am no one special."

He reached out, unable not to feel her. Sebastian ran his finger across her jaw, tipping up her face to look at him. "You are wrong. So wrong. I think you're lovely." He did not know where the words were coming from. All he did know was that they were true. She was unlike any of the simpering fools who followed his coattails in London, hoping for a match. That she was cautious of him, not swayed by his pretty words, meant more to him than he thought they would.

She was different, and he was different when around her. The realization was humbling and telling simultaneously, and he needed to mull on that before their paths crossed again.

A SHIVER of awareness trembled down her spine at the feel of his touch. They were alone in the gardens, free from prying eyes, and his words, oh, such sweet words, were doing odd things to her stomach.

If she were as bold as Georgina, she would close the space between them and kiss Lord Hastings. The wicked glint in his eyes told her he would not be in opposition to such actions. "Ye think I'm lovely? I think ye may have had too much wine this evening." She grinned, trying to make light of a situation she wasn't entirely sure she had control of. Never had she been in such a position, never had any gentleman touched her so intimately.

It left her discombobulated and unsure of what to do next.

"I have had hardly any wine, my lady. It is not the wine that has intoxicated me."

*Oh my. Had he really said such a thing?*

"You are not fond of compliments, I think. Mayhap you have not heard enough of them." He reached for her, taking her face in his hands.

Elizabeth gasped, unsure what to do, what to say, or think. Was he going to kiss her? She'd never been kissed before, and now, in his arms, she could not think of anything she wanted more. He was so overwhelming, handsome, his dark-blue eyes and strong jaw, his lips that made her want to close the space between them and touch her mouth to his.

If only she could be so bold.

Like a dream, he slowly leaned down, and then his lips brushed hers. They were as soft as she imagined, and then the kiss changed. He closed his mouth over hers, his tongue slipping against her lips, and a heady ache settled between her legs.

Elizabeth reached for him, wrapping her arms about his neck and slipping into his arms. He let go of her face, wrapping his arms about her waist, crushing her to him. Her breasts grazed against his waistcoat, sensitized and heavier than they normally were.

His mouth moved, teased her to open for him. Elizabeth copied his movements, hoping she was doing the right thing and not making a fool of herself.

"That's it, open for me, darling." He kissed her hard, and then the world on which she stood tilted, threatened to tip her off.

His tongue slid into her mouth, tangling with hers. She moaned, kissing him back with as much need, as much desire as that which coursed through her blood like an elixir.

The kiss went on and on, both of them taking from the other. His hands slid over her back, sometimes lower than what was acceptable in a dance. She wanted him to dip his hand lower still, knead her flesh. On second thought, she wanted his hand elsewhere too. Her breasts ached, her nipples tingled. Liquid heat pooled at her core, and she tightened her thighs, wanting to sate the throbbing there.

Elizabeth fisted his hair into her hands, holding his nape, and slipped her tongue against his. The sensation was odd but delicious. He moaned, and if there ever was a sound she wanted to hear, again and again, it was that one.

She pulled back, meeting his dark, hooded gaze. "Do you like my kiss, my lord?" she said, sipping from his lips yet again.

He swallowed, a small smile quirking his mouth. "I think you need to kiss me again." He closed the space to do exactly that, and Elizabeth stepped away, holding him back with her hand.

"If I kiss ye again now, ye may have your fill, and I cannot have that." She grinned as understanding dawned on his face. He smiled, bowing.

"Good evening, then, Lady Elizabeth."

"Good evening, my lord." Elizabeth turned, biting her lip to stop the squeal of delight from passing through. How delicious it was to be in his arms, to have his kisses bestowed on her. However was she to ensure she received more of them? No man would kiss a woman like Lord Hastings kissed her unless their interest was piqued. Hope blossomed through her. Did this mean that finally she would receive an offer, be courted, flirted with, and kissed for her Season in Scotland?

She smiled, crossing the lawn and stepping back up onto the terrace before heading indoors. Perhaps this year she would be her own good-luck charm and not anyone else's.

Lucky Lizzie indeed.

# CHAPTER 8

T hey returned to Edinburgh two days later to commence their Season in town. Elizabeth greeted the butler at Georgina's townhouse, handing a nearby footman her gloves and hat. They were all tired after their journey and hectic few days in the country, but Elizabeth couldn't help but feel energized and excited over the weeks to come.

She had watched Lord Hastings leave the country estate the day after the masked ball. Only hours after their kiss in the gardens. He had looked back at the estate before climbing up into the equipage, and she could not help but wonder, hope, that he had been looking for her. Glancing back to see if she were watching him go.

Of course she was watching. She had not stopped thinking of him since the moment he kissed her. Oh, and what a glorious kiss it had been.

He would already be back in Edinburgh, and she hoped he would be at the ball they were attending in a few short hours. Elizabeth strode into the front parlor, going over to the silver salver to see what other events they had been invited to since leaving town.

She shuffled through them all, absently listening to Georgina and Julia discuss their wrinkled traveling gowns before Georgina ordered tea and refreshments in the front drawing room.

"Oh, I'm so happy to be back in town, but what a wonderful masked ball ye threw, Georgina. I'm sure everyone is talking about it," Julia said, slumping down on a nearby chair.

"Of course they are, but I just received word," Elizabeth said, holding up a missive and waving it about, "that Marianne Roxdale is holding an outdoor ball. She states here in her letter that it's to be a reproduction of a night at Covent Gardens in London."

Georgina huffed out an annoyed breath. "She does this to make her event the event of the Season. How dare she compete in such a way and so soon after my own entertainment? It's because I secured Lord Dalton's affections, and she did not. Not that it helped me much since he died two years into our marriage. She's fortunate enough that her husband is still alive."

Julia chuckled, patting the seat beside her for Georgina to sit. "That is quite a callous statement, my dear. It would be best that ye did not state those words again to anyone but us. They will think ye are unfeeling."

"I am unfeeling," Georgiana stated matter-of-fact.

Elizabeth joined them just as their refreshments and sandwiches were brought in. "Do ye think you'll see Lord Bridgman at the ball tonight, Julia? I think he compliments ye well and he seems quite taken with ye, which shows an intelligence otherwise masked by his roguish ways."

Julia grinned. "I may see him tonight, but what I would like an answer to is where you disappeared to on the night of the mask. I saw ye walk off the terrace with Lord Hastings and disappear into the gardens."

Elizabeth had not told her friends what had happened between them. For some reason, she had wanted to keep it to herself, just for her to savor and dream over. During the carriage ride back to Edinburgh, she had ensured they spoke of anything and everything that had nothing to do with the gentleman occupying her life at present.

If she told her friends of her hopes, it would make it doubly worse when he left for London after the Season, and she was still without an offer. The humiliation would be enough if it were simply she who knew her hopes, nevertheless her friends.

"We walked in the gardens, took the air, that is all. Nothing happened between us, and nothing will, I'm sure. We're friends, no more than that."

"Oh," Julia said, disappointment marring her face. "Well, never mind. I'm sure now that we're back in town, and ye have managed to know one another better that he will soon be falling at your silk-slippered feet, begging you to be his wife. No one with any intelligence could deny you."

"I concur. Julia is right. He would be a simpleton if he was not interested in your sweetness."

"We shall see what happens, but I will not get my hopes up, not with Lord Hastings or anyone. I'm in Edinburgh to enjoy the Season here with my two closest friends. That is pleasure enough."

Georgina grinned, sipping her tea. "I agree. Men complicate the situation in any case. They make your mind all fuddled and unable to think straight. When I was married to Lord Dalton, and after our wedding night, I dinna think that I would ever think clearly again. A look, a touch, and I was powerless to his charms." She sighed, throwing them a sad smile. "Until ye have a man who will love ye as Lord Dalton loved me, we shall all keep our options open and not be fooled by pretty words or devastating kisses."

Elizabeth met Georgina's pointed stare and hoped the heat blossoming on her face wasn't visible. Did Georgina know she had kissed Lord Hastings? In the future, she would have to ensure she was more careful. The last thing she needed was to be forced into a marriage with a man who saw her as a diversion during a Season and nothing more. A loveless marriage was a state she could not abide.

Her brother had married for love, adored his wife, and Elizabeth wanted the same sort of commitment. Anything less was not to be borne.

THEY ARRIVED at the ball later that evening when the event was already in full swing. Each of them, exhausted after their travels, had rested over the afternoon and slept late. Now, refreshed and ready to throw themselves into the full swing of the Season, they entered the room, paying their regards to their hosts before procuring a glass of champagne each from a passing footman.

Marianne Roxdale strolled past, giving them each, but Georgina especially, a cool nod of welcome before disappearing into the crowd.

"I think ye may be right, Georgina dear. Marianne is hosting her outdoor event to spite you. Seems she has not forgiven ye for winning Lord Dalton."

"No, it would most certainly seem that way."

Elizabeth glanced about the room, taking in those who were present. She looked down at her dark-emerald silk gown, the pretty gold embroidery over the bodice a favorite feature of her dress. The color suited her, and she could not help but hope that Lord Hastings was present to see.

A voice in her head taunted her that she'd dressed in one of her best gowns in the hopes he would see her, be pleased and appreciative of her appearance.

She picked up the diamond-encrusted cross that sat about her neck, fiddling with it, a nervous flutter in her stomach when she could not locate him. There were many parties and balls in the city tonight. He may have attended another event.

"Shall we take a turn about the room?" Georgina said, setting off, Julia by her side.

Elizabeth followed them, stopping to talk to the guests whom she knew. The outdoor ball Marianne Roxdale was holding the *on dit* for conversation.

Leaving the small group a little while later, she turned to find Georgina and Julia but could not see them anywhere. Continuing on, she watched the dancers as she made her way around the room before she ran nose-first into a muscular chest positioned right in front of her.

"Oh, I do beg your pardon," she said, stepping back and holding her glass of champagne out to the side to stop assaulting the gentleman with her drink, along with herself.

"Good evening, Lady Elizabeth."

Shock rippled through her at the silvery words. Her eyes flew up, meeting those of Lord Hastings. "Ye came," she blurted, forgetting herself a moment and wishing she could pull those words back into her mouth. "I mean, good evening, my lord. I did not think ye were here."

"I just arrived," he stated, taking her hand and kissing her gloved fingers. The breath in her lungs seized, and if she were the fainting type, she was sure she would need smelling salts right at this moment. His devilishly handsome face, his eyes that held wicked intent, made her want to forget the ball and just walk out of the room, away from everyone here so they may be alone.

*What else could he do to you if you were alone?*

The thought came out of nowhere, and heat bloomed on her face, not the best appearance for a red-headed woman with freckles.

"Will you dance with me?" he asked, not letting go of her hand.

Elizabeth felt herself nod and allowed him to lead her out onto the floor. The strains of a country dance sounded, and couples hurried onto the floor to take their places. Elizabeth stood beside Lord Hastings, feeling as though her heart would burst outside her chest, it pumped so fast. The man made her nervous, made her all jittery inside. Did this mean she liked him as much as she hoped he wanted her? She sent up a silent prayer it was the case and that she would not yet again be labeled Lucky Lizzie for others here in Scotland as well.

The dance started, the steps taking them from each other only to join up yet again. His stormy-blue eyes bored into her, not shifting to the other couples about them. He was all-consuming, made it impossible to concentrate on anything else.

"I'm glad to see you back in town, Lady Elizabeth. I missed saying goodbye to you at Lady Dalton's estate."

"Ye left early, my lord. I was not out of bed by the time you departed," she lied, having been up for several hours, unable to sleep with what happened between them at the ball. The kiss, the clutching, his moan.

Oh dear lord, that sound he had made when she touched her tongue to his. Even now, it made her want to repeat the embrace, hear it again, fell him against her, in her. This must be what her sister-in-law Sophie meant by desiring one's husband, an essential ingredient Sophie had said was required for a happy and enjoyable marriage.

*Desire…*

Did that mean she desired Lord Hastings? Was this what she was feeling? She also liked him very much, he was amusing and a lovely dancer, but other than that she did not know him much. Only that his brother had passed, and he inherited his father's title.

"I must ask, my lord. What do you like to do when you're not paying court to ladies such as myself or dancing away your nights at balls and parties?"

"Well," he said, twirling her before setting her back in line with the other women dancers. "I take care of my estate. I have not had it for long, you see, and there is much to learn. I'm in Scotland to look over Bragdon Manor as you know, ensure all is in working order before I return to England."

The idea of him leaving for England after the Season shot a pang of sadness through her. If he did not ask her to be his wife and came to know him even better than she did now, she was sure to miss him. Mourn the idea of them she had started to imagine quite more than she should.

"My brother has said I may move to Halligale after the Season, especially if I do not marry. I'm not a young debutante, and my brother does not believe I need to live quite so strictly as an impressionable young woman ought. I shall have my independence, at least, if not a husband."

"Your brother is very accommodating to allow you such freedom. I do not think I would allow my sister—were I to have one—such liberties. Who knows what rogues are lurking about, just waiting for their moment to swoop in and seduce them to scandal?" He waggled his brows, grinning.

Elizabeth laughed. "What fun to be had if they did," she said, teasing him.

"Hmm," he murmured, the sound making her insides quiver. "With me as your neighbor, mayhap, it will be me who'll knock on your door late at night and ask to share a nightcap."

She gasped, and he pulled her against him, spinning her yet again in the dance. "When can we be alone, Lady Elizabeth? I cannot wait much longer to have you in my arms once more." His words whispered against her ear sent delicious shivers down her spine. Did he mean what she thought he did?

"There is no place here for such rendezvous, my lord. You will have to be content to have me in your arms, such as we are now." Although the idea of sneaking away, of allowing him to kiss her as he had before, was more tempting than anything else in the world right now.

He was dangerous, not only to her reputation but to her ability to deny him. She bit back the smile that wanted to burst from her lips. How she loved every moment of his inappropriate words.

And the dark, hungry look he had that promised everything she'd ever wanted and more.

# CHAPTER 9

Sebastian wasn't sure where the need to have Elizabeth all to himself was coming from, but it was there, as certain as the air he breathed, the wine he drank, he wanted her. The last day of not seeing her had been the longest in his life. It was totally unlike him to constantly think of one particular woman. And yet, that is exactly what he'd one.

He'd wanted to see her on the morning that he'd left Lady Dalton's estate but had not marked her in the breakfast room or any of the other downstairs parlors open to the guests. He wasn't sure what he was going to say to her had she been there. Maybe he needed to remind himself that what they had shared was not an imagined fantasy, that she had kissed him back, sunk into his arms, and allowed him to take his fill of her as much as he'd desired.

He wanted to kiss her again. To feel her pliant and needy in his arms. But how to get her to be alone with him? That was the question.

"Will you come for a drive with me tomorrow? We can travel past Edinburgh Castle or go out into the country if you prefer?" He waited with bated breath to hear her answer, hoping she would say yes.

Her eyes brightened. "I would like that very much."

"Wonderful." He smiled, holding her hand through the dance. He could not remember the last time he looked forward to such an outing. He'd never before invited any particular woman for a carriage drive or to spend the day together. He supposed she would need to bring a maid, but he wasn't so worried about that. Servants knew when to blend into their surroundings and give privacy.

Sebastian reminded himself he was going to all this trouble because he wanted his ancestral home back. Not because he found her enchanting, pretty as a peach and a woman who excited him, made him feel more alive than he had in, well, forever.

"I shall pick you up at eleven if that is agreeable?"

"That will do very well," she replied, smiling up at him as if he'd just bestowed on her a bunch of flowers.

She would suit holding a dozen red roses. It would bring out the fierceness of her hair, make her eyes shine. He leaned close, spinning her and moving her off the ballroom floor and behind a large gathering of potted ferns.

Without warning, he spun her, so she was partially hidden behind him and the plants, and then he did what he'd wanted to do all evening. He kissed her. For a moment, she stilled in his arms, but then like a flower, she opened, bloomed, and kissed him back.

Her fingers slipped around and gripped his lapels, holding him close. By God, his body roared with possession, with need. He took her lips in a punishing kiss, stepping her back farther, if only to prolong his time with her. A bark of laughter pulled him back from the brink of ruining the woman in his arms. He clasped her hand wrapped about his clothing, pulling it away. He breathed deep, putting space between them.

His breathing ragged, Sebastian watched as she too fought to control her reaction to him. Her lips were red, swollen from his touch. Her breasts rose and fell with her heightened breaths, and his body hardened. He damned the ball going on behind them that it stopped him from taking his fill. From kissing her until they were both sated, which, right at this moment, he was decidedly not.

"You should go back to your friends before you are seen behind here with me, Lady Elizabeth."

Her eyes widened farther, and then she was gone, brushing past him, the scent of lavender all that remained. Sebastian closed his eyes, breathing deep and calming his racing heart. For how long he stood there, gaining control of his emotions, of his needs, he could not say, but tomorrow, *tomorrow*, he would see her again. Alone this time, save her servant and for as long as they both wished.

Edinburgh had fewer eyes than London, and he was starting to enjoy his time here more than he thought he would. Winning the heart of a Scottish lass was turning out to be more enjoyable than first thought. Now he just needed to ensure he did not lose it just as his brother lost their estate.

ELIZABETH PACED in the front foyer of Georgina's Edinburgh home, listening for a carriage to roll to a stop out the front of the house. She stopped every now and then and peeked out the front windows beside the door, careful not to move the lace curtains that hung there, lest Lord Hastings made an appearance and she was seen as too eager.

And she was impatient to be gone, alone with his lordship. Her maid sat on a nearby chair, a book clasped tight in her hands and not the least interested in what Elizabeth was doing. After their kiss last night, she'd barely slept. The thought that he'd snuck her behind some palms and kissed her until her toes curled in her silk slippers shocked her still. Her heart beat fast at the memory of it and her stomach clenched in delicious flutters.

Would he kiss her again today? Something told her he would, that the sole reason for inviting her out on this ride was to be alone with her, just the two of them. Her maid could be distracted easily enough and not be bothered too much by what Elizabeth did. Not that she intended to ruin herself, but a kiss could not hurt, surely.

A highly sprung black, open carriage rolled to a stop, and she knew he was here. His lordship tied the reins to the carriage before jumping down with carefree ability she wished she could enjoy. Having to wear a dress most of the time stopped her from having such freedoms. But none of that mattered, not right now.

She stood at the window, admiring the sight of him walking up the steps to the front door, his dark hair falling over one eye and giving a roguish edge to his appearance.

There was a small smile playing about his mouth, and she hoped he was as eager for their outing as she was. This was her first such foray with a gentleman, and she couldn't help but hope that it was true. That he was genuine in his regard of her and wasn't playing her a fool.

It would be a great lark indeed to deceive Lucky Lizzie in her home country as well as England.

A rap on the door sounded, and she stood aside, allowed the footman to open the door. Elizabeth met Lord Hastings as he stepped onto the foyer's parquetry floor, giving him her hand. "Lord Hastings. You are most prompt," she said, not letting him know that she was as well. That for the past half hour, she had been in this foyer waiting for him.

"I never leave a beautiful woman waiting." He reached for her hand, kissing it, his eyes meeting hers as his lips touched her glove. Heat thrummed through her, and she took a calming breath. Her reactions to him were maddening and sweet, all at the same time. She loved what he did to her, but it frightened her too. There was so much at stake, her heart for one, should he be the type of gentleman who paid court during his time in town only to turn about and leave without a backward glance or offer.

The humiliation, the hurt, would be unbearable.

She fought not to grin like a debutante on her first turn about the dance floor. He held out his arm, and she allowed him to help her down the steps toward his carriage. The day was warm, not a cloud in the sky, a perfect day to visit and explore Edinburgh and its surrounding lands.

Her maid perched herself on the back of the equipage, and they were soon rumbling up the hill toward the ancient fortress. They could not get too close, only the Royal Mile, due to the castle being an army garrison. Lord Hastings pulled the horses to a stop, and for a moment, they stared up at the high walls, the shouts of men behind the building's walls barely audible.

His lordship turned the equipage about, heading back along the mile toward Holyrood House. The palace gates were too closed, yet the sight of the beautiful gardens beyond all but begged to be explored. "I wonder if the royal family is in residence." she said, staring at the magnificent building.

"I do not believe so," he replied, clicking his tongue to move the horses on. "We shall drive to Arthur's Seat. I assume you know where I'm taking you."

"Of course." Elizabeth adjusted the small blanket that sat over her legs, already enjoying herself immensely, even though they had not traveled far or seen too much. "We used to picnic there as children when we came to Edinburgh with Mama. I will admit that my seeing it again is long overdue," she said.

"Well then, I'm glad to be the one to reacquaint you."

His sweet smile made warmth flow through her veins. This courting business was really quite lovely, especially when one enjoyed being courted and found the man quite to her tastes.

No man would go to all this trouble to merely turn about at the end of the Season and leave. Oh no, it was looking almost certain Lord Hastings was leading up to ask her to be his bride.

Would she say yes if he did? She shot a look at him, inwardly sighing at the sight of his perfect profile. His lovely, dark hair was long enough for the breeze to flutter as they trotted through the streets of Edinburgh.

Yes, she would agree to marry him should he ask, and she would revel in every kiss and touch he bestowed on her from that moment on.

Her heart beat fast, as she imagined being his wife. If she were fortunate enough to have a marriage with affection and love like her brother and Sophie enjoyed, she would be well pleased. Could this be where they were headed? He certainly seemed to like her.

*No more Lucky Lizzie for others, but for herself.*

They made the base of Arthur's Seat on Edinburgh's outskirts just as the sun rose high in the sky. Lord Hastings jumped down, coming around to help her alight. She reached for him, placing her hands on his shoulders. A squeal rent the air when he pulled her from the carriage, lifting her as if she weighed nothing but a feather. His action slipped her against him, and, with devastating slowness, he dropped her to her feet.

Elizabeth felt every muscle in his chest, every flex of his arms, the warmth of his breath against her face, his closeness that made her forget herself, before her toes hit the ground.

Absently she heard her maid jump down, but she couldn't foster enough caution to step away and out of his hold. His gaze held hers, a promise of some kind lighting his eyes.

"This way," he said, taking her hand and starting up a well-worn path lined with the undergrowth from the trees.

"Have you ever been here before?" she asked him as they came to a clearing. Lord Hastings let go of her hand at the sight of other people and placed it on his arm instead.

"Once, several years ago now, but it has not changed. I should have thought to bring a picnic basket and blanket so that we could have shared and enjoyed a meal."

"Perhaps next time," she suggested, hoping there would be more of these carefree days, away from Society's eagle eye.

"I would like that," he said, cocking his head to one side. "Come, we shall walk a little farther."

"Tell me, Lord Hastings, do you visit Scotland often now that you have an estate here?" She hoped he would, that he would make Scotland his permanent home, especially if he offered for her hand. She could quite happily live in her home country with the man she was starting to care about above anyone else in the world.

"I do, at least once a year, for several months. My English estate in Nottinghamshire, while beautiful, is not where my heart resides. My childhood was spent more in

Scotland than in England, and I have always said it is more my home here than anywhere else."

"Really?" Elizabeth met his gaze. "But I thought your home in Scotland was recently acquired. Did you used to live elsewhere, or did your family have a home that you have not told me?"

# CHAPTER 10

Sebastian stilled, his mind whirling to form a reply and to remember all the lies he'd told so far. Lady Elizabeth was no fool, and one slip of the tongue from him and his ability to win her, win back his estate, would be over.

He wished he could swallow his own stupid tongue. How to get out of this mess of words he'd created? "My mother was Scottish and had a home here, but I was too small to remember where." He closed his eyes a moment, hating the fact he'd just made himself sound like an idiot.

"How lovely that ye have a connection here too. I like ye even more now."

Her teasing words made his blood burn. Damn the maid who followed them a few steps back. He wanted Elizabeth alone so he could kiss that delectable, pouty mouth. Somehow in the few days that he knew her, she had started to wiggle her way under his skin, and he had at times had to remind himself the reason he was courting her in the first place.

To gain back Halligale. Become the lord of the grand Scottish estate that Lady Elizabeth's brother stole in a baseless game of cards. Not because she made him want to be around her, made him look forward to each new day he woke up for on this great land.

"When do you think you shall return to Halligale?" he asked, needing to change the subject off of himself.

"At the end of the Season. My brother has said that I can live there so long as I have a companion or husband." She threw him a curious look. "Ye too must be for Bragdon Manor soon. I will not forget that ye promised me a tour."

The idea of having Elizabeth alone with him at his home made him almost groan aloud. What fun they could have if that were the case. "I have not forgotten. I should like to have you in my home for more than a visit if you were open to the idea."

She stopped walking, staring up at him. A small frown marred her brow. "I apologize, Lord Hastings, but can you ask that question again to ensure I heard you correctly, for I'm not entirely certain of your meaning."

Sebastian glanced at the maid. "Please turn about a moment and ignore all that you're about to hear," he said to the young woman.

"Yes, my lord." The young woman turned about without questioning his decree.

"Lady Elizabeth Mackintosh, would you be willing to marry me? I know that we have not known each other long, but I do believe we suit." He had not meant to ask her so soon. Hell, he barely knew her, but what was the point in delaying his suit? He liked her and he needed her to gain back his ancestral estate. There was no point in postponing the inevitable. She would either say yes, or he would have to persuade her to do so.

She stared up at him, her eyes wide in shock. "You're asking me to marry you?"

He nodded. "I am." He leaned close, kissing her cheek,

the lobe of her ear, her neck. She shivered in his arms, and he smiled against her neck, breathing deep her sweet lavender scent. "Say yes and marry me so we can be together without a maid in tow."

She gasped, her hand reaching out to lay on his chest. She pushed him back a step and met his gaze, hers cloudy with desire. Heat licked along his spine that she was so attuned to him. That her reaction to him was so alike his own. Made him burn with a longing that cried to be sated. How fortunate that the woman he needed to marry made him react so.

"Ye are not trying to fool me, my lord? Ye are in earnest?" she asked him.

Sebastian had the overwhelming desire to strangle the gentlemen in London, and ladies too, who had teased her. Made her believe she was useful to gain other people offers of marriage and not one for herself. The fact he too was fooling her made his stomach churn. He did not wish to hurt her and telling her the truth of why he wanted the alliance would surely do that.

No, this was better. If she agreed to be his wife, he could marry her, gain Halligale back, and Elizabeth would never be the wiser. What one did not know would not hurt them, as the saying went.

*Her brother will work out your motive.*

Sebastian pushed the unhelpful thought aside. he'd worry about that when it happened. "I want you, and no one else. I promise you that, above my honor as a gentle-man." Which was also true. He did want her, and no one else. The mere idea of her marrying someone else made him want to gnash his teeth. "Marry me, Lady Elizabeth. Be my wife."

She smiled, her pretty mouth tempting him before she

322

said the words that placed him one step closer to his home. "Yes, my lord. I shall marry you."

He whooped, picking her up and spinning her about before taking her lips in a searing kiss. She kissed him back, held nothing from him, even though they could be come upon at any moment.

"Call me Sebastian. No more my lord or Hastings. To you, I'm merely Sebastian." He kissed the smile off her face, enjoyed her reaction to him, the bank of desire she released in him each time he was with her.

"Ye may call me Elizabeth in return," she said, wrapping her arms about his neck, her smile as warm as the sunshine on his back.

Sebastian liked the pleasure his proposal brought forth in her. To make her happy made him so. It was a novel experience, one he'd not experienced before with a woman. He liked it. He liked her.

"When shall we announce it? I need to write to my brother."

The idea of telling her brother tempered his enjoyment. He was an intelligent man from all reports, and Rawden was right. He would suspect his motives. Undoubtedly know he was the late Lord Hasting's brother and see his proposal for what it was.

"May we postpone telling your brother?" he asked her.

Her shoulders slumped, and he knew he'd disappointed her. Sebastian pulled her into his arms, holding her tight. "I do not say this to upset you or cause you to doubt my offer. I merely want to enjoy the Season here with you a while longer before the madness of a wedding pulls you back to Moy and your family. I do not wish for you to leave."

Her fingers played with his hair. Damn it all to hell, she

was sweet and his if he could manage to keep her. Keep her brother from ripping her from his arms.

"I understand, and I shall not tell Brice, but," she said, looking up at him with beseeching eyes that he feared he'd never deny. "May I tell my friends? I would like to share my happy news with them."

Sebastian saw no impediment to that idea. "Of course, I would love them to share in your happiness."

She leaned up, surprising him with a kiss, and he took the opportunity afforded him and kissed her back. The kiss spiraled into something that was hot, needy, and altogether not appropriate for where they stood. They needed to marry and soon. He wasn't sure he could live without her in his bed every night for too much longer.

So long as her brother didn't cause him any more trouble, more than he already had. He would not lose Elizabeth, or his childhood home for a second time.

Elizabeth stared at her friends, hoping the shock of her betrothal would enable them to speak, and soon. Both women stared at her, mouths agape, their eyes wide.

"Say something, will you? Ye know I dinna like it when ye do not state your opinion."

Georgina spoke fist, blinking out of her stupor. "You're marrying Earl Hastings? When did he start courting ye in earnest?"

"More importantly," Julia stated, her mouth still gaping. "How did I miss his interest in ye went beyond innocent flirtation to an offer of marriage!"

Elizabeth held out her hands, calling for calm. "It's been a whirlwind, I know. My brother has not even been informed, but I think Sebastian and I suit. He's amusing, attentive." She wanted to go on and tell her friends his kisses were devastatingly toe-curling, but she did not. Some things she wanted to keep just for them, their own sweet secret. "I like him, and he grew up in Scotland at his mother's estate, so he understands the country and our way of life here."

"He's English. What will ye brother say, do ye think?" Julia asked, sitting back on her chair and crossing her legs up under her.

"Brice married an English woman. I dinna think he'll care."

Georgina laughed, a tinkling sound that held an edge of sarcasm. "Oh, he'll care. While Julia and I both enjoy the company of an Englishman at balls and parties, it is no secret that our family would prefer a Scotsman to be our husbands. Yer brother may have married a Sassenach, but that dinna mean he wants ye to marry an Englishman. Yer brother will be no different."

Elizabeth bit her lip, worrying it between her teeth. Would Brice dislike her choice? She did not like the idea of her brother being against her marriage. She wanted Brice and Sebastian to become friends as well as brothers-in-law. To share their children's childhoods, spend Christmas together, and more Seasons in town both here and in England.

"I dinna believe so. Brice will be happy for me and my choice. He'll not cause any difficulty, I'm sure."

Julia raised her brow. "When do ye think you'll tell your brother?"

Elizabeth frowned, unsure herself when that would happen. "He's preoccupied at home at the moment. Sophie is *enceinte*, and there are complications. I dinna want him rushing to Edinburgh to approve my impending marriage. I would prefer to travel home and let him know in a few weeks." Or, the idea of arriving home already married was tempting as well. Her brother could not disapprove of her Englishman then.

Not that she expected him to dislike Sebastian. English or no, there was nothing wrong with her choice. He was titled, rich, sweet, and kind. What was there to dislike?

"Oh, my dearest, why did ye not tell us about Sophie? We will both hope for the best for her."

Elizabeth smiled at her friends. "Thank ye for your kind thoughts. Her brother and his wife Lady Clara have arrived to assist them, but I'm to return home at the end of the Season before the child is due."

"What does Lord Hastings think of postponing ye telling your brother?" Julia asked, watching her keenly.

The look on her friend's face made her choose her words carefully, not wanting to let them know that it was, in fact, Sebastian's idea not to tell Brice. To give them time to enjoy more of the Season, just the two of them, before the madness of a betrothal sent Edinburgh into a flurry and her family along with it.

"He is happy to comply with my wishes." Elizabeth pasted on a smile, willing the seed of doubt that settled in her stomach that he had not wanted to tell her brother because, by the end of the Season, he intended to cry off and return to England.

No, he wouldn't do that to her. Elizabeth had to move away from the doubt Lucky Lizzie had instilled in her. His courtship, his affections were true.

She swallowed the panic threatening to bring up her breakfast. "I hope you're both happy for me. For all that the situation has come about quickly, I am happy with my choice. I think that given more time I could fall in love with my husband."

Georgiana smiled, standing and pulling her up to give her a tight hug. "We're happy for ye, Elizabeth. Lord Hastings is a lovely man, and if he has captured your heart or is on the way to doing so, how could we not love him in turn?"

Tears sprung to her eyes, and she hugged her friend

back, laughing when Julia joined in with their show of affection.

"Ye know what this calls for," Julia said, not letting either of them go. "We need to go shopping for your wedding night. A lovely nightgown is required for these Englishmen with a profile and jaw, such as Lord Hastings has. You need to shock his stockings off when he sees you for the first time alone in a bedchamber."

Butterflies took flight in her stomach at the thought of being alone with Sebastian in such a way. She supposed that would happen soon, and a new wardrobe would be required. As the new wife of an earl, she had to look her best. She had waited years to be married and to be able to wear whatever she wished. Rich, dark colors that suited her red hair and pale skin.

SEBASTIAN LEANED against the wall at the Season's latest event. A day after proposing to Elizabeth, and he could not keep his gaze from following her about the room as she waltzed with Lord Fairfax. There was something different about her tonight. Her smile was brighter, her eyes more alive, and as for her dress, well, he did not think he'd seen anyone more beautiful in his life.

He reminded himself their marriage, was a means to an end. A way in which he could gain control of his ancestral home his brother lost. To Elizabeth, however, he had started to think that she cared for him more than he deserved.

He didn't like to deceive her. It wasn't her fault his brother had been an ass and lost their estate in a game of cards, but neither should Elizabeth's brother been so quick to take advantage of his stupid sibling.

A quiet voice told him Laird Mackintosh was free of any misconduct just as much as his sister.

He rolled his shoulders, his eyes narrowed when Lord Fairfax's arm slid low on Elizabeth's back, and she was forced to reach around and lift it away from her derrière.

Her gaze met his over the gentleman's shoulder, and she threw him a wink. Sebastian choked on his whisky, receiving a whack across his back from Rawden for his effort.

"Whoa, Hastings. We don't need you to choke to death before you make that delectable Scottish morsel your wife. I'm assuming by your glower that you've laid claim and asked her to be your bride as planned."

He nodded once, clearing his throat. "I have, and she said yes. As for Lord Fairfax, if his hand moves lower again on her person, I will be forced to break his arm before the waltz ends."

Rawden chuckled, a knowing light in his eyes. "Talking of women, I must say Lady Julia is driving me to distraction. Since our return to town, she has refused me each time I've asked her to dance or stroll about a ballroom. I think she is testing me in some way."

"Or she is trying to let you know in the nicest possible way that she is not interested in you."

Rawden looked at him as if he'd sprouted two heads. "Don't be absurd, man. How could she not! I'm the second son of a duke. An alliance with my family would benefit anyone."

"Except she's an heiress with her own estate here in Scotland. She no sooner needs to marry you than Lady Elizabeth needs to marry me. I, however," he said, throwing his friend a smug glance, "just happen to be more fortunate than you in that I have secured my bride's affections."

"She isn't your bride yet," Rawden reminded him, gesturing to the two women as they were reacquainted after Elizabeth's dance. "What are you going to do if her brother refuses your suit?"

Sebastian had been thinking about the issue, which was foremost in his mind. If Elizabeth heard of his brother's gambling problem that led to his ancestral home being lost to a game of cards and that the house in question was now her dowry, she would run for the Highlands and never marry him.

"I'm thinking of eloping with her. Now that she has agreed to be my wife, and she's of age, I do not see the impediment. We could return to Moy Castle, inform her brother of her married state, and deal with the fallout then. I will be sure to consummate the marriage before then."

Sebastian took a deep, calming breath as the idea of having Elizabeth beside him, under him, on top of him sent a lick of heat up his spine. It would be no chore to make the fiery redheaded Scotswoman his. He looked forward to plundering her. In fact, the idea kept him awake most nights since he'd met her.

Rawden whistled. "He'll call you out or just murder you if you marry her without him knowing. From what I know of Laird Mackintosh, he's not a small lad and not one to be crossed."

Sebastian sipped his whisky, thinking over his friend's words. "Married and with the union consummated, there would be nothing he could do. He certainly would not want to kill his sister's husband. And with Halligale back in my hands, should Elizabeth take offense to the truth, at least I have time to win her back, try to make her see my side of the argument. She may be angry for some time, but I believe that too shall pass."

"Do you really think that'll happen? She will never forgive you if she finds out that you're marrying her for her property. If she did not have it in her name, would you be in Scotland right now chasing her skirts about?"

No, Sebastian would not, but that was beside the point. It also didn't factor, not anymore. There was something about Elizabeth that he liked. He enjoyed her company, was glad to have met her, to have her as his wife. They suited, no matter what the reasons were for bringing him here in the first place.

"I will have to try to ensure the truth does not pull us apart."

"You sound like a man falling in love and regretting his choice. I wish you luck with that, Sebastian," Rawden said, stepping out into the fray of guests and disappearing soon after.

He could make Elizabeth understand, explain how much Halligale meant to him. If she knew the truth, she would forgive him eventually. After all, it was not as if he did not like her. He did very much. More than anyone he'd ever met before in his life.

# CHAPTER 12

A hand reached up and smoothed the line between his brow, and he realized Elizabeth was standing before him, a precious, knowing smile on her lips.

"You're woolgathering, my lord. Penny for yer thoughts?" she asked him, stepping to stand beside him.

He picked up her hand, kissing it and not caring who noticed. Her eyes widened, and he grinned. "Good evening, my dearest. I see I was too late to claim you for the waltz."

She chuckled, wrapping her arm tight about his and holding him close. "There is to be another. I have been assured of that from our hostess this evening."

It pleased him that she wanted to reassure him. He wished the gnawing ache in his gut would also dissipate. However, something told him that it would not, not until he told her the truth and faced the consequences.

"I'm glad to hear it," he replied, tugging her to walk with him. He needed to move, to remove them from the gathered throng. He needed to have her to himself. "We should leave. I need to speak to you alone."

Her eyes widened, but she nodded. "I can tell Julia and Georgina I have a headache and need to return home, but we need to be careful to leave separately, so as not to raise suspicion, if you dinna want my brother to know of your suit. Everyone in Edinburgh knows him, and no doubt are updating him weekly on my progress."

Sebastian had not thought of such a thing, which made his need to get her away from Edinburgh, away from her brother's reach, more imperative. "Have your carriage take you home. I shall meet you there."

She nodded, sending him a small, conspiratorial smile, and then she was gone. He watched her disappear into the throng and wondered when he'd become such a cad. A bastard who offered marriage to a lady who was as high on the peerage ladder as he, who was as kind and sweet as anyone he knew, and all for an estate.

Who had he become?


ELIZABETH DID AS SEBASTIAN ASKED, meeting him at the mews behind Georgina's townhouse. He pulled her up into his carriage just as it rolled to a stop, calling out the address as he slammed the door closed.

"Why are we going to Dalmahoy?" she asked, as the carriage lurched forward. "That is an hour away, at least."

"I need to discuss something with you, and I need you not to answer the question until you at least ponder it a moment in your mind."

"Very well," she conceded, settling back on the leather squabs and clasping her hands in her lap. "I'm listening."

He took a fortifying breath. "I do not wish to wait for your brother or the banns to be called. I want to marry you now. I want you to be mine and no one else's. From this night forward."

For a moment, Elizabeth fought to control her racing heart. The idea of being his, of him wanting to marry her now and not in several weeks, soothed the small amount of anxiety she had had over his request to wait.

It seemed his lordship had a change of heart. "Why do you wish to marry me now? I haven't even told my brother that you asked me. Do you even have a special license?"

He glanced down at her hands in his, studying them, playing with her fingers. "I do not do this to steal you away from your family, but why wait, Elizabeth? The Season is young, and I do not want to spend it having to keep my hands off you. Being careful how I touch you and what I say. I want you, more than you'll ever know. More than I thought I would ever want anyone."

His words melted her heart, and she sighed. "This is all such a rush, Sebastian." Her stomach churned in knots. "You're not trying to deceive me in any way, are ye?" She had to ask. She would be a fool not to.

He swallowed, reaching for her face. "No, of course not," he managed. "Know this for it is true. I want to marry you because I adore you. I want you to be my wife, my countess. I want you because I desire you so dearly. The thought of anyone touching you, Lord Fairfax in particular after his wandering hands this evening, made me want to throttle the bastard. Never doubt those words for they are true."

Elizabeth met his gaze, trying to settle her nerves over what he was saying, hoping he wasn't playing her the fool. "So we're to Dalmahoy then?" she asked, smiling a little.

"If you say yes to my proposal, my plan, then yes."

She thought about it a moment, but she already knew what her choice would be. "Yes, let us elope, and then I can return home and celebrate with my family. They will be overjoyed to know that I'm married. We can always take our vows again in the chapel at Moy Castle."

He kissed her quickly, meeting her eye before he said, "I would adore that, just as I adore you."

SEBASTIAN PULLED her into his arms and kissed her hard. She opened for him immediately, no fear, no hesitation, and his body roared with need. He should be kissing her with sweet, luring strokes, but he could not. His body, his mind had other ideas. Tonight when he'd seen her dancing with Lord Fairfax, he'd all but had to force himself to remain where he was. It would be impossible for him to stand aside, watch her be courted by other men this Season, and all the while be secretly engaged to her.

No. He could not endure it. He wanted to dance, to flirt, and be inappropriate with her if they wished before society. He did not want to watch his manners or his conduct. If he wished to kiss her in the middle of a waltz at a ball, then he damn well would.

She pushed into his arms, her breasts grazing his chest, and his wits spiraled, crumbled into a pile of rubble.

He wanted her with a longing that would take out his knees had he not been seated. His body burned, hardened, and he wanted her to touch him, to run her hands over his body, clasp, and stroke him, give him pleasure.

She moaned, and he realized his hand was kneading her breast, rolling her nipple between his thumb and fore-finger. He needed to see it, to taste, and revel in her warmth.

Sebastian broke the kiss, pleased when she lay her head back, pushing her breast into his hand. He ran his finger along the top of her gown. "Your skin is so unblemished, like milk." He slowly slipped her bodice down with patience he did not know he possessed, exposing her flesh. He could not wait a moment longer. He dipped his head and kissed her pebbled peak, licking its pinkened surface, making it bead farther.

Her fingers spiked into his hair, pulling him near. He fought for control. He would not take her here, in a carriage of all places. She was a maid, a lady, and soon to be his wife. She deserved better than this. With a strength he did not know he possessed, he wrenched away, breathing deep to control his need.

Sebastian threw himself into the squabs, facing forward, and refused to look at her mussed hair, her flushed face, and swollen, well-kissed lips as she set her gown to rights.

He looked out the window and found they were not far from the small village where he had organized the reverend at St. Mary's church to marry them.

She reached out, touching his arm, and he closed his eyes, fighting not to wrench her onto his lap and continue what they had started.

"Sebastian, what is the matter?" she asked, trying to catch his eye.

He shook his head, grinding his teeth. "We're not married yet. I should not have touched you as I did."

A seductive, knowing chuckle sounded at his ear, and he shivered. She leaned close, clasping the lapels of his jacket. "You dinna see me stopping ye."

He took a calming breath. "I know, but it does not make it right. I want to marry you, and I do not want to ruin you in this way. You deserve better than a romp in a moving carriage."

She bestowed the loveliest smile, and it was equal to a fist to the stomach. He ought to tell the truth. Tell her that his courting of her had been born out of greed. The need to have his ancestral home back and nothing else.

But how could he tell her such a thing? She would never marry him then, and that goal had now changed. Morphed into something new and real, something true that made his heart full.

"You said you would marry me," he continued. "I have a reverend waiting for us. Married acquaintances of mine who live on an estate just outside of Dalmahoy will meet us at the church and be witnesses to our vows."

"However did you organize all this so soon?" she asked him, her eyes bright with wonder and excitement.

"You are over one and twenty, so we do not need your family's approval. I paid a hefty fee today to secure a special license. Not easily found here in Edinburgh. Our union will be legal, then nothing can come between us."

The carriage lurched to a stop, and Sebastian turned to her, taking her hand. "We're here. Are you ready, Lady Elizabeth to become Countess Hastings?"

She squeezed his hand in return, nodding once. "I am ready."

And so was he.

# CHAPTER 13

E lizabeth walked up the aisle alone, wishing her family could be here with her, and yet, overjoyed at the idea that she was about to marry a man she adored. Seeing Sebastian waiting for her before a stone altar, the reverend smiling as he stood with his bible in hand, made butterflies take flight in her stomach. Soon she would be his, and she could be with him always. A small part of her had to admit she was marrying him for more than the mere reason she enjoyed his company and found him amusing, not to mention, devastatingly alluring.

Her heart had been speared by love's arrow, and for several days now, she had come to realize she did not merely like Sebastian, but loved him. Loved his humor, his conversation, and kisses. His hot, commanding gaze that even from across a room made her skin singe.

After all the legalities were dealt with, the thought that she would be alone with him, and as his wife, set her senses rioting.

Absently she heard the reverend declare them husband and wife, and before she had a chance to thank the father, she was caught up in Sebastian's arms, his mouth taking hers in a searing kiss.

Elizabeth wrapped her arms around his neck, kissing him back. The day was simply perfect, and when she returned home to Moy, she would celebrate with her family and friends, but tonight, right now, was her time. A time to savor with her new husband.

He set her back down on her silk slippers before turning to his friends and the reverend. "Thank you for tonight. I shall not forget your kindness for our sake."

"You are most welcome, Hastings," Lord Pitt said, smiling at them both and holding his wife's hand atop his arm. "I took the liberty of preparing a room at our estate if you wish to rest."

"That is most kind, Pitt. I do not know how to thank you," Sebastian said, smiling down at Elizabeth a moment.

"Ah, it is no trouble at all," his lordship said, waving Sebastian's concerns aside. "There are plenty of rooms at the big house, no need for thanks."

They quickly signed the register, making their union legal, before Sebastian paid the reverend handsomely and they were on their way. Soon they arrived at the dark-gray stone home of Lord and Lady Pitt, where they would spend their wedding night.

During the short journey neither of them spoke, but Sebastian held her close, his arm about her shoulder, his thumb idly sliding against the skin on her arm and sending her wits to spiral.

She could not wait for them to be alone.

They made their way upstairs. The mansion with its dark, rich woods and heavy window coverings was too sullen for Elizabeth's taste, but it was still opulent and comfortable. Lady Pitt pointed out several rooms, the servant's stairs, the upstairs parlor if they cared to use it.

Finally, they came to their room, and she gestured them inside, looking about and checking everything was in order.

"If you need anything, ring for a servant, the bellpull is beside the mantel, and they will assist you." Lady Pitt wished them good night and closed the door softly behind her.

Elizabeth walked about the room, taking in the furnishings of rich, mahogany wood and deep-green velvet coverings both on the bed and the chairs that sat before the fire. Animal skins covered the wooden floors and the curtains had been pulled closed to keep out the night's chill.

She went and stood before the fire, turning to face Sebastian, who leaned against the door, slowly untying his cravat, his wicked, heated gaze focused solely on her.

Heat pooled at her core, and she could hardly wait for him to touch her. To be with him as a wife should be with a husband.

"When you stand before a fire, I can almost see through your gown. Did you know that?"

She flushed but did not move. Instead, she reached up, pulling out the pins in her hair and letting her long, red locks fall about her shoulders. "No, I did not know, but I thank ye for letting me be aware of the fact. I'll be sure not to stand before any fires when I'm next in a ballroom."

"You have lovely legs, wife," he said, stepping closer still, his jacket and waistcoat thrown onto a nearby chair without care. His hands reached down, pulling his shirt out of his buckskin breeches. He reached behind his head, slipping it off.

Elizabeth swallowed, having never seen him naked before. A delicious part of her reveled in the knowledge he was hers to admire, to have. That no one else would ever see him thus again. Not unless that person was her. She met him halfway across the room, not willing to sit idly by, wait for him to take her in his arms.

He pulled her close and shuffled her toward the four-poster bed, making quick work of the hooks at the back of her ballgown. Before she had a chance to be shy, he'd stripped her of her gown and shift, turning her quickly to unlace her corset.

Sebastian stood back and took her in, his eyes running over her body like a physical caress. Elizabeth took a calming breath, unsure of what was going to happen, what was expected of her. If he liked what he saw.

"Dear God, you're stunning." He scooped her into his arms and deposited her in the middle of the bed, following and pinning her beneath him.

She slid her foot along his calf, the feel of his hairy legs tickling the base of her feet. He still wore his breeches, a fact that now with her beneath him, she wanted to amend. "Undress, Sebastian. I want to feel you."

He kissed her quickly before kneeling on the bed. Like his other clothes, he made short work of his breeches, throwing them somewhere on the floor at the base of the bed. Her mouth dried, her eyes fixed on his manhood. She swallowed, nerves pooling in her stomach and something else, a warmth, a need, at the sight of him.

*Would they even fit together?*

As if reading her thoughts, he chuckled. "We'll fit, my darling." He joined her, kissing her deep and eliminating all the fear that had spiked through her at the sight of his sex.

Their tongues tangled, and heat pooled at her core. She undulated against him, her body afire, and seeking something she did not know but was certain she would soon understand.

He surged against where she burned, and pleasure

spiked through her blood. She gasped, clutching at his back as they kissed deep and long, as he prepared to make her his.

It was too much. She needed him now. Enough with the teasing. They had played that game. Now it was time for her to have him fully. To claim him for herself.

"From the moment I saw you, I wanted you," he admitted, a truth that had nothing to do with why he'd married Elizabeth, but certainly why he pursued her without caution. She was a beautiful woman, but what made her especially different from all the rest in his vicinity was her intellect, her kindness. A woman like her should have been scooped up and married years ago. She should have a hoard of children already.

The thought that tonight he could get her with a child, that she could grow round with his children, fortified his growing feelings for her. Emotions he could no longer deny. He had long ended merely liking her. He now realized, with trepidation, he was falling in love with her.

"Did ye really?" she gasped, arching her back and giving him the ability to kiss her neck, the tops of her breasts. Her skin was flushed, her hair long strands of red hair curled about the pillows. His heart stuttered.

She was so beautiful it hurt.

"What did you think of me?" he questioned her, kneading one breast, bringing it up to his mouth to kiss and tease.

She moaned, trembling beneath him. "I thought you extremely handsome, but English," she teased, watching him as he licked her nipple. Their eyes met, and he teasingly bit her flesh. Elizabeth pouted but purred, spiking her fingers in his hair to hold him against her.

He wasn't going anywhere. Tonight was just for them, and he would savor every minute he had her in his arms. A gentleman partook in one first night with his wife, and Sebastian wanted to make the most of it with Elizabeth.

Her skin smelled of jasmine, and he kissed his way down her stomach. Her breathing was ragged, and he intended to make it a lot more so before their night was over.

He pushed her legs apart, sliding his hand on the inside of her thigh, running his finger across her mons. She moaned his name, clutching him.

"Do you trust me?" he asked her, settling between her legs.

She nodded, watching him with wide, clear eyes. He kissed between her legs, smiling that it was the same shade as her head before kissing her fully. She gasped, tried to twist out of his hold, but he held her still, suckled on her sensitive nubbin. Within a moment, she stopped, waited to see what he did next. He teased her flesh, kissed and licked his way along her slit, loving her with his tongue.

He slid one finger into her hot core. So damn tight. The thought of her wrapping around him made him almost spend. The fear that he would hurt her spiked fear in his soul and he worked her into a fervor, needing her to be ready, to be wet, out of her mind with need before he claimed her virtue.

It did not take her long to relax, to lift her taut ass off the bed, and undulate against his mouth. He held her there, bringing her closer and closer to release, but never quite giving her what she wanted.

"Sebastian, please," she moaned when he flicked her nubbin with his tongue before giving her one last kiss. He came back over her, settled between her legs, and thrust into her core, taking her virginity.

She stilled beneath him, and he stopped moving, giving her time to adjust. He swallowed hard. The urge to take, to satisfy himself, bore down on him. "I'm sorry, my darling. It'll only hurt for a moment or two. I promise."

With the slightest nod, he felt her relax with each breath, and with the slowest, most excruciating thrusts he'd ever known, he started to make love to her while she adjusted to his size.

It didn't take long before she had grown used to him, was moving with her own rhythm. She lifted her legs, clamping them about his hips, and pleasure licked up his spine, hot and demanding.

"Harder, Sebastian," she gasped, her hands clutching his shoulders. He kissed her neck, pumped into her, taking her as she wanted. It was all the approval he needed to increase his pace, give them both what they craved.

He claimed her with abandon, reached down, lifted her bottom. She moaned, and he could feel her tighten about his cock. So good. So damn tight that he was sure he would see stars. Her core pulled at him, and then she broke.

"Sebastian," she cried, clutching at him as he continued to give her what she wanted. What they both needed. Her climax brought on his own, and he came, deep and long. Allowed himself his release to spill into the first woman ever in his life.

He cried out her name, kissing her as his orgasm licked up his spine and didn't seem to abate.

Sebastian breathed deep, trying to calm his racing heart. Damn, he'd never come so hard, gained such pleasure before in the bed of a woman. But this was not any woman. This was his wife.

He lay beside her, pulling her into the crook of his arm

before kissing her fiery-red hair. "Are you well? I hope I did not hurt you too much."

She rolled against him, running her hand idly over his chest. "No, ye dinna hurt me at all." She met his gaze, touching her palm to his cheek. "I cannot believe we're married in the truest sense now." She kissed his chest, her lips skimming his flesh and tickling him somewhat.

"You do not regret your choice?" he asked her, needing to reassure himself he was who she wanted. An absurd reaction considering what they had just done, but he could not help himself. Their union had been so fast, not that he regretted a second of it, but he hoped that she would not. Not ever, if he could help it.

"No, of course not," she replied. "I couldn't be happier to be your wife."

"I am glad," he replied, leaning down to kiss her sweet lips that he doubted he would ever tire of. "Because I'm so happy that I'm your husband." The words truer than he ever thought possible, especially since he'd courted her for one reason and one reason only; what she brought to the marriage.

Not anymore. His ancestral childhood home he cared little for, he realized. So long as the woman in his arms was his, he was home wherever she was, and if that so happened to be at Halligale, then all the better.

# CHAPTER 14

Three days later, after telling her friends in Edinburgh her great news, they were on their way south and toward Moy Castle, her childhood home. Julia and Georgina were beyond thrilled by her marriage, if not somewhat put out about her eloping. But once Elizabeth had promised them both she would renew her vows after the Season, they were both willing to let the slight go.

They had several hours to go, and having just broken their fast at an inn several miles back, the carriage ride ahead did not seem as long and arduous as it normally would. Not with the handsome gentleman sitting across from her in the vehicle. She watched him read the newspaper, a small frown between his brow, and couldn't quite believe she was married. That this year it had been her turn to find a husband.

As if he sensed her regard, his eyes flicked over the top of the paper and met hers. The heat banked in his deep-blue orbs made her stomach clench in desire. They had barely left each other's sides these past days, and the bedroom even less.

At the time, Elizabeth had thought there may be something wrong with her that she wanted him as much as she did. That every time he threw her a lazy smile, or knowing look, a wink or grin, she was powerless to deny his pull.

They had made love in numerous places in Georgina's home while she was packing her things to leave, some of them long, delectable hours of lovemaking, while others were quick, sinful tidbits that sated her until they came together at night. Some of the things Sebastian had done to her made her wiggle on her chair. She had been so green, so unaware of what could be between a man and a woman.

She was no longer so innocent.

He set his paper down, a lazy smile across his mouth. A mouth that was as wicked as his tongue. "What are you thinking, my Lizzie?"

He had started to call her that. *My Lizzie.* Every time she heard the name, it made her heart flutter and gave her hope that someday there would be an unbreakable love between them. It had not escaped her notice that neither of them spoke of the emotion or the lack of such a declaration. Elizabeth knew in her heart she was well on the way to loving the rogue sitting across from her and giving her one of his wicked come-hither looks that she could never ignore.

But did he love her? She knew he enjoyed her company, had chased her down over the past weeks until she was his wife, so he must like her very much, but was he falling in love with her? That she could not say, but she hoped and dreamed he would and declare his heart soon. She did not want to be the only one in the marriage, falling in love.

"Nothing of importance, merely admiring my handsome husband."

He chuckled a deep, husky sound that promised all sorts of delicious pleasures. He leaned back in his seat, studying her in turn. "The green velvet you have on today makes your eyes look fiercely bright and absolutely stunning."

Warm appreciation thrummed through her at his words. How had she come to be so lucky to have secured his hand? She glanced down at her gown, running her hand along the gold thread at her bodice. "I had it made especially for the Season this year. I'm glad you like it."

"Come here," he said, his eyes darkening with hunger.

Elizabeth moved to sit beside him. The carriage lurched, and she glanced out the window, noting there was still some time to go. Nothing but fields and forest darkened the view.

A light kiss on her neck startled her a moment before she tipped her head to the side and allowed him to continue his seduction.

"Hell, you smell sweet." He reached for her, tilting her to face him. Their gazes collided, and she knew he wanted her. His eyes burned with need and determination.

Heat pooled at her core, and she went to him, kissing him with all the passion she felt. His hands wrenched her onto his lap, jerking her dress to pool at her waist. Cool air kissed her stockinged legs as her body craved his touch.

He wasn't gentle. He ripped open the front falls off his breeches, his hard manhood spilling against her mons. Elizabeth pressed against him, trying to sate the need that coursed through her body. She wanted him, had watched him for hours, and hoped they may come together in the carriage before they reached her childhood home.

It was naughty, wicked fun to be with Sebastian in such a way. They were husband and wife. There was no real harm in them behaving so, even if it was utterly roguish.

He kissed her hard and long, his tongue tangling with hers. He clasped her hips, his fingers biting into the velvet and her skin beneath. Elizabeth wrapped her arms about his neck, using her knees to place him at her core, before lowering onto his erection.

They both moaned as he settled inside her, fulfilling her every need. Their lovemaking was frantic and fast, both of them needing to sate themselves of the other. He helped her take her pleasure, rocking onto him, pushing her closer to release. He whispered delicious, naughty things in her ear, his whispered breath sending a shiver of desire down her spine.

"Come for me, my darling. Take your pleasure," he gasped, so hard, so large that she thought she may die of the delight of it all.

She kissed him, took his lips, and claimed him as the first tremors of her release shuddered from her core to spike throughout her person. So good that she wondered how she had lived without such a thing for so many years. If it was better known that a woman could find such pleasure with a man, there would certainly be more weddings or love affairs, Elizabeth was certain.

They stayed locked together, their breathing ragged. Elizabeth wondered after the fact what had possessed her, what had made the truth whisper from her lips, but before she could rip the words back from her mouth, she uttered the three weighty words that changed so many people's lives. Their lives forever.

"I love you, Sebastian."

AN AWKWARD SILENCE fell between them. Of all the things he'd expected to fall from Lizzie's lips, it had not been the word love. Even so, the words no longer terrified him as they once would have. In fact, he'd had the opposite reaction, had felt nothing but hope and adoration for the woman in his arms. He'd even tried to form his own lips and tongue around the words himself, but they would not form. They became tangled, muddled, and would not declare themselves to her.

Instead, he opted to kiss her, show her with his body what she meant to him. What her honestly made him feel.

What she made him feel.

Love.

# CHAPTER 15

A few hours later, the carriage rocked to a halt before a dark, stone building that looked like a magnificent fortress. Sebastian jumped down, helping Elizabeth alight, his eyes fixed on her childhood home.

A feminine voice called out Elizabeth's name, and he turned to see the late Duke of Law's daughter, Lady Clara, pull Lizzie into a warm embrace, kissing her cheek. Lizzie seemed pleased to see Lady Clara and held her in turn.

Lady Clara's attention turned toward Sebastian and cooled, became guarded. He steeled himself for the reception he would receive here. Did they suspect his motives? Had rumors of their attachment made it to Moy?

"Lord Hastings, whatever are you doing traveling with Lady Elizabeth?"

Lizzie smiled at her friend, letting go of her ladyship's hand to come back to him, clasping his. "Lady Clara, may I present my husband, Lord Hastings."

He'd never seen Lady Clara without words, but here it was, the first time for everything he supposed. The shock and wariness that entered her eyes did not bode well for their announcement.

"Husband? You're married!"

"Who is married?"

Sebastian bowed as Mr. Stephen Grant came out to join his wife, wrapping his arm about her waist. "Elizabeth is married, Stephen. Did you know?"

He frowned, looking between Lizzie and Sebastian. "No, I did not." He turned that frown on to Elizabeth. "Does your brother know?"

"No," Lizzie said, her voice unfazed, but he could feel the tension in her stance, feel the slight shiver that raked over her skin. He gave her a reassuring squeeze, and she threw him a wobbly smile. "I'm here to tell him."

Lady Clara seemed to shake herself out of her shock and came and gave Elizabeth another hug, kissing him, too, on the cheek. "Congratulations to you both. This is wonderful news."

Lizzie relaxed somewhat at her ladyship's words, but the felicitations did not ring true to Sebastian. "Is Brice home?"

"He's in his office," Mr. Grant said, throwing Elizabeth a small smile.

"Thank ye." She turned to him, taking his hands. "I think I should speak to Brice on my own. It'll be a shock to him to hear this news, and I dinna wish to upset ye by his initial reaction."

There was no way he was allowing Elizabeth to face her brother without him. If the laird jumped to the conclusion that the marriage was for the initial reason it was, he needed to be there to defend himself.

*You cannot defend the indefensible.*

Sebastian ignored the warning voice in his head. As much as he was relieved to know Halligale was back in his hands, that his children would grow up and inherit the estate, the union between him and Lizzie was so much more than the ancient pile of bricks.

After her declaration of love, the words had been spiraling about in his mind, taunting him to admit what he felt for the woman staring up at him with nothing but affection in her beautiful green eyes.

"No, I shall come with you. Your brother needs to hear from both of us, a united front, husband and wife."

With the slightest of nods, she pulled him forward into the home. The estate rivaled even his in Notting-hamshire. The ancient, medieval wooden beams, the staircase, and entrance to the great hall were enormous. Yet, the house did not feel cold or unwelcoming. Large tapestries and family portraits hung on most walls, roaring fires burned in the grates, and he could hear laughter and a woman's voice somewhere else in the home.

"Brice should be through here," he heard Lizzie tell him as he followed.

Sebastian had never met the Laird Mackintosh, had heard his brother mention him with nothing but loathing and anger after he'd lost Halligale in the card game. The man who met his eyes was not what he expected.

He'd assumed the laird to be similar to him in stature and height. He was wrong. The laird was a behemoth of a man, tall and muscular, a Scottish warrior of years past. Sebastian swallowed, pushing down the fear that the man before him could strike him down with his bare hands, and without much effort.

"Brice." Lizzie walked quickly over to her brother and into the man's open arms. He kissed her crown, holding her a moment before he raised his head and spied him standing in the doorway. He hated to think what the Scot thought of him. Sebastian felt as though he had not measured up to his standard from his cool consideration.

He spoke, his voice deep and commanding. A voice that, when spoken, others listened to. "Who is your guest, Elizabeth?"

She came back over to him, taking his hand and pulling him into the room. Sebastian made certain he put some of the desk between the two of them.

"Brice, I would like to introduce you to my husband, Sebastian Denholm, Earl—"

"Hastings," her brother finished for her, his eyes pinning Sebastian with ire. "Husband?!"

Sebastian did not want to flinch or show any sort of fear before the laird, but his yelling of the word *husband* had been unexpected and did catch him off guard. He pulled Lizzie beside him, holding her close. "That is right, my lord. We were married several days ago in Dalmahoy."

The laird's glower did not bode well, not for either of them. "Ye are the brother to the late Earl Hastings?" he queried, his brogue a lot heavier than his sister's. Sebastian also did not miss the thread of wariness in his tone.

"Yes. Emmett Denholm was my elder brother."

"And ye are in Scotland for the Season, hell-bent on catching my bonny sister's hand in marriage by the looks of it. Why are ye not in England like all the other Englishmen marrying English ladies?"

He shrugged, smiling, knowing that from the tone of Lizzie's brother, he did not like Sebastian at all, or the fact he'd made her his wife. "Is not your wife English, my lord?" he put in, not allowing the continual slights to pass unde-fended. He would only put up with so much before words had to be said.

The laird's eyes narrowed, and Sebastian wondered how far he could taunt the Scot before he had a solid crack across his jaw. He held no regard for the fiend, not after the laird had stolen Halligale from under his brother's nose when he wasn't in the position to gamble and think straight in the first place. Practically robbing his family of their inheritance, their land. If the laird thought he would bow down to his supposed superiority, he was delusional.

"And ye married my sister without my consent, without marriage contracts being signed. Where is the paperwork, Elizabeth?" the laird said, not sparing Elizabeth a whisp of a look, his eyes pinning Sebastian to the spot.

Sebastian choked on his words, having not expected the Scotsman to be so cold. He met Lizzie's eyes and found them wide with alarm. "Brice, I'm not sure I appreciate yer tone. Lord Hastings is my husband. I'm Lady Hastings now. Do not be so cutting and rude."

The laird looked at him, nonplussed, seemingly ignoring his sister's words. "And I'm not sure if I appreciate ye marrying a rogue we dinna know much about, other than the fact he's the brother to a man I trusted less than the Jacobite army trusted King Charles II."

"Brice," Elizabeth gasped, glaring up at her brother. She had mettle, his wife. Few would look up at such a giant of a man and chastise him. "I shall tell Sophie what a beast you're being, and then you may realize your mistake."

The laird crossed his arms over his chest. "Ye will do no such thing. Ye know Sophie is unwell and needs rest. She's not to be troubled with this dilemma you've tangled yourself into. I shall deal with this false marriage and extradite ye from it."

"You will not." Lizzie took a step forward, using the desk to lean on and press her point. "The marriage is consummated. There were witnesses and a reverend. There is nothing ye can do to change the course of my life.

I married the man I love, and I shall remain so no matter the reason ye dislike him so much."

"Mayhap ye would like to know, sister, where my dislike comes from." the laird said, a muscle working in his jaw.

Dread coiled in Sebastian's stomach. This was the moment he had been dreading. If Elizabeth found out the truth as it once had stood, she would never forgive him. He would lose her.

"Come, Elizabeth," he said, clasping her hand and trying to drag her from the room. "We shall return to England. Maybe in time, Laird Mackintosh will cool his ire and think more clearly and fairly regarding our union."

"Unlikely," the laird said, glaring at him. The laird turned to his sister. "Come, Elizabeth, we need to speak, and alone. Ye deserve to know the truth."

"Pardon," she said, clearly confused. "What on earth has ye like this, Brice? I dinna understand."

The laird, instead of coming over to Sebastian, taking him by his shoulders and hoisting him back out into the hall, he walked about his desk, sitting as if he had not a care in the world. "Sit, ye will need to be off ye feet when ye hear what I have to say."

Lizzie threw him a cautious look, and Sebastian knew she was fearful of what her brother knew, and she did not. What Sebastian had possibly kept from her that would have changed her opinion of him. Kept her from marrying him.

The thought he could lose her in a matter of minutes sent panic to coil through his gut, and he fought not to sweat. He sat beside Lizzie, taking her hand in the hopes to calm her when she learned of his brother and her inheritance.

The laird sighed, rubbing a hand across his jaw. "I knew the late Lord Hastings. In fact, when he was here the

Season before last, I ran into him in Edinburgh while up there on business. A game of cards was played, Lord Hastings was a terrible gambler and lost often, and yet, it dinna stop him from being a fool and thinking that was not the case."

Lizzie squeezed his hand, throwing him a concerned glance. "I'm sorry your brother was troubled, Sebastian."

He raised her hand, kissing it. "It has nothing to do with us, my dear. Do not concern yourself with my sibling."

"Even so, I'm sorry."

His heart thumped hard in his chest that she was worried for him. That she cared. Sebastian met the laird's hard gaze and prepared himself for the axe to fall across his neck.

"The late Lord Hastings, low on funds, opted to gamble his Scottish family estate. A house that his mother had inherited not long after her marriage. The estate that I gifted ye, Elizabeth."

Sebastian took a moment to steel himself before he could bring himself to meet Elizabeth's startled eyes. That she had taken but moments to understand what her brother was saying said a lot about her intelligence. Her eyes filled with tears and his heart crumbled in his chest. He reached for her, but she wrenched away, standing and moving over toward the desk.

"You married me to gain back ye family estate?" She paused a moment, swallowing hard. "Is that what ye did, Sebastian?"

He shook his head, standing. "No, I did not."

The laird growled, literally growled. "Dinna make a fool of my sister a second time, Lord Hastings. Own the truth and shame the devil, boy."

"I am not a boy, and you'll be best to remember that,"

Sebastian roared, having about enough of being treated like the worst person on the planet. "At first, I may have seen the opportunity, Lizzie, but it has since become so much more than an estate. I love you as much as you love me. I no longer care about Halligale."

"You're a liar. Ye courted me, pursued me and no one else, and the stupid, blind fool that I was imagined it to be because ye truly wanted me. Wanted no one else but me, but all ye wanted was what I bought to the marriage."

Sebastian held up his hands, hoping to make her understand. "I admit, I came to Scotland to try to gain Halligale back in some way. When I found out that you had been given the estate, my mind, of course, came to the conclusion that a union with you would be the easiest course. I could have simply asked to purchase it back, Lizzie, but I did not. Not because I couldn't afford the estate, but because once I got to know you, I found you were a gift that I had not thought to receive. I fell in love with you and your sweet nature. I no longer care for the estate. I want you."

"Really," she said, her tone one of disbelief. "Then, when I sign the house back over to my brother, removing ye from gaining the estate, ye will still profess your love. Still wish to remain married to me."

"Of course," he said, knowing that such a transaction would be impossible. She was his wife now. What was hers was his by law. "Forget what we bring to the marriage, and please remember what we're like together. How much you love me. How much I love you."

# CHAPTER 16

How much she loved him? Elizabeth almost scoffed at the absurd notion. She had been played the fool, and she had been the only one who had not known it. How many other people attending the Scottish Season knew Lord Hasting was there with an ulterior motive? To marry her and gain his ancestral home back.

*What a slimly, English bastard.*

"How dare ye? I was the laughingstock of London before, and now ye have made me so a second time. I shall never live down the shame of marrying a man who tricked me into the union simply to gain his old estate back. It will not be you, an earl, who'll suffer the snide remarks and snickering giggles as ye walk past. Oh no, they will be reserved solely for me."

"No one will say such things, Lizzie. I shall not allow it, and it is not true."

"That is absolute horse dung, Sebastian." She paced away from him, a fury running hot through her blood. "That you say ye no longer care what happens to the estate is also a lie. You care, quite a lot, and it was why ye were so keen on an elopement so soon into our courtship. Ye did not want me to form any affections with anyone else. Ye have taken from me the ability to make a match with solid foundations. Your love is a pack of cards similar to your brother's, which were destined to crumble."

He ran a hand through his hair, and she could see the frustration thrumming through his body. "Yes, I did court you originally to regain the house, but it was days only before that all changed. I want you, Lizzie. And no matter what your brother says," he said, pointing to Brice, "what I feel for you is stronger than anything I've ever experienced before. I have never told a woman that I love her. And I do love you so much. I do not want to lose you."

"And yet ye will for you are the worst of what lives beyond the Scottish border. A selfish, self-serving Englishman who dinna care for anything or anyone except himself."

Her brother grunted his approval to his sister's words.

"You stay out of this argument. This is not your battle." Sebastian pointed at the laird, glaring at the bastard.

The laird stood, his chair scraping on the wooden floor. "Ye best stop talking now, Lord Hastings."

Sebastian heard the warning in his tone, but he refused to listen, to concede. He needed Lizzie to believe him. To love him and be with him as she'd promised she would. He could not lose her now. Not for this reason, not when that reason no longer mattered to him.

"Make me," he said, prepared to defend himself, defend his future with Lizzie.

"Enough!" Elizabeth's voice cut between them, pulling Sebastian out of his impending thrashing with the Laird

Mackintosh. "Brice, please give me a moment with Sebastian."

Her brother glared at him one last moment before he stormed from the room, the door slamming hard behind him.

Sebastian did not move, scared that if he did, she would bolt, and his chance of explaining, of getting her to understand, would be over. "Lizzie, please try to see the situation from my side. I did not mean to hurt you."

"No, I suppose you did not. You did not expect me to find out. A stupid assumption considering who my brother is and his association with yours. What made you think that you would not be called out for your shady actions?"

Before he had a chance to answer, she waved his words aside. "You never thought to not get away with it, did you? You knew my brother would make the connection, see your reasons for marrying me, and call you out on it. But if I was already married to you, the marriage consummated, well, there would be naught my brother or anyone could do to undo our union."

When put like that, Sebastian could see he looked like a right bastard. He had pushed her quicker than he ought, needed their marriage watertight before he met her brother. What she said was true, and he could not defend himself against the charge.

Even if he now loved her, wanted her above anything else in the world, his words would fall unheard by her, for he'd ruined what chance they had by being dishonest.

"For what it is worth, I do love you, Lizzie. I may not have set out with honorable intentions, but for me, I have long thought of no other than you. I want our marriage to be a happy one. Please forgive me."

She shook her head, anger all but thrumming through her. "No, I cannot. Ye are not to be trusted. You're a liar, a thief dressed in fine, superfine coats and polished hessian boots. I want nothing to do with ye." She strode over to the desk, scribbling on a piece of parchment before folding it and flicking it to the edge of the desk.

"What is this?" he asked, picking it up.

"Give the note to Mrs. Gardener at Halligale. She knows my signature and will believe that you're my husband. You wanted the estate back, well, now ye have it. I hope ye enjoy your pile of bricks."

"Lizzie, the home was my mother's. The one place that all my happy memories were made. Please do not do this."

"Get out," she said, her voice hard and brooking no argument. "We shall remain married because I cannae change that fact, but know, from this day forward, we're no longer husband and wife. I dinna want anything to do with ye."

Sebastian debated going around the desk and taking her in his arms, holding her and trying to push his reasoning. But her eyes burned with hurt and anger, and he would not force himself on her. He would try again. Another day he would return and attempt to win back her affections.

"I'm sorry," he said, striding from the room and heading straight out the front door. The carriage was unloaded, but he did not miss the fact that his trunks were still tied to the back of the equipage. The laird stood to the side, giving the driver orders, his arms crossed over his sizable chest.

"Ye are to return to England. If I hear of ye going to Halligale, I shall have ye disposed of where no one will hear from ye again. Dinna think just because ye are my sister's husband that I'll forgive ye for tricking her into marriage so to gain her estate. Ye are never to set foot here again, or anywhere near Halligale."

"I own the estate beside Lizzie's, and I shall return there if I wish. Not you or anyone will tell me what I can and cannot do."

The laird's mouth curled up into a snarl. "Obviously, you do whatever ye want and dinna care for the consequences."

Sebastian turned and climbed up into the carriage. He ignored the laird who stood in front of the home as if to keep him at bay. He scanned the windows, wishing to see Lizzie, even if for one last time. He did not know when he would see her, and the thought of never seeing her again made him want to cast up his accounts.

No, this was not the end, not their friendship or marriage. She loved him as much as he loved her. What did it matter that he happened to fall in love with the woman who had inherited his ancestral home?

*You did not tell her the truth, and that is the problem.*

He closed his eyes a moment as the carriage lurched forward. It did not matter, and yet that was all that mattered, really. He had not been honest, and in by doing so, by setting out to first deceive, he had ruined any chance for them.

He glanced back at the house, despair clasping his chest when he found the windows empty of her—his Lizzie.

# CHAPTER 17

E lizabeth stayed at Moy Castle for the night before heading to the estate her brother had gifted her. A home she had come to love but now was no longer so sure she wished to keep. She could sell it, she supposed. Her brother had mentioned the option if she could not bear to keep it.

The carriage rolled to a stop before Halligale, a rambling and whimsical home she'd come to love. She jumped down without waiting for assistance and looked up at the estate. Her mind, try as she might, could not help but imagine Sebastian here as a child. Running about the large home, the manicured gardens, being chased by his brother, nanny, or mother.

She had not been listening to him as much as she should have, she supposed. As a woman who came from a loving family—her brother, at least—she could understand Sebastian wishing to gain his estate back. The one place he had the happiest memories of childhood.

Sighing, she headed inside. The housekeeper greeted her in the foyer. Elizabeth ordered a bath and the fire to be lit in her room, exhaustion nipping at her heels. After her travels these past days, and the emotional toll that accompanied her, all she wished for was a relaxing bath and sleep.

To be alone and sort out her life, what she would do, how she could move forward with the truth she now had to live with.

Her room was just as she remembered it, warm and welcoming, the light drapes and bedding giving the space a feminine feel and lighting up the dark-timbered woods. She sat on the edge of the bed, watched as the maid fussed about with her trunks and gowns, a scullery maid working hard to light a fire in the grate.

"Would ye care for ye dinner to be served, Lady Elizabeth?"

She nodded, ignoring the fact they were still calling her by her unmarried name. Of course, they would. They did not know that she had been married, and was now the wife of Earl Hastings. A countess.

"I will have it in here in an hour. Thank ye," she said, not wanting to use the dining room.

Two footmen carried up a copper bath and set it before the hearth before a whole line of servants brought up bucket after bucket of water. Her bath was soothing, relieved her aching bones, and relaxed her for the first time in two days.

As she climbed into bed later that night, she couldn't help but wonder where Sebastian was. Had he returned to London? Was he at his new estate next door, or was he in Edinburgh? A small part of her hoped he was at Bragdon Manor so she may see him, have him explain to her yet again what his reasoning was to break her heart. Anything to make her understand, to believe that she had not been duped into marriage all for the sake of a house.

. . .

DAYS PASSED, and she had been back at Halligale for almost a week when Julia descended from Edinburgh to visit her. Elizabeth poured them tea in the downstairs drawing room. She had not written to her friends telling them of her pain, her situation as it stood with Sebastian. So why was Julia here? She was curious to find out.

Julia held her tea in her hands, her attention traveling over Elizabeth and not missing one detail. Thankfully her friend was polite enough not to mention the dark shadows beneath her eyes or that she had lost weight and none of her gowns fit her properly anymore.

"Georgina and I had a visit from Lord Hastings several days ago," she said matter-of-fact. "He suggested that we travel down to Moy Castle and see you. Georgina could not get away from Edinburgh, but I came, only to find that you had decamped from Moy and were back at Halligale. I'm glad to find you at home here."

Her friend's guarded words put her on edge. She sipped her tea, studying Julia. Whatever had her friend heard? That Sebastian had gone and seen them, well, she wasn't sure what she thought of that. If he thought involving her friends, getting them to side with him would help his cause, he was delusional.

"Sebastian visited ye. I suppose ye were surprised to see him and without me in attendance."

"We were both surprised, and before you ask, no, he did not say why we should come here and see ye, only that he was concerned and thought ye may need a friend."

Elizabeth bit the inside of her mouth, fighting off a flow of tears that up until right now she'd been able to blink away. She would not cry. She would not allow anyone to make her succumb to tears again. After her embarrassment in London—Lucky Lizzie—she had sworn never to cry over trivial things.

*This is hardly insignificant, Elizabeth.*

She stared down at her hands, at the wedding ring that now circled one finger like a beacon of her failure. "Lord Hastings married me because this house that we now sit in was his childhood home. His brother lost it in a game of cards to my brother two years ago, or thereabouts. I was his means of getting it back."

Julia's mouth gaped, and for several moments she did not speak at all. Elizabeth shoved away from the embarrassment that wanted to swamp her. This was not her fault. This was Sebastian's fault. He was the bastard who had set out with this plan. She had been merely the innocent party in the affair.

"Lord Hastings did what?" Julia's teacup rattled on its plate, and she set it down with a clank. "He told ye this?"

Elizabeth nodded. "He did, yes. When we traveled to Moy, my brother made the connection and saw through his marriage to me. Sebastian could not deny it, tried to make me see the reasoning as to why he did what he did. I still cannot believe it myself." Elizabeth stood, walking over to the window and looking out over the estate. The grounds that Sebastian thought more of than she did. "He grew up here with his mother, who was Scottish. A lot of happy memories, so it would seem. An ancestral home he was loath to lose and therefore thought to trick me into marriage as an easier way in which to get it back."

"But surely," Julia said beseechingly. "He loves ye. I'm certain of it. Is there a chance that he fell in love with ye during his courting of ye as well? And so, his fixation on the estate shifted to ye, and the home became secondary. I simply cannot believe any man could treat a woman with so little respect. I cannot believe it of him. It is too awful."

Elizabeth shrugged, unable to turn and face her friend. "That is what he says. He says that he fell in love with me while working toward his original plan, but I cannot suppose that." Or perhaps she did, but she could not forgive him for his treachery. That all those sweet words, the long considerations across a ballroom floor, the waltzes they had shared had all been a ploy, a game for him to see how hard it would be for her to fall at his feet.

Heat rushed her cheeks. She had been uncommonly easy to form an attachment, had barely given anyone else a chance after Lord Hastings had started to follow her skirts about town. What a mindless fool she had been. What a cad he had been in turn.

"He looked wretched when he came to see us, Elizabeth, as if he had hardly slept."

"Good," she spat, harsher than she ought. Julia did not deserve her wrath, her disappointment in Sebastian. "I'm sorry. Please know I'm not angry at ye."

Julia came and joined her at the window. "Know that I'm on your side, and I shall defend and support ye to the bitter end if that is what you wish of me, but before you make any hasty decisions, ye must think on this. There is the possibility that Lord Hastings may have started out with underhanded intentions, but that they were soon scuttled when yer charm and warmth, and it caught him unawares. He loves ye, does he not?" Julia asked.

Elizabeth nodded once. "So he declares."

Julia clasped her hands, shaking them a little to gain her attention. "Ye are loveable, Elizabeth. No matter what nickname London termed you. Lord Hastings ignored all that, he came to know ye, the real ye, and he fell in love with that woman. If he did not care, he would not have come back to Edinburgh to your friends and beg them to go to Moy. He would have turned about, traveled to

London, and set his lawyers for Scotland to gain back this estate."

"There is still time. He may have already done such a thing for all that I know."

"He was still in Edinburgh when I left."

Elizabeth did not know what to think. Over the past days, her emotions had experienced a range of highs and lows. Of hope and despair. It was no surprise he had not chased her down to Halligale after she had told him she did not wish to see him again. But she knew she needed to take Julia's words into consideration. People do change. Was it possible that Sebastian had done so?

"When people find out that I inherited Halligale and that the previous family who owned it is none other than my new husband, there will be talk. I'll be ridiculed at every party I attend, pitied because people will think Sebastian married me for his lost estate."

"They may say such things," Julia agreed. "But after years of a happy marriage, of children and love, Elizabeth, what can they say after that?" Julia smiled. "They will say they were wrong, and ye can make them eat their words. Ye can live a happy marriage and not care what their opinion is."

For the first time in what felt like weeks, she smiled. Julia was so very smart and insightful. When one was melancholy and unable to see straight through their pain, she was always the one friend who was honest and offered a different point of view.

Not that Elizabeth had not been hoping, wondering the same thing, but it was nice to hear it from someone else all the same.

She would face talk, snickers, and giggles as she walked by, reactions she had come to loathe after her embarrassing Season, but she could survive it. With Sebastian by her side, with his support and love, she could sustain anything.

"I need time to think all of this through, to decide what I wish to do." Elizabeth pulled Julia into a quick embrace. "Thank ye for coming down here to see me. To tell me what ye have. You are the best of friends."

"I want ye to be happy, Elizabeth, and something tells me that yer heart too was touched with Lord Hastings. Without him, I fear you will never be content. Think about everything I said, decide your path. As I declared earlier, Georgina and I will be there for ye, no matter your choice."

"Thank ye," she said, more grateful than Julia would ever know for her insight. "I know that ye do."


SEBASTIAN COULD NOT STAY in Edinburgh long. The Season held no appeal for him or the city now that Elizabeth was not within its walls. He traveled down to Bragdon Manor, took daily walks, and thought over how he could win her back.

So far, he'd failed at the task. Any way he looked at his predicament, a solution, nothing proved he loved her more than the estate.

The way he set out to win Elizabeth had been wrong, ungentlemanly, and cruel. Of course, he'd never meant for her to find out. That idea more than imperative after he realized he was falling in love with her.

A foolish ideal that would never happen. Not with her brother knowing the truth and seeing his motives.

Now that she did know his motives, he would forever be frowned upon in her family if he ever came within a foot of them again. After the laird's dismissal of him, Elizabeth's too, he doubted that would ever occur.

"Damn it all to hell." He swiped a long stick he held in his hand over the tall grass he was walking through on the boundary of his estate and Elizabeth's. He'd found out by a footman that she was in residence there, alone. Her friend Lady Julia had visited last week but had returned to town after staying but a few days.

He stopped, staring over toward his childhood home, watching as the afternoon sun made the west-facing windows reflect the golden rays. Several chimneys bore smoke, a homely, welcoming place he had to admit he no longer cared too much about.

What he cared about was the woman who sat within its walls. What was she thinking? Had she calmed down somewhat after the explosive truth had ruined what had been between them? He did not know, and right at this moment, he was too fearful of finding out. The fear of her reaction of her pushing him away a second time made him want to cast up his accounts. How on earth could he make her see he loved her? Truly loved her and not her inheritance.

A twig cracked somewhere to his right, and he turned to see the startled face of Elizabeth, her bonnet hanging idly in her hand by a blue ribbon. Her light-blue afternoon gown made his heart stutter in his chest.

Hell, he'd missed her. Her beauty, hair hanging loose over her shoulders, held off her face by a few pins, her green eyes wide with shock at seeing him again. He stared at her for a long moment, captivated by her charm. "Lizzie," he said at length, not moving for fear she'd bolt.

"You're at Bragdon Manor?" she asked, glancing quickly toward his estate.

"I am, but not for long. I'm having my things packed and readied for transport to England. I'm selling the property and going back to Nottinghamshire." Lizzie did not deserve to have him living near her in Scotland, certainly if she did not wish him to be near her again. He would honor her wish, give her what she wanted and live in the hope that one day she would forgive him and return to his arms.

"Oh." Was all she said, nodding slightly. "I suppose since the law states what is mine is yours, you have your ancestral home back and do not need two estates side by side."

"That is not why I'm selling," he corrected her, hating that she believed what was no longer true. Had not been the truth for him for several weeks. "I do not want Halligale either. You can do whatever you want with the estate. I shall not stand in your way."

"Really." The word was curt and held an edge of suspicion to it. As if she did not believe a word he said.

The one way he could prove he did not care about the estate was to leave, go back to England, and continue his married life alone. "What I say is the truth, Lizzie. I no longer want Halligale, for I've come to understand that it has to hold those you love within it for a house to be home." He took a cautious step toward her, and yet she stepped back, out of his reach. "I could take the estate, live there, but I would not be as happy as I was as a child, for you would not be there with me. In gaining the estate, I would lose you, and nothing is worth that."

She studied him a moment, but he could see she was unsure of his words. Distrusted him. Would he ever earn her trust again, relish in her love and warmth once more? Hell, he hoped he did.

"I know you do not believe me, and that is why I'm going. I cannot change our situation. We're married, and there is no undoing that." He shrugged. "This is the only way in which to think to prove myself to you. To leave, but know," he said, trying to take her hands and failing a second time, "I do love you, Lizzie. Somewhere in my grand plan of gaining back what was mine, I captured something so much more precious."

She swallowed, her eyes glassy and bright. "And what was that, Lord Hastings?"

He flinched at the use of his title, but what did he expect? He'd lost the right for her to call him Sebastian. Husband. Lover.

"Your heart." This time, Sebastian clasped her upper arms and kissed her quickly on the cheek before turning and striding away. This was for the best. He could not stay. To do so may push her further away. If he had any chance of winning her back, England was where he had to decamp. Wait and hope she would one day arrive on his front step.

Ready to claim what will always be hers.

His love.

# CHAPTER 18

Three months passed and what Sebastian had told her the day out on the heather-strewn land, that he was leaving, still held true. He had not come back to Scotland in all that time, had remained at his estate in Nottinghamshire. What town gossip she did receive from family and friends in England stated, in any case.

From all accounts, the once rakehell, most sought-after bachelor in London had eschewed the city's delights and secluded himself away at his country estate. She had not believed he would sell the estate next door, but within weeks the home was sold, and the new owners were already living in and enjoying their Scottish abode.

When the home had sold, and news reached her that Sebastian was safely back in England, and the distance gnawed at her like a cancerous tumor.

As the weeks turned into months, his absence weighed her down, and for the past few weeks, she had started to look at her situation a lot more clearly. See past her initial anger and disappointment and understand why he'd done what he had.

He may not have banked on falling in love with her, but he did, and she now believed that more than anything else. She had visited Moy several weeks into his departure and found out Sebastian had signed over any claim to Halligale. If she wished to, she could sell the estate and be done with the connection, but no matter how mad he had made her, she could not do that to him.

The estate had been his childhood home. The very walls, rooms and gardens she had come to love, she adored even more because of the boy who grew up within its stone and mortar.

She could not sell it just to prove that he loved her.

His leaving, giving up of the home, the despair she had read in his eyes the day out on the land when their paths crossed, told her his affections toward her were true.

He loved her. Had fallen in love with her despite his initial plan, and if it were the estate she had inherited that had brought about that love, then she would cherish the house forever.

The carriage turned into the gates of Wellsworth Abbey, and Elizabeth moved to look out the window at the large Georgian mansion that was Sebastian's English estate.

It was more formal than the wild, rugged one his mother had owned, and yet it was just as beautiful. Nerves tumbled in her stomach at the thought of seeing him again after so many months. Would he admit her? Did he still love her?

Elizabeth knew to the core of her being she loved him. Had missed him, no matter how much she may have tried not to at the beginning of their separation.

Their estrangement, no matter how painful, was required, however. She needed time to think, time to heal, and move past her hurt. To forgive him.

The carriage rocked to a halt, and a footman bounded up to the vehicle, opening the door. Elizabeth stepped down, stretching out the soreness in her bones that miles of travel had wrought on her body.

A gentleman rounded the corner of the house, his attention on the paperwork in his hands, his head down, and not looking where he was going.

Warmth ran through her like whisky at the sight of Sebastian. He was dressed in tan breeches and black hessian boots that were covered with dust. A shirt and waistcoat, no jacket, and the sleeves of his shirt were rolled up to his elbows. Had he been out and about the estate, looking in on his tenant farms, the fields?

As if sensing company, he glanced up and skidded to a stop, his eyes darting from her to the carriage and the abundant of traveling trunks stacked on the back of the vehicle.

"Hello, husband. Are ye not going to greet me?" she asked him, amused somewhat by his shock.

"Lizzie?" Her name came out with an exhaled breath, and her heart pinched at the disbelief that ran through his tone.

He had not thought she would come. Perhaps he never thought to see her again. Silly man. When women were angry, and especially Scottish women, one must understand that time is required to forgive and move forward in life.

She stepped toward him, smiling. "Sebastian. Ye look well," she said, aware that they were being watched by an abundance of staff.

"I am as good as I can be." He frowned, taking in her wrinkled gown, and Elizabeth knew she had several strands of hair loose about her face.

"You must be tired." He clasped her hand, kissing it.

Without letting her go, he turned for the door, barking out orders for her trunks to be unpacked in the countess's rooms beside his own.

"Come, we can speak in my library."

Elizabeth followed him, taking in his home. Marble floors, family portraits, and rich tapestries hung on the walls. Dark-chestnut doors led into numerous rooms. She saw little of them before she was rushed into the library, where he closed and locked the door.

She strolled over to the fire, warming her sore muscles. She turned and found him staring at her with something akin to disbelief.

"Ye did not expect me," she stated, knowing that after months of separation, not many people would, certainly not after the way they parted.

A small frown set between his brows, and Elizabeth had the overwhelming desire to wipe it away, to take away his fear. "I did not think I would ever see you again. It has been so long."

He moved toward her, but not close enough that she could reach out and touch him.

"Our separation has given me time to think, Sebastian." She unhooked her pelisse, throwing it over a nearby wingback chair. "And while I dinna agree with how ye set out to win my hand, I am not unhappy that we're married. Not anymore."

She closed the space between them, staring up at him. He looked good enough to devour. His eyes burned with hope and fear both. His slightly disheveled appearance gave him an air of ruggedness that she liked. Not so much the lord of the manor, but a man, delightful, strong, husband of hers.

"You do not regret being my wife?"

She shook her head. "No. I want to be yer wife."

He reached out, clasping her hands. "But what about what I did to you? How I tricked you into marrying me?"

"Well, the fact that fate had you falling in love with the woman ye set out to fool, I consider myself the victor in this, for you are mine to command. Mine to love."

"I am yours," he declared, kissing both her hands in turn. "I'm sorry, Lizzie. I have missed you so much." He pulled her against him, holding her tight in arms that locked about her, like an impenetrable band.

"When my brother told me ye had signed any rights of Halligale over to me, I knew that ye loved me, for I knew how much that house meant to ye."

"It means nothing to me without you in my life." He reached up, pushing the loose strands of hair away from her face, his thumbs idly sliding over her cheeks. "I have missed you so much."

She blinked back tears. They could move forward, have a life together, a marriage. "I missed ye too. Once I decided to forgive ye your stupidity."

His lips twitched. Oh, she'd missed him, everything about the man in her arms. Even if he had been absurdly stupid, to begin with. "Are you here to stay with me?"

"I am," she said, looking about the room. "And when ye want, we can travel to Scotland to your home there as well. I want ye in my life, Sebastian, and from this day forward, I never wish to be parted from ye again."

"I love you. So much." He wrapped her in his arms a second time before pulling back and taking her lips in a searing kiss. Her body heated, liquified at the feel of him again, his warmth, the commanding way he took her mouth.

It did not take long for the kiss to turn from beckoning and sweet to hot and needy. The months apart acted as a kaleidoscope of need. Elizabeth wrapped her arms around his neck, kissing him back with undisguised desire.

His hands were everywhere, teasing and touching, stroking and tweaking. She moaned when one hand covered her breast, rolling her nipple between his fingers.

"I want you," he gasped, bending to scoop her into his arms. He carried her over toward the fire, laying her down on the thick Aubusson rug beneath them. And then he was atop her. His powerful body settling between her legs, atop her chest.

Lizzie reached down, fumbling with the buttons on his breeches. One of his hands supported his weight, the other making quick work of her gown, wrenching it above her hips. He thrust into her, taking her with hard, deep strokes. She sighed. This was right, what she wanted. Had missed so very much.

Lizzie wrapped her legs about his hips, letting go and giving over to his desire, the desperation in each thrust, each touch, and kiss he bestowed on her. She ran her hand through his hair, clasping his nape, trying to calm him.

"I'm not going anywhere, Sebastian," she said, slowing their kiss. "Not ever again."

He quieted his lovemaking, and it was more devastating than anything she had ever known. In every kiss, every touch, she could feel the reverence he felt for her, the care and love he had.

"I love you, my darling wife."

She arched her back, enjoying this newfound pace particularly. "I love ye too. Now and forever."

"Yes. Now and forever."

# EPILOGUE

*Halligale Estate, 1813 Scotland*

Sebastian threw his son in the air, catching him as he giggled and screamed at the game. He was a strapping lad, already a young hellion and a handful for his mother. Ewan Sebastian Brice Denholm, Viscount Trent, future Earl Hastings, was the most perfect boy. Watching him stumble and run to his mama made Sebastian's heart twist in his chest.

Lizzie and Ewan were everything to him, and every day he thanked the stars in the heavens he had not lost his wife due to his own foolish actions.

"Stop throwing him in the air, Sebastian," she said, setting their boy back on his feet and watching as he ran back to him. "He'll be sick all over himself before Brice and Sophie arrive."

Sebastian inwardly groaned, seating himself on a nearby settee, content to watch his son pick up and play with the wooden blocks at his feet. Brice had eventually forgiven him for his conduct, but it had taken two years after their reunion. Still, even to this day, three years into their marriage, he sometimes wondered if the Scottish laird believed he loved his sister.

Not that he cared what Laird Mackintosh thought, so long as Lizzie loved him, that was all that mattered.

"He likes being thrown in the air. He will not be sick. He's too tough for that nonsense."

Right at that moment, his son coughed, spitting up some of his lunch over the front of his clothing. Lizzie threw him a knowing *I told you so* look and called for his nurse.

"No, I shall take him up and change him." He scooped his son up in his arms, leaning down to kiss his wife as he walked past. "I shall not be long."

"Good." she grinned up at him, laughing when Ewan reached for her face, kissing her cheek. "Thank you, my darling boy," she said, kissing him back.

Sebastian chuckled, pulling their son away.

He did not think he could have been any happier than the day she arrived at his estate, forgiveness in her heart, but he was wrong. Right now, every day since that day. had been better than the last.

The birth of their first child, her body rounding again with their second. Hell, he prayed for a girl, a wee lass with fiery red hair and brilliant, green eyes just like her mama. Their life was perfect, happy, and blissful.

When his brother had lost the estate, and he had set out to win the woman who inherited it, little did he know how much he owed his foolish sibling. He owed him his life. His happiness.

"Darling," Lizzie called as he started out the drawing room door.

"Yes?" He turned to her, counting down the hours until he had her in his arms once again. Alone in their room.

Her eyes warmed as if she knew what he was thinking. Understood the secrets of his heart. "Nothing really, only that I love ye."

He winked, tickling his lad when he wiggled on his shoulder, letting out a squeal of laughter for his efforts. "I adore you too," he replied to her. Reveling in her beauty and the love that shone from her eyes. And he always would.

His own perfect Highland Rose.

Dear Reader,

Thank you for taking the time to read *Kiss the Wallflower box set, books 4-6*! I hope you enjoyed the stories.

I'm forever grateful to my readers, so if you're able, I would appreciate an honest review of *Kiss the Wallflower Books 4-6*. As they say, feed an author, leave a review! You can contact me at tamaragillauthor@gmail.com or sign up to my newsletter to keep up with my writing news.

If you'd like to learn about book one in my Royal House of Atharia series, To Dream of You, please read on. I have included chapter one for your reading pleasure.

*Tamara Gill*

# TO DREAM OF YOU

The Royal House of Atharia, Book 1

*After months spent in hiding, Princess Holly is finally ready to take her rightful place as ruler of Atharia. All she has to do now is survive her murderous uncle's attempts to steal the throne for himself. But when a mysterious gentleman washes up on the shores of her beach, she's shocked to realize she needs his help almost as much as he needs hers …*

*When Drew Meyers left his estate, his plan was to escape the arranged marriage, his scheming father brokered for him. The storm that nearly killed him was not part of the plan. Neither was meeting her. Holly is everything he ever wanted, and he will do anything to keep her safe and get her home—even if doing so means he'll be forced to let her go forever…*

*A union between a princess and a lowly future duke is forbidden. But as intrigue abounds and their enemies circle, will Drew and Holly defy the obligations and expectations that stand between them to take a chance on love? Or is their happily ever after merely a dream?*

# CHAPTER 1

*Sotherton Estate, Suffolk, 1805*

*My Lord Balhannah,*
*Drew...*
*I write to you today from necessity and desperation, and I hope you*
*shall heed my words and help me due to our friendship. There is no*
*doubt in my mind that in the coming days your father shall demand*
*that our marriage takes place forthwith. In fact, as I write this, my*
*father is readying the coaches to travel two days hence. I assume a*
*marriage license has already been procured and contracts signed, unbe-*
*known to us of course...until today.*
*Know that as much as I admire and care for you as a friend, I do not*
*love, nor do I wish to marry you, as I'm sure you do not want to*
*marry me. You see, my heart has long been given elsewhere, and I will*
*not, not even on pain of disinheritance, give up the man I love.*
*When we arrive at Sotherton, please do not be there, unless you wish*
*to break my heart and give yourself to me before God, when you know*
*that I shall never love you how a wife should love a husband. If you*
*can provide me with time, my love has promised to come and collect*
*me at Sotherton, where we shall run away to Scotland and be*

*married. I'm sorry to be so frank with my words, but I'm desperate to get this letter to you and, with it, stress how much I do not want such a union.*

*Please do whatever you can to dissuade this marriage from going ahead.*

*Forever your friend,*

*Myrtle*

D rew placed the missive from Myrtle into the fire in his room and went to the window. He pulled back the heavy brocade velvet curtains to gauge the weather. A perfect spring day, and from his window, he could see the sea and the cove where his small sailing raft was kept.

Absently he listened to his valet, Jeffries behind him go about his duties in his room. He could not stay here. Not with Myrtle so heartsick over their impending marriage. With his decision made, he turned and faced his servant. "I'm going sailing and may even travel down the coast to visit Sir Percival's at Castle Clair in Kent. I will meet you there. Please pack me a small bag to get me through until we meet again. Nothing too fancy, mind you, we'll be mostly hunting or taking our leisure about the estate. Maybe only two dinner jackets."

Jeffries stared at him, his eyes wide with this change of plans. Drew raised one brow, waiting for him to comprehend he was serious with his demand.

"Of course, my lord." Jeffries started for the chest of drawers, pulling out cravats and buckskin breeches before walking into Drew's dressing room to collect a trunk. "Will His Grace be aware of your travels, my lord, or are we keeping this excursion a secret?" Jeffries asked, from the small room.

Drew went to his chest of drawers and pulled out the oldest buckskin breeches he owned. He stripped his perfectly tied cravat from his throat, along with his waistcoat. Rummaging through his cupboard, he couldn't find his old woolen waistcoat that was warm and what he liked to use for sailing. "I cannot locate my..." Drew smiled when Jeffries passed it to him, a small smile on the man's face. "Thank you," he said, slipping it on, along with his coat.

Drew walked over to his desk and scribbled a short note to his father. Folding it, he handed it to his manservant. "Have this sent from London when you move through there. The duke may travel to town and demand answers, he will try to find me, but he will not succeed. Under no circumstances are you to tell him where I've gone. I will send a word in a week notifying you, God willing, of my safe arrival." His father was ruthless when it came to having his way, the marriage to Myrtle no different. He would lose his allowance, Drew had little doubt, but what of it? It would not be forever. Myrtle would run away and marry, and then Drew could return home.

Thank heavens Miss Landers was also against the union and only needed time to ensure their marriage would never happen. And time is what he was buying now.

Jeffries handed him a small black valise. "Yes, my lord."

Drew pocketed some blunt and left, leaving via the servant's stairs and the back door, two places his father's shadow never darkened. He ran a hand through his short locks, pulling on a cap to disguise himself further.

The brisk, salty tang of sea air hit him and invigorated his stride. Drew walked through the abundance of gardens his mother had so painstakingly cared for before passing last year. Memories of running about the garden bombarded his mind. Of hidden vistas and large oaks that any young boy enjoyed frolicking around whenever he could. His mother had designed the garden to incorporate hidden vistas perfect for children. Plants that camouflaged the old Roman ruins on the south side of the park, so it wasn't until you were almost upon them did the ruins reveal themselves, the long-lost castle of the Sotherton dukes who came before them.

Drew had spent hours playing on his own within the walls of this green sanctuary. As much as he disliked having the idea of a wife at this very moment, he couldn't help but look forward to the day his children would run about the beautiful grounds and enjoy what he always had.

The crashing of the waves echoed through the trees. Stepping free of the manicured grounds, Drew stood at the top of the small cliff and looked down on the beach's golden sands below. Many years ago, he'd had a small boathouse built to house his sailboat, and as the tide was high, it would be no problem pulling it out and dragging it the short distance to the water.

Taking the winding path down to the shore, it didn't take him long to haul the boat into the shallows and throw his bag under the little compartment that would keep it dry. The sky remained clear, with only the slightest sea breeze. It would help him travel down the coast to where his friend and closest confidant Sir Percival lived. The trip should only take a few days, and he couldn't get far enough away from this estate. To be forced into a union, not of his choice, or Miss Lander's, was reprehensible. The year was 1805, for heaven's sake. His father really ought to get up with the times. Step into the nineteenth century and embrace the new era. He was a grown gentleman, fully capable of making his own decisions. For his father to demand he marry, simply because he'd stumbled across an heiress, was offensive.

Drew pushed off from the shore, releasing the sail. The wind caught the sheet and pulled him out to sea at a clipping pace. He steered south and smiled. His father would forgive him in time, he was sure of it. The duke was never one to hold a grudge for long, and no matter how mad he'd be at finding out Drew left, he would get over it in time.

Want to read more? Purchase To Dream of You today!

## LORDS OF LONDON SERIES
## AVAILABLE NOW!

Dive into these charming historical romances! In this six-book series by Tamara Gill, Darcy seduces a virginal duke, Cecilia's world collides with a roguish marquess, Katherine strikes a deal with an unlucky earl and Lizzy sets out to conquer a very wicked Viscount. These stories plus more adventures in the Lords of London series!

Lords of London

# LEAGUE OF UNWEDDABLE GENTLEMEN SERIES AVAILABLE NOW!

Fall into my latest series, where the heroines have to fight for what they want, both regarding their life and love. And where the heroes may be unweddable to begin with, that is until they meet the women who'll change their fate. The League of Unweddable Gentlemen series is available now!

LEAGUE OF UNWEDDABLE GENTLEMEN

# THE ROYAL HOUSE OF ATHARIA
## SERIES

If you love dashing dukes and want a royal adventure, make sure to check out my latest series, The Royal House of Atharia series! Book one, To Dream of You is available now at Amazon or you can read FREE with Kindle Unlimited.

A union between a princess and a lowly future duke is forbidden. But as intrigue abounds and their enemies circle, will Drew and Holly defy the obligations and expectations that stand between them to take a chance on love? Or is their happily ever after merely a dream?

## ALSO BY TAMARA GILL

Royal House of Atharia Series

TO DREAM OF YOU

A ROYAL PROPOSITION

FOREVER MY PRINCESS

League of Unweddable Gentlemen Series

TEMPT ME, YOUR GRACE

HELLION AT HEART

DARE TO BE SCANDALOUS

TO BE WICKED WITH YOU

KISS ME DUKE

THE MARQUESS IS MINE

LEAGUE - BOOKS 1-3 BUNDLE

LEAGUE - BOOKS 4-6 BUNDLE

Kiss the Wallflower series

A MIDSUMMER KISS

A KISS AT MISTLETOE

A KISS IN SPRING

TO FALL FOR A KISS

A DUKE'S WILD KISS

TO KISS A HIGHLAND ROSE

KISS THE WALLFLOWER - BOOKS 1-3 BUNDLE

KISS THE WALLFLOWER - BOOKS 4-6 BUNDLE

A MARRIAGE MADE IN MAYFAIR
SCANDALOUS LONDON - BOOKS 1-3 BUNDLE

High Seas & High Stakes Series
HIS LADY SMUGGLER
HER GENTLEMAN PIRATE
HIGH SEAS & HIGH STAKES - BOOKS 1-2 BUNDLE

Daughters Of The Gods Series
BANISHED-GUARDIAN-FALLEN
DAUGHTERS OF THE GODS - BOOKS 1-3 BUNDLE

Stand Alone Books
TO SIN WITH SCANDAL
OUTLAWS

# ABOUT THE AUTHOR

Tamara Gill is an Australian author who grew up in an old mining town in country South Australia, where her love of history was founded. So much so, she made her darling husband travel to the UK for their honeymoon, where she dragged him from one historical monument and castle to another.

A mother of three, her two little gentlemen in the making, a future lady (she hopes) and a part-time job keep her busy in the real world, but whenever she gets a moment's peace she loves to write romance novels in an array of genres, including regency, medieval and time travel.

www.tamaragill.com
tamaragillauthor@gmail.com

Made in the USA
Middletown, DE
26 March 2021